THE RISE OF ISIGAR

The Rise of Isigar

Copyright © 2025 by J. M. Kidd

Visit the author's website at www.authorjmkidd.com

All rights reserved.

No part of this publication may be reproduced, distributed, or transmitted in any form or by any means, including photocopying, recording, or other electronic or mechanical methods, without the prior written permission of the publisher and copyright holder.The story, all names, characters, and incidents portrayed in this production are fictitious. No identification with actual persons (living or deceased), places, buildings, and products is intended or should be inferred.

Book Cover Design by Krafigs Designs

Editor: John Matthew Fox

ISBN: 978-3-00-080977-4

First edition: January 2025

THE RISE OF ISIGAR

J.M.KIDD

For T and J

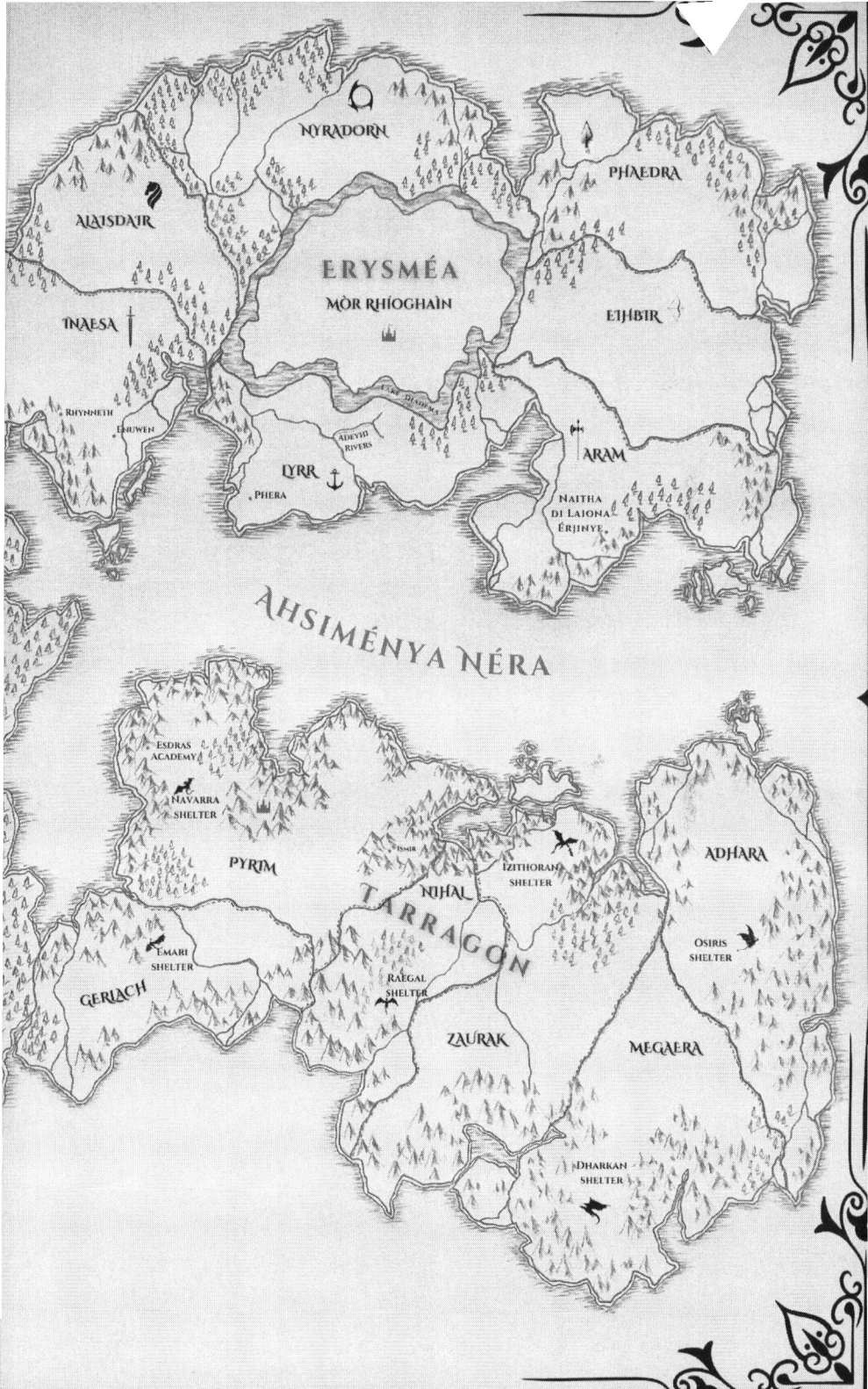

CHAPTER 1

Not this time, Aleirya thought, her knees clutching her dragon's back as she leaned forward.

Her sharp gaze pierced through the darkness as she scrutinized the shoreline below them.

Jaw clenched and ready to plunge toward the roaring waves from their hiding place, she waited, ignoring the bored hum that reverberated from her dragon's throat.

"This is ridiculous," said the dragon and huffed, black smoke bursting from her nostrils. "We're supposed to be on patrol, and instead, here we are hunting some tiny creature."

Readjusting her grip, Aleirya kept eyeing the coastline bordering the enormous, jagged cliffs and replied, "You mean a draspith, Takhéa. The two of you aren't so different."

This time, the dragon growled.

"They are simply fortunate enough to have hatched from a dragon's egg, but that's where our similarities end. I am nothing like a draspith… pitiful, small critters," Takhéa muttered.

"They are dwarf dragons," Aleirya began, but she stopped when her dragon snapped her teeth.

Takhéa turned her enormous head toward her, growling again, and Aleirya saw the dragon's large eyes, the one violet, the other a bright silver, widen as the slits of her pupils thinned to fine black threads.

She could feel her dragon's onyx scales vibrate beneath the tips of her fingers just before the strange sensation climbed up her arms.

With a grin, she tapped Takhéa's shoulder in apology and then fixed her eyes once again on the shore.

They had seen the draspith, or dragonspark, return to this place many times before; here where the enormous cliffs of Tarragon, the realm of the Dragon's Kin, ended and bordered onto the Dhaharran Forest—a vast terrain expanding over thousands of acres, separating Tarragon from the elven kingdom.

The forest was home to the mysterious Metatari, or shapeshifters, half human, half beast, with a pair of heterochromatic eyes defining their race and symbolizing their coinciding wild and hominid nature.

The clever creature had always managed to escape, but tonight Aleirya was determined not to let that happen.

The rock began to crack and crumble beneath Takhéa's talons as the dragon shifted, crawling along the face of the cliff.

Rubble came loose and plummeted toward the waves below when Aleirya warned, "Careful, you'll give us away!"

The dragon snorted and answered, "You give the draspith too much credit." She paused before adding, "Why is this so important to you, anyway?"

Aleirya let out a long sigh, trying her best to concentrate on the hunt, and replied, "I overheard Zannia and Thoran talking the other night. It was something about my father, or at least I think it was. Either way, I have to know if it's true."

"You assume the draspith can tell you if it is?" Takhéa asked in return.

"Yes. I read that their magic can decipher the truth," Aleirya answered.

"And you discovered this in one of those books you stole from Sir Odynn's library?" asked the dragon.

"Borrowed—you mean borrowed. I intend to return it," she muttered.

"Hmm…" Takhéa replied. "Even if that is true, I doubt the draspith will let you use its magic after you render it unconscious and capture it."

"I'll figure out a way," Aleirya snapped.

"How did you get the sleeping powder, anyway?" Takhéa continued to probe her. "I doubt Kalithea gave it to you without asking questions. Talk about sticky fingers…"

Aleirya set her jaw and ignored the last of her dragon's words.

"I got it from the dragon shelter about a week ago. I'm going to put it back as soon as I'm done with the draspith," she answered.

"Be careful! That powder is used to put an actual dragon to sleep. There's no telling what it could do to a draspith should you use too much. Perhaps you'll kill it," said Takhéa.

"I will not kill it," Aleirya grumbled. "I know what I'm doing."

A sound akin to a chuckle bubbled from her dragon's throat. But before Takhéa could add another snide comment, Aleirya interrupted. "There it is!"

Leaning forward over her dragon's massive shoulder, she pointed to the bottom of a steep slope ahead that abutted the stony shore.

There, along the side of the cliff, a small dark shadow scaled the rocky wall.

Something must have spooked it, as the draspith spouted a bright gust of flames while it scampered along the shore and up the cliff side, catching Aleirya's attention.

The corners of her lips twitched upward, and she spoke. "Now!"

With one powerful thrust of her legs, Takhéa pushed off the mountainside and plummeted toward the shore.

Bending forward, Aleirya's whole body stiffened, and she pressed her knees harder against her dragon's back. Excitement bubbled within her as the wind whistled past her ears, and her stomach lurched from the plunge.

She clutched the last large spike of Takhéa's ridge that trailed down her long neck and ended in between her shoulder blades, holding on as tightly as she could.

The dark sky concealed Takhéa's black hide, making her almost impossible to spy. She would only become noticeable once it was too late.

They had almost reached the slope when the draspith turned its head and caught sight of them.

A high-pitched screech shot through the air from its gaping mouth that made Aleirya wince, and the creature scrambled into motion.

Takhéa spread her wings wide just in time to slow their flight before her talons buried themselves into the face of the cliff where they landed above the draspith.

The rocky surface gave way at first, and they slid down the slope before the dragon secured her hold.

Takhéa's whole body shook at the roar that rose from her throat while her long neck curved downward toward the small creature.

She crawled toward the draspith, forcing it to retreat, the waves crashing loudly below them.

Having cut off its path upward, the only escape was flying or dropping into the icy water below; both of which Aleirya knew the dragonspark would try to avoid, since its short wings wouldn't carry it far, and like an actual dragon, a draspith hated water.

Tugging at the spike on Takhéa's back, determined to grab her dragon's attention, Aleirya spoke calmly. "Remember, I only need you to secure it. I need it alive."

Another rumbling sound reverberated through her dragon's teeth when she replied, "I'm not making any promises."

"Takhéa," said Aleirya, but the dragon refrained from replying.

The draspith let out another screech, its body glowing from the fire that built inside it.

As if meaning to distract the great dragon before it, the dragonspark let out a burst of flames and, all at once, flapped its undersized wings and sprang from the rock. Transitioning into the air and barely gliding over the rolling tide, it dropped onto the escarpment and scampered away.

Takhéa leaped after it and landed on the shore. The dragon swung her neck forward and nearly seized the draspith's tail, missing it by a hair's breadth before it jumped and crawled inside a fissure in the cliff side.

Aleirya quickly slid down Takhéa's back and ran toward the cleft where the draspith had disappeared.

It seemed to continue deeper inside the cliff, and the space was just wide enough that she could squeeze inside.

"Hurry and be careful, Aleirya," her dragon warned from behind her. "We are awfully close to the forest… We shouldn't stay here for long."

The dragon had stretched its long neck to its full length and gazed outward toward the imposing line of trees near them, where the Dhaharran Forest began.

Aleirya smirked and shrugged her shoulders. "Relax. The Metatari never venture this far outside their territory. We'll be out of here with the draspith before you know it."

She cast one more look at Takhéa over her shoulder, winked, and then slipped inside the cleft.

As quietly as she could, she continued through the narrow passage, listening for the slightest sound of the draspith.

The darkness grew thicker around her as she followed the winding trail that led her deeper and deeper inside the cliff, the path before her as clear as if cast in daylight thanks to her inherent dragon's blood.

A strange scratching sound like the scuffing of boots against the ground or something scurrying across gravel echoed from the cool depths of the cleft.

Instinctively, Aleirya's hand wrapped around the hilt of the dagger strapped to her right thigh, the practiced tug of her wrist tacitly drawing the blade from its sheath.

The scraping grew louder as she got closer to its source; then Aleirya heard a thud as if something had tumbled or someone had tripped and fallen.

Her heart beat fast, and holding her breath, she whirled around the corner, prepared for anything lurking ahead.

A whistle chased through the dark space as the dagger's edge cut through the air, following the movement of her body; but its threat was pointless.

Aleirya frowned as she stared at the dead end of the tunnel. Nothing explained what she had heard.

Irked, she kicked at the ground, her boot striking a pile of rocks just as a small burst of flames flared through the darkness from above her, and she jumped.

Her gaze swept upward toward the direction of the fiery light, and she saw it.

Its body glowed once more from the blaze that had erupted from its throat, the spikes along its spine and tail gleaming bright red. Its tiny wings fluttered and an orange tongue flicked from its mouth as the lizard-like creature stared down at her, tilting its head from side to side while perched on a small ledge protruding from the rock above her.

There you are, Aleirya thought as she eyed the draspith.

The creature continued to tilt its head back and forth, releasing a chirping sound as it continued to watch her.

The draspith was only a fraction of a normal dragon's size. Having hatched from a dragon's egg as a dwarf dragon, their existence was brought about by a rare mutation no one had yet understood.

They could not speak or bond with one of her people, but like the true dragons, whispers abounded they did harbor some magical power as well.

Aleirya remembered wanting to have one of them as a pet while growing up. But a draspith was no pet.

They hated being touched, able to scorch flesh with the same blistering heat of a regular dragon's fire, and they preferred living in the cool environment of caves or rocky outcroppings, hidden away from other larger creatures.

Keeping her eyes on the draspith, Aleirya carefully sheathed her dagger and let her right hand subtly drop to her side before she fumbled for the vial in her pocket that contained the sleeping powder.

The draspith seemed to stretch its neck toward her, and its nostrils widened as if it had detected the scent of something in the air when her fingers folded around the lid.

Steady now, she thought to herself, as if she were trying to soothe the creature.

Then, holding her breath, she flicked the lid from the vial and swung her hand toward the draspith.

THE RISE OF ISIGAR

The powder rose into the air and toward the creature. But the draspith seemed to have sensed her plan.

Through the bluish cloud that veiled her view, Aleirya spied the dragonspark's squirming body and heard scratching claws and rocks tumbling down from above.

Stepping through the cloud, Aleirya lunged and tried to grasp its tail, but her hand came up empty.

The fog cleared, and she saw the draspith had vanished from its perch. All that remained was a small hole in the rock it had burrowed through.

With a grunt, Aleirya tried to pull herself up along the wall and peer inside the small opening, but it was too high up.

She could hear its faint scampering beyond the thick stone barrier between them and let out a sigh.

Not wanting to give up yet, she inspected the wall in front of her. A large piece of rock towered before her, imitating the appearance of a door. She let her hands run along its grooves, wondering if she might remove some stones and create a space large enough for her to crawl through and follow the draspith.

Stepping back, she glanced at the spot where the draspith had vanished, suddenly feeling a hand over her mouth as someone grabbed her from behind.

Aleirya jabbed her elbow into the attacker's side and immediately reached for her dagger, but the stranger was faster.

His grip fastened tightly around her wrist under the wince that left his lips, followed by a low muffled sound, like a growl.

Aleirya was about to jam her heel into his foot but found herself suddenly unable to move.

Her limbs stiffened and froze in position while her breath quickened under his grasp, and she felt her shoulder blades dig into his chest. She could only assume by his large frame that it was a he, unable to see the stranger's face.

Only her mind seemed untouched by the odd paralyzing sensation that flooded her body.

She wanted to bite his hand and force him to loosen his grip on her, but she couldn't.

Then, out of the blue, she heard his voice.

He had not spoken and yet she had unmistakably picked up the sound of the deep dulcet tones that echoed through her mind.

What are you doing here? he asked.

The skin on her neck and arms turned to gooseflesh, and she felt the disquieting sensation travel down her back and into her legs.

How did he make it past Takhéa? she wondered. *Is she alright?*

Your dragon is unharmed. His low voice trickled through her thoughts.

Aleirya was certain that if she had been able to move, her whole body would have jerked at his surprising answer.

How is he doing this?

Aleirya heard him let out an annoyed sigh, and then her eyelids fluttered, and she felt a strange haze settle over her.

What are you doing here? he asked again, this time with a little more bite.

Aleirya struggled to fight the odd influence that seemed to render her mind powerless over his questioning and found her thoughts forming under his bidding.

I hunted the draspith, but it escaped, she replied.

You shouldn't be here, so close to our borders, dragon girl, said the stranger.

Aleirya could sense him loosening the spell he had placed over her, and she seized the chance.

What's your name, and what do you want, shapeshifter? she blurted, letting the questions flood toward him.

But there was no reply. Instead, suddenly, she was shoved forward, stumbling as her legs gradually recovered their strength, and she caught herself just in time.

A bright light pierced through the darkness of the cleft when she whirled around toward the stranger and released her dagger from its sheath.

Squinting, she lunged at him.

Her fingers snagged his right wrist just before she clutched his cloak at the shoulder and shoved him backward against the wall of the cleft's passageway. Behind her, the odd beam of light flickered and widened, but she ignored it and tucked the blade of her dagger beneath his chin.

All she could see underneath his dark hood was the pale skin of his sharply angled chin and his lips that contorted into a snarl.

Instead of freezing under her grip, the stranger muttered something under his breath, releasing a rippling force from the center of his left palm that slammed into her chest, knocking the breath out of her. Then he snatched her dagger by the blade held to his neck, and with a curse and a hiss, he tore the weapon from out of her grasp, flinging it into the darkness behind her.

The walls of the cleft, as well as the ground beneath her, seemed to shift, blurring her vision, and before she knew it, Aleirya felt her back meet the cold hard rock behind her with a smack just as she glimpsed her attacker leap into the beam of light beside her.

Every trace of him vanished. The light extinguished, and her eyes fluttered shut right before she sank to her knees.

When she came to, Aleirya lay prostrate, face downward against the ground of the cleft's passageway, her dagger an arm's reach to her right, the blade smeared with blood.

Blinking, Aleirya shoved herself to her feet and winced as a sharp pain rose to her head.

What in the dragon's name just happened?

Her mind drew a blank as she tried to gather her thoughts, and she could not recall a struggle or any incident that explained her ensanguined weapon.

The draspith… It must have escaped. Did I wound it?

A pulsating ache climbed up the nape of her neck and spread up the back of her skull, making her wince and draw in a sharp breath.

A heavy fog lay over her mind as she rubbed her eyes and then trudged forward before stooping down to retrieve her dagger.

Her fingers wrapped around its hilt just when she noticed a strange, small object lying beside it.

Her brow furrowed as she wiped the dagger's blade clean on her trousers, sheathed it, and then scooped the item into her hand.

Straightening, Aleirya focused her attention on the piece that lay in the open face of her palm.

It was a small wooden charm, like that belonging to a bracelet. The carving showed a stag's head with one of its ears and antlers missing.

Aleirya continued to stare at it, uncertain where it had come from.

The piece was beautifully made, and she rubbed it between her fingers for a moment, taking in its smooth wooden surface.

Then, without further thought, she tucked it away inside her pocket and with a sigh and one last look at the cleft's dead end, the draspith nowhere to be seen, she turned and made her way outside the cliff.

Emerging outside the cleft, her gaze immediately locked onto her dragon's, the huge scaly creature sitting before the narrow opening with her tail beating against the ground like an impatient cat.

"What took you so long?" the dragon asked, stopping when she noticed Aleirya was empty-handed. "It escaped? How?"

Aleirya ignored her dragon's questions and stepped closer to rub her snout.

"Bad luck. It found a small hole to escape through before I could capture it."

The dragon muttered something incomprehensible as Aleirya approached her side.

Something made her stop, and furrowing her brow, Aleirya turned and cast a glance over the rolling tide and the thick line of trees that marked the edge of the Dhaharran Forest.

Unsure about what she sought, yet unable to ignore the feeling of unease, she hesitated.

"What happened in there?" Her dragon spoke, drawing her attention back to the present. Her remarkable eyes were fixed on her as she awaited Aleirya's answer.

Aleirya lowered her gaze to her hands that rested against her dragon's scales and replied, "Nothing... It just escaped."

Takhéa snorted and spoke. "So much for 'I know what I'm doing'... Seems like you could have used some help in there."

Aleirya couldn't help but grin, knowing her dragon only meant to tease.

"Ah, yes, help would have been nice. If only your head weren't so large, you could have joined me."

The dragon growled and lowered herself so that Aleirya could climb up onto her back.

"Whatever... We should get back. The deception spell on your tracking stone shouldn't last much longer," the dragon muttered.

At her words, Aleirya's hand immediately traveled to the pendant that hung from her neck. She was to wear it at all times as a cadet of the Esdras Academy, the training institute for Tarragon's dragon warriors.

With Takhéa's help, Aleirya had placed a spell over the pendant that concealed their true location, enabling them to stray from the designated patrolling route and pursue the draspith.

Her dragon was right. If they didn't turn back now, their ruse would be discovered.

Aleirya nodded wordlessly and climbed up her dragon's side. Hoisting herself onto Takhéa's back, she replied, "Let's go."

CHAPTER 2

A gust of the night's brisk wind tore through her hair when Aleirya saw the towers of the guard post appear in the distance.
She could taste the salt from the spume of the roaring waves on her lips, and the cool air brushed her face while she closed her eyes.

"I'm sorry we lost the draspith," said Takhéa.

With a sigh, Aleirya opened her eyes and dropped her shoulders before she answered, "It's alright."

For a moment, she allowed herself to concentrate on the sight before them and relished the comforting sound of the waves beating against the rocky cliff side.

This was home, and nothing came close to it.

The moon cast a perfect glow on the ocean water, causing shadows to form on the surrounding cliffs and making them look all the more terrifying and majestic.

She was proud to call Tarragon her kingdom.

Her dragon's scales vibrated as Takhéa hummed, sensing her delight, before she spoke again. "What was it you wanted to learn about your father with the help of the draspith's magic?"

Aleirya riveted her gaze on the full moon, studying the subtle nuances of gray that tinged its otherwise perfectly white surface, and she replied, "Thoran spoke of my father's service as a dragon warrior and how he…" Aleirya stopped. Her throat itched, and she swallowed before she went on, "He deserted the king's army during the Eskhàra Uprising—right before he died—which would make him a—"

"Traitor," the dragon interrupted gently.

Aleirya clenched her fists and forced the lump down that had built in her throat, thankful that her dragon hadn't made her say it aloud.

Their conversation ceased briefly until she heard Takhéa speak again. "I'm sorry…"

Aleirya nodded wordlessly and diverted her attention onto her dragon's lilac wings that shimmered silver beneath the light of the moon, and she let their graceful movements entrance her.

"I just had to know if it was true," she said.

Aleirya had been born during the last days of the Eskhàra Uprising, the violent rebellion of a hybrid warrior race, half elf, half Dragon's Kin, that had sought to overtake their ancestral races in a gruesome series of battles seventeen years ago. According to those who had survived, only the alliance between the elves and the Dragon's Kin, and the combined forces of their armies, had saved them and led to their victory over the Eskhàra.

Aleirya had lost her parents in the Uprising as an infant, too young to remember anything about them; her foster parents, Thoran and Zannia, never spoke of them, claiming to know hardly anything about her father and nothing of her mother.

The palms of her hands tickled at the hum that bubbled from Takhéa's throat, and she answered, "But does it really matter? You are a born rider, Aleirya, a dragon warrior… Perhaps the two of you have that in common, but your father's story doesn't have to be your own. It won't be."

The dragon slowed her flight, getting ready to descend toward the barbican of the guard post that emerged ahead just as Aleirya smiled.

"I know… You're right," she said and stroked her dragon's neck.

"Of course I'm right," the dragon grumbled and huffed a cloud of black smoke. "You should really know that by now."

Aleirya laughed. Takhéa was one of a kind. Not only because of her sense of humor, but also because of her black hide.

Black dragons were scarce; only a handful of them had ever been seen.

Takhéa's uniqueness was what Aleirya loved most about her; that and that she wasn't afraid to share the pieces of her mind with anyone, often in a sarcastic yet amiable manner.

Aleirya stared at the enormous archway that rose in between the twin towers of the barbican just as her dragon expanded her wings, stretching them to their full length, and settled into a glide before releasing a precise sequence of bursts of flames.

The fortified outpost was manned by a pair of guards, and opposite them, perched on the battlement of the barbican's right tower, was a bronze-scaled dragon, its wings angled and raised above its beastly shoulders while it glared at them with its yellow eyes as they drew closer.

Upon recognizing them, the dragon lifted its chin skyward and spouted a golden blaze. The guards undid the magical wards and granted them entrance, and Aleirya watched the space below the archway ripple and clear, the invisible barrier vanishing before them.

Tarragon's kingdom was mainly built on cliff terrain. The realm's borders formed a jagged ring of massive stone walls, towering into the sky and surrounding the territory of the Dragon's Kin.

Inside these walls, most of the royal residential buildings, public halls, the Esdras Academy and, of course, the palace, had been crafted, shaped by the smoldering blaze of dragon's fire.

In the center of Tarragon, a broad cleft ran from the northeast to the southwest corner of the kingdom, making the overall outline appear as if it had been built inside a canyon. Inside the cleft and spread out across the entire realm were the villages, markets, meadows and farmlands, and lastly, the six dragon shelters. Each was named after one of Tarragon's founding dragons. Osiris, Navarra, Dharkan, Emari, Raegal, and Izithoran established the kingdom of the Dragon's Kin under their leader, Tarragon, and his rider, Arthurion, who marked the beginning of their ancestry.

Perched on top of her dragon's back, Aleirya watched the world below her shrink, mesmerized by the countless dots of gold dusting the kingdom that had fallen under the cover of night while Takhéa climbed higher and set course for the Esdras Academy.

Takhéa touched down on the landing field atop the Esdras Academy in a swift gallop. How her dragon managed to so elegantly transition from her flight to the ground, considering her powerful stature, never ceased to amaze her.

The dragon bowed her head, and Aleirya descended from her back.

Her boots struck the ground, and while remaining close to Takhéa, she gently placed her hand on her dragon's neck, just behind her jawbone.

She could feel Takhéa's steady pulse as her fingers traced the course of the large artery beneath the scales.

"Mea corem èdyanur, ouvéa en arès, pareiis e pnaema," said Aleirya.

Created by the first group of the Dragon's Kin, the phrase declared the rider's admiration and heartfelt gratitude toward their dragon. Spoken in their ancient tongue, Rymédrakai, or roar of the dragon, it was typically shared between the rider and his or her dragon before battle.

Strength of my heart, ally in battle, counterpart of my soul. Aleirya cherished the words of the phrase, letting them echo through her mind while she lingered at Takhéa's side for a moment.

Takhéa hummed and offered Aleirya a subtle wink, batting her purple eye, and then carefully nudged her cheek with her snout.

"See you tomorrow?" she asked, smiling at her dragon.

Takhéa dipped her head in a nod and added, "Don't do anything too mischievous without me."

Aleirya laughed, taking a few steps back while she watched her dragon turn and ready herself to take flight again.

She whistled, meeting her dragon's gaze, and then tapped her right hand over her heart before Takhéa gave a roar and leaped from the rooftop of the academy, vanishing almost seamlessly in the night sky right before her eyes.

The tall stone doors of the academy's main entrance roared and creaked as they drew open, and Aleirya stepped inside, crossing the atrium between the two giant dragons carved out of stone that bid her welcome.

Diorys and Diadyrèm were what her people called them, guardians of the dragon warriors, or Dimardraki.

Like two prowling beasts, the stone dragons emerged from the walls opposite each other, perched on all fours, wings arched and raised, and the spear-headed points of their scaly tails meeting in the center of the vaulted ceiling above her.

Passing Diorys on her right, Aleirya tapped the dragon's chin, grinning as she passed him by and veered left, following down the torch-lit halls.

Her gaze swept along the walls decorated with carvings and tapestries depicting their people's history, maps of the world as they knew it, as well as famous warriors and legends of the greatest dragons to have ever lived.

As always, her stride slowed a bit once she came by a renowned piece showing a scene of both elves and Dragon's Kin gathered around a large table strewn with silver and golden figurines of soldiers and dragons—the last council of Tarragon and Erysméa's royal court.

Pausing, Aleirya stopped and eyed the forms of the elven figures worked into the stone image.

Her knowledge of the elves and their realm was limited to what she had been taught at the academy. Her lessons focused on the elvish military, their combat style, and the history between the kingdoms of Tarragon and Erysméa.

For a brief period in their joint past, elves and Dragon's Kin had lived in unison, sharing their kingdoms' wealth, wares, and cultures—all the way up to the coming and ending of the Eskhàra race, the result of romantic relationships between an elf and a Dragon's Kin.

THE RISE OF ISIGAR

After the Eskhàra had fallen, the kingdoms had been sealed off from each other and a law had been passed, forbidding any sort of relation between an elf and a Dragon's Kin. The punishment for breaking this law was death.

Of course, not all subjects kept to this rule; over time, an illicit underground trading scene, known as the Black Market, had been formed and grown—a secret alliance between elves and Dragon's Kin established for dealing with specific commodities, as in armor and weaponry forged by the Dragon's Kin, elven spells, elixirs, spirits, and even the exchange of secrets between both kingdoms.

No one knew for sure if the authorities were oblivious to these dealings or if they concealed their awareness and occasionally obtained certain services for themselves when it was convenient.

Finally, Aleirya pulled her gaze from the portrait and continued down the hall.

Her steps carried her into an enormous cavern illuminated by countless stalactites that glowed like fiery embers, and strewn throughout its expansive grounds were several stone platforms for exercise and training for the cadets of the Esdras Academy.

By this hour, most had retreated to the academy's dorms, and the cavern was all but cleared out except for a single field. It was the largest training surface located at the center of the cavern.

Aleirya halted before it, crossing her arms in front of her chest and leaning against one of the stalagmites that wrapped around its entire platform like a colonnade.

The corners of her mouth quirked upward as she laid eyes on the group of aspiring dragon warriors engaged in excited conversation, dance, and ritualistic games in celebration of the impending bonding ceremony that was to be held by next sundown.

The Dragon's Kin were an elite warrior folk, gifted with amplified senses and physical abilities by their inheritance. Unlike any other race, they shared a unique lifelong bond with the dragons, and once pledged to each other, a warrior could channel their dragon's power into magic.

Every year, the Esdras Academy welcomed a new class of riders who had bonded with a new generation of dragons and who would begin the five-year journey into becoming and joining the ranks of Tarragon's dragon warriors.

Her gaze swept over a group of five cadets who sat cross-legged on the ground and were arranged in a circle over a game of 'wings of conquest.' The painted board in their midst was strewn with dice and dragon figurines as they chanted an ancient battle cry while shaking their fists as one of them cast the dice. Aleirya smirked and looked to the next group beside them, tossing cards into the center of their gathering in a match of 'scales' where the object of the game was to collect as few cards as possible marked with the diamond-shaped image of a dragon's scale.

A catching tune rose in her ears, and her fingers started to tap to the rhythm of the song that played.

A young Dragon's Kin strummed vigorously on the lute in his hands. Another accompanied him, enthralling the audience with the lighthearted harmony of his flute. All at once, others joined in with the clap of their hands and the stomp of their boots, adding a beat to the merry tune that tickled the soles of Aleirya's feet to move, but she resisted the urge and let her eyes take in the sight instead.

A pair of boys stood in the center of a circle, swinging their sparring swords, but not in practice of combat. Every clash of the wooden blades echoed the beat of the melody as their light feet shuffled and leaped across the floor, their bodies moving in graceful twists and turns.

Aleirya continued to watch and smiled, warmth spreading through her chest at the joyful scene, clapping her hands as the tempo sped up.

The cadets encircling the two boys whistled and cheered as the song neared its end, their movements now a blur of rapid steps and twirls until, all at once, the instruments stopped and the hall succumbed to silence before the eruption of applause.

The crowd dispersed, returning to their conversations and games, when a familiar figure skipped toward her.

"You came!" the young girl exclaimed excitedly. "How was patrol?"

"Not as much fun as you've been having here," Aleirya answered and grinned.

The girl's name was Emmarie. Aleirya and Emmarie had been introduced to each other after Emmarie had successfully completed and passed her orientation year.

As part of the Esdras Academy's mentorship program, which Aleirya had volunteered to partake in, she was to guide and encourage one of the new applicants throughout their first year of training.

For weeks now, Emmarie had been following her like her own shadow, watching her train and looking over her shoulder as she visited her regular classes.

It was the very first time Aleirya was a mentor to one of the prospective dragon riders, and she hoped desperately that Emmarie's initiation would go well and that the girl would be chosen and bonded during the ceremony tomorrow.

If she was, it would not only mean the birth of a new dragon rider, but it would also serve as an advantage for Aleirya, since it would enable her to assume a higher rank whenever she enlisted in any of Tarragon's armies. Successfully completed mentorships were commended amongst new warriors. It proved that one had already established leadership skills and could take on responsibility for fellow soldiers.

The girl tugged at the end of her long braid that hung over her shoulder, a nervous habit Aleirya had noticed in her.

Looking up at Aleirya, she asked, "You wanna join us in a round of scales? A few of us were just getting ready to start a new game in case you'd like to play?"

Aleirya smiled back at her, but before she could answer, she spied a pair through the crowds standing on the opposite side of the court and replied, "Maybe another time."

"Oh, OK," said Emmarie.

Aleirya tapped her shoulder and walked past her, steering toward the couple she had noticed when she suddenly stalled her stride.

Then, leaning toward Emmarie, she spoke. "You'll be fine. Try not to worry so much. You were meant for this."

She watched Emmarie's brow relax and her expression change as her smile reached her eyes, and she nodded before turning to rejoin her friends.

Aleirya watched her briefly and then continued to forge a path through the crowd.

Her attention froze on the two familiar figures standing at a distance from the ongoing celebration. The one was burly, a head shorter, and significantly older than the other. Sir Odynn's silver hair was neatly kept and combed back, matching the long beard that covered the bottom half of his face and hung from his chin. Creases ran along his brow and his right hand hovered before his mouth, his index finger resting above his lips as he inclined his head toward the taller figure beside him whom Aleirya recognized at once.

The young woman stood with a poise more innate than could ever be learned.

Princess Kalithea, eldest daughter of King Ethuriel, had replaced her royal gown with a set of leather armor and riding gear that draped around her slender figure and fit her like a glove. The image of two fire dragons, their necks wrapped around each other, each spouting a gust of flames in the opposite direction, had been worked onto her leather breastplate; an individual sigil she had designed for herself and her rank as the Royal Dragon Guard.

Aleirya was no stranger to the princess, having known her since childhood thanks to her close friendship with her younger sister Izidora. Throughout the years, they had formed quite the bond, making Kalithea more an elder sister to her than anything else.

Kalithea's arms hung at her sides, but Aleirya recognized the tension stored within them and the subtle play of her fingers with the golden tassel that hung from the decorative dagger at her hip. She did so whenever something unnerved her; it was the only and the faintest crack in the otherwise impenetrable façade of her royally composed manner.

The princess continued to speak quietly to Sir Odynn, her piercing emerald eyes scanning the crowd as Aleirya approached.

"Your Highness," Aleirya said and failed to suppress a grin at the sight of the princess's frown. Kalithea wasn't one for etiquette, and she despised flattery of any sort.

Turning toward Sir Odynn, Aleirya gave a respectful bow and added, "Sir Odynn."

Her academy scholar smiled familiarly and replied, "Cadet Perèdur, I half expected to receive an alarming word from the guard post that you hadn't yet returned from patrol. I trust your flight was pleasant, no surprises?"

Aleirya folded her hands neatly behind her back and answered, "Takhéa and I wouldn't dare unsettle you so, Sir Odynn."

Her words earned a chuckle from him before she added with a grin, "It was a splendid evening to be on patrol assignment. I have nothing out of the ordinary to report."

Something pricked at her neck at her response, and a brief sense of alarm rushed over Aleirya that she couldn't explain, but she ignored it and swallowed, redirecting her attention onto the princess.

Her eyes searched Kalithea's strained expression, and a knot formed in her stomach.

The princess was not herself. In fact, she hadn't been for weeks now.

Sir Odynn must have read Aleirya's concern and the silent wish to speak to Kalithea alone off her face, for she noticed him turn toward the princess and heard him speak up. "I shall be in my quarters should you wish to resume our conversation at another time, Your Highness."

He then gave a bow and retreated gracefully, surveying the young cadets spread across the training field as he walked away.

Once he stepped aside, Aleirya grabbed hold of Kalithea's arm and led her away from the platform and out of earshot of the rest of the celebrating Dragon's Kin.

"Are you alright? You don't look well," said Aleirya.

Kalithea lowered her gaze to the ground, shaking her head.

She gave a sigh and then replied, "No, not really."

Aleirya studied the princess again. She observed the faraway look in her eyes and the slightly paler tint of her complexion that her handmaiden had undoubtedly tried to conceal with rouge that dressed her lips and cheekbones. Yet the telltale signs of Kalithea's concern were as apparent to her as the faint scent of lavender and orange blossoms from the princess's perfume that lingered about her.

"It's the bonding ceremony," Kalithea began again. "I fear for the dragons' safety, Aleirya… and my father, he—he just won't listen."

Pausing, she looked up and met Aleirya's gaze.

Kalithea took her role as the Royal Dragon Guard seriously, and there was no one in the kingdom more suited for the position than she.

She knew everything there was to know of the dragons and cared for them with every fiber of her being.

Along with the responsibility of fostering and training the young dragons, delivering medicinal care to the wounded or ill, her position required the maintenance, resource management, and supervision of all the dragon shelters—a position that had been gravely challenged throughout the past months.

All throughout the kingdom, young dragons had been disappearing while others found their way to the shelters injured or gravely sick.

Despite these rather strange occurrences, and after the many investigations of each reported case, so far, all incidents had been declared coincidental.

Kalithea had been busy monitoring the disappearances and caring for the young dragons whilst trying to determine what was happening and what plagued their health.

Aleirya pursed her lips to speak when Kalithea added, "Something about the illnesses, the disappearances… It seems off. It can't all be coincidence. I don't believe it."

Aleirya swallowed, pondering her response carefully.

Before she opened her mouth to reply, a woman passed them by, bearing a tray of tall glasses filled with mulled wine.

Aleirya snatched two of the chalices without stopping the woman and handed one to Kalithea.

She raised her glass to her own lips and took a rather large sip, grimacing before she spoke. "You're certain your father's investigators are wrong?"

Aleirya half expected an angered expression on the princess's face when she looked up from her chalice, but instead, she caught Kalithea staring into the distance again as if lost in thought.

After a moment's pause, the princess nodded and then responded, "Yes. Perhaps they didn't know exactly what to look for when they examined the dragons. I think the matter deserves more attention, and we should postpone the ceremony until any criminal intent is ruled out—but Father says it is for the people."

She stopped and then raised her glass, emptying the chalice before she sighed and went on, "I can still hear his speech in my mind. 'It represents our heritage as Dragon's Kin, which we are to honor, Kalithea.'"

Aleirya noticed the princess's fingers clutching the chalice in her hand while she continued, "Yes, the dragons have been prepared for the bonding ceremony and the young cadets have been diligently training for this day for a long time. But what good does it serve if we celebrate our heritage as Dragon's Kin but can't protect our own from harm?"

Her gaze flicked back toward Aleirya.

"He hopes I can accept and come to understand this as I am to succeed him as queen."

The last part of her words sounded more spat out than spoken, and she grimaced.

"Maybe," Aleirya began, but she was cut off when the princess muttered, "Anyway, Mother will be quite pleased with his dismissal of my plea. The celebration of the bonding ceremony entails another ball, another flock of potential suitors, and another chance to twirl me into the arms of some vainglorious nobleman more enthused by the prospect of the role of 'future king consort' than a marriage to me."

"Wow," Aleirya said and smirked. "How long have you been waiting to let all that out?"

Kalithea sighed and matched her crooked smile. "You have no idea."

Aleirya laughed.

"Speaking of suitors… I believe yours is looking for you," said Kalithea, dipping her chin and beckoning Aleirya to look behind her.

Aleirya knew who she meant even before she glanced over her shoulder at the soldier approaching.

Nathanael Haliskar.

"He's not," she protested, narrowing her eyes while she turned to face Kalithea again.

"Whatever you need to tell yourself," the princess remarked, arching an eyebrow before staring into the empty chalice in her hand with dismay.

Aleirya grinned and crossed her arms over her chest. At least the princess seemed in a good enough mood to tease her.

"I should get back to the palace… minimize the extravagance of the frock I am to wear to this ball tomorrow. You know they have guards now secretly reporting my comings and goings to my parents? Ugh…"

Aleirya smiled sympathetically and nodded just as Kalithea's shoulder brushed her own, and the princess walked away.

Aleirya turned to look after her and spoke. "I'm sure, in time, all will be resolved, Kalithea…"

The princess met her gaze and smiled appreciatively before she gave a nod and took her leave.

Aleirya overheard the quiet echo of the words, "Your Highness," as Nathanael passed Kalithea and offered a bow before continuing toward her. Aleirya watched as Kalithea grumbled something inaudible and waved a hand in response, not even looking Nathanael's way as she slowly disappeared from view.

"Perèdur," Nathanael said, coming to a stop beside her, "what in the dragon's name did you say to the princess to make her so…"

"Princess-y?" Aleirya asked, cocking an eyebrow at him.

Warmth flooded her chest at his company, and she smiled, tucking her arms tighter around her ribs while continuing, "I did nothing of the sort. In fact, I hardly said a word to her. She's unnerved; says she fears for the dragons' safety, and then went on about her stubborn father and marriage-minded mother and the extravagance of frocks…"

"Hah!" Nathanael chuckled. "Well, then I sure missed an exciting conversation."

Aleirya noticed the dimple on his left cheek deepen upon his grin, and her own smile widened.

"Not really," she answered, swaying on her feet, and letting her shoulder bump into his gently.

Both of them fell silent for a moment and let their attention stray back to the ongoing celebration until Nathanael spoke up again. "Are we still on for later?"

Aleirya clicked her tongue, turning toward him, and narrowed her eyes.

Ever since she had been enrolled as a cadet at the Esdras Academy and every night before the bonding ceremony, they had snuck into the arena where the ceremony was to be held and watched the stars until dawn through its open roof.

Having enrolled two years before Aleirya, Nathanael had brought her there three years ago before her very own bonding ceremony to help calm her nervous mind. After that, she had made him promise to make it a tradition the two of them would repeat every year.

"Nathanael Haliskar, are you blowing me off?" she asked.

Shaking his head, he answered, "I wouldn't dare."

"Hmm," said Aleirya. "Well, good. 'Cause it's tradition. A promise, and you know—"

"A promise is a promise," Nathanael interrupted. "I know."

Aleirya held his gaze and returned his foolish grin before she uncrossed her arms.

Speaking of suitors… I believe yours is looking for you. Unbidden, Kalithea's words came back to her.

But Aleirya ignored them. Nathanael didn't think of her that way. They were friends, the best of friends. Anything else was silly to imagine.

Ignoring the goosebumps that spread all over her skin, she said at last, "Then you know where to find me."

CHAPTER 3

Camouflaged in the foliage of the blue coniferous trees, Nathanael's dragon dipped his snout and batted a golden eye at them, signaling it was safe to move.

Aleirya slid down the dragon's forearm after Nathanael, landing with a soft thud in the tall grass.

The corners of her mouth tipped upward at the rush of excitement, leaving a trail of goosebumps down her arms, and she looked up to nod a thanks at the sapphire-scaled dragon. The majestic creature crouched low to make himself as small as possible and winked at her in return.

Without wasting time, Aleirya and Nathanael tackled the final distance to the arena through the moonlit fields on nimble feet, careful not to alert the night guards standing watch.

THE RISE OF ISIGAR

The arena rose before them, emerging from out of the face of a cliff that overlooked the canyon of Tarragon's kingdom, its villages and rivers glittering in the distance below them and mirroring the starry sky.

The arena had been built in the shape of an enormous dragon skull with its powerful jaws agape.

The lower jaw modeled the ring surrounding the field of the arena where the attraction was displayed. But instead of a solid band, a wide chasm ran through it, providing a generous space for spectators to stand in. Large, jagged columns of rock emerged asymmetrically out of the walls forming the chasm like fangs.

The upper jaw extended at a steep angle to its counterpart and towered into the sky. Inside its cavity, spacious balconies had been designed for the esteemed guests, such as the royal family and high-standing representatives of the king. The roof resembled the bone structure of a dragon's snout and skull and shielded His Majesty and his guests from direct exposure to the blistering sun or from being drenched by rain in poor weather conditions, though those were rare in Tarragon. Four symmetrical excavations aligning with the bony orbita and nares created a passage for a comfortable draft to pass through during the hot summer days, and similar jagged rock formations, like stalactites, sprouted out of the periphery of the upper jaw line, imitating a dragon's sharp set of teeth.

Aleirya and Nathanael scaled the outer wall of the arena and slipped through the opening in the roof above the balcony reserved for the royal family before climbing down to its center stage.

Catching her breath, Aleirya stopped, her mouth dropping and curving to a wide smile while she took in the sight.

Instead of seeing the otherwise ordinary bare architectural design, she now marveled at the elaborate decoration of the arena that had been arranged during the previous days in preparation for tomorrow's celebration.

Beautiful garlands made of intricate braids of eucalyptus and wild vine matched with ivory lilies and, of course, in honor of tradition, dragon roses, dressed the balconies and the columns of the arena.

The dragon rose showed seven sepals enclosing several layers of petals in various colors. Upon exposure to magic, it would glow, shimmering in different shades of the petals' color.

The colors of the dragon roses for the annual ceremony were chosen in accordance with the hue of the dragons that were to be bonded with the young riders. On this night, the arena glowed in an aurora of blue, purple, and green.

Tiny water droplets perspired from the dragon roses into the air, emanating light in the colors of the roses like a thousand stars.

Aleirya stood breathless in the middle of the arena, remembering the very first time she had been there.

This year's ceremony was particularly special.

It was the very first time Aleirya was a mentor to one of the aspiring dragon riders.

Her thoughts strayed briefly toward Emmarie.

Not only did the outcome of this year's bonding ceremony matter so much to her, but it had also been the very first for which she had witnessed and partaken in the extensive preparations for the bonding of the future riders and dragons. She recalled the months of careful assessment of the young dragons who were ready and willing to enter the unbreakable bond with a warrior.

Alongside the academy leaders, dragon wardens, and the other mentors, Aleirya had helped choose the dragons for this year's ceremony, and for the very first time, she had witnessed the ritual of the dragons' selection of the fourteen cadets who were to be bonded.

Though it had all transpired months ago, Aleirya remembered it like it had been yesterday.

Gathered on the top of Mount Yévaèd, where, according to the legends, Arthurion of Isgerèl had been transformed by the dragon and reborn as the very first of the Dragon's Kin, they had awaited the dragons' answer.

Side by side, they had stood before fourteen braziers of iron resembling the image of dragon eggs. The bowl-shaped vessels had been arranged in a half circle before the cliff's edge, and a mural had been painted over the stone in their midst. It depicted the image of Arthurion's rebirth as the warrior kneeled before his dragon, Tarragon, clinging to the hilt of a sword that had been set ablaze. A phrase decorated the rim of the mural written in their ancient tongue.

Born of ashes, raised in fire, a true dragon shall not burn.

THE RISE OF ISIGAR

She recalled not being allowed to look up as, one after the other, the dragons selected for the ceremony had approached the peak of Mount Yévaèd and set fire to the braziers.

When all the iron vessels had been lit and the last dragon had departed from their midst, one by one, each of the mentors had stepped forward and held the ceremonial sword of the dragon's promise into the flames of a brazier. Withdrawn from the fire, the blade would reveal the name of the cadet who had been chosen. The name would fade once the blade cooled and was passed on to the next mentor to hold within the flames of the next vessel. This would continue until all the names had been revealed.

Each dragon's choice of their rider was to be honored and kept secret from all.

Even those assembled during the ritual could not know which dragon had given which name.

Though having been selected by a dragon was a promising indication that one would become a rider, it was only the first part of the choice.

They called it the linking of minds.

The union of heart and soul had yet to follow, and as the second part of the choice, it was the one they celebrated as the dragon's promise or Dharveiannir.

Though it was rare, it had happened before that a dragon had reversed their decision upon searching the heart of their rider and had turned away from them during the ceremony. This meant that the unfortunate Dragon's Kin would not be bonded.

Each aspiring rider was granted a second chance to bond with a dragon. But it had been a common wisdom amongst their ancestors that if once rejected, the dragon had found one's heart not fierce enough, and it was most likely that a bond was then impossible.

Aleirya shuddered at the thought. She couldn't imagine the pain of being rejected by a dragon after having prepared to become a rider all her life.

While everything else about who she was and where she had come from was a mystery, becoming a dragon rider was the only thing she knew to be completely true about herself. It was all she wanted. With Takhéa, the emptiness she had always felt within concerning her parents didn't feel quite as devastating.

Beside her, Nathanael pulled out a frayed quilt and spread it out neatly over the ground. He then lay down on his back and placed his hands comfortably behind his neck. Aleirya joined him, resting her head on his stomach.

"Quite the sight, isn't it?" he asked.

Aleirya nodded and answered, "Every year I think I know what it will look like. Yet every year, I'm amazed all over again. It's like seeing it for the first time."

"I'd say that's a good thing," Nathanael commented.

"It is," said Aleirya.

Captivated by the mesmerizing ambiance as they lay perfectly content in the arena, Aleirya smiled. She felt calm, enjoying the momentary oblivion of her mundane worries. Then she laughed.

"What's gotten into you?" Nathanael asked, taken a bit by surprise by her sudden outburst.

She turned her head to look up at him and answered, "I was just thinking of how ridiculously upset I was with you when you suggested we come here the first time. I remember yelling that sitting in the middle of the arena at midnight would not make me feel better or less nervous about the ceremony… And all the while you stood there with that smug grin of yours making me even more furious and knowing full well that I'd end up loving it."

Pausing shortly, she averted her gaze from him and then added, "And it did really help. After that, I wasn't nervous or scared anymore. All I could think about was how excited I was about being a part of all of it."

Nathanael smiled. "I'm glad."

For a while they lay there in silence, enjoying the sight, when Nathanael said, "I just knew what it was like: the anxiety, the fear of perhaps not being chosen after all; I don't think I slept for a minute the night before the ceremony. And I was indeed the last of my fellow cadets to become a rider that day.

"So, I thought, if you could remember this, it would help distract you from doubting yourself and what you were made to be and that is a rider. Also, I was so nervous that day that I don't even remember what the arena looked like, and I think you'd agree that you're definitely missing out if you haven't seen this."

Aleirya nodded and let the quiet settle between them once again.

Under the aurora of lights that glistened in the sky above her, she let her mind drift from the present moment, to Takhéa, to Emmarie, to her parents…

"Thank you for this," she said, at last.

Then she closed her eyes, hoping to preserve the memory of this view in its smallest detail while she drifted off to sleep.

CHAPTER 4

Beautiful music filled the spacious rotunda of the royal dining hall, resonating in Izidora's ears.

Like all the other rooms in the palace, this one had been designed to the nines, all under the queen's specific orders.

Exquisite paintings from acclaimed artists all across the kingdom dressed the walls, emanating an atmosphere of warmth and pride for the Medina name, as many portrayed tales of the family's history and their valiant forefathers. Other than enthrall their welcomed guests, they often provided a much-needed rekindling of entertainment in moments destitute of conversation.

Izidora had therefore often wondered if her mother had chosen them precisely to encourage long-lasting conversations, since it was part of the queen's responsibilities to keep the guests of her king well entertained. It was a purpose she doubted they would serve on this morning, as the joyous laughter and lively conversations of their guests brought the dining hall to life.

The previous weeks had been very busy around the palace as King Ethuriel and his queen, Cassiopeia, had welcomed the royal party of advisors and lords traveling with their families from all over Tarragon to the palace to celebrate Dharveiannir. Izidora didn't mind a bit of excitement every once in a while, yet, amongst all the commotion, she yearned for some quiet.

A little bored and not in the mood to take part in the conversation with the other young women seated at the table beside her about which dress she was going to wear to the ceremony, she let her eyes trace the paintings on the walls while she gazed across the hall.

She knew these paintings by heart, since it had been a habit of hers to study them whenever she was made to sit through long dinners and other sorts of gatherings as one of the king's daughters.

Observing each of the elegant designs, she pitied the many artists that had spent weeks and months expertly adorning the walls with their unique handiwork under the watchful eyes of her mother. Nevertheless, she was grateful for their diligence, since the art had always made her feel at home. Looking up at the ceiling inside the hemispherical dome that formed the roof of the dining hall, she gazed at the hauntingly beautiful artwork.

It was her favorite painting in this room, displaying the magnificent image of a dragon. Its outspread wings, head, neck, and chest revealed a harmonious flow of various shades of metallic blue, gold, and green.

The wings, expanding to the left and right side, covered most of the ceiling inside the dome and overshadowed the assembly seated at the table below as if they meant to offer protection from the outside world. The dragon's long scaly tail extended along the ceiling down to the base of the dome, where it ended in an elegant curve.

Her mother's sense of design and creativity continually amazed her.

She could remember watching her mother spend hours comparing colors and fabrics and sketching designs for furniture pieces, which she would then present to the carpenters.

When she wasn't drawing, directing the redesign of another room in the palace or attending scheduled civil or political audiences with Izidora's father, you would most likely find her in the music room. She was an artist through and through.

As little girls, her father had told her and her sister, Kalithea, about how their mother had captured his heart with a single song.

It had so happened that their grandfather, Aristaeus, had arranged a ball for his son, hoping to orchestrate a marital engagement and inviting all the noble maidens of Tarragon. Countless young women presented themselves adorned with their most precious jewels and extravagant gowns before the handsome prince, trying to charm him with their flattery, yet to no avail.

The prince, being young and having absolutely no desire to marry, was annoyed by his father's doing and planned to escape the ridiculous celebration as soon as an opportunity arose. When one had presented itself, he skillfully withdrew from the festivities and wandered off toward the more secluded parts of the palace. Slipping silently through the halls, he overheard music echoing from one of the rooms.

Following the sound, he caught sight of a young woman seated at the grand piano in the music room. She looked like she had evaded the party as well, dressed in a beautiful red gown. Her long golden-blonde hair lay loosely over her left shoulder, looking like it had been released from its upswept hairstyle.

Not wanting to startle her or cause her to interrupt her playing, he had settled on the floor in the hall, eavesdropping on the sweet melody for what seemed to be hours. When he could no longer bear his own curiosity about who the enchanting young woman was, he gave up hiding and gently approached her.

She had then continued to play for him until the early hours of the morning and had so won his heart. Izidora's father had named that very song 'Cassiopeia's Lullaby,' and her mother still played it for him whenever he wished.

Now, that same grand piano stood in the parlor's corner before the arched entrance of the dining hall. It had been purposely moved there because of the ongoing festivities.

Izidora rose from her chair and elegantly excused herself before she crossed the room to the grand piano. Carefully arranging her dress so that it would not wrinkle, like her mother had shown her, she seated herself at the piano and started to play. Her mother had taught her many beautiful compositions over the years, all of which she knew by heart.

After she began playing, she glanced over at her parents. The tension in her mother's shoulders seemed to recede at the sound of the music, and she noticed her father reach for her mother's hand, pressing it gently while a smile crept over his face.

She continued to play when a little girl in a yellow ruched dress approached. She looked up at Izidora with her big brown eyes and curly chestnut-colored hair that, judging by the yellow bows in the girl's hands, had been intentionally loosened out of its braided style.

Her cousin, Danae, looked like a dress-up doll, undoubtedly uncomfortable in her formal attire.

"Can I sit with you?" she asked in her sweet, small voice.

Smiling, Izidora interrupted her playing and lifted the girl up onto the bench beside her.

When she resumed, Danae remarked, "I like this song. Can you teach me how to play it?"

"If that is what you'd like, sure. Let me show you how it starts and then we'll take it step by step," Izidora answered.

Danae's eyes sparkled with excitement as she watched eagerly as Izidora placed one hand on the piano, moving her fingers slowly and gliding one by one over the keys. The two of them went on, Izidora playing a few notes first while Danae tried to imitate the sequence with vigorous ambition. She hadn't noticed how much time had passed until the sound of pebbles thumping against the large window behind them caught her attention. She turned and looked out to see Aleirya standing outside with another set of pebbles in her hand. Izidora waved, signaling that she had seen her and remembered that they had meant to meet before the ceremony.

It must already be past noon, she thought to herself in surprise.

Gently, Izidora helped Danae off the piano bench, and after promising her she would teach her the rest of the song another time, she sent the little girl off to her family and made her way to her bedroom.

Stepping inside her childhood room, Izidora wasn't surprised to see Aleirya sprawled out over her bed on her stomach, propped up on her elbows and resting her chin on her palms. She looked a bit disheveled.

"You look like you just rolled right out of bed," Izidora said. "Don't tell me you slept in those clothes?!"

Aleirya was wearing a tight-fitted, long-sleeved white shirt that tied together at its neckline and black leather trousers as part of her riding gear. Her long, tousled hair fell over her back and shoulders in its familiar waves when she looked up at Izidora with a smug grin and yawned before answering, "Actually, I did. And I slept just like a child. You know, not everyone has servants to dress and style them when they get out of bed," she teased.

Izidora gave her an unsympathetic look. "I can dress myself, thank you very much. So, what have you been doing all day besides sleeping?" she countered as she stalked over to the dressing table and sat down.

Aleirya rolled over onto her back and then sat up on Izidora's bed.

"Well, I helped prepare and serve breakfast for the prospective first-year cadets this morning. You should've seen how nervous they were, especially Emmarie. Some of them looked like they had just learned how to walk."

"You speak of them as if you were so much older," Izidora remarked, amused. "I'm sure you had the same skittish look on your face when it was your turn."

"Not my point," Aleirya replied, suppressing an affirmative smile.

Izidora laughed.

"And then," Aleirya interrupted, "I might have snuck back to my room to take a quick nap before I came to see you."

"I wouldn't call a few hours a quick nap, but alright," Izidora teased again and received a soft blow from the pillow Aleirya threw at her.

"If you're so exhausted, what were you doing up so late last night?" she asked Aleirya.

"I was out with Nathanael. You know, our little tradition before the ceremony?" she said, messing with the tangles in her hair that she had noticed.

"Ah," Izidora replied, raising an eyebrow, and crossing her arms over her chest before passing Aleirya a curious look.

"Don't look at me like that. We do this all the time! He's my friend," Aleirya asserted.

"Yes, but 'just friends' don't spend the night watching the stars together," she said.

Aleirya didn't answer and turned away, rolling her eyes and trying to hide the smile that crept over her face.

Izidora noticed and smiled back at her.

"Alright, we don't have to talk about it anymore. But I think you two should figure out whatever this is with actual words. Don't you want to know how he feels about you?" she asked.

"Ugh, you sound like my mother. 'You guys should talk,' 'Tell him how you feel,' 'You're perfect for each other,'" said Aleirya. "Zannia loves me and wants me to be happy, but in truth, she wishes I'd prefer settling down over wielding swords and riding dragonback. But that will never happen. Nathanael and I are friends. I don't want to mess up what we have with… feelings. Besides, Takhéa and my future as a dragon warrior are more important than anything else."

"Hmm," Izidora simply replied and nodded.

"What?" Aleirya asked.

"Nothing," she answered and shook her head. "It's just you're avoiding the inevitable. Everyone knows and sees it."

"Knows and sees what?" Aleirya asked.

"Just that," Izidora began, getting up from the dressing table and backing up as if expecting Aleirya to pounce at her at any moment when she added, "you would make an adorable couple."

"It's not like that!" Aleirya insisted, grabbing more of the pillows on the bed just as Izidora dove for cover, catching the revealing expression on her friend's face.

After the cheerful laughter had ceased and both of them, exhausted from their friendly battle, sat side by side on the floor against the bed, Aleirya spoke. "I hope everything goes as planned and that Kalithea will enjoy the celebration tonight as well."

"Me, too," Izidora replied. "This morning she was late for breakfast, and when she joined us, I thought she looked like she had been crying. When I asked her about it, she said she didn't want to talk about it. But one of her maids mentioned to me that one of the injured dragons died last night. Kalithea had cared for it for weeks, and she had thought it would recover, but then…"

Aleirya took Izidora's hand and said, "I'm so sorry."

Izidora nodded.

"It would be nice to see her relax a bit." She spoke with a sigh. "Otherwise, I fear she will turn into our mother soon; always so worried, always so tense."

Aleirya laughed aloud.

"Don't you dare tell her I said that!" Izidora protested.

The two smiled at one another. She and Aleirya had been friends for as long as Izidora could remember.

Aleirya was always a welcome guest in their home, and Izidora knew it had offered Aleirya a lot of comfort throughout the years to be so close with her family, giving her a sense of belonging, as she had once said.

"We should probably start getting ready," said Aleirya, drawing Izidora out of her thoughts.

Izidora grinned.

Aleirya had little to call her own, and the wages she received serving Tarragon's military she used to aid the maintenance of Thoran and Zannia's forge.

Izidora didn't mind sharing her vast wardrobe with Aleirya.

Besides, she enjoyed the challenge and the excitement of transforming her friend's everyday look into something absolutely breathtaking.

"Indeed," said Izidora. "And it's a good thing you came by so early, since it's going to require something near to magic to get you to look presentable."

At that, she received another well-deserved blow from Aleirya with one of the pillows before she raised her hands in a mocking gesture of surrender.

* * *

The banquet hall of the palace overflowed with Dragon's Kin engaged in excited conversation and laughter as the festivities began.

The double cube-shaped hall welcomed its guests embellished in extravagant floral garlands and royal blue banners decorated with the royal insignia showing the majestic head of a golden dragon spouting its fire in pride.

Illuminated by the marvelous light provided by the enormous candelabra, every detail of its exquisite architectural design, such as the decorative plasterwork adorning the walls, ceiling, and stone columns, emphasized its glory. Upon the upper level, surrounding the center of the banquet hall, the musicians arranged their ensemble and prepared their instruments for playing.

Izidora and Aleirya arrived at the banquet and immediately sought shelter from the busy crowds, dodging into a corner under the gallery.

Not far away from them stood Nathanael amongst his comrades, surrounded by a group of dolled-up women giggling and affectionately stroking the men's arms and shoulders.

Aleirya felt a brief pang in her chest that quickly shifted into a feeling of pity for the girls for parading themselves so desperately before the soldiers. She saw Nathanael notice her and waved to him before returning to her game with Izidora, watching the guests waltz into the hall in their fancy attire and making fun of some of the ridiculously extravagant costumes.

Deeply enjoying their sport, she hadn't noticed Nathanael make his way over to them. It provided her with such a scare that she jumped when he spoke, suddenly standing behind her and Izidora.

"Now that is a hat I must have!" he joked, referring to the stout lady who had just entered the hall wearing an extravagant ball gown and matching headdress that only seemed to accentuate her corpulence.

Sipping wine from his chalice, he looked at them, grinning, knowing very well what they had been up to. They looked back at him in guilty astonishment that he had caught them in the act of their rather offensive game. But unable to help themselves, they laughed.

Taking a subtle bow before Izidora, he spoke. "Princess."

He then turned toward Aleirya, smirked, and added, "I almost didn't recognize you all tidied up, Lady Perèdur! Impressive work, Izidora, I must say."

Aleirya punched his shoulder and said, "Hey, what makes you think I didn't do this all by myself?"

Nathanael just looked at her, grinning wider, and took another big sip from his chalice.

"I sense it is my time to leave the two of you to your devices," he cunningly answered, and with another elegant bow to Izidora and a wink, he retreated.

"I think in his tongue that meant that you look beautiful," Izidora whispered, nudging Aleirya, who was watching Nathanael disappear back into the crowd.

Izidora had picked out a pale blue slender gown for Aleirya with fine silver-colored lacework, almost evanescent, and beginning at the middle of the bodice before spreading into the skirt of the dress. The heart-shaped neckline extended around the upper parts of her arms, baring her shoulders. She had dressed the loose waves of her dark, ash-blonde hair with small pearls and pulled back two strands in single braids to form a crown around her head.

Before Aleirya could answer, an announcement echoed through the hall. "Gentlemen, lords and guests, I present to you His Majesty, King Ethuriel, and Queen Cassiopeia!"

Cheerful applause and exclamations of "All hail the king" resonated throughout the banquet hall as the king entered with his queen by his side.

"That's my cue!" Izidora exclaimed and then darted off, squeezing through the crowds to the entrance, where she hoped to resume her spot next to her sister before they were announced and bid to enter. She must have made it just in time as the following proclamation resounded, "Next, may I present to you His Majesty's daughters, Kalithea Arienne, first-born and successor of the Medina legacy, and their younger daughter, Izidora Eydis Medina!"

The applause and cheering continued as the sisters stepped into the hall. Both wore elegant gowns that draped their figures in royal blue and gold, the colors of the royal family.

Izidora had skillfully interwoven the thick tresses of her hair in several braids that joined at the nape of her neck, held together in a bun by a golden clasp that was shaped like a wreath of fine leaves. A few dark brown curls hung loosely at the sides, lining her warm features and golden-brown eyes.

Next to her, Kalithea's golden-blonde hair, like their mother's, cascaded in glossy waves down her back. A side-to-side braid adorned with a golden floral headpiece, beset with sapphire gems, decorated the back of her head.

Countless curtsies and formal greetings later, Izidora found Aleirya amongst a few of her fellow cadets of the academy.

Rubbing her cheeks in a circular motion, she said in pain, "I warn you, if you make me smile one more time, I will have your head!"

Groaning, she tried to relax her face and let out a long sigh of relief.

"Now to the fun part of the evening," she said and then pulled Aleirya over to the side before grabbing two chalices of wine and handing one to Aleirya to toast to their, at last, free evening. After taking a sip, Izidora nearly choked, lifting the back of her hand to her mouth.

Clearing her throat, she quickly whispered to Aleirya, "Quick, hide me!"

"Hide you? What? From whom?" Aleirya asked, confused, while she let Izidora seize her arms and drag her aside, ducking while she used her as a shield.

"Damian," Izidora grumbled through gritted teeth. She continued to tug at the sleeves of Aleirya's dress, drawing her toward one of the marbled pillars supporting the gallery when an all-too-familiar, slick-sounding voice rose from behind Aleirya. "Princess Izidora, what a delightful evening it is!"

"Wings and talons!" Izidora cursed quietly as she rolled her eyes and then twirled around Aleirya to face the boy.

Aleirya watched her force a pleasant smile and lower herself in an elegant curtsy just as he went on, "Forgive my forwardness, Your Highness, but you look… exquisite."

Damian bent forward, taking Izidora's hand, and planted a kiss on the back of it. Behind him stood his two bootlickers, Lucius and Cassian, who snickered noticeably under their breath.

Aleirya cringed and set her jaw at the sight of the three of them.

Damian Astraea was a highborn and the eldest son of one of King Ethuriel's advisors. He had inherited his father's looks and ambitions, but certainly none of his tact or wits, and his intentions toward Izidora were as obvious as were his charms.

"Damian," Izidora replied.

Damian then turned toward Aleirya.

The two of them had crossed paths many a time at the academy, as Damian was a fellow cadet and one of Nathanael's peers. But as quickly as she had gotten to know him, she had equally learned to avoid him, as he harbored a renowned dislike for any female comrade-in-arms.

He eyed her before he opened his mouth and asked, "And who might this enchanting acquaintance of yours be?"

He reached for her hand as well, but Aleirya quickly folded it behind her back and answered, "Spare me the displeasure, Damian. You know who I am."

Straightening, he smirked and replied, "You can hardly blame a man for not recognizing you, Perèdur. I must say, the skirts suit you better than the swords."

"Hmm," said Aleirya, and she flashed an amused smile back at him. "I could say the same of you. At least I know how to handle myself with both."

Damian chuckled, but Aleirya caught the flicker in his gaze that betrayed his annoyance over her response.

Redirecting his attention back to Izidora, he went on, "Princess, you must allow me to steal you away from this rather brutish company. Perhaps you might favor a dance with me?"

"Actually, I believe I was promised a dance with the princess," said another male voice from behind them as Nathanael joined them.

Nathanael dipped his head in a bow and then extended his hand toward Izidora, saying, "Princess, it would be an honor."

Izidora smiled and curtsied before accepting his offer and letting him escort her to the dance floor.

Walking away, Nathanael halted briefly, and placing his free hand on Damian's shoulder, he leaned closer and spoke to him. "Surely there is yet an entire flock of desirable young women who will not be able to resist your charming offer."

Aleirya thought she had heard a snarl slip past Damian's curled lips while he fixed Nathanael with a glare and watched him walk away with Izidora by his side.

His pointed gaze darted back to Aleirya. Looking her up and down once more, he sneered at her before he backed away and bumped into a server bearing a tray laden with chalices.

The sound of shattering glass drew an echo of gasps from the onlookers who turned at the commotion. Damian cursed and whirled on his polished heels, vanishing in the crowd of gawkers.

A shower of heat trickled down Aleirya's neck and shoulders in anger as she watched Damian disappear without a word and the servant slowly push himself to his knees, shards of the crimson-stained glass scraping the ground beneath his palms.

Careful not to drown the trim of the gown Izidora had given her in the pool of wine that spread over the tiled floor, Aleirya stooped down to help the servant and gathered some of the glass shards.

The young man wore a black patch over his left eye that drew her attention to his face and stalled her working hands. It struck her as odd that the palace staff would allow one with such an obvious impediment to serve His Majesty's royal guests at the banquet, but before she could purse her lips to question him, she noticed his hand was bleeding, a long cut running across his palm.

"You're hurt. Let me help you," she said and tried to reach for his hand, but he pulled away.

"Don't trouble yourself. I'll be fine," he answered roughly.

Aleirya withdrew her hand but hesitated to get up and leave.

The young man continued to gather the heap of broken glass together when she found herself staring at him.

He seemed to notice her lingering gaze as his jaw tightened, but he kept his eyes trained on the floor and continued to tend the mess as if it were nothing unusual for her to watch him.

"What happened to your eye?" she asked without thinking.

The servant stopped for a second, and then he answered, "I lost it to an infection when I was a child."

Aleirya's brow softened, and she leaned forward, extending her arm and releasing the fragments of glass she had gathered on the servant's tray before she answered, "I'm sorry."

He didn't answer, only nodded in reply, and then rose to his feet.

"Apologies, my lady," he said.

Aleirya stood and nodded just as he gave a bow and then quickly moved past her, eager to flee the scene.

Aleirya turned and let her eyes follow the path he had forged through the banquet's guests, suddenly feeling inexplicably odd.

The dainty patter of heeled slippers rose from behind her just before two hands gently grabbed onto her shoulders, and she heard Izidora speak. "That

Nathanael of yours sure is a knight in shining armor, swooping in with his white-scaled dragon just in time to save me from the slippery hands of that priss."

She giggled and spun Aleirya around to face her.

"Are you alright?" she asked, letting her hands drop back to her sides. "I'm sorry if that was awkward… me and Nathanael taking off like that to dance. I—"

"It's fine, Iz," Aleirya interrupted her.

She smiled and waited for Izidora to catch on before she added, "I'm fine, and you're lucky he came around, because I was not going to take you to the floor. I love you, but for a princess, you're a horrible dancer."

Izidora grimaced before she smiled and slapped Aleirya's arm. "I am not! It's these shoes! I swear, I'd move as gracefully as a deer if it weren't for these murderous heels…"

"Try a clumsy fawn," Aleirya teased before she let Izidora drag her out from underneath the gallery.

"I'll prove it to you," she exclaimed.

"Please, don't," Aleirya interjected. But it was too late. Izidora had already reached under her skirts and taken off her shoes, spinning and skipping toward the dance floor of the banquet while she laughed infectiously and beckoned Aleirya to follow her.

Chapter 5

T he sun had not yet set when the ranks were filing inside the arena. As the dragon roses glowed, the last of the people entered.

It was finally here, Aleirya thought, Dharveiannir, the celebration of the dragon's promise.

She stood beside Izidora on a balcony that overlooked the center of the arena. It was about to begin.

Even a few of the dragons had come to celebrate with the people and surrounded the outskirts of the arena. Some spouted fire in excitement while others bounded through the air, forming spirals to entertain the spectators.

The chattering crowds grew quiet when fourteen young men and women dressed in black leather riding gear marched into the center of the arena and then formed a large circle. Each wore a royal blue sash with a gold dragon rose pin at their left shoulder and a sheathed sword draped over their right side.

Aleirya didn't need long to find Emmarie. Her black hair was tied together in the traditional braided style the female dragon riders wore for the celebration.

Several small braids ran along both sides of her head and joined at the base of her neck where her hair folded together to a knot that resembled the shape of the dragon rose.

Aleirya saw the girl glance up at her, smiling from ear to ear, her odd reddish-brown eyes sparkling with excitement. She couldn't help but grin and waved back at her from the balcony.

When all had fallen silent, each of the aspiring riders, one after the other, drew their sword and thrust it into the ground in front of them. Kneeling behind their blade, they then bowed their heads toward the ground.

When the last had kneeled, an angelic voice started to sing.

They called it the hymn of Dharveiannir.

Aleirya closed her eyes as the first verse resonated within the arena.

Irèn éra thythèmnir,
Though I may fail,
Éda mea èdyanur thyrsmai,
My strength subside,
El veiannir iskharzon diar èda éra inphernyss aellistai,
The promise made between you and I shall forever prevail.
Oris éra yvedi treazimn diar mearys,
As I vow to keep you by my side,
Mea èdyanur,
My strength,
Mea gédi,
My guide,

THE RISE OF ISIGAR

Ouenam corea simeron oris pnaemari elkyran,
Our hearts alike as our souls intertwine,
Tésa min perodir,
All that I have,
Etha is diador
May it be thine.

There was no applause to be heard after the hymn had been sung. Instead, an eerie silence followed that broke at the sound of a crescendo coming from the stroke of the powerful wings of an approaching dragon.

All eyes of those watching turned toward the roof of the arena as the first dragon hovered over the kneeling young men and women in the center of the arena.

The dragon's scales displayed a magnificent shade of purple like that of an amethyst gem. A beautiful golden design adorned the crown of its head like a diadem, displaying the words: 'Néa ardurnai,' meaning *new beginning*.

The dragon circled above them for a while, eyeing each of the individuals below, before gradually descending in a kingly manner to the center of the arena amidst the fourteen.

Aleirya clutched the skirt of her dress, feeling her own pulse pounding in her throat as she watched.

She froze, and her eyes darted toward Emmarie and then back to the dragon as it drew closer to the ground.

Aleirya pinched the soft fabric between her fingers even harder at the thudding sound of the dragon landing amidst the aspiring riders, and then her heart sank.

The dragon folded its wings neatly, coming to a halt before a young boy.

Letting out a long sigh, she shut her eyes.

It's only the first. She still has a chance.

For a moment, it seemed as if the whole assembly held its breath, anxiously awaiting what was to come next.

The dragon bowed its massive head toward the ground, eyeing the blade before the boy. Then it pulled its head back, and out of its throat, it produced a burst of violet-tinted flames that set the sword ablaze.

Aleirya forced her hands to loosen and let go of her dress as the congregation erupted in a choir of delighted shouts and cheers, and the young man rose and raised his head to look at the dragon.

He then approached the dragon, setting his right hand at its neck and gently placing his left hand on its snout. Closing his eyes, the new rider then recited a spell that was inaudible for the surrounding audience.

Suddenly, the purple flames that encircled the sword vanished. The only remnant was a single name etched into the blade of the sword. It was the dragon's name, chosen by his rider and sealed under the spell that now bound them as one.

The boy took hold of the hilt of the weapon, and after drawing it from the ground, he raised it toward the sky and proclaimed, "People of Tarragon, it is on this very night that I solemnly pledge my allegiance to the throne, serving my king first and then you, the people, until my last breath! I vow to serve you wholeheartedly, remaining faithfully at the side of Eleftheria!"

In the very moment he proclaimed the dragon's name, Eleftheria, the engraving on the blade glowed, and the arena erupted in cheers and applause.

Aleirya joined the crowds in their excitement as Eleftheria took her place behind her rider, clearing the field for the next dragon to arrive.

One after the other, the second, third, fourth, and fifth dragons approached and chose their rider. By the eighth, Aleirya felt sick from the excitement and her concern for Emmarie.

The next one will be hers, she told herself.

She wondered if this was just as terrible for the other mentors.

Nine, ten, eleven, twelve... Aleirya's heart seemed to sink further and further inside her ribcage, causing her to not look up when the thirteenth dragon arrived.

Aleirya stared down at her feet, wondering when her head would stop spinning and when the weight on her chest would lift so that she could breathe more easily again.

She closed her eyes and tried to think of something else.

The crowd's voices quieted again, but Aleirya couldn't bring herself to look up.

"Aleirya! Aleirya." Izidora whispered in her ear, grabbing her shoulder. "Look! Isn't that…" Izidora added and pointed toward the center of the arena.

Aleirya's head snapped upward. She knew exactly where to look, having memorized the exact spot where Emmarie kneeled before her sword. Her gaze locked on the girl, who somehow looked smaller.

Perhaps she has lost hope, Aleirya thought.

Aleirya bit down on her lip, her breath lodged in her throat, and sweat broke across her palms as the green dragon lowered its snout, sniffing at the ground before Emmarie.

It gave a snort, releasing a burst of black smoke when it took another step toward the blade that protruded from the ground in front of Emmarie.

Do it. Aleirya felt her lips move to the sound of her thoughts while she watched.

Her hands folded into fists and shook. Her chest tightened when, suddenly, the dragon stepped back and raised its head.

It seemed to eye Emmarie, and then it turned its neck and it looked out over the crowds instead.

No. No! Aleirya heard her own voice screaming inside her, fearing the worst.

The dragon roared, and then whipping its neck back in Emmarie's direction, it spouted its fire.

The sword glowed gold amidst the green flames, and Aleirya gasped.

She thought she saw Emmarie's body tremble before it proudly rose upright, and the girl raised her gaze to that of her dragon's.

Aleirya whistled as loudly as she could and drove her palms against each other, clapping so hard it hurt.

Emmarie's face shone with pride as the people rejoiced, and then she took to her dragon's side.

Aleirya threw her arms around Izidora and smiled, nodding her head against her friend's while Emmarie turned toward the crowds and proclaimed the dragon rider's oath.

The girl's light voice now roared through the arena as she spoke at last. "I will remain faithful at the side of Idrahzel!"

"Yes!" Aleirya shouted, cheering as she joined the people's elated voices; letting go of Izidora, she straightened and took in a deep breath, smiling.

But just as Emmarie had proclaimed the name of her dragon, a terrible series of shrieks and roars filled the sky.

Horrible, mournful cries reverberated across the arena's center where the newly bonded dragons stood by their riders. Then, one after the other, they leaped into the air and scattered across the heavens as the crowds filling the spectators' ranks stirred and surged against the walls of the chasm. The people's screams rang through the arena, several hands pointing down toward the kingdom's canyon where Aleirya saw billows of black clouds and smoke rising in the distance, erupting from the ground out of seemingly every direction.

The bells of the villages' watchtowers tolled from afar under the blackening sky, intercepted by soul-wrenching cries of dragons. Aleirya felt her chest constrict, tears stinging her eyes at the agonizing sound.

"We're under attack!" someone shouted.

"The dragon shelters, the villages, they burn!" others joined in as the smell of charred wood and flesh wafted through the arena.

Aleirya and Izidora looked at each other and then up to the king and his royal guests. He stood surrounded by his guards, and it looked like a messenger was yelling something at him over the loud cries of the people who deserted the arena in a frenzy. The king's face was unreadable as he shouted commands at his guards, and the assembly moved toward the entrance.

Kalithea, who had been standing close to her father, froze and her face had gone ghostly white. When she hesitated to follow the evacuating crowd, a guard gently reached for her, leading her away to follow along with the rest.

Aleirya's eyes darted from Kalithea and the king to the arena's center, searching for Emmarie.

Relief overcame her at the sight of a group of soldiers who gathered the young riders together, shielding them from the chaos that broke out around them and shoving them toward the exit of the arena.

THE RISE OF ISIGAR

With the certainty of Emmarie's safety, Aleirya quickly grabbed Izidora's hand, and then the two of them fought their way through the frantic crowds as fast as they could back to the palace.

Chapter 6

The elf across the room looked as lifeless as the corpse a group of farmers had found an hour before sunrise.

Pulling his arms tighter around his chest, cold bleeding into his skin at the nape of his neck like a clasp of icy fingers, Valeirys swallowed and trained his eyes on the soldier.

"Tell me your name," said Commander Rheiavirn. His strapping frame was bent over the large table that occupied the center of the room, his hands resting on the marbled top showing a three-dimensional map of Erysméa, the kingdom of the elves.

"Gwenaël, Sir Rheiavirn," the elf answered. His body appeared as if it had shrunk within his armor, and his complexion seemed to have worsened within a few shaky breaths that whistled past the crooked pair of white lines marking his lips.

"Tell me what happened, Gwenaël," Commander Rheiavirn went on.

Pushing off from the table, the commander straightened, and the light that flooded the room caught the sigil of the sword embossed upon his pauldrons, the league of Altair, and the military force under Valeirys' father's command.

Valeirys' gaze moved between Gwenaël and the tall dark-haired elf known as no one other than Trajan Rheiavirn, the youngest soldier to have ever achieved the rank of commander amongst the seven leagues of Erysméa's military, and Valeirys' father's second.

"The body… It's the third now in just two days," said Gwenaël.

Dark rings had gathered beneath the elf's eyes, and he looked as though he had not eaten or slept in days, his cheekbones and chin standing out in sharp angles.

"I've seen dead before… bloodied, impaled, even cleft in two. But this was an entirely different evil."

He paused and stared down at his boots, his face growing ashen.

"Like the others, this victim was a child. Half of its body was bruised and mutilated, the other half of its flesh was scorched," Gwenaël added.

Valeirys' throat tightened as an unwanted image of the described sight rose before his mind's eye. His gaze flicked toward Trajan, who continued to look at the soldier, and he noticed the slightest twitch in his jaw.

He didn't have to guess what went through his friend and mentor's mind.

It had been months since young elves had disappeared all throughout the kingdom without a trace; the first dead had surfaced a few weeks ago.

Valeirys had heard whispers of corpses washed up on the shores of Lyrr or drawn out of the water by fishermen; now, three bodies had been discovered in Inaesa, the region under his father's command and his home.

Every soldier at their disposal had been called into action. But every effort, every search, every lead had proved unsuccessful. Whoever was committing these atrocities was laughing in their faces, and while Erysméa's leadership feigned confidence against this enemy, the façade was steadily crumbling.

Gwenaël's lips quivered, and he spoke. "The people are afraid, sir. Every day, another village falls under the control of the rebels. Quelling the violence and protecting those loyal to His Majesty has become our daily effort.

"Just yesterday, half of the unit stationed to protect Enuwen was severely injured. The rebels poisoned the rivers; when we sent healers to cleanse the waters, the soldiers guarding them were attacked. We need reinforcements or we will lose control."

Trajan's brow furrowed, the dark brown of his eyes fixed on the soldier across from him, while his hands clenched at his sides.

Valeirys' stomach twisted. He knew the truth. The forces of his father's league were already stretched thin... Reinforcements seemed a luxury they did not have.

"The sword has not lost its power," said Commander Rheiavirn. "Continue to hold Enuwen. I will have Rhynneth send as many soldiers as they can spare until the injured reclaim their posts. They should reach you by nightfall."

He rearranged the silver figurines marking the units deployed throughout Inaesa's region before glancing up at the elf once more.

Gwenaël bowed as if to retreat, but the lag in his steps betrayed his hesitation. "Sir Rheiavirn, if their children can't be saved, then at the very least, the people need some proof that the transgressors will be found and that justice will be done." His voice seemed to falter in the end, as if his courage had left him.

Valeirys swallowed, and lifted his chin, his chest tightening at the tension that encompassed the room; he watched as the commander's resolute expression softened for just a moment before he nodded and replied, "These crimes will not go unanswered, Gwenaël. It is up to us to restore hope to our people. Rest assured, these perpetrators will be found and tried for their wickedness. Now, remember your oath, return to your post, and do not forget the power of your blood."

The soldier froze and his cheeks blanched before he bowed and retreated, almost tripping over his feet as he exited the chamber in a hurry.

Valeirys watched the entrance fall shut behind him, the silence growing louder once again before he moved, desperate to shake the cold rigidity that had settled in his legs from hours of standing still.

His eyes skimmed the tall arched shelves lined with books, scrolls, and maps before they wandered back to the table over which the commander continued to hover, an array of crossing swords supporting it in the middle.

Coming full circle around the room, Valeirys approached the commander's side, letting his eyes pass over the table's masterfully crafted marbled top showing an accurate display of Erysméa's lands.

Erysméa had been an elven heroine who had defied the evil King Izurion.

The king's mind had been corrupted by his practice of a dark sorcery, causing him to commit the greatest atrocities one could have imagined, only to satisfy his pleasure of violence.

To protect her people, Erysméa had led a rebellion along with the allied forces of the Dragon's Kin into victory over Izurion at the cost of her life.

In order that her sacrifice would be remembered, the elven people had named their new kingdom after her.

Erysméa was separated into seven regions by rivers that bled into Lake Diadéma, which surrounded its capital, Mòr Rhíoghaìn.

The seven regions, Alaisdair, Inaesa, Nyradorn, Eibhir, Aram, Lyrr, and Phaidra, were governed each by one of seven lords appointed by the king.

Like his grandfather had been, Valeirys' father, Uryiel Altair, was now Lord of Inaesa; as one of the elven lords, his father was not only responsible for the well-being of the people who lived in Inaesa, but also head of one of the seven military leagues divided among the elven realm.

A unique sigil had been given to each league, symbolizing their expertise and their region. The league led by Uryiel Altair bore the family's sigil of the sword.

Valeirys knew the remaining six sigils by heart.

There was the chakram of Lord Zelathiel, the spear of Lord Yeva, the anchor of Lord Tarquinius, the battle ax of Lord Cenric, the archer representing the lordship of Sir Fearghail, and the stallion of Lord Rhaegalisron.

Resting his hands on the smoothly rendered stone of the map, Valeirys let out a sigh before he spoke. "Why haven't we found him yet?"

Trajan shook his head and did not look up to meet his gaze when he replied, "We will find him."

With every corpse, the rebellion thrived. For weeks now, they had sought to unmask the rebellion's leader, trying to infiltrate their inner circle, but to no avail.

The only progress they had made was the detection of a pattern.

Whenever a new body surfaced, the rebellion's activity gravitated toward the location where the dead had been found. Their numbers soared, usually coupled by a surge of violent protests, robberies, arson, and other crimes within the village or region where the body had been discovered. It was as if they fed off the people's fresh misery, capitalizing on their sorrow and desperation. It was a cruel but effective tactic.

But this time, it was different.

"Three bodies and the rebel leader hasn't made his move… something is off," said Valeirys.

Trajan pursed his lips to speak just as the doors of the chamber burst open, followed by a cascade of heavy footsteps.

A tall, able-bodied elf strode into the room, a team of soldiers flanking his sides.

His father's presence immediately established command of the room; Valeirys thought he had noticed the guards lining the doors of the chamber stiffen at the sight of their lord.

Uryiel's chest was emblazoned with the sigil of the sword that gleamed across his breastplate, and an emerald cape flowed down his back. His long black hair was pulled back behind his pointed ears in its usual braid, and his striking azurite gaze froze on Valeirys before he gave a curt nod and spoke. "Any news of the scoundrel?"

Valeirys straightened, clasping his hands behind his back, and with the dip of his chin, he answered, "No, my lord."

Uryiel continued to eye him with an all-too-familiar stern expression. He was not known for his warmth. He was a strict father and an even fiercer leader. Relentless discipline and ambition, a strong mind and an even stronger spine were the sort of qualities he valued.

His father proceeded toward them, coming around the table, opposite Valeirys, to stand beside Trajan.

Without glancing in his direction, Uryiel spoke to him. "Reach out to our spies again. I want word back by nightfall. If anyone so much as whispers the word 'rebellion,' I want to hear of it. You are dismissed, soldier."

Valeirys nodded, and without delay, he bowed and stole out of his father's study.

Drawing the doors shut behind him, he blew out a breath and turned down the hall.

Billows of light flooded the spacious rooms and halls of Valeirys' father's manor through the windows that lined his path, the glass interwoven with ivory tracery that reminded him of the veins of a leaf.

All throughout the manor, the floors and steps were tiled in marbled stone. The trims of the high ceilings were decorated with beautiful plasterwork, and the smoothly rendered walls reflected a bright glow of light, emanating an elegance and an unmet tranquility.

Reaching the end of the hall, Valeirys' gaze halted on the grand winding staircase, leading both up and downward, that rose in front of him from the center of the atrium.

Its ivory stone handrails had been carved into a sinuous branch from which twigs sprouted and trailed down to the steps, forming the spindles that crossed and interlaced one another in a webbed pattern.

Veering right, Valeirys reached for the lock stiles of the manor's main entrance, shaped in the image of a downcast sword. Its guard extended to the left and right, forming the middle rail of the entrance, and skillfully inscribed onto the segment that resembled the fuller of the blade stood the familiar engraving, 'Altair,' his family's name.

With a push, the heavy doors opened, and Valeirys watched the sword split into two equal halves, clearing the path onto the portico and the gardens that preceded his home.

A gentle breeze swept past him, the rich scent of the garden's flowers and the calling of the songbirds engulfing his senses as he strode onto the pathway leading onto the lands that surrounded his family's estate.

The rustling of the trees and the briskness of the morning were a much-welcomed reprieve to the hours spent inside his father's study.

Valeirys continued along the cobblestone path, relishing the quiet until his feet slowed, his eyes narrowed, and he recognized a figure in the distance standing on the private training grounds, an arrow strung taut and ready to fire.

The arrow made a snapping sound before it plummeted into the center of the target.

"Whew," Valeirys whistled. "An aim like that would put Father in his place."

"Ah, wouldn't be much of a challenge. Rumor has it he's a terrible shot," the elf answered and turned around to face him, a smile lighting his features.

Across from Valeirys stood Eyvindr, the true-born son of Uryiel and Yessenia Altair.

Valeirys himself had been brought to Uryiel and Yessenia as a babe with no parents to claim him as their own, and henceforth, he had been adopted and raised as their own. Although two years older, Eyvindr looked much younger than Valeirys.

Despite his age, his fair skin and triangular-shaped face had kept their childlike appearance; while Eyvindr's slender physique seemed rather frail, Valeirys had a muscular figure, perhaps brawnier than was characteristic of an elf.

Eyvindr's thick, onyx-colored hair fell over his forehead and ears where it curled at the ends, and he had inherited the same piercing azurite gaze of his father.

However, despite their physical similarities, Eyvindr was no soldier. He had been born with feeble bones that broke like glass, and no magic had been able to cure his ailment. Throughout his childhood, he had suffered an insurmountable number of broken bones, and even now he wore a brace over his left leg after dismounting his steed in a hurry.

Extending the bow and quiver of arrows toward him, his brother spoke. "You want to give it a try?"

The right corner of his lips quirked upward, and Valeirys grabbed hold of the bow and took position.

With the lift of his arm, he held his breath and took aim at the target in the distance. But before he could release the arrow, his brother interrupted, "Wait."

Valeirys peered at him past his raised arm just as Eyvindr gently reached out to touch him. Having made a few slight adjustments to his posture and handling of the bow, his brother stepped back, eyeing the target ahead, and then spoke. "Now."

Valeirys loosed his grip on the arrow and watched it explode into the air with a crack.

Reaching the target, it split the arrow of Eyvindr's finest shot in half, burrowing into the center of the bullseye.

Valeirys grimaced and muttered, "Show-off."

Out of the corner of his eye, he caught Eyvindr smile before he leisurely strolled aside.

Valeirys knew his brother had made a promise to himself to master at least one weapon in order to not conform to the impression of the weak son his father had of him, and so he had chosen the bow.

Eyvindr enjoyed the challenge it presented because of the high amount of precision work it required; also, it gave him the advantage of avoiding close combat, such as was necessary when wielding a sword, and thus avoiding more broken bones.

However, though he had truly come to master his craft, he still wasn't fit to enter the military service as an archer. For it was required of every soldier to compete with other weapons, such as the sword, chakram, or spear.

It was something Eyvindr couldn't manage as a warrior due to the fragility of his bones.

"How goes the search for the rebellion's leader?" Eyvindr asked, staring at the target just as Valeirys released another shot.

Frowning, he lowered the bow and replied, "We're nowhere close to unmasking him. By now, he should've made his presence in Inaesa known. I don't know what he is waiting for."

Valeirys stared blankly into the distance, his mind spinning through various ideas.

"Perhaps he's not waiting for anything. Perhaps he's playing a different game this time," said Eyvindr.

"What do you mean?" Valeirys asked and looked at him.

"Well, I am no soldier or, better yet, evil mastermind—" Eyvindr began when Valeirys interrupted, "You're smarter than anyone I know. What are you thinking?"

Indeed, what his brother lacked in physical prowess, he more than made up for in academic brilliance. Eyvindr had an extraordinary imagination and an ingenious understanding of military strategy, despite not being able to serve as a soldier because of his condition.

Eyvindr grinned foolishly, a spark in his eyes, and he spoke. "Well, it's been months now that every league has been monitoring the rebellion's actions, trying to unmask their leader's identity. By now, they certainly know that we're aware of their habits."

He paused and tilted his head to the side before adding, "Maybe the goal is to unsettle you. Maybe they're just planning to do something unexpected?"

"Maybe," Valeirys answered and clenched his teeth. They were always three steps behind…

Eyvindr strolled off the training site, and Valeirys joined him, pondering his brother's words.

"Considering the circumstances, it seems ironic that we are to celebrate our military at the king's banquet tomorrow," Eyvindr said beside him.

Valeirys nodded, his gaze trailing the cobblestone path before them when he answered, "According to Father, King Yevandrielle has been adamant about upholding the tradition to honor those in service of the realm; now more than ever. He refuses to have the banquet postponed."

"Hmm," said Eyvindr.

They had reached a crossway when Eyvindr turned right and Valeirys spoke. "Where are you off to?"

"Mother's apothecary. I promised I'd assist her today," he answered. "And you? What errands does Father have you running for him?"

Dipping his chin in a goodbye, Valeirys turned left and replied, "I am to visit the aviary."

Chapter 7

A choir of birdsong drifted along the warm and sweet-scented breeze that swept through Inaesa's public aviary. The joyful chirping, trills, and whistles mingled along the rustling of the trees and the tranquil pattering of the fountains spread throughout the vast array of orchards and gardens spanning over ten acres of land.

The gravel beneath Valeirys' boots crunched as he walked, and his eyes skimmed the parterres of flowers; hues of red, lilac, and blue melding together like dappled blots on a painted canvas.

Shadows danced over the ivory trellises and the sculptures under the swaying crowns of the trees, the stone telling of elven legends, tales of love, hope, and peace.

The sun dusted the path before him in pale gold as Valeirys continued along the pathway ahead that curved around a gazebo formed by a ring of birch trees, their crowns intertwined to a blossoming roof. A fountain splashed in its midst, the droplets of water catching the day's light and reflecting beads of color.

Moving past the gazebo, Valeirys trod onward until his gaze caught on the sight of a bench that stood atop a circular patio. Decorative plasterwork dressed the center of its back, showing an intricate design of a staff encircled by a flight of swallows.

Climbing the pair of steps and crossing the patio, Valeirys stopped and turned to sit down.

Warmth nestled at the nape of his neck and spread along his shoulders from the sun's rays as he moved his lips to form a whistle. The melody dispersed into the morning breeze, vanishing as quickly as it came.

Looking up, Valeirys studied the sky until a soft flutter of wings rose to his right, and he grinned.

Curious black orbs stared back at him as the small bird cocked its head from side to side and gave a chirp.

A sìthyra or 'a whisper' is what his people called it; a creature born of elven magic. Its obsidian feathers glittered beneath the sun, a white crest curving around its neck.

Carefully, Valeirys stretched out his hand toward it, and the sìthyra came to rest on his finger.

Gently, he stroked its silken coat and spoke. "Sìthyra, sìthyra tahvei imos ena igra, eios naphernae yen yndrefim di pervaes mikos."

Whisper, whisper, travel far and travel fast, bring word to thy friend of secrets passed.

He smiled and raised his arm just as the bird took flight, its body a silhouette of black vanishing in the blue above in the blink of an eye.

Now, all he had to do was wait.

The shadow cast by the gnomon had moved two hour lines before the sìthyra returned. Averting his attention from the sundial that expanded over the patio at his feet, Valeirys stretched out his hand and drew the sìthyra closer.

The creature dipped and inclined its small head toward him, cooing as he stroked it; Valeirys cast his attention on the crest, circling its neck just as its color changed from white to bright yellow.

The canary cage.

Smiling, he rose to his feet, the message received.

With the sìthyra riding his shoulder, Valeirys passed through the gardens, headed straight for the meeting place.

He could see the dome of the canary cage peek through the grove of trees just as his silent companion chirped a farewell and took to the sky.

The tall gates of the enormous cage rose up in front of him, the entrance drawn open.

The decorative ironwork forming the rotunda gleamed bright silver from beneath the cluster of exotic flowers and vines that twined around its frame.

Valeirys strode inside, and his gaze was immediately drawn toward an opera of canaries singing overhead, flickers of bright yellow swirling and darting across the space beneath the dome.

"Ah, a tune to the ear, is it not?" said the voice of an approaching figure.

Valeirys cast a sideways glance toward the elf.

Black hair lined with gray brushed his shoulders, a scruffy beard covered the parts of his face the sun had not bronzed, and a pair of olive-colored eyes peered at him from beneath the rim of a straw hat.

The elf's pale tunic was rolled up to his elbows, an apron was tied around his waist, and a pair of tall, dirtied boots covered his feet.

"Did you know the canary can develop a distinct manner of singing?" he asked, stopping beside Valeirys and crossing his arms over his chest.

Valeirys grinned. The key's answer was already resting on the tip of his tongue.

"Yes," he replied. "That is because they can distinguish a sequence of sounds, minimize them, and reproduce them."

The elf's eyes narrowed ever so slightly before he dipped his hat and said, "Clever little creatures."

He moved along with Valeirys as both trod outside the cage's rotunda.

Valeirys did not know the elf's real name, only his alias: Korah.

Strolling along the gravel pathway, Valeirys inclined his head toward the elf and spoke. "I need a name."

Korah shook his head and replied, "I'm afraid he remains nameless, soldier."

Valeirys gritted his teeth, his stride not slowing as he glanced into the distance before looking back at the elf and muttering, "How many more bodies must be found before he makes his move?"

"I know Lord Altair grows impatient, as do we all," Korah interjected.

He paused and seemed to take his time as they ventured further through the aviary's gardens before he stopped and came to face Valeirys.

They were alone, standing amidst a quercetum of white oak trees, and yet he caught the flicker of the movement in Korah's gaze as he assured himself of their privacy.

Then Valeirys watched the elf's hand reach inside the pocket of his apron as he withdrew a folded piece of parchment and said, "I believe the incident with the waters in Enuwen was meant to deflect our attention, but from what I am not yet certain. The rebellion seems to be slumbering…"

He stopped and let out a breath before adding, "Of late, our unit has noticed a surge in business of the printing presses; an influx of shipments and deliveries containing excessive amounts of vellum and inks. Nowadays, any subject itchy to write and able to get their hands on a quill seems eager to print a word of scandal or conspiracy. Nevertheless, we investigated. Nothing stood out, except this one: It's new, and the only print every press seems to be producing and distributing."

Korah unfolded the piece in his hand and held it out to him.

The parchment showed an image of a serpent, its fanged mouth agape, and an arrow piercing its head.

A spasm chased along his jaw as Valeirys clenched his teeth, and his fingers pinched the leaflet.

"Every few days, the image changes ever so slightly, a new detail worked into the design. Once, we thought to have noticed the letter 'L' drawn inside the fletching of the arrow. Another time, there was a detail set inside the serpent's scales, like a sigil of sorts; the latest was the grotesquely exaggerated fork of the tongue," said Korah.

The elf let out a sigh and then went on, "The artist is unknown. I have my unit watching the comings and goings of the printing presses, trying to identify the maker of this specific piece. But it seems this fellow uses different errand boys to deliver his sketches to the printers to remain anonymous. Whoever it is, I have no doubt he or she is tied to the rebellion."

Valeirys stared at it, scrutinizing every detail.

Perhaps he's not waiting for anything. Perhaps he's playing a different game this time.

Eyvindr's words rose in his ears, and with a jerk, he lowered his arms and averted his gaze from the printed image.

A huff burst from his mouth, and his lips pressed against each other to a hard line before his eyes found Korah's, and he spoke. "It's a message. He has something in mind, and he's growing bolder by the day, dangling the secret of his plan in front of our faces…"

Korah's expression seemed to darken as he listened and then gave a nod.

"The only question is, what does he intend to do?"

***

Yessenia could already see the small apothecary shop ahead on the outskirts of the village as she walked down the road. Her family had owned it for generations. Since her father had died and her mother had grown too old to maintain the business, it had been passed on to her to look after.

A sigh swept past her lips when she noticed a pair of children huddled together on the ground before the shop's entrance.

Lately, it had been nothing unusual for customers to gather in front of the shop even hours before it opened, anxiously awaiting her arrival. Yet despite wanting nothing more than to help, her heart never failed to sink a bit at the sight.

Drawing in a deep breath, Yessenia took in the fresh morning air one last time before she slowed her steps and came to a stop before the two boys.

She looked down into their pale and frightened faces and offered them a comforting smile when they peered back up at her.

Then she nodded toward the shop's entrance and spoke. "Follow me."

The siblings rose to their feet while the younger seemed to help the older up.

Opening the door, a small bell rang as she entered the shop and held it open for the children to follow her inside, passing under the sign over the doorpost that read: 'Trageian's Apothecary.'

She had worked as an apprentice under her father, Samyiel Trageian, as one of Inaesa's finest healers for years and had thus acquired quite the expertise.

She loved her father's apothecary; she had kept to his trade even after her marriage to Uryiel and her claim of the title Lady Altair.

From childhood, Yessenia's father had always told her that her blood and her magic were special, and that she should use her abilities to help those in need.

Motioning toward a small bench to her left, she instructed the boys to sit down while she removed her cloak.

Quietly, the children did as she asked, the younger boy eyeing her with an expression of both worry and awe.

Yessenia knew that look well. Healers were well respected, since their trade was a difficult one to master, but their appearance seemed to always strike a bit of fear in those who came to ask for help.

Approaching the children, she kneeled before them, leveling her gaze to theirs. Studying the elder one for a moment, she noticed him bite his lip while fidgeting nervously with his hands that lay curled in his lap. His fists were skinned and blood smeared. He tried to avoid glancing at her from underneath his hood until she spoke softly. "How can I help?"

The boy looked up, his dark eyes staring back at her while he hesitated to answer.

"Show her," his younger brother said and carefully nudged his side.

His light voice sounded timid and shook a bit.

The older one sighed and pressed his lips together, watching her closely before he lowered the hood of his cloak.

Yessenia's expression remained still, even when she saw the deep gash that ran along the right side of his head and past his ear. Dirt and dried, crusted blood clung to his light brown hair, surrounding the ragged lines of the wound. A bruise was forming beneath his right eye and upper jawbone. She didn't need to ask to know what had happened.

Yessenia shifted her glance from the wound to the boy's eyes and then to his hands. Carefully embracing them with her own, she said, "I'll be right back, and then we'll clean you up. Everything will be alright. The wound will heal well."

She squeezed his hands lightly and offered a weak but reassuring smile before she rose to her feet.

She began to turn away when the younger boy leaped from the bench and spoke. "Please, don't tell our parents!"

"Najim," the other child cautioned.

Yessenia looked at him, a bit surprised. The boy seemed terrified and looked back at her with a longing expression. "Aetius was only trying to keep me safe. He didn't mean to get involved in the fight."

"Najim, stop!" his brother growled.

But he skipped out of his reach and went on, "The blacksmith and the watchman, they were fighting again. The blacksmith was yelling something about spineless soldiers and how the king will rue his failures, and then the watchman told him to shut up, and then they just started beating each other. More joined the fight, and I was just trying to get away when I bumped into one of them and fell. Aetius was trying to pull me away when he got hit. I, I don't even know how it happened, but there was just blood, lots of it, and—"

"It's alright." Yessenia stopped him, coming closer to the boy and placing her hands on his arms.

Inspecting him for a moment to make sure that he was unharmed, she added, "As long as the two of you promise me you'll continue to look out for each other and try to stay out of trouble, I promise to let this be our secret."

She waited for the boy to nod at her in agreement, a tiny spark of relief glistening in his brown eyes.

"Now, wait here," Yessenia said before she turned away and walked to the back of the shop.

Sadly, it hadn't been the first time something like this had happened.

Throughout the past weeks, she had received many such visits from injured villagers or grief-stricken families searching for some potion or treatment to ease their brokenness. The people's suffering had grown by the day ever since the young elves had disappeared without a trace, and the circumstances seemed to worsen, many growing violent as their anguish and frustration boiled over.

All these injured reminded Yessenia of war.

Most of the time, a healer would be called or visited to treat the common ailments of the people. But they were also often requested by the military during seasons of battle to cure infections, treat wounds, and provide relief from pain and fevers and sometimes nightmares and illusions that befell the traumatized soldiers. Yessenia still recalled the images and sounds of the battlefield in excruciating detail. A rather unfortunate result of her elven nature, as the elves possessed an extraordinary perception and memory. It enabled them to sense feelings of others and recall their memories up to the smallest detail, sometimes even after years had passed.

Thankfully, she had only experienced war as a healer once. When soldiers and healers were being called upon before the battles of the Eskhàra Uprising, she had volunteered to go in place of her father.

Yessenia returned to the front of the shop with an assortment of vials, herbs, and ointments to treat the boy's wound, grateful that she could make herself useful in this way.

Although all elves could practice magic, not every elf possessed the same magical power. While many, of course, found their strength in applying their abilities in battle, some could draw and manipulate the natural elements better than others. They served the realm managing large plantations or worked in forges as blacksmiths, fashioning weaponry with their own fire that burned hotter and made the weapons more resistant and durable than others, almost like those of the Dragon's Kin, which were forged in dragons' fire.

Several found their fortitude in the more artistic scene and could create illusions so convincing that they appeared to be real to the untrained eye. Their ability brought them quite a fortune, as it increasingly developed into a public attraction their spectators would handsomely pay for. Others expressed their magic in creating elegant façades for the homes of the wealthy, sculptures, and other sorts of decorative elements, shaping the stone by their magic in accordance with their imagination.

And at last, there were those such as Yessenia and her ancestors who had been gifted with the unique magical ability to detect and heal the ailments of the body.

Turning the corner, she breathed a subtle sigh of relief when she saw the boys were still there, given their earlier frightened state.

Having set everything down onto a cart beside the bench, she gently cleansed the wound and then dipped her fingers into the ointment before placing them over the boy's injury.

Whispering a spell, she let the incantation take its effect and let her fingers direct the closing of the wound.

Usually, and unlike other magic, the power to heal or affect the mind or body of another could only be translated onto an individual by physical contact or by the ingestion of an elixir or potion. The only exception to this rule was if the elf practicing the magic was more powerful by nature, or if a deeper, intimate relationship existed between the elf using the magic and the recipient.

The gash was almost sealed when the shop's bell rang again.

Completing the spell, Yessenia turned around and saw Eyvindr rush inside, breathless from running.

"I'm here, I'm here," he said, still trying to catch his breath and bending over his knees. "Sorry I'm late," he added, still huffing.

To Yessenia, her son, Eyvindr, was the greatest reminder that all magic had its limits.

Every elf knew that magical power required energy to work. Every action performed with magic also demanded a different amount of energy. Sometimes, an elf could use their own inherent strength that would recede and likewise increase again when the elf recovered, or they could draw power from their surroundings, such as the energy from the earth.

It took a significant amount of practice and training to learn the art of extracting the energy and how to use it. Also, each source was different and needed to be understood before it was drawn from.

In Yessenia's line of expertise, not every affliction could be healed, just as it wasn't possible to bring a loved one back from the dead through magic.

Some assumed that it depended on the severity or complexity of the pathology that afflicted the sick. Others believed that the energy required to maintain the spell long enough to take effect, and thus heal the ailment, was simply too great.

"It's fine," she said and waited for Eyvindr to meet her eyes.

When he did, she added, "Go to the back and bring me some more of the hypericum ointment." She smiled at him briefly and watched him nod at her before he went on, and she returned her attention to the children once again.

Yessenia finished tending the gash on the side of the boy's head and treated the bruising beneath his eye and along his jaw, while Eyvindr healed his injured hands under her precise instructions.

It wasn't long before every trace of the fight was removed from the child's body, and Yessenia bid the brothers goodbye with a warning to be careful.

Closing the shop's door behind her, she let her shoulders sag and expelled a sigh.

Pinching her eyes shut, she tried to force the image of the brothers' scared and bloodied appearances aside.

The king will rue his failures. The younger brother's words lingered in the forefront of her mind, and a shudder chased down her spine. When would the violence and the hatred stop? When would the terror that plagued her people end?

Chapter 8

The crisp timbre of the violins twirled above the laughter and elated voices from the crowd in attendance of the king's banquet and sent a tingle of goosebumps down Valeirys' arms.

The brooch bearing his family's sigil of the sword pressed painfully against his shoulder. He felt hot, and his skin itched beneath the embroidered collar that folded around his neck.

Resisting the urge to scratch, Valeirys clutched the sleeves of his doublet, incredibly uncomfortable in his formal attire, and let his gaze stray across the elaborate space before him.

The Great Hall was a sight to behold. Four perrons led up to the majestic structure that overlooked Mòr Rhíoghain's city below. Its walls were fashioned almost entirely out of glass, and a colonnade of enormous ivory pillars encircled its outline.

Carved into the white stone of the moldings of the gallery and the high vaulted ceiling was a finely detailed stucco rendering a beautiful portrait of Erysméa. The heroine was depicted with her sword raised overhead and mounted upon a powerful stallion. Her hair had been tossed back by the wind in the captured scene, and a diadem graced her forehead.

Valeirys blinked at the twinkle of lights that broke over him like stars shaped as floating orbs, drawing and scattering the light that poured into the hall from the windowed walls. The spheres reflected the wealth of colors from the bouquets, the ladies' gowns, and the golden glow of the candlelight, warming the scene of the king's banquet.

The tables overflowed with trays of venison, roast oxen, heron, and glazed chickens, as well as tarts, custards of dates and honey, and platters of pastries and candied fruits too decorative to seem edible.

The sweet and savory aromas, the smells of herbs, salt, and garlic were enticing enough to make a full stomach grumble for more.

Any other time, the feast set before Valeirys might have made his mouth water, his eyes close at the warm, delicious smells that engulfed his nose and drawn him to the table to taste the lavish meal. But not on this evening.

Instead, a lump swelled in his throat, and his stomach sank.

The king's banquet was meant to be a merry occasion. But any sense of pride for his service to the kingdom and any enjoyment of the evening's riches were lost on him.

His head ached from the frustration and the exhaustion that wore on him from the last days, weeks, even months. The reminder of the dead elves, the families torn apart by tragedy, and the fruitless chase of the rebellion's leader roused an anger within, exhausting his patience and his composure.

Valeirys' glance trailed the decorative twist and turn of the flower garlands molded around the generous display of foods spread out over the tables, and his hands curled to fists at his sides as the menacing image of the serpent hovered before his mind's eye.

Blinking, he looked away.

Eyvindr stood beside him, nursing the crystal chalice in his hand, seemingly lost in deep thought.

His brother cleaned up nicely. His deep black locks of hair were neatly combed back, baring his fine features and striking eyes. Though both had had their celebratory attire fitted to them, the fine clothes suited Eyvindr much better. Dressed in their family's colors of emerald and silver and bearing their sigil, Eyvindr looked regal.

Valeirys swallowed and tugged at the cuffs of his sleeves and tried to adjust his collar again, but it still didn't seem to fit quite right.

Clearing his throat, he forced himself to stop fiddling with his clothes and set his eyes back on the crowd spread throughout the hall.

His gaze halted on a tall silver-haired elf toasting to a group of soldiers, a personal guard glued to his sides, when he spoke. "Do you think it's true what they say about Lord Zelathiel?"

He cast a sideways glance at his brother, whose head jerked upright at his question; and Valeirys watched the azure circlets of his eyes search and freeze on the elf at the opposite side of the hall.

"That he's awfully suspicious and won't go anywhere without his guards or that he orchestrated the deaths of his older brothers to claim his father's lordship?" Eyvindr asked in return.

Lord Amulius Zelathiel was the youngest of nine sons of the late Lord Zelathiel; while it was publicly known that the Zelathiel family had suffered a tremendous series of tragedies, losing eight of their sons to illnesses and ill-fated hunting expeditions, rumors abounded about Amulius' unlikely succession.

"With that crooked smile, I'd say the latter," Eyvindr added, leaning closer to Valeirys, who couldn't help but smirk at his answer.

Then, taking another sip of his wine, his brother added, "But, if I had to choose, I'd rather be considered devious and cold-blooded than say, well, a promiscuous fool like Lord Yeva."

Boisterous laughter drew Valeirys' attention to the elf Eyvindr had just mentioned, who was traipsing into the auditorium surrounded by a flock of bejeweled noblewomen. Lord Yeva was a notorious philanderer and enjoyed flaunting his newest conquests before the public's eye. Though one could debate whether the women's hearts had truly been won or if he had simply purchased their affections for the right price.

Claiming a chalice from the server who passed them by, Valeirys drank and then continued to observe the rest of the guests.

He could easily pick out the remaining five lords and leaders of Erysméa's leagues.

Lord Rhaegalisron stood beside his father. His hand gripped the stem of his chalice and cast a blinding gleam, as it was decorated with five priceless rings, one on each finger.

As the wealthiest of Erysméa's lords, he made no secret of his riches. Valeirys had heard the stories of the family's manor, which some would say was only second to the palace itself, and Lord Rhaegalisron's latest acquisition of twelve Akahl-Teke stallions with coats that shone gold beneath the sunlight had been enviously frowned upon.

Moving on to another pair, Valeirys recognized Lord Fearghail and Lord Cenric, the lords of Erysméa's southeastern regions.

A peculiar scar ran along Lord Fearghail's face from the bow of his upper lip to the corner of his right eye, an injury he had apparently acquired in his very first battle as a soldier. Though some cruel voices whispered that the young lord had simply been too clumsy with the blade.

Lord Cenric stood beside him, engrossed in the conversation. His head was shaven on both sides, and the design of a battle ax was worked into the peculiar cut of his black hair.

And lastly, there was Lord Tarquinius. The elf's cheeks appeared flushed from the wine in his chalice. He had not moved from the side of the grand table laden with delicacies, his left hand picking at the marzipan depicting the sigil of the stallion. He was known for his weakness for sweets, and what sort of magic kept him so thin was beyond Valeirys.

The song played by the string quartet switched, inviting the king's guests to join in the dance.

Through the swish and sway of the couples that had taken to the floor, Valeirys glimpsed the table marking the head of the banquet where His Majesty, the royal family, and the members of the king's council had been seated.

"Your gorgeous princess is here," said Valeirys, nudging Eyvindr's shoulder. "You should ask her for a dance. After all, you got all dressed up for this. It would be a shame if it had all been for nothing."

Eyvindr followed Valeirys' gaze that halted on the Princess Diyara, a well-practiced smile rounding her lips and lighting her gentle features.

"She's been forced to compliment, smile at, and perhaps entertain every spruced-up lordling in this room with conversation. I'm sure she'd be delighted to dance with another. Especially one who just might break a leg should I trip over my own feet on the dance floor and drag her down with me," Eyvindr responded.

"You're too hard on yourself," said Valeirys. "For all you know, she just might prefer your company over the endless charade of noblemen begging for her attention."

"Hmm," was all his brother answered before he raised his chalice and drank again.

Smacking his lips, he gave a sigh and then said, "Is it too soon to leave? Surely, we've made enough of an appearance to avoid rebuke or the punishment of Father's withering stare…"

Valeirys chuckled and answered, "You know as well as I do that he will not take kindly should we do so. Besides, even without watching us, he will know the minute we leave. It's like when we were children and the room got too quiet for both his and Mother's taste…"

Nodding, Eyvindr took a step forward and placed his empty chalice on the table beside them. Looking back at Valeirys, he said, "Then I will at least step outside for a moment. The air in here has grown increasingly stale and, well… pretentious."

He gave a half smile and then turned on his heels, disappearing in the crowd.

Shaking his head, Valeirys directed his attention from his brother toward His Majesty and the ranks of Erysméa's royal council. He immediately recognized the Lord Councilor Calaedorn seated beside the king. He was the overseer of the seven leagues and master of weaponry, and a face every soldier knew.

Standing off to the right of His Majesty, and perhaps the most prominent of the king's councilors, was the unmistakable Lord Councilor D'Arthragnan.

Leaning on his cane, the Lord Councilor inclined his head toward Prince Malik as they spoke. The elf was impossible to overlook. Given his crippled state, Lord D'Arthragnan's instatement as member of the Erysméan court by King Yevandrielle had been an unprecedented occurrence.

Though no one had dared question or openly criticize His Majesty's choice, by most, Lord D'Arthragnan was considered inadequate for the position because of his disabled condition. It hadn't mattered that he had faithfully served Erysméa's military for most of his life, beginning as a squire to the former king and Yevandrielle's father. Cripples were not meant to bear the honor of possessing a high rank or a public office, such as advisor to the king.

Valeirys' throat tightened, and he swallowed as his thoughts briefly strayed toward Eyvindr at the sight of the crippled lord.

If an ailment was incurable by elven magic, the elf afflicted was considered cursed, unable to serve the realm efficiently, and therefore reduced to a subject of lowest worth in the kingdom's eyes. It was proof of the vanity of Erysméa's highborn society only a few would care to admit.

Silence broke as the music ceased. The crowd dispersed and gathered along the outskirts of the Great Hall or took to their seats, lining the tables, and King Yevandrielle rose from his position.

Behind him, seven banners of different colors ran down the wall. Each depicted one of the seven sigils of Erysméa's leagues and was mirrored in the king's livery collar that hung over his chest and shoulders. His crimson robes shone dark against the bronze of his eyes and his silver hair.

With his chin slightly raised in a manner befitting his royal blood, King Yevandrielle pursed his lips and spoke. "Kin of elven blood, soldiers, warriors tried and true. We gather here to honor you; for your devotion, for your loyalty, and for your courage until death."

A hush settled over the king's assembled guests as the voices stilled and the sounds of a few clearing their throats stopped.

Valeirys folded his arms across his chest and let his eyes sweep over the people toward the king when a flicker of movement caught his attention.

King Yevandrielle continued to speak, but his words blended to a muffled sound, fading into the background of Valeirys' mind as his glance ran over each corner of the hall and up toward the gallery.

His pulse began to pound, a pressure building in his throat as his focus flitted back and forth along the balcony above that curved around the celebratory space.

His eyes narrowed, but whatever he might have seen was lost in the shadows.

Drawing a deep breath, he forced himself to calm, gritting his teeth at the sense of paranoia that overcame him.

His focus trailed back toward the king and the crowd, still immersed in his speech, and he ignored the prickling sensation that moved down his neck and back.

"Our kingdom bleeds, our people suffer under the darkness of an evil that has claimed far too many of our own," King Yevandrielle's voice thundered.

The clink and clatter of a glass shattering arose from somewhere across the hall. The faint noise drew hardly any of the people's attention from His Majesty. Valeirys felt his chest tighten, and his gaze sharpened as he scrutinized the scene before him.

"But even amid this peril, we stand unbroken. Our bond is inseparable, and our love and loyalty to our people and the great who have gone before us shall remain unshakable. We shall overcome this and any enemy that dares to rise against us. Our very blood, our spirit demands it, and united, we shall not fail," said King Yevandrielle.

Somewhere behind him, Valeirys glimpsed a few servants wading a path through the guests, the stir of movement jabbing at his sense of alertness once again.

Swallowing, he straightened and riveted his concentration on His Majesty as his speech neared its end.

"The crown is nothing without your faithfulness. Your resilience and your bravery are seen. They are cherished, and tonight, they shall be celebrated."

For the length of a breath, the crowd fell silent before a choir of cheers and clapping resounded.

Valeirys drew a breath, the tension loosening his shoulders, and he lowered his arms to his sides.

King Yevandrielle smiled and raised his chalice in a toast, the deep red of the wine shimmering through the clear crystal. His guests imitated the gesture when, suddenly, a loud crack sounded and an arrow struck the king's goblet, tiny glass shards bursting from his hand in a crimson splatter.

Everyone ducked and screams followed as another arrow soared past the king's head and slit the banner behind him, engulfing it in flames.

Heat flared in Valeirys' limbs, a jolt racing down his spine, as a flight of flaming arrows descended upon the banquet's guests.

Diving for cover behind the pilaster to his left, Valeirys' glance snapped toward the king. Relief flooded his chest at the sight of a unit having flocked to His Majesty's side. With shields raised in protection over him, they escorted him out of the line of fire.

Chaos claimed its control over the frenzied gathering. Guests scrambled in a wake of screams, upturned chairs and tables, and the hall caught fire. Black pillars of smoke towered toward the vault of the ceiling where the banners had once hung.

Valeirys' hand folded around the hilt of his sword, and his eyes darted toward the gallery above in search of the archers just as a series of cries broke out and mounds of parchment were released into the smoke-filled air, obscuring the view above.

Figures emerged through the dense cloud of fumes and vellum that sailed toward the ground and veiled Valeirys' vision, their voices rising in bellows. "Liberator! Liberator!"

Dressed in servants' garb, their faces smeared in inky black, they continued to scream and fell upon the banquet's guests, a crumpled piece of parchment in their left hands, while various items, no doubt to be intended as weapons, were grasped in their right.

The high-pitched ringing of weapons drawn rang in Valeirys' ears, his jaw clenched before he dove into the middle of the brawl.

The tussle of bodies enveloped him while he worked his way through the mob of protestors, a silver platter as a makeshift shield in his right to protect himself from the arrows that swarmed above.

With a grunt, he drove his heel into the gut of a boy no older than himself and knocked the elf to the ground before rendering him unconscious with a strike to his temple. Valeirys was about to grab the elf's collar and drag him out of the open and reach of the archers when a pair of bodies were hurled onto the floor beside him.

Crouching low to catch himself, Valeirys glanced to his right and recognized the prince himself tackling one of the protestors.

Prince Malik tore a candelabra from out of the elf's grasp. His ink-stained hands clawed at the prince's face, smearing it with streaks of black while he screamed curses on him.

With a punch to his ribs and then a blow to his jaw, the prince silenced the elf as his head lolled sideways.

Malik stood when something whizzed past Valeirys' left ear, and without thinking, he threw himself at the prince. Valeirys raised his shield high just as a shower of arrows rained over them.

More shrieks paired with a cascade of shrill cracking sounds split the air and drew Valeirys' attention to the hall's east flank that had been hit, and he watched in horror as sharp twisted lines tore through the once immaculate surface.

The glass creaked loudly, as if it was about to shatter. Several elves rushed toward it, raising their hands before the cracks, and causing layers of ice to form over the broken surface, intending to prevent it from crashing to the ground.

But just as quickly as the magic took effect, the side of the building was struck again, the glass exploded, and the wall came down.

Splinters and fragments of glass scattered everywhere. For a moment, Valeirys' vision blurred, and a shrill tinkling sound flooded his ears.

His senses numbed, and he heard his own breath and the muffled cries of the guests. The ground seemed to vibrate from the thundering footsteps as people raced past him.

The noise of glass scraping against the floor beneath the scampering soles of their shoes followed the sound of their flight like a shadow.

"Are you alright?" Valeirys shouted as he and the prince staggered to their feet.

Pushing forward, Valeirys moved toward the hall's entrance, the battered tray in his left still held high to guard the prince, who met his eyes and nodded.

They had almost reached the doors of the hall when a pair of soldiers came toward them and Valeirys let them take the prince.

The floor of the banquet teemed with armed elves and lords reclaiming control of the tumult. Some belted out commands, and Valeirys heard a group of voices cry out over the commotion, "To the gallery!"

Valeirys' head snapped upward, and his eyes raked the space above.

A figure moved, and Valeirys caught the swift flutter of a dark mantle just before someone spun away from the balcony of the gallery. The guileful gleam of the stranger's argent gaze still lingered in Valeirys' line of vision in the space where he had stood watching just seconds ago.

The elf's face had been hidden behind a mask, and yet Valeirys had no doubt of the smirk that disfigured his features before he vanished from sight.

A scourging heat coursed through Valeirys' veins at the ire that erupted within him.

The muscles in his legs jerked, his feet ready to take off from the ground, when he noticed something stick to the sole of his boot.

Reaching down, Valeirys ripped the piece of parchment from his shoe and brought it close. A scribble of black ink bled into the paper trapped beneath his left hand; his body went rigid as he read:

Let this be a warning to all ye of noble blood and claim.
We will not be silent.
With your cowardice, you have declared yourselves an enemy of the people.
We will avenge the suffering of our own.
We will cut off the head of the snake.

The Liberator

Chapter 9

Aleirya winced as the sharp edge of the beam dug into her shoulder. With a gasp, she readjusted her grip, her palms burning and prickling from the splintered wood; gritting her teeth, she dug her heels into the muddied ground and pushed.

"Lucius, Cassian, lift!" the cadet in front of her cried out. "By the dragon, if only they'd quit complaining and put that energy to good use!"

Ashamed, Aleirya realized she had already forgotten her name, having seen so many unfamiliar faces throughout the past weeks while helping clear the ruin sites of the destroyed dragon shelters under the king's command.

"Not so loud," Aleirya muttered breathlessly. "Otherwise they might feel insulted and drop it all together."

"Wouldn't make much of a difference," the other girl countered and then gasped for air. "Argh, why does this have to be so heavy?"

Ahead, the boys heaved the other end of the beam higher, raising it above their shoulders when the group finally reached the cart.

With a grunt, Aleirya helped shove the charred piece of debris forward and finally let go.

She stopped to catch her breath and rubbed her smeared hands against her thighs. They started to turn back to continue their work when they heard one of the academy's instructors call out, "Everyone, take a break!"

Shielding her eyes against the sun, Aleirya straightened and instantly caught sight of the small group of investigators that approached the shelter's remains.

"Off you go, step away! Let the investigators do their work," the instructor yelled again, waving his hands as if to herd them together like a group of children and lead them away.

He turned his back to them, when Aleirya quickly slipped behind the girl beside her and crouched low before sneaking over to a pile of wreckage.

"Where are you going?" the girl asked, trying to keep her voice low but loud enough for Aleirya to hear her.

"To relieve myself," Aleirya whispered back and waved her off. "I'll be right back."

The girl didn't believe her but only shrugged her shoulders and said, "Tsk, whatever."

She followed the others who moved toward the tents for a break when Aleirya smirked and moved on.

Settling down on the ground, she rested her back against a charred stack of wood and waited.

She was close enough to hear the investigators approach as they began their examination near the shelter's entrance; for a while, the only audible sound was the echo of their footsteps pounding against the remains of the shelter's old foundation.

Aleirya sighed impatiently, her shoulders sagging against the heap of soot-stained wood that granted her cover when, all at once, their footfalls grew softer and a pair of voices rose in muffled tones.

Aleirya cursed silently. She had to know what they were discussing.

Creeping along the remains of the shelter's outer walls, she drew as close as she dared to the group of the king's investigators.

The bitter and smoky odor of the scorched wood made her wrinkle her nose as she peered through a jagged hole in the west flank and watched as Sir Odynn held up a piece of debris into the sunlight.

"What do you think?" said the man to his right. According to Izidora's description of the lead investigator hired by His Majesty himself, she was certain that he had to be Sir Hothwin.

Sir Odynn studied the piece a bit longer before he replied, "It was indeed dragon's fire that burned the shelter to the ground. The evidence is undeniable. When held into the sunlight, any object destroyed by it casts the same violet sheen."

"Hmm, Princess Kalithea will not be pleased to hear this," said Sir Hothwin.

Sir Odynn nodded and handed the piece off to another, who stood beside them, and said, "I'm afraid it is indisputable. Even if we do not believe that the dragons did this of their own accord, the shelters were burned by dragon's fire."

As soon as he had spoken, the rest of the investigators joined them, and nodding, one of them said, "The talon marks are deepest along the west wall and continue toward the ceiling. The fire must have started on the opposite side."

Aleirya immediately ducked out of sight when she saw him point in her direction while explaining his findings.

Crouching low, she continued to listen as he went on, "We also discovered the same marks as proof that magic was used to aid the destruction of the shelter. It seems incredible that no one witnessed anything."

"Well, those who were close when the shelter caught fire and who might have seen anything were killed. The autopsies revealed that some of the victims might have even been struck down by this magic before their bodies were burned," said Sir Hothwin.

Aleirya felt her spine tingle at his words and pressed closer to the wall.

"Yes, but didn't some survive? I thought the count was seventeen. One of them ought to have something to say about that night," another chimed in.

"You can hardly speak of surviving," Sir Hothwin responded a bit pointedly. "Most of them were stable boys who worked at the shelters. I'm afraid if the reports are to be believed, their minds are lost. They will be lucky if they ever manage to speak a simple sentence again."

"This must have been the elves. Perhaps they were trying to steal the dragons from us?" a voice spat angrily.

"It seems an awfully grave risk for them to take, considering that the dragons would never side with them against us," another investigator replied.

"That is, if we believe it was an attack from the elves," Sir Odynn joined in. "We have yet to determine the magical source of this power, Sir Tallith."

The man he had just identified as Sir Tallith snorted and replied, "As if there were anyone else who despised the dragons more than the elves."

"Perhaps we should leave the political discussion to His Majesty and his royal council." Sir Hothwin's voice rose between them, interrupting the debate. "We are here to investigate and simply inform King Ethuriel to the best of our knowledge."

A set of heavy footsteps sounded as someone approached the group.

Daring to look up once more, Aleirya saw the instructor stop before the investigators and ask, "Sir Hothwin, could I be of any assistance to you?"

"I believe our investigation is almost concluded," Sir Hothwin answered, nodding politely. "However, for the sake of completeness, I would like to examine the remains of the roof if you would be so kind as to direct us to where you have put them?"

"Of course, Sir Hothwin. If you would follow me," he replied with a nod.

Their voices quieted as they left.

Going after them, Aleirya tiptoed toward the shelter's main entrance where the investigation had begun.

Stopping at the end of the wall, she watched the group walk away when Sir Odynn suddenly stopped and hung back.

Aleirya froze. Her heart pounded, and she held her breath. Had he seen her?

Unable to look away, she then saw him crouch down and pluck something from the ground.

Aleirya let out a sigh of relief but slid a little further behind the wall, just in case.

Rising to his feet, he called out to the others a few paces ahead, "Instructor, would you happen to know where the keeper of this shelter is?"

They all stopped at his words and turned toward him.

The instructor walked back to Sir Odynn when he answered, "I'm sure he is around here somewhere. I can summon him if you'd like."

"That would be most kind of you," said Sir Odynn.

The instructor nodded and quickly retreated from his side.

The rest of the investigators drew closer to Sir Odynn once again when he spoke aloud. "Aggyreidimos idiss… I cannot believe I didn't notice it earlier."

Raising his hand so they could see, he held out a plant before them. It looked like a weed, bearing several small white blossoms.

"Already bored with this investigation, Sir Odynn? Why the sudden interest in botany?" Sir Tallith teased.

The others chuckled.

Sir Odynn went on as if he hadn't heard him. "I've never seen its kind here before. It isn't known to grow in Tarragon."

"What exactly is it?" said another.

But before Sir Odynn could answer, the instructor returned along with the shelter's keeper.

"How long has this been growing here?" Sir Odynn asked.

"I couldn't say for certain. We had a new groundskeeper manage the land. I could speak with him and have word brought back to you," the shelter keeper replied.

"Good," Sir Odynn answered when Sir Hothwin interrupted, "Oh, for wings and talons, Jasper! What is it with this plant?"

Looking back at him, Sir Odynn answered, "Aggyreidimos idiss… translated, it means silver tongue. It is rather uncommon; first mentioned centuries ago. If the recordings are true, with the right spell, its properties can force any truth from the mind of the one subdued by its effects."

"What would this have to do with the fires?" Sir Tallith asked.

"I'm not sure. I'd need some time to study it, and I have yet to research the effect it would have on a dragon. But its discovery here is quite unusual," said Sir Odynn.

With a sigh, Sir Hothwin answered, "Very well. If anything should come of it, do not hesitate to share it with the rest of us."

Sir Odynn nodded, still studying the plant in his hand as the group moved again, leaving the shelter behind.

Once they were far enough away, Aleirya stepped out from her hiding place and walked toward the tents to join her fellow cadets.

Her mind itched with more questions after what she had learned.

Why would the dragons destroy the shelter? What sort of magic was at play here?

Aleirya continued to ponder the conversation she had eavesdropped upon, her eyes trailing the muddied ground before her as she went until she halted.

Squinting, she crouched down, having spied something in the dirt. Drawing it out of the mud, she rose and rubbed it clean. It was a small piece of wood that looked like a twig adjoined to an oval-shaped piece at the bottom. Dangling from its other end was a tiny metal ring that had been broken.

Eyeing it, Aleirya couldn't help but think that she had seen it before, though that was impossible. Playing with it in her open hand, she inspected it a while longer before she gave up and tucked it away in her pocket.

The motion felt oddly familiar and yet she couldn't tell why.

Shrugging off the peculiar sensation that she had somehow done this before, Aleirya continued to march toward the tents.

Still confused and distracted, she almost ran into someone when she reached the camp. Looking up just in time to avoid colliding with another cadet passing her, she dodged them and twirled sideways.

A weight slammed into her chest when she stopped and saw Nathanael standing by one of the tents up ahead.

He wasn't alone.

Across from him stood a girl, smiling and going on about something that appeared to be terribly amusing.

Glancing from Nathanael to the girl, Aleirya didn't recognize her. But the simple observation of her gown gave away that she wasn't a fellow soldier from the academy, and the way she stood there so elegantly, even the style of her hair, made Aleirya think she was one of those girls who didn't enjoy getting their hands dirty.

She watched Nathanael smile back at the stranger, seemingly taken by their conversation.

The girl moved closer to him and stroked his arm before leaning forward to whisper something to him.

Aleirya's stomach knotted while she watched her step back and slowly walk away from him.

She looked back at Nathanael, but he had already turned and left in the opposite direction. Aleirya's brows furrowed as she stood there motionless for a moment, wondering what exactly she had just witnessed.

The knots in her stomach didn't loosen, but she refused to pay them any more attention, and instead, she turned and joined a group of cadets that passed her, heading back toward the shelter to resume their work.

A warm breeze rustled the fields tinged in orange and gold when Aleirya finally reached her parents' home.

Plodding through the tall grass, she could see Takhéa and the old fire dragon, Brandr, basking in the last rays of the evening sun as they lay before the cottage and Thoran's workshop. The fire dragon had once been bonded to her great-grandfather, and ever since his passing many years ago, he had remained with the Perèdur family, offering his service to the forge.

Now under Thoran's care, Brandr provided the forge with the dragon's fire they needed for the crafting of Tarragon's finest weaponry.

Brandr lay on his belly in the fields with his enormous head perched up on a rock that had been warmed by the sun, sleeping soundly. Compared to him, Takhéa, who was resting not far away from the great red dragon, looked like a fledgling that had just hatched.

Takhéa lay curled up with her tail wrapped around her body and its point tucked under the side of her head while she slept.

What a life, Aleirya thought, grinning at the sight of her dragon.

When she was close enough to touch her, Takhéa opened her silver eye, keeping the other shut, and remarked, "You know, I don't know what it is you're thinking, but I can sense jealousy."

Aleirya laughed.

"It's alright," she replied, stroking her dragon's snout, and then added, "I'm glad one of us is enjoying a good life."

"Mmm," was all Takhéa remarked before Aleirya walked on by, and the dragon turned her head to face the other side, drifting back to sleep.

Shaking her head, Aleirya smiled contently.

She had almost reached the cottage when she heard Thoran call her name.

Stopping, she looked up and met his gaze while he approached from the right, having come from the forge.

Thoran was in a good mood, and coming to a stop beside her, he brushed the delicate ridge of her nose, leaving a black mark from the soot that was on his hands.

Aleirya grinned at him, both amused and annoyed, and asked, "Really?"

Thoran laughed.

"Well, you know, you've looked so pale these days that I thought you could use a little color," he said.

"Thanks," she answered.

He laughed aloud once more and then threw his arm around her shoulders, waiting for her to smile before he asked, "How was your day?"

"Fine," Aleirya muttered as they headed on inside the cottage.

Zannia was already waiting for them and urged them to hurry and clean up before supper.

After they had eaten, they settled down by the small fireplace of the cottage where Thoran fell quickly fell asleep in the rocking chair that looked very much too small for his brawny form. For a while, Aleirya and Zannia sat closely beside each other before the hearth, sharing the contents of their day before they both fell silent, staring at the fire and enjoying the soothing warmth together.

When the flames had dwindled and only glowing embers remained, Zannia turned in for the night. She covered Thoran, who was fast asleep, and planted a kiss on Aleirya's head.

"Good night, my little dragon warrior," she said and lovingly stroked Aleirya's cheek before retreating to her bedroom.

"Good night," Aleirya whispered after her.

Still wide awake and longing for her dragon's company, Aleirya rose and grabbed a quilt before quietly sneaking outside the cottage. Takhéa was lying on her side, not far ahead, with her back toward Aleirya. Her long neck extended in the air as she looked out over the fields.

Cast in the moonlight, her lilac wings and spikes that ran along her neck and tail shimmered silver.

Aleirya climbed over the dragon's forearms and shins folded in front of her and halted before the spike emerging from the joint of her left wing. When Takhéa didn't move it to let her crawl into the hollow of her side, she asked, smiling, "Are you going to let me in?"

Takhéa stared down at her for a moment, hesitating before she huffed a grunt and then slowly raised her wing.

Aleirya's breath caught, an ache gripping her chest, and she swallowed.

Even under the faint light of the moon, the talon marks across her dragon's side were visible.

Her fists clenched, and she whirled to face her dragon as she spoke. "Who did this to you? What happened?"

Takhéa lowered her head, closing the distance between them so that Aleirya could place a hand on her snout. She waited until Aleirya's breathing slowed before she batted her eyes and answered, "Unbound dragons attacked us while we were scouting the cliffs for abandoned caves for the nesting season. Since the shelters are unusable, Princess Kalithea asked for our help while our riders were busy helping clear the ruin sites. At first, I thought we must have gotten too close to another nest, but these dragons were looking for a fight."

Aleirya's jaw clenched, and she shook her head before closing her eyes and resting her forehead against her dragon's scales. She tried her best to push away the thought of her dragon finding herself in harm's way without her there to help her.

Takhéa hummed.

"I know I didn't tell you," her dragon began. "But after everything that happened, I wanted to do something… The attacks, the deaths of the young dragons, they have unsettled the Unbound."

Slowly, Takhéa pulled away, and Aleirya looked up to meet her gaze.

"I knew the Unbound dragons despised us for our choice to bond with you, but to turn against us, their own kind, when someone out there clearly intends to harm us... I don't understand."

Aleirya swallowed and spoke. "I'm sorry, Takhéa."

Her dragon shook her head and went on as if she hadn't heard her. "Brandr said it won't be the last time something like this happens. He's warned me from now on not to hunt on my own. And there's more."

Her dragon's head swung back toward her, and Aleirya froze at the ferocity in her wide eyes.

"Already fewer dragons are returning to Tarragon and to the Dragon's Kin to have their young. Kalithea fears they have lost faith in your people's protection. She said it means that fewer will be born and raised amongst the Dragon's Kin and that would result in fewer desiring a bond with them, meaning—"

"The end of the riders," Aleirya interrupted breathlessly.

Her gaze dropped from Takhéa to the ground at her feet, and her heart sank. How could this be?

Aleirya's arms stiffened at her sides, warmth flooding her chest as her gaze narrowed and then darted back up to her dragon.

"What can we do?" she asked.

Takhéa turned toward her and nudged her cheek with her snout before she replied with a growl, "I think we need to figure out who did this and destroy them for it."

Chapter 10

Dressed in her riding gear, Aleirya waited for Takhéa to return from her hunt with Brandr.

Anxiety crawled up her spine, not only after what had happened to her dragon the last time they were apart, but also because, today of all days, she could not be late. The cadets had been called to return to the academy after having helped the builders prepare for the new construction of the dragon shelters; considering the recommencement of their training, the academy's instructors had organized a tournament all trainees had been invited to take part in.

Crossing her arms over her chest, she huffed a breath and bit down on her lip, counting the seconds that ticked by relentlessly.

These competitions were open to the public, though far less attended compared to the royal tournaments which were hosted by the king once a year. However, they weren't simply attractions or a means to test one's skills for fun.

Representatives of Tarragon's warlords always visited official academy tournaments. It was a means to scout the younger generations of warriors for new recruits for their armies. If she did well, she would be remembered, and a good performance today could raise her prospects by bounds. If the representatives liked what they saw, it could lead to her having her pick of one of Tarragon's finest armies to join and better her position for bargaining over her wages while serving the warlord as a dragon warrior.

Prepared to leave, she stared out into the distance, searching the skies for any sight of her dragon when she heard Zannia approach her from behind.

Aleirya turned and smiled once she drew close, wrapping her arms around her in a hug.

"We're going to miss having you around so much," said Zannia, letting go of her and stepping back.

In the background, she could hear Thoran's voice call out to her, "Wait!"

He hurried to the door, holding something in his hand. The object was wrapped in thick leather, and handing it to Aleirya, he said, smiling, "Open it."

Aleirya looked at him curiously and unwrapped it.

Inside was a chakram. Its sharp edge had been decorated with the signature engraving she recognized from other weapons the Perèdurs had made.

Five sharp points extended from the circular blade. A part of the chakram had been wrapped in leather for a handle that seemed to fit the width of her palm perfectly.

"It's beautiful," Aleirya said and looked up at Thoran with a smile. "Thank you!"

"It was my father's and your grandfather's. He had it with him in battle when our warriors aided the elves in their war against King Izurion. As you know, it isn't a weapon the Dragon's Kin commonly use. But when he forged weapons for the elves back then, he made this one for himself.

"It's smaller than the traditional chakram the elves use but just as deadly. I found it the other day when I was cleaning out the storage. I thought, since you're the warrior in our family now, you should have it. He would have given it to you himself if he were here, I'm sure," said Thoran.

Aleirya carefully re-wrapped the chakram in the leather and threw her arms around him.

"It's perfect. Thank you!" she said.

Thoran smiled and answered, "I'm glad you like it."

Aleirya carefully packed the chakram away in a small pouch on the side of her trousers, just below her left knee.

Peering over her shoulder, she could finally see the dark silhouette of her dragon's form approaching in the distance.

Hugging her parents once more, she hurried outside and ran toward Takhéa, who began to land.

"You know from now on, every time you're late, I'm going to be worried," said Aleirya.

Takhéa began to lower her chest toward the ground when she replied, "I'm not late. I just measure time differently; besides, Brandr was with me. Any dragon would have to be out of their right mind to attack him."

Aleirya shook her head and started to climb up her dragon's side. Once again, her breath caught when she pulled herself upright onto Takhéa's back and noticed the scratches along her dragon's scales that ran down her side from her left shoulder.

Swallowing, she opened her mouth to reply, but all that came out was, "I can't be late."

Takhéa huffed as if having taken offense and responded, "You won't be… that is as long as you hold on tight."

And with that, the dragon leaped into the air and took flight.

Brusquely, Aleirya pushed through the hundreds of cadets who had gathered around the central training field of the Esdras Academy, ignoring the annoyed glances and the retorts telling her to watch her step.

Anger thrummed through her veins; a fresh surge of heat consuming her body at the pain and frustration over what had happened to Takhéa.

How could those dragons have attacked their own blood?

If only she had been at her dragon's side.

Shoving past another group of bystanders, Aleirya reached the large platform beneath the open-roofed court and crossed it, joining the other cadets who had signed up to partake in the competition.

In her fury, she barely felt the weight of her armor.

The Esdras Academy was buzzing with life and packed to the rafters as the tournament was about to begin.

Four different platforms and training sites, spread throughout the academy, had been prepared for the upcoming event, giving the cadets an opportunity to demonstrate their skills in different disciplines.

Besides the dual wield competition for which Aleirya had signed up for, the tournament's remaining contests comprised a hand-to-hand combat tourney, an archery contest, the dragon races, and the game of spells, a competition that tested one's magical abilities.

Perhaps things were far worse than they thought...

With lips pressed to a hard line, Aleirya set her helmet down beside her and fastened her hair in a braid while her mind continued to overflow with concern.

What if the Unbound truly blamed the Dragon's Kin for what happened in the shelter fires and turned against them? How were they supposed to fight and survive a battle on two sides, facing an unknown enemy with vast magical powers and the dragons of the Unbound?

A hand came to rest on her shoulder, and she jumped.

Wincing at the sudden volume that arose around her from the ongoing event, having seemed to have drowned it out completely, Aleirya looked to her right.

"Is everything alright?" Nathanael asked, grinning. "You seem a little nervous."

Shrugging off his hand, she replied, "I'm not nervous."

Beside him stood a tall stranger, or rather, a contestant.

Wanting to avoid any further conversation with Nathanael, Aleirya extended her hand toward the other cadet and spoke above the noise. "I don't believe we've met before; my name is Aleirya."

THE RISE OF ISIGAR

The young man shook her hand and replied, smiling, "The name's Kajetan. I've heard a lot of good things about you, Aleirya."

Letting go, she returned the smile and said, "Ah, well, then remember those when I beat you. It's really nothing personal."

Kajetan laughed and then answered, "I think I like you already."

She could feel Nathanael's eyes on her when she stepped back and averted her gaze toward the crowds standing on the opposite side of the court, pretending not to notice.

In her distraction, contemplating the attack on her dragon, she hadn't even thought to scan the masses for any sight of the warlords' representatives.

Her heart pounded at the sudden reminder of the significance of the next hours that lay ahead.

The cheering grew louder when one of the academy's lead instructors stepped out onto the platform. Welcoming the guests and fellow trainees for their attendance of the competition, he began by stating the rules of the contest. Brute force against the opponent was to be avoided as well as blows to the head or neck; the goal was to hold the opponent at sword point to surrender or disarm them.

"Finally," he proclaimed. "In light of the attacks on the dragon shelters, the winner of this competition shall be granted the rare privilege of joining the royal investigation of the threat against our kingdom. Rest assured, this is not an opportunity you want to miss out on, as it will allow you to prove the first fruits of your training to no one other than King Ethuriel himself."

His gaze passed over the crowds that cheered and clapped before he spoke, at last. "Let the tournament commence!"

One by one, the names of the first contestants were drawn to determine the contenders of the following duel.

Kajetan was one of the first cadets to be called; when he headed onto the platform, Aleirya sent him off with a whistle, joining in on the cheering that rose about them.

Looking back at her over his shoulder, he winked teasingly before picking up his pace, jogging toward the center of the court to meet his opponent.

The fight only lasted a few minutes and had undoubtedly impressed the spectators.

By only a handful of maneuvers, Kajetan had disarmed his opponent, forcing him to surrender.

Despite his tall muscular form, he had moved soundlessly and with an agility that both fascinated Aleirya and made her stir with envy. Perfect focus and precision in every strike of the blade had proven him the dominant swordsman, a worthy contender, and a challenge she yearned for.

Watching Kajetan walk off the field victoriously, she couldn't help but smile.

Rejoining them, he resumed his spot beside Nathanael and removed his helmet, shaking his head while he forced the stray strands of his blond hair out of his eyes.

"Not bad," said Aleirya, looking past Nathanael at Kajetan, "though I thought you could best him quicker."

Still breathing a bit heavily, Kajetan replied, "I'm just warming up for our duel."

"You're that confident it'll be so easy to best me?" she asked.

"Easy, no… but fun, yes," he answered with a smirk.

"We'll just have to see about that," she replied, grinning back.

Then she returned her attention to the next match already unfolding in front of them, silently betting which of the contestants would be the winner. This went on, fight after fight, until she shifted from one leg to the other, and her skin itched from the wait, wondering when it would finally be her turn.

Nathanael hadn't spoken another word to her, standing beside her and observing one match after the other while wrapped up in conversation with Kajetan.

Observing him from the side, it seemed as if he were trying to ignore her as well.

Something lurched in her gut at the thought.

Aleirya wondered if it was because of the girl she had seen him with. Perhaps things were changing between them.

Chewing her lip, she pushed the thought aside.

How had they gotten here? She hated this, hated the way things were between them.

Staring at him, she overheard the first call of her name as the instructor drew the names of the next cadets for the upcoming duel. She only realized she had been called when Nathanael suddenly looked back at her and held her gaze for a moment that seemed to drag on for minutes. Pursing his lips, she waited for him to speak, when her name sounded again, and he seemed to change his mind.

Tapping her shoulder, he shouted over the noise, "Knock them dead."

He smiled as if nothing were off.

Nodding, she grabbed her helmet and headed toward the middle of the training platform, silently cursing herself for growing so distracted by him.

Shrugging every thought aside in order to clear her mind for the duel, Aleirya continued to trudge forward, scanning the court for her opponent.

She hadn't heard the name the instructor had called upon announcing the next fight.

When her eyes fell on the person moving toward her, already her disappointment rang through her mind. Not him.

Across from her, Damian Astraea began to take the field.

The boy continued to raise his hands as if to rouse the crowds to cheer him on, a contemptuous smile on his face while he neared her.

Reaching the middle of the platform, he slowed to a stop, purposely stepping into her path so that their shoulders bumped against each other when she tried to walk past him.

Her left fist clenched, and she stopped beside him.

She hated that she had to look up at him to see his face but did her best not to let it show.

Winking at her, he leaned toward her and whispered, "I promise I'll play fair."

The notion made her want to grit her teeth, but she forced a charming smile instead.

When he straightened, she looked into his eyes and answered, "I don't play, I win."

A hint of surprise at her words flashed across his face before his smug expression returned. Ignoring him, she turned and walked away, stretching as tall as she could while she headed to her side of the field.

Coming to a stop, she spun around and resumed staring back at Damian, who stood with his back toward her on the opposite corner of the court, still flirting with the crowds.

Envisioning him dropping to his knees in defeat, she drew her helmet over her head.

Its black steel appeared as if covered in scales, matching the breastplate, vambraces, cuisses, and greaves of the rest of her armor. Two tear-shaped openings formed the slits for her eyes to see through. A pair of dragon's wings formed the helmet's sides, beginning from the front at the height of her chin and ending in two sharp points that stuck out above her head.

She went on studying Damian until a boy approached her from the side.

Finally, looking away from her opponent, she unsheathed both her swords from her back and cast them downward before handing them over to the boy.

Nodding, he accepted them and then walked toward a brazier set alight by a white flame. It wasn't a fire, but a spell displaying the illusion of a flaming shape. An instructor and their dragon had cast it before the beginning of the tournament.

With a razor-sharp gaze, she watched the boy draw each of her blades through the white blaze, sealing them with a magic that would protect her opponent from any injury.

She had forged the swords herself, having learned under Thoran's tutelage, and she prided herself on them.

As their maker, she had named them Ismené and Valdr, meaning wisdom and ruler.

Aleirya kept her eyes on them while the boy turned and walked back to her. Unlike the elven soldier, a Dragon's Kin warrior was traditionally taught to fight with two swords. The double-edged blades were curved and had two sharp points at the ends, imitating the shape of a dragon's wings.

Reaching her side, the boy returned the twin swords.

Taking them back, she nodded a silent thank you and then redirected her gaze toward the center of the court, waiting for the instructor to call her and Damian together.

When he summoned them, she approached the middle of the platform, Ismené and Valdr gripped firmly in both hands.

Coming to a stop at the instructor's signal, she looked straight at Damian.

The boy was in good shape, broad shouldered and about a head taller than herself. Optimistically speaking, her odds for a victory weren't as good as his, if solely judged on their physical appearances. Despite her lean and wiry form, wrought from years of training, she couldn't rely on sheer strength when pitted against him.

But perhaps quickness and endurance would do the trick.

Damian still hadn't put on his helmet. Most assuredly he had done so to further intimidate her. Without it, she could clearly see the pompous expression that crossed his face and the same haughty look in his eyes every boy she had ever fought against had had when contending against her for the first time.

She had heard he was a good fighter, and he had a reputation for his formidable skills, but she would not let that unsettle her.

His arrogance was as easy for her to read off him as it was to tell the color of his eyes, and she would use it to her advantage.

Pride was good, but overconfidence could cost any warrior, no matter how great, their victory.

When Damian smiled back at her, it was as clear as day that he was certain she had no chance against him.

Though she knew he couldn't see her expression hidden away beneath her helmet, she grinned. Anyone was defeatable if only you could find their weakness, and Damian's was his egotism.

Standing tall, with her feet firmly fixed on the ground, she waited for the instructor to step back. She and Damian were far enough apart for the tips of their extended blades to touch.

When the instructor gave them both a nod, Aleirya took one step forward and raised Valdr to meet Damian's left blade.

"Foratis méa dukero," both of them said.

Courage guide me. The words rang true within her.

Lowering her right arm, Aleirya then drew Ismené, crossing it with Damian's right sword and spoke along with him. "Diagoni eta èdyanur méa annae inoeram."

Honor and strength be my wings.

Then she took one step back, dropping onto one knee like her opponent.

She crossed both of her swords before her with the words, "Eta unum méa vaspiron edrakai magveiis praena."

And may my dragon's blood grant me victory.

As she spoke, her eyes were on Damian until she rose, pulling both swords back down to her sides.

Having completed the Dimardraki's ritual, the dragon warrior's pledge, Aleirya took her position for the duel to begin, at last.

CHAPTER 11

L eft foot forward, Aleirya held Valdr raised above her shoulder, its point directed at Damian's chest.

With Ismené grasped tightly in her left, she held the blade steady and aimed at his gut.

The whole place quieted as she blocked out the noise of the crowds surrounding the court. The cheering spectators' waving arms and their shifting bodies melted into one blur while her eyes focused on Damian's form alone, the sole object of her attention.

Eliminate the distraction, keep your eyes on the opponent, and never underestimate their strength.

The teachings of her training circled in her mind like a mantra.

Both of them continued to move in an almost simultaneous motion, circling the court on nimble feet.

Now that Damian wore his helmet, she wished she could see more of his face. This way, it was much harder to guess how confident he felt or what he perhaps meant to do. Staring back into his blue eyes, ridden with determination, she noticed the slightest flicker in his gaze before he lurched.

Aleirya moved upon instinct and deflected the strike before they both skipped out of reach of the other within a heartbeat.

The space around them exploded in bright light as her senses heightened.

She could feel her own breath against her skin tinged with a taste of steel, and the initially faint clinking sound of their armor, that shifted along with the motion of their bodies, rose to a volume that made her ears hum.

Damian charged at her anew.

His left blade whipped toward her from above, while his right swung from below in a horizontal arc toward her waist.

Aleirya repelled the dexterous move and retaliated.

Time slowed to a trickle while a screech tore through the court as Valdr's point grazed his breastplate.

Damian leaped backward; when they broke apart, Aleirya caught his glare, piercing through the slits of his helmet, and she knew.

She was not what he had expected.

Satisfaction kindled the flames that licked at her heart, and she threw herself back into the fight.

Like a set of drums, the steady beat of her pulse gave her rhythm as she glided across the platform.

Aleirya followed his attack with a swift maneuver, feigning left with a hint of a thrust before slashing Valdr at Damian's left arm.

He grunted at the hit but held onto his weapon.

Without thinking twice, Aleirya advanced onto him again and threw her weight against his block, driving him backward.

Under each thrust of her arms, the pulsating flow of her own blood grew louder, reminding her of the powerful stroke of her dragon's wings, and she smiled in defiance of her opponent.

He would remember this fight… She would make sure he did.

Damian's next strike came quickly and with a force that sent jolts down her arms as she parried the blow of both his blades, crossing her swords above her shoulders.

His attacks were growing fiercer. He was growing impatient.

The corners of her lips twitched upward to a grin.

Then, feigning high, she struck low, jabbing both her swords toward his abdomen.

Damian almost tripped but escaped the blow.

He countered swiftly, but she guessed his next move and returned the favor with an equally quick riposte, forcing him to retreat with a growl.

Good, Aleirya thought, and she smirked. He didn't like that she wasn't the easy target he had made her out to be.

The soles of her feet stung from the constant shuffling, and cold sweat ran down her spine as her body burned from the lithe twists and turns following the twitch of each muscle.

Blots of color danced in the periphery of her vision as the crowd's stirring increased, but not once did she dare take her eyes off her opponent.

The following blows came hard and fast as the steel cracked and shrieked between them, sending flashes of silver through the space around them as their shadows danced across the field below the midday sun.

Aleirya lunged at Damian, hurling her blade toward his knees.

Dodging the strike, he attacked in return, but she sidestepped his advance with a quick spin to the right.

All she needed was to provoke him into making a mistake.

Jabbing Ismené toward his center, Aleirya swung Valdr low, aiming to slash the sword along Damian's waist.

He heaved an angry breath as the blade barely missed its mark and then retaliated.

Again, she escaped his reach, making him shout, and in the blink of an eye, he came at her again.

Both his swords came crashing down at her at a blinding pace that forced her to retreat once she parried the hit.

A surge of energy seemed to course through Damian as he swung his blades anew in a similar motion, making use of the momentum he had gained.

Aleirya wanted to wince at the weight of his thrust that broke over her, and she found herself counting each hit, wondering how many she could parry before her knees gave way.

She couldn't overpower him; he was too strong. She had to stop him, and she would.

A gasp reached her ears as Damian began to tire under the effort of his blows.

But she couldn't wait for exhaustion to overtake him and grant her the win.

The next hit sent a sharp pain down her spine, and she bit her lip, tasting blood.

Suppressing a cry, Aleirya pushed back as hard as she could.

If she could make him believe he had won, if he thought she had given up, perhaps she could surprise him.

The next clash of their swords threatened to deafen them both as Aleirya fended off the strike and forced some space between them. He was driving her toward the opposite side of the court and into the corner of the platform.

Falling back, Aleirya feigned a stumble backward, catching herself on her right leg.

Taking the bait, Damian drew closer and struck at her again, swinging one sword after the other in a downward diagonal motion over his shoulders.

Instead of blocking the hit, Aleirya leaned backward and retreated just enough for Damian's blade to miss its mark.

She let him attack her a few more times, evading each blow by simply moving out of reach, acting as if her strength were failing her.

A gleam darted across his eyes while he marched after her.

It was working.

Dragging his right sword after him, he stepped toward her and raised his left blade, prepared to cast one final blow and claim his victory.

Now! her mind screamed, and she charged.

Bounding toward him, Aleirya hauled Ismené upward and deflected his sword with a backhanded block before propelling Valdr with as much strength as she could muster into his left side.

Damian buckled at the blow, bending forward just as Aleirya withdrew Valdr and brought the sword down onto his right arm.

Damian's right blade slipped from his grasp, and he stumbled backward.

His hands fumbled around the hilt of his remaining weapon, but before he could strike back, Aleirya had already swung both her swords overhead and against his defense.

The force of both blades caused him to loosen his grip.

Aleirya saw it and responded without a moment to spare.

With a deafening shriek, Ismené's true edge clashed against Damian's sword, blocking it, and immediately, Aleirya raised Valdr to his throat.

The boy froze.

Holding him at sword point, she spoke. "Drop it."

All at once, the commotion of the crowds came crashing over her in a crippling capacity as her focus shifted from Damian to her surroundings.

Aleirya's body jerked, threatening to collapse, but she stood tall.

When Damian finally dropped his weapon, she stepped closer so that both their helmets almost touched.

With Valdr's edge pinned against his neck, she looked directly into his eyes.

Got you, she thought, hearing her own proud voice resonate within above the crowds' gleeful voices that blared around her.

The air that filled her lungs as her chest rose in a deep breath never felt better; even the taste of her own blood that still lingered in her mouth seemed sweet at the thrill of victory.

The sun beat down on them when the tournament concluded.

Squinting at the bright light, Aleirya watched as the heat waves rose from the sandstone platform, blearing her surroundings.

Her muscles ached, the palms of her hands stung, and she longed to put her feet up, standing in the middle of the court beside the other high-ranking contenders of the dual wield competition.

Out of the fifty contestants, she had come in fifth place; best of her division and the only younger cadet to make it into the final rounds along with the academy's graduates.

The shed dragon scales worked into her armor prevented her from overheating. Nevertheless, she grew increasingly uncomfortable, and in the merciless heat, slowly but surely, the weariness set in.

She couldn't wait to get out of here and clean up before finding Takhéa.

The thought of soaring aimlessly through the sky without the pressing weight of her armor, the wind tearing through her open hair, made her want to sigh.

Her gaze shifted to the left just as more applause erupted from the ranks of the crowds at the announcement of the contest's winner. They whistled and cheered while the instructor placed the garland of golden dragon roses around Nathanael's neck.

Aleirya watched, unable to suppress a grin while he bowed his head slightly before the instructor and then accepted a pin showing a fiery ring with two crossed swords at its center.

Upon claiming his reward, Nathanael stepped back, rejoining the rest of them.

Clapping, she joined in on the praise bellowing forth from the crowds when Kajetan, who stood beside her, tilted his head toward her and spoke. "One day that will be you."

She looked back at him and nodded appreciatively.

"You did great. It wasn't at all easy to best you, and definitely not as much fun as I thought it would be," he teased.

"Thanks," she replied, recalling the memories of their match.

It was the one she had learned the most from and perhaps also the one she had enjoyed the most.

She had managed to keep him shuffling across the court until his breath came in quick strokes, challenging each of his attacks with a dexterity that had forced him to always think several steps ahead. They had both fought splendidly, but in the end, he had bested her with her own tricks, using a moment of her distraction to force her to surrender, landing her in fifth instead of fourth place of the competition. The result of the fight had cautioned her never to get too comfortable with her strategy and be prepared to change course even when least expected.

Her focus shifted back toward the present once the instructor turned toward her and the remaining three contestants awaiting their reward.

Each of them received a garland with dragon roses bearing a splendid royal blue and a sealed scroll, stating their accomplishment and ranking position in the competition.

After accepting the scroll and bowing her head at the instructor who remained standing across from her, she took a step back and drew one of her swords, extending the weapon before him.

An enormous dragon head then peered out over the frame of the open roof and cast a relieving shadow over her. With the hilt of her sword aligned horizontally, Aleirya held Valdr before her and observed the instructor raise his hand to hover over its fuller.

Aided by his dragon's magic, she watched him drag his fingers through the air until a tiny spark arose and moved along the steel of the blade in a mixture of circles and lines, forming an engraving of a dragon's head. At the center of the creature's eye, instead of the slit pupil, a downcast sword appeared; a token of her achievement for all to see.

When he had finished, the instructor nodded back at her with a grin and moved on to the next contestant beside her, repeating the procedure.

Lowering her sword, Aleirya pulled it closer to herself, admiring the new mark.

A ray of golden light bounced off the fine steel as the dragon above shifted, moving its head so that the sun poured over her once more. Blinking as her eyes adjusted to the light, she caught her reflection in the fuller of her sword and smiled.

With her ears thrumming from the hours of clashing steel and the commotion from the crowds who dispersed as the tournament ended, Aleirya walked off the platform.

She had almost reached the edge when someone stopped her from behind, and she turned at the familiar sound of his voice. "Hey, great job out there! You really didn't go easy on Kajetan."

Aleirya smiled and nodded, looking back at Nathanael standing across from her.

She stared into his eyes, forgetting to say anything for a moment before a reply stumbled from her lips. "Thanks—well, and you; I mean, you won! That's amazing! I mean not that it was surprising at all; you're one of the best…"

Shut up! she cursed at herself. She never rambled on like that around him.

A simple 'thank you' and 'congratulations' would have been enough…

Lowering his head briefly, Nathanael grinned, making the dimple in his left cheek deepen. Aleirya felt something tug at her from within at the sight of it.

When he looked back at her through the wavy strands of his dark brown hair that hung over his forehead, a heat flashed over her, rippling from her head and neck and down into her arms and legs.

Ignoring it, she swallowed and forced a neutral smile before Nathanael spoke again. Involuntarily, her gaze dropped to his lips as they moved, and she resisted the urge to grit her teeth.

"A few of us are heading to Killian's tonight to celebrate if you'd like to join us. You can bring Izidora, too," he said.

Intent on keeping her reply short this time, Aleirya nodded and answered, "Sure."

She shrugged her shoulders just to add a bit of casual flare to her response, as if he hadn't flustered her at all.

A strange pause lingered between them before Nathanael's smile deepened, and he added, "Pick you up before sundown at the front gate?"

This time, she only nodded and then watched him turn away with an amused grin and a final glance over his shoulder.

When she had lost sight of him in the crowds, the same gut-tugging sensation returned, and she clenched her fists, feeling stupid.

Why had she said yes? She was mad at him for keeping secrets from her, and now she had simply agreed to tag along with him like all those other silly, stupid girls desperate for a boy's attention. She should have said no. Why hadn't she said no?

"Miss Perèdur," another said, approaching from her right.

Immediately, Aleirya's mind snapped out of its grumblings, and she turned toward him, recognizing the instructor's voice.

"Sir Bradan," she replied, bowing respectfully.

"That was quite a performance, Cadet Perèdur. I see the absence from the academy has not harmed your training. I look forward to seeing how you progress this year."

"Thank you, sir," Aleirya said.

Instructor Bradan nodded in return and spoke. "You can be very proud of your accomplishments today."

He eyed her for a moment before adding, "I believe there are some people who would like to speak with you."

He tilted his head to the left, gesturing at a group that stood a bit off to the side, avoiding the visitors who continued to file outside of the academy.

Aleirya recognized them as the representatives of four of Tarragon's armies, each decorated with a pin that showed a dragon with scales of a different color, depending on the warlord they served.

Bronze, green, red, and purple… Lord Oberon, Lady Anthea, Lord Eldread, Lord Zadock… Aleirya eyed each of them while she analyzed the group. She had caught the attention of four out of six of the representatives. It was a result she was quite content with; for now…

"Would you like me to introduce you to them?" Instructor Bradan asked, interrupting her thoughts.

"Yes, sir," she answered, trying not to sound too eager.

They began to walk toward the group when he spoke to her again. "If you are interested, perhaps I could have you train with some of our graduates this term?"

Ecstatic over the opportunity he had just offered her, Aleirya slowed her steps and exclaimed, smiling, "Yes! Yes, of course!" and then re-gathering her composure, hoping the representatives hadn't noticed her enthusiastic reaction, she added in a more collected manner, "I mean, absolutely, sir. I would be honored, sir."

Grinning slightly at her excitement, he answered, "Very well, then. I will arrange for you to join us soon. After all, young talent is to be furthered."

"Thank you, Sir Bradan," Aleirya replied just before they closed the distance to the group of representatives.

Chapter 12

Izidora sat with her legs tucked up against her chest in one of the far corners of the gallery that overlooked the council chamber, eavesdropping on the councilors of the king who were arguing below. Far too curious what her father and his advisors were planning to do about current matters, she and Aleirya had developed a habit of sneaking into the private meetings of the council for weeks now. Izidora had left one of the gallery's windows open across from where she sat huddled for Aleirya to sneak in after her. Aleirya had climbed the outside façade of the building and pulled herself up onto a broad ledge that extended from the wall and waved to her.

Izidora signaled it was safe for her to crawl inside when the voices from the assembly below grew louder.

"What did I miss?" Aleirya whispered, huddling down on the floor beside her.

"Nothing we didn't already know. Sir Hothwin just explained what you told me. The dragons' own fire and some sort of foreign sorcery destroyed the dragon shelters. He mentioned something about strange marks that were identical at each shelter and that prove the use of magic; ever since then, they've been arguing over how all of this could even be possible," Izidora whispered back.

Stretching their necks as far as they dared, they could see King Ethuriel, beside him Kalithea, who had recently been allowed to take her seat next to him in the council, the royal administrators, and Tarragon's warlords.

Unlike the military structure of the elves, Tarragon's military was divided into six separate armies. First, there was Tarragon's royal army led by King Ethuriel himself and his right hand, Lord Jarek, which was the largest of the six. After the royal army, five military units, smaller, yet still each a respectable force, were led by Tarragon's warlords. The warlords were subject to the king's command and pledged allegiance to His Majesty to protect Tarragon whenever there was an imminent threat. However, each warlord had independent authority when it came to the government of his or her own soldiers.

As a soldier or dragon warrior, one was free to join any of the military forces, granted the warlord in charge or, in case of the royal army, Lord Jarek accepted one's request.

The five warlords who sat at the table below were Lord Zadok, Lord Oberon, Lord Eldread, the Lady Anthea, and the most savage of them all, Lord Varlam. Lord Varlam was not known for his tact. As a matter of fact, one could doubt he even had any sense of proper courtesy or understanding for anyone but himself. He was a man of war and a prideful one at that. He had made a name for himself by his military feats, though he was much more popular for his brash behavior and especially for his hatred of the elves, which he often vocally demonstrated. Throughout the years, his unruly tongue had cost him many close alliances with any of the other warlords, and the council didn't seem to be very fond of him either.

"Silence!" The king's voice rang out from below.

The assembly quieted at his command.

"Sir Hothwin, if you would please proceed in explaining these marks," King Ethuriel went on.

Sir Hothwin seemed nervous, and his hands shook while he hesitated.

Before he could answer, Izidora saw Sir Odynn approach him from behind and gently place a hand on his shoulder.

"I believe I can be of some assistance in this matter," he interrupted.

Gratefully, Sir Hothwin nodded at him and stepped back when Sir Odynn went on, explaining, "The ability for any living soul to practice magic is based on what we would describe as an inborn element. It is, as some prefer to explain, embedded in our blood or a fiber of the complex design of our being; that which makes us part of the living. In order to avoid more confusion, I shall cling to the first as I proceed."

Sir Odynn paused shortly and then shifted in his stance, as if to make himself more comfortable standing before the royal assembly. Then, leaning on his cane in his left hand, he continued, "As magic, or rather the ability to wield such power, is in our blood, it is irrevocably tethered to our identity. Meaning that whenever one wields magic, it leaves a trace; a mark that is unique and precisely linked to the one who practiced the magic that was used. No mark is like the other."

"As you have spoken, are we to be led to understand that the threat could therefore stem from amongst our own people? Could one of our own have done this?" King Ethuriel asked.

Sir Odynn shook his head at the king's question and answered, "I believe not, Your Majesty, for there are certain exceptions to this rule. You see, as Dragon's Kin, our ability to wield magic is quite unique in its nature. Our magic is not inherent, meaning we cannot raise it from nothing within our own strength. Instead, we can only summon it from magical beings, such being the dragons. The magic we use is therefore, in truth, not our own. Having said this, when a Dragon's Kin performs a spell of any sort, they leave no mark."

He paused and then continued, "In all the years of my studies of magic, never have I come across an explanation for this. The most common attempt to interpret the meaning of this is that since the magic is drawn from the dragon and flows through the Dragon's Kin who wields it, the mark of the dragon vanishes somewhere within the bond between the two. Perhaps it is an innate means of protection the dragons possess to conceal their identity or perhaps not. We do not know. However, this does, in our humble opinion, rule out a threat from within our own kingdom."

The unmistakable sound of Lord Varlam's voice resounded through the chamber as he rose angrily from his seat and spoke. "This very crime reeks of elven nature, my king. As we have all been clearly led to understand by these experts, these fires were no result of a tragic accident. They were intentionally set. Someone wanted to destroy what is ours!"

The council seemed to awaken under Lord Varlam's interruption. Their discordant murmurs chased through the chamber when Lord Varlam spoke again. "Your Majesty, as we have just heard, there is evidence that magic was used to commit these crimes. As we all know so well, the elves are the very beings that pride themselves in their magical power. It is their strength and their greatest weapon against us. This cannot be a coincidence!"

"Lord Varlam," Lord Jarek warned.

Nervous looks passed through the rows of lords and advisors, and the murmuring continued.

"I do believe we should be cautious in our assumptions," Sir Odynn began.

But his voice was drowned out by Lord Varlam who didn't seem to care for his opinion and went on in a loud voice, "So many were cast to their deaths, and if we are to believe what we have been told, most of them not because of the fires. They were murdered! Our people! Not with just any weapon, but with magic. This can only be a malicious plot by the elves! And I say it is time we gather our armies and show them we are a force to be reckoned with!"

The other lords raised their voices in outrage at Lord Varlam's call for battle when the king interrupted loudly, "Traces of magic alone do not stand as sufficient evidence of an elven attack, Lord Varlam! There are others besides the elves who possess the power to wield magic and this without the help of a dragon. We have yet to prove beyond a doubt that this is their doing."

The warlord was about to speak up again when the king raised his hand in a warning for him to not say another word.

Angrily, Lord Varlam slammed his fist into the table; dropping into his chair, he held out his chalice and called out to the cupbearer, "More wine!"

A moment of silence passed through the room until the king spoke firmly. "The findings of this investigation are dire and to be taken under serious consideration, indeed. However, Lord Jarek and I led a thorough search after the night of the fires and had many questioned concerning the days and weeks before the bonding ceremony. There was no sighting nor evidence of an elven invasion into our lands around the occurrences of the fires. Without definite proof, I cannot justify an attack on Erysméa. Yes, the evidence for their involvement is compelling, but it is not enough to strike with force as of this moment. We could start another war between our races after so many years of peace."

Izidora thought she had heard Lord Varlam scoff just before her father went on, "Sir Hothwin, Sir Odynn, is there anything else you have to report to this council?"

Nodding, Sir Odynn answered the king, "There is one more rather interesting discovery, Your Majesty, though I must admit I am not yet certain of its role in the attack."

"Go on," said the king.

"Very well," said Sir Odynn. "We made the strange discovery of a plant, known as Aggyreidimos idiss, sowed on the grounds of the shelters. We had missed it at first as most of it had been destroyed in the fires, but upon a second examination, remnants of it were found at every shelter."

He paused and then added, "Translated, Aggyreidimos idiss means silver tongue. First mentioned centuries ago, its origin is unknown. However, it is not commonly found in Tarragon. Throughout my research, I discovered it was primarily used during seasons of war and administered to captured spies or prisoners as a potion, forcing them to reveal secrets of the enemy against their will. It rendered the victims powerless against the probing of their minds; a cruel, but very effective instrument of interrogation; and this does not even conclude the uses of silver tongue. Having studied recordings of it, I found it can bind one mind to another and force it under its control for as long as the victim is subdued under its effects. I am uncertain of its power over a dragon, Your Majesty, but it could explain the unnatural behavior of the dragons that led them to destroy the shelters."

Whispers chased through the chamber upon Sir Odynn's report.

"Could this provide the investigation with any direction as to who might have attacked the shelters?" the king asked.

Sir Odynn shook his head and answered, "Since I am certain that it was planted intentionally, we have asked that the groundskeeper be found. According to the shelter keeper's word, the groundskeeper would most likely know how long it has been growing by the shelters and perhaps even who planted it, if it wasn't he himself. Unfortunately, we have not yet received word from him."

Nodding, King Ethuriel spoke. "Then, by order of the king, I shall issue a search warrant for the groundskeeper. He is to be found and brought before this council for questioning."

Murmurs of agreement flowed through the ranks of the council, and then the king said, at last, "Sir Hothwin, Sir Odynn, I thank you for your insight and for the tremendous effort you have devoted to this investigation. We shall consider your findings and meet again. For now, you are dismissed."

The two nodded respectfully and then, having offered a final bow before the king, they retreated from the council chamber.

Once they had left, Lord Varlam began to speak before the assembly again. "My king."

He had lowered his voice as if to force himself to express himself calmly before His Majesty, but there was a rough edge to his words that gave away his temper.

"It is no secret that the elves have always envied our power and our bond with the dragons. They want what they cannot have," he said. "Though they refuse to admit it, they have always held an ancient fear that the dragons might rise to destroy them someday. It has driven them against us as they consider us the dragons' loyal subjects."

Then his voice rang louder as he continued, "The evidence brought before us today is clear. They have sought an opportunity to attack and so try to weaken our united force. Who else would have reason to rise against us or feel threatened by a power such as ours? If we do not act now, they will surely strike again until we are too weak to contend against them!"

Izidora's hands balled into fists, and her throat tightened under her anger over Lord Varlam's disrespectful tone. How desperately she wished to be a part of the council and not have to hide her presence. Her mind flooded with ideas of the things she would like to shout into Lord Varlam's face right now.

"I am not blind nor ignorant of the nature of the elves or their fears of an attack by the dragons, Lord Varlam," Izidora heard her father say.

"What you have said has been heard and will be considered in the further course of our joint investigation. As soon as they prove themselves guilty of the crimes committed, we will act appropriately as the strong, united force that we are. But until then, Lord Varlam, not a sword shall be raised against them," King Ethuriel added firmly.

Angrily Lord Varlam growled in reply, "My king, it is with all the respect I can muster that I warn you of your foolishness!"

"That is enough!" Lord Jarek shouted and added, "How dare you speak to your king in such a manner?"

Izidora dug her nails into the wooden panels of the floor and felt her mind grow distracted from the sharp pain that shot through her fingers. It was the only thing she could think to do to keep herself from leaping to her feet and hurling a string of insults at the imbecile who disregarded her father's authority.

The rest of the council began to dispute aloud once again. Some joined Lord Jarek as they cautioned Lord Varlam, angrily reminding him of his station before the king.

When the shouts grew louder and louder, King Ethuriel arose from his seat and yelled over the chaos, "This meeting is over!" He glared at the crowd. "Unless any heads want to roll. You are all dismissed."

There was a commotion as the lords and ladies rose and left the chamber with no further resistance. Only King Ethuriel, Lord Jarek, and Kalithea remained behind.

Still seated, Kalithea looked up to the gallery where Izidora and Aleirya were hiding. Izidora and Aleirya both locked eyes with her briefly as she passed them both a concerned and warning look.

Then she looked back at her father when Lord Jarek began to speak. "He should not be allowed to speak to you in such a manner before this council, much less remain in a position of so much power, Ethuriel.

"Given what we have learned today, we have enough to be concerned about. We do not need another hazard to burden ourselves with. I warn you, he is unpredictable, and his anger makes him especially dangerous. If we are not careful, he could just as well lead us into a war against the elves."

"He would seal his own death, Lord Jarek, should he rally against the elves," King Ethuriel replied calmly. "I agree. He is not to be underestimated. But I will not be bated to act forcibly. And so far, besides his foolish tongue, he has done nothing for me to justify stripping him of his rank. I will not be provoked by his words and neither should you let yourself be impressed by his lack of ability to control his temper. However difficult it may be."

The king rose, and, at last, the three exited the room, Kalithea following her father.

She turned once more to look up at Izidora and Aleirya before shutting the chamber doors behind her.

"I would have liked to punch that moron in the face! Who does he think he is, speaking to my father like that?" Izidora exclaimed angrily, jumping to her feet.

"Lord Varlam, warlord of the third army of Tarragon and self-anointed king of fools, if you ask me," Aleirya remarked.

Izidora paced back and forth, grumbling.

"Hey, in case it makes it any better, I have the greatest respect for your father for not letting an idiot like Lord Varlam provoke him to any rash behavior," said Aleirya.

It hardly helped, and Izidora still boiled with anger.

Forcing herself to calm down, she said, "You're right. I guess it's a good thing I'm not queen. Otherwise, he wouldn't have a leg to stand on anymore."

Aleirya still sat on the floor of the gallery, leaning against the banister with her arms wrapped around her knees and stared down at her feet.

"Who do you think did it?" she asked Izidora quietly without looking up at her. "Who would dislike us that much to do such a thing? And the dragons? I don't want to imagine how much they must have suffered."

Then she met Izidora's gaze.

"I don't know. I don't know what to make of it all, to be honest," said Izidora, clenching and unclenching her fists at the thought.

She sat back down beside Aleirya and added, "I hate to even think that there's a chance Lord Varlam isn't completely wrong and that the elves are responsible. Although there's been peace between us all these years, it's not impossible. They are powerful, and they are masters of their magic."

Aleirya sighed and answered, "I guess you never know whom you can trust."

"Well, that's not all true," Izidora said and tried to smile. "We can trust each other," she added and gently placed her hand over Aleirya's.

Aleirya nodded and tried to smile, but the grin faded ever so quickly from her lips.

"Is everything alright?" Izidora asked.

Something else seemed to bother her.

Izidora watched Aleirya play with her fingers for a while before she looked back up at her and spoke. "Can I ask you something?"

The question seemed strange, considering their long-standing friendship, but she nodded and replied, "Of course."

Aleirya looked down at the floor again and bit down on her lip before she turned toward her and went on, "Is Nathanael seeing anyone?"

"What?" Izidora blurted. She wanted to cover her mouth with her hands at her sudden outburst but hugged her ankles tightly instead. "Why would you think that?" she added quickly.

Eyeing her closely as if to determine whether her reaction had been genuine, Aleirya stared back at her and went on, "I saw him the other day with a girl."

She let the back of her head roll sideways along the beam of the banister behind her, directing her gaze forward while she continued to speak. "They seemed quite interested in each other. I didn't recognize her, and I'm sure I've never seen her around the academy... I just thought it was strange he didn't tell me, and I wondered if you had perhaps heard something of the sort?"

Izidora felt her chest tighten as she listened to Aleirya. She had feared for her friend that this day might come.

If only she had told Nathanael how she felt. Perhaps now it was too late.

Shaking her head, she answered, "I haven't heard anything about that. I'm sorry."

"Sorry?" Aleirya replied. It almost sounded as if she were scoffing.

"Why sorry?" she added and pulled herself to her feet. "There's nothing for you to feel sorry about."

Izidora rose with her. Standing an arm's length from her, she replied with a sigh, "Come on, Aleirya. It's okay to be upset about this."

"I'm not upset! It just would have been nice to know what was going on in his life. I thought we were friends," she answered.

She had crossed her arms over her chest, looking rather defensive.

Izidora noticed her raise her chin and straighten, letting her arms sink to her sides when she noticed her studying her as well.

"Did you really think he would wait forever?" she asked carefully.

Izidora thought she had noticed Aleirya's eyes glisten but couldn't have been sure.

Aleirya shrugged her shoulders as if casting off the weight of her pain, and she smiled.

"I'm glad he's found someone. Maybe we'll even get to meet her tonight. He invited me to tag along to Killian's to celebrate after the tournament. You'll come with me, right?"

Izidora studied her friend thoughtfully and hesitated before she sighed and nodded. "Sure. If I can get Kalithea to cover for me, count me in."

Aleirya smiled mischievously before she spun around to leave. Izidora followed and draped her arm over her friend's shoulder once she reached her side.

Chapter 13

Nathanael pushed the door open for Aleirya and Izidora to step inside the bar. Sounds of loud laughter, music and song, paired with the smell of sweat and spilled ale, greeted them as they entered.

Aleirya could see Killian wiping off the counter of the round bar that stood in the middle of the room and shouting orders at the lads and girls to carry out the large jugs of ale to his guests. As usual, the bar was packed and noisy.

"Over there!" Nathanael shouted behind them, pointing to one of the round tables in a booth in a corner of the bar.

Pushing through the crowds, they made their way over to the group, dodging the waiters and waitresses who struggled to move back and forth between the bar counter and the tables with several overflowing jugs of ale in their hands.

Most of the crowd consisted of soldiers. Some were of the royal army and others of the armies of Tarragon's warlords, who stayed close to the capital because of their leader's required presence at the many council meetings with the king.

After having arrived at the booth, thankfully unscathed, Nathanael introduced them to the group seated in front of them.

Aleirya recognized Kajetan immediately, returning his wide grin with a smile of her own before her eyes scanned the rest, following Nathanael's cue. The corners of her lips flattened when her gaze froze on the last member of their small gathering.

"And this is Kara." Nathanael spoke loudly over the noise.

Aleirya had seen her before. She was the girl Nathanael had been with several days ago at the shelter site.

Aleirya felt a punch to her stomach but ignored it.

Kara smiled at her and waved, and she imitated the gesture politely but quickly averted her attention from the girl, sensing the same annoying tugging in her stomach she had felt when she had spoken with Nathanael earlier that day.

Like Aleirya and Nathanael, most of their group were dressed in black leather armor decorated with a gold pin at the chest showing two crossed swords behind a dragon's head, the signet of the Esdras Academy.

Nathanael then bade them to slide onto the bench beside Kajetan while he sat down beside Kara across from them.

Aleirya couldn't help but glance in their direction, watching Kara smile from ear to ear and lean close to Nathanael, folding her hands around his arm.

Her jaw tightened at the sight of him turning toward her, wrapped up in their private discourse.

With noise blaring all around them, Aleirya continued to stare at both of them as if she meant to read each line of their conversation off their lips when the wave of a hand flashed through her vision.

"Hey, there! Are you alright?" Kajetan asked.

Aleirya squinted, shaking herself out of her thoughts before answering, "Uh, yes. I'm fine."

She seemed to lose track again when Kajetan went on, leaning closer in order to not have to shout, "You know, it's rude not to introduce me to your friend."

Aleirya shook her head, completely missing the fact that he was just teasing her and spoke. "Sorry… Iz, this is Kajetan. He's a graduate from the academy. Kajetan, this is Princess Izidora."

She caught on to his game and added, "… as you should know."

Gritting her teeth, she cursed herself for acting so silly.

"Oh, please don't call me princess here," Izidora said while she shook Kajetan's hand and smiled.

"Agreed," he said, grinning back at Izidora.

Just then a waitress arrived at their table and breathlessly distributed the jugs of ale among them, setting one of them down before Aleirya and Izidora, each with a thump that made some of the ale spill out of the jug and all over the table.

"But we didn't—" Aleirya protested when Kajetan interrupted, speaking into her ear and raising his voice above the commotion, "Don't bother! The crowd is drunk and merry! They keep ordering one after the other, unable to keep count, and the waitresses don't know whom to serve the ale to anymore! You're bound to get a few of those without asking for 'em tonight!"

With that, he raised his jug to theirs, and a loud echo of shouts of, "Cheers," resounded through the bar.

And so, they sat through one song and round of ale after the other, sharing each other's stories and jokes and laughing.

Every once in a while, Aleirya would steal a glance at Nathanael, and once or twice he met her eyes before she quickly looked away.

Nothing had to change between them; they were still friends.

She reminded herself time upon time that it didn't bother her to see him with Kara, though she couldn't quite ignore the tightening of her throat and the sting that shot through her chest whenever they exchanged looks.

Aleirya took a big sip from the cup in front of her, downing the rest of the ale in it before rejoining the friendly chat between Izidora and Kajetan.

More sets of jugs reached their table as the night progressed, and eventually, Aleirya and Izidora fell into the routine of simply passing them on to be drunk by one of the young men. This continued until Izidora could bear it no more. Pitying the poor waitress, she told her to spare herself the trip to their table and continue to serve the ale to a group of brawny soldiers closer to the bar's counter.

"I believe you are that poor girl's hero tonight, Izidora," Kajetan yelled.

Izidora smiled at him and yelled back, "By the looks of her and the others, I'd have these men pick up their own ale at the counter if I were running this place!"

"Aye! I see you have the true mind of a queen!" he remarked and winked at her before beginning to down one of the last remaining jugs at their table.

Aleirya turned toward Izidora and smiled, raising an eyebrow at her and nodding in Kajetan's direction. Izidora rolled her eyes and turned to look away, smiling sheepishly before receiving a gentle nudge from Aleirya.

Shifting their attention to the center of the bar, Aleirya and Izidora watched along with the rest of their group as the crowds grew louder and some chanted, "Varlam! Varlam! Varlam!"

It was then that they saw Lord Varlam leap onto the counter of the bar with one overflowing jug of ale grasped in each hand. Stretching his arms outward, he raised the jugs above his head and shouted, "Good men and warriors of Tarragon! Tonight, let us drink to our power and the heritage of our dragon's blood!"

Shouts of delight resonated through the bar as the men drank and cheered.

Lord Varlam gulped the ale from both his jugs down to the last drop and released them from his hands when he finished. They struck the counter with a loud thump, earning loud laughter and shouts of amusement from the men standing below him.

Lord Varlam then raised his voice anew. "Men of valor! I know the pain and suffering of our people, and I see the threat and the wretchedness of our enemy! But King Ethuriel is weak. He's afraid, and he has no faith in the strength I see in you as one of your own!"

More shouts, louder than the previous, arose from throughout the bar, and they chanted his name once again. Some of the loyal soldiers and men listening who had not succumbed to drunkenness reached for the grip of their swords, carefully watching the crowd.

Aleirya saw Izidora's hands clench into tight fists while she stared at Lord Varlam, and she gently placed her hand on her shoulder, cautioning her to remain calm.

Lord Varlam yelled, "I swear to you, if I were your king, I would lead our armies into victory over the scum of this world that call themselves elves and rid us of the plague that they are!"

"What is he speaking of?" Aleirya heard one of the young men at the table ask amongst their group.

The men standing before Lord Varlam continued to shout and raise their jugs, cheering and calling out his name.

"But," Lord Varlam shouted, "who can blame the man for growing weak? For all these years he has been surrounded by women softening his heart and mind!" he added and chuckled loudly.

The bar roared with laughter, but before Lord Varlam could continue his speech, another voice echoed loudly from one of its corners.

"Treason!" Izidora yelled.

"Treason!" she cried again. "What you mistake for weakness is sensibility and strength to govern a kingdom wisely; abilities your acclaimed self has and will always lack!"

She had climbed onto their table and stood above the horde of men across from Lord Varlam as if a cleft separated the two.

The crowds were dumbfounded and fell silent, curiously awaiting Lord Varlam's reply.

What are you doing, Izidora?

It was all Aleirya could think while her eyes darted back and forth between her friend and Lord Varlam, who seemed to fume with anger.

"I see that not only have you succeeded in dulling the mind of your own father, but you also attempt to manipulate the minds of these men to turn against me and follow your father into his own doom! You foolish girl, to think that you can teach me sense when you have none yourself! Otherwise, you would know better than to question my authority!" Lord Varlam shouted.

"You are a fool if you think you can so openly slander my father's name, Tarragon's king! You have no authority that is worth my respect," Izidora answered fiercely.

Lord Varlam growled and jumped down to the ground, parting the crowds between him and Izidora, who remained standing atop the table.

"How dare you speak to me like that? I shall have you learn your place, Princess! Perhaps it will provide your father with the valuable lesson not to leave his women unleashed!" Lord Varlam spat angrily and moved toward her.

Some soldiers who were brave enough to stand against him immediately rose to stop him from approaching the princess, a few even drew their swords.

The stale air was laden with tension, emotions boiling amongst the cluster of inebriated men thirsty for a brawl; then the first fist flew as a grapple began amongst the soldiers.

Chaos broke out, sides formed, and the men fought.

Aleirya pulled Izidora down from the table and started to push her toward the entrance when Nathanael yelled, "Aleirya! Take her out back! Go!"

Aleirya nodded and swore under her breath as they turned and pushed through the crowds, regretting that she was weaponless.

Izidora stumbled before her as they moved as fast as they could.

They had almost reached the bar when a goblet flew toward them, coming from a pair of men clobbering each other before they crashed into a nearby table.

Aleirya jumped, throwing herself onto Izidora and shielding her body as they fell to the ground. Above them, she heard a crack and turned to see the goblet rolling across the wood floor, having smashed into a wall and leaking the dark brown liquid of the ale it once held.

Forcing herself and Izidora back onto their feet, Aleirya pushed her friend toward the bar just in the nick of time. She had barely started to run after Izidora when a soldier stumbled and fell behind her, having been punched in the face.

His attacker had already leaped after him as Killian rushed toward the men to break up the fight.

Passing her, Killian glanced at her and yelled, "Keep moving!"

Without hesitating, Aleirya and Izidora jumped over the counter of the bar and made for the kitchen.

Skidding into the room first, Izidora came to an abrupt stop when another man crossed their path.

Hurrying after her, Aleirya didn't wait to see what he would do and yelled, "Duck!"

Izidora did as she said, covering her head with her hands, and let out a scream when she bent forward.

Coming from behind her, Aleirya grabbed hold of the handle of a large pan that hung on the wall and swung it with all her might. It struck the man on the head and sent him crashing to the ground, unconscious.

"Run!" Aleirya shouted.

Izidora jumped over his slumped body and ran toward the back door of the bar's kitchen that led outside into a courtyard.

Aleirya stopped and stooped down to find the man still breathing and his pulse beating against the tips of her fingers.

He'll survive, she thought, and then hurried to follow Izidora.

Shoving the door open, Aleirya stepped out into darkness, shortly thereafter hearing the door swing shut behind her.

"Izidora!" she yelled while her eyes searched the thick darkness that settled around her.

Before they had adjusted to the blackness, she heard a whimper coming from somewhere in the dark. "Izidora!" she called again and felt a tension spread throughout her entire body as she readied herself for a fight.

Then Aleirya heard a scream followed by the sound of heavy footsteps and something being dragged through gravel.

Her hands clenched into fists while she tried to detect where the sounds were coming from. Aleirya turned in circles, eyeing her surroundings and looking for anything in the courtyard she could use as a weapon.

She didn't feel afraid. Her whole body was alert, ready to pounce at whatever was about to emerge out of the darkness in front of her.

Besides a shovel that leaned against the wall of the bar and a few sconces that lay on the ground next to several barrels of wine, the courtyard was void of anything remotely usable as a weapon.

Steadying her footing, Aleirya slowed her breathing and concentrated as the sounds and footsteps grew louder. There was another scream, and then she saw a tall dark figure come forward.

"Are you looking for your precious princess?" the unmistakable voice asked once the figure emerged from the shadows toward her.

Aleirya watched as Lord Varlam stepped forward, dragging Izidora behind him by her hair. Izidora's frightened cries pierced the air as she screamed while twisting and turning and clawing at his grip.

"It would be wise of you to leave, girl, if you wish to keep your life," he added.

Ignoring his threat, Aleirya shouted, "Let her go!"

Lord Varlam stopped and laughed. "Hah! Do you really think you stand a chance against me? You are nothing but a little girl. And beyond that, you have no weapon to wield against me! Go on, before I change my mind and finish you first!"

Aleirya stood unmoved.

"I said, let her go!" she shouted again.

Lord Varlam growled. Then he pulled Izidora up by her hair and struck her hard before dropping her to the ground.

A hot surge of anger filled Aleirya. She crouched down, grabbing a handful of sand and gravel and tossed it into the air when Lord Varlam stepped closer.

He cursed and spat as the cloud of sand reached his face, and he wiped it from his eyes, giving her time to run and grab the shovel that stood by the bar's wall.

Aleirya gripped its wooden shaft and swung it while turning around to face him. She had intended to strike his knee, but before it could reach his side, he grabbed hold of the blade and handle grip.

Lord Varlam snarled at her as they stood face to face, Aleirya still holding on to the shaft of the shovel as she stared up at him.

Then, leaning against his hold, she jumped, pulling her legs up to her chest, and driving her feet into the pits of his arms, she let go of the shovel and pushed him backward.

Taken by surprise, he stumbled and tripped before falling on his back.

This gave Aleirya time to snatch the sconces she had noticed lying beside the wine barrels.

With one in each hand, she ran back toward Lord Varlam who rose to his feet, this time drawing his sword.

Aleirya had almost reached him when he raised his weapon.

But instead of dodging the strike, she leaped into the air and swung the iron sconce in her left hand downward.

Lord Varlam's blade caught hold inside the crown of the sconce with a screeching sound.

Unable to pull the sword free, he growled and raised his weapon higher so that Aleirya hung above the ground.

Mustering as much strength as she could, Aleirya swung the other sconce in her right toward him, where it met the left side of his face.

Blood splattered as he screamed and dropped his blade, sending Aleirya back down to the ground.

Quickly, she scrambled to her feet, clinging to the bloody sconce in her right hand.

Angrily, Lord Varlam spat blood from his mouth and stomped toward her.

Aleirya raised the sconce in defense to strike again, but this time he caught hold of it before she could thrust it at him.

Single-handedly, he tore it out of her grasp and sent it flying into the darkness and out of her reach.

His right hand then fastened around her neck, and he heaved her upward into the air.

Aleirya choked and tried to wring herself free, kicking and clawing at him.

Lord Varlam laughed, and Aleirya saw blood trickle down his mouth and over his chin.

"You've fought your last fight, child! Or should I say first?" he snarled, and then he flung her up and through the air, sending her crashing into the wall of the bar.

Her back struck the hard surface first, knocking the air out of her lungs. Aleirya gasped, and a wave of pain coursed through her from her head along her spine and into her legs. For a moment, she lay motionless.

When she opened her eyes, her vision swam, yet she could still make out Lord Varlam's large form in the darkness.

She heard him laugh while he made his way over to Izidora, who had stirred and moaned, obviously taking Aleirya for dead or at least unconscious. Izidora began to scream and whimper as Lord Varlam neared her. Then he pulled her up by the neck, forcing her to look at his face.

Aleirya struggled to move and felt a piercing pain in the side of her left leg, but she didn't dare look down.

She overheard Izidora gasp for air as Lord Varlam choked her, tightening and loosening his grip around her neck while he laughed.

Her mind raced hopelessly in search of a way to save Izidora, Lord Varlam's horrible voice echoing through her mind.

Do you really think you stand a chance against me? You are nothing but a little girl!

Suddenly, a thought crossed her mind. She wasn't weaponless at all!

Aleirya reached down to the side of her left leg above her knee where she had just before felt the piercing pain.

A flaming burn ran through her hand when she pulled out the chakram Thoran had given her and cut her hand. She felt the blood run over her palm and down her wrist as she winced and propped herself up against the wall with her right arm.

Hearing Izidora let out another cry, Aleirya adjusted her grip on the chakram in her left hand and tried to set her blurring focus on Lord Varlam, who stood with his back to her, still holding Izidora up in front of him.

She could feel her strength ebbing from her as her consciousness faded, and she felt no longer in control of herself.

Drawing a sharp breath and willing all the strength she had left into her grasp, Aleirya thrust the chakram forward, sending it sizzling through the air.

There was no scream to be heard when the chakram met its target. Instead, Aleirya heard a loud thump as Lord Varlam fell forward to the ground with one last gasp of air before everything went dark before her eyes.

Chapter 14

Aleirya awoke lying inside the infirmary of the Esdras Academy. Her whole body heaved as she gasped for air.

She continued to draw several deep breaths, reassuring herself that she was still alive before she sat up and let out a yelp of pain. Her chest and back ached, and it felt hard to breathe, as if someone were standing on her chest. There was a sharp pain in her left leg, and her left palm had been bandaged.

Beside her bed sat Sir Odynn.

Upon hearing her awaken, he rose from his chair.

Placing his book down, he came to sit on the edge of her bed.

"Now, now, you shouldn't get up. You are safe, Aleirya," he said.

Aleirya drew another sharp breath when another wave of pain passed through her.

"What happened? Is Izidora alright? Where is she?" she asked.

Sir Odynn gently pushed Aleirya back into a lying position when she tried to get up again.

"It's alright. Izidora is alive and recovering, thanks to you. She is with her family. You do not need to worry, and you need to rest yourself," Sir Odynn cautioned.

Giving in, Aleirya sank back and stared up at the ceiling.

Clenching her fists, she swallowed and asked, "And what about Lord Varlam? Have they imprisoned him? Will they ensure justice is done for what he did?"

"He's dead," Sir Odynn said dryly.

Aleirya's head snapped toward him, and her heart lurched.

"Dead? As in, gone for good?" she asked.

Her hands trembled at the thought. She had killed a man. She had irrevocably taken a life from this world.

Sir Odynn watched her thoughtfully before he spoke. "They call it a hangman's fracture, usually caused when an extreme force is applied to the upper vertebrae. Though instead of being hanged, they found a chakram embedded in the back of his neck."

He paused and continued when she remained silent. "In most cases, the injury is lethal."

Aleirya couldn't look at him, averting her gaze to stare up at the ceiling once more and told herself to breathe.

Sir Odynn laid his hand over her bandaged one and spoke softly. "Aleirya, look at me."

Aleirya took a deep breath and swallowed, forcing herself not to cry before finally looking at him.

"Everything will be alright; I promise you that. What you did was brave," he said and gently squeezed her hand.

Not knowing what to say, she simply nodded at him.

"Aleirya?" Sir Odynn asked.

Aleirya looked at him and replied in a choked voice, "Yes?"

"What do you remember from that night?" he asked again, curiously.

Aleirya stared at him, unsure of what he was after or what it was exactly that he expected to hear from her.

Then averting her gaze from his, she swallowed hard and began, "There was a fight at the bar. We tried to get out, and I, I remember running. It was dark and I, I couldn't, I couldn't see him. I only heard the screams," she said with her voice shaking.

Remembering the sound of Izidora's helpless cries caused her eyes to well up with tears.

Aleirya drew a deep breath and forced them back. Her throat felt dry and ached. She sat up and tried to reach for the pitcher of water beside the bed when Sir Odynn rose to help her. He handed her a cup, and she drank.

When she had finished and he had taken the empty cup from her hands, she continued. "I must have fallen. I hit something hard. I couldn't breathe, and I was losing my vision. Everything was turning black." Aleirya stopped for a moment and then went on, "When I woke up here, I almost thought that it had all been a bad dream."

Sir Odynn looked at her thoughtfully for a while, not saying a word.

"So, you don't remember throwing the chakram?" he asked.

"Not really," Aleirya said, shaking her head.

At her words, his expression turned quizzical.

"What do you mean by 'not really'?" he asked.

Aleirya's hands shook. She wasn't certain what exactly had happened or how she had managed to throw the chakram, delivering such a deadly blow. How was she supposed to explain it to him?

Aleirya tightened and released her fists before answering, "I remember thinking that it had to stop. He had to stop hurting her," she said in a choked voice. "I don't know how I did it. I couldn't see, but I had to stop him. It was as if…"

Aleirya couldn't finish the sentence, for the doors of the infirmary burst open and Thoran and Zannia came running in, pushing past the guards at the door.

Aleirya's first thought was to wonder why they had set guards before the infirmary. She wasn't a criminal, or was she now?

She quickly pushed the thought away when Zannia reached her bedside, collapsing to her knees as tears started running down her face. Thoran came to the other side of Aleirya's bed and gently reached out to touch her cheek while grabbing hold of her right hand with his.

"My child, what did he do to you?" Zannia said, sobbing.

Sir Odynn spoke before Aleirya had the chance to answer. "She needs to rest, but she will be alright. She has broken a few ribs and injured her left leg and palm, but there don't seem to be any other severe injuries. She was quite fortunate. I had assumed much worse when I saw her brought to the infirmary."

Then Sir Odynn approached the left side of the bed and uncovered Aleirya's left leg before beginning to remove the bandage above her knee.

His expression looked startled when he finished pulling the bandage off her skin. There was a long cut along the side of her left shin, ranging up to the middle of her thigh, which appeared to have already healed shut.

Faded patches of yellow and green skin covered her leg where it had been bruised.

His surprise turned into a stern look, masking his entire face, and he spoke. "It appears she is healing quite quickly. I will go send for a healer to tend to her and provide a fresh bandage for the wound."

He rose to leave and began to walk away from them, mumbling under his breath, "If that is even necessary."

"How much longer must she stay here?" Thoran asked.

Sir Odynn stopped, turned, and answered, "A few more days, I suppose. I will inquire of that from the healers and have word sent to you."

Thoran nodded gratefully and turned to look at Aleirya.

Confused, Aleirya sat up and asked, "How long have I been lying here?"

Sir Odynn looked back at her and replied, "Three days. It's been three days, Aleirya. They have kept you here in the infirmary for care and observation, and so far, only I have been allowed to see you."

Aleirya looked at him, speechless.

When she said nothing, he added, "But your family is here now, and I suppose they will be able to take you home soon. But this shouldn't concern you now. You need to rest. I will return in the morning, and we can talk some more."

Not knowing what to say, Aleirya just nodded and let herself sink back into her bed. Closing her eyes, she wished it had all just been a dream.

Chapter 15

An uncomfortable pulse chased up Valeirys' wrists and into his shoulders from the impact as he leaped backward, his blade skidding off the edge of Trajan's sword with a shrill screech.

His chest rose and fell under the quickening of his breath while he circled the training platform across from his mentor. With a huff and a grunt, his eyes narrowed, Valeirys charged again, leaning his whole body into the strike.

An ear-splitting crack broke through the air as Trajan warded off the hit, the noise ricocheting across the open-roofed platform that overlooked Valeirys' father's lands.

"Not bad," Trajan shouted.

The commander gave him a moment to catch his breath before he riposted, his blade aimed to slash across Valeirys' torso.

The edges of their swords clashed as Valeirys blocked the attack, but more swiftly than he had expected, Trajan twisted beneath the high cross of their weapons and dragged his blade along the right side of his abdomen.

Valeirys doubled over, and the tip of his blade struck the stone beneath him. Thanks to the magic coating their weapons, the hit was not lethal, but it would leave a bruise.

"Anger is a powerful fuel, but you can't let it blind you," said Trajan. He stopped and sheathed his sword, turning to face him.

Valeirys nodded breathlessly before he straightened.

The briskness of the morning transformed into a comfortable breeze under the risen sun as he looked out over the planes of green before him.

Sweat lined his brow, and his muscles burned, exhausted from the training session.

Drawing his lips to a firm line, Valeirys turned, returning his sword back to the scabbard strapped to his side and spoke. "What's the count with this morning's dead?"

Trajan met his gaze, his expression immediately darkening. Hesitating at first, he then sighed and answered, "The fourth protestor took his life before sunrise."

Valeirys' shoulders sagged in exasperation, and he shook his head.

A week had passed since the attack at the banquet. Several of the king's guests had been injured. An arrow strike had fatally wounded three, and the bodies kept piling on. Just last night, word had reached them from Aram that another group of corpses from the kidnapped elves had been found.

The days following the rebellion's attack had been consumed with interrogations of the protestors who had been seized and imprisoned. But the only knowledge they had gained was that this Liberator had gone to extraordinary lengths to keep his true identity hidden, even from those willing to follow him.

"Loyal to his madness until death," Valeirys muttered and joined Trajan's side as they walked off the training site. "They might as well crown him their king and be done with it…"

"He's made use of their youth and impressionability," said Trajan.

Their footsteps echoed along the cobblestone pathway as they headed toward Valeirys' father's manor.

"He never showed his face to them. They never knew his name," the commander went on. "It was smart."

"It was devious!" Valeirys blurted. "Cruel and manipulative. He did it knowing that his identity would remain a secret when his foot soldiers were caught and tried for their crimes."

Trajan nodded and spoke. "Yes. But it was smart."

Valeirys scoffed, his knuckles cracking under the tight balling of his fists.

The commander's steps stalled, and he waited for Valeirys to stop and look back at him.

"His time will come, Valeirys. Despite how it seems, the attack on the banquet wasn't as devastating a loss as it appears to have been."

Taking a step closer to him, Trajan added, "He gave us a name, not his true name, but nevertheless a name. It is only a matter of time before his boldness brings his downfall."

Valeirys nodded and swallowed before directing his gaze forward as they resumed their return to the manor.

"Besides." Trajan spoke again. "Perhaps the tides are about to turn. Yessenia will have reached Aram with your father by now to observe the dead. Perhaps her skills will reveal the truth of the enemy we face and finally bring an end to the misery that started all of this."

* * *

Yessenia drew a deep breath as the heavy doors were drawn open, and she entered the morgue.

Naitha di Laiona Érjinye, hall of everlasting peace, was what her people called it.

It was a great cathedral built upon a cliff that overshadowed the sea at Aram at Erysméa's southeastern border.

A part of her had dreaded this moment ever since they had set off on their journey in answer to the king's summons. Her heart stuttered in her chest, and ice flooded her limbs as something fiercely protested within her, begging her to turn back.

But as if moving against a current, Yessenia riveted her eyes on the hall of the nave before her and forced herself forward with Uryiel walking closely beside her.

Tall pillars surrounded her left and right, their semblance both solemn and soothing as she let her eyes run across the stone of their forms and that of the tiles beneath her feet that were covered in names; the names of the beloved her people had lost.

It was the way the elves honored their dead.

After their bodies had been burned, the families would have their names engraved inside the stone to ensure that they would never be forgotten.

For in the stone, there is a permanence and a peace that is indelible by the change of our world.

Her father's words rose in her ears, the memory of his voice bittersweet but a comfort all the same as she kept on going.

The cathedral was flooded with light through its tall windows and ceiling, and a cool gust of air rushed through its halls.

The vaults were made of glass, and the intricate silver ribs resembled the blossoming crown of a tree when gazed upon from below.

Reaching the end of the nave, Yessenia and Uryiel passed under a grand arch that led them into the chapel.

Unlike other cathedrals, walls didn't enclose the chapel of Naitha di Laiona Érjinye. The chapel was built as a roofed terrace with stone columns lining its outer rectangular circumference; at its center stood an altar upon which a delicate figure lay draped by a white cloth.

A shiver raced down Yessenia's back from her head to her heels when she saw it, and her eyes fixated on the body now only a few steps before her.

Uryiel remained standing at the entrance of the chapel when Yessenia carefully approached the altar.

Only when he spoke did she notice that someone had been standing beside it, waiting for her.

"Yessenia Altair, born Yessenia Elyra Trageian. Welcome," the elf began and gave a bow.

His voice held an uncanny gentleness that instantly lifted the veil of sorrow and lightened the crushing weight of horror that had lain heavily on her shoulders these past days.

"My name is Bérètharomyr, Guardian of the Unforgotten," he went on. "You have a great gift, daughter of Irèptiss."

Irèptiss had been the greatest healer Erysméa had ever known, blessed with an incredible power so that it had become a custom among the elves whenever one spoke of a great healer to call them 'son or daughter of Irèptiss'.

No one had ever called her that before.

Yessenia bowed her head in return and looked at him. She guessed that Bérètharomyr was about her age. His white hair lay straight over his shoulders, and like hers, his eyes shone bright gold.

Yessenia sensed the elf held a great power of his own, one she couldn't quite comprehend. Even from the distance at which he stood to her and without physical touch, she could feel his thoughts link with hers as she held his gaze.

Forcing her curiosity over Bérètharomyr aside, she returned her concentration to the task before her. Then she nodded, signaling to Bérètharomyr that she was ready, and the elf lifted the covering from the body.

A wave of numbness crashed over her when she saw it.

The elves had preserved the body in the state it had been found.

Before her lay the lifeless form of a young elf, no older than Eyvindr or Valeirys.

His entire right side had been scorched, and all over the skin of his left side, up to his neck, there were cuts and scars. His face was bruised, his lower lip had been split, most likely from being beaten, and the right side of his face and ear showed more black patches of burned skin.

Yessenia's eyes examined the body from the crown of the young elf's head to the soles of his feet, forcing herself not to imagine what the nature and appearance of the innocent child must have been like before this evil had befallen him.

Circling the altar and halting at its left side, she inspected the cuts on his ghostly form more closely.

Her breath came in shallow puffs as she studied them.

With lips pursed as if to speak, she stretched out her hands toward the body while she inwardly recited the steps she was to take to perform her examination.

The tips of her fingers had gone cold and rigid like the corpse that lay before her. She had not yet touched the boy's marred skin when she heard Bérètharomyr speak. "I would not advise to lay hands on the dead."

Stopping, she looked at him curiously just as he lowered his voice and went on, "Though his spirit has left, something still dwells within the boy's form. I cannot quite explain what it is, but I sensed an essence of a foreign… entity. I felt it whilst conserving the body."

It was strange the way he had said it. He had spoken so quietly, as if he had intended for only her to hear him.

Yessenia shook her head and replied, "I do not wish to offend you, but how else am I to determine the source of this evil or the cause of his death?"

"I can tell you how he died," Bérètharomyr answered calmly and stepped closer.

Approaching the opposite side of the altar, the golden hue of his eyes seemed to brighten while his glance swept over the boy, and Yessenia wondered whether it was grief or anger that stirred within him.

"The flames that burned him only destroyed what was left of his physical form… If left alone with his wounds, surely the decay of his flesh would have poisoned the rest of his body. But I do not believe that it was the fire that killed him," he began.

"So, the scorching of his skin was meant to conceal the true cause of his death?" Yessenia whispered back to him.

He looked at her and hesitated for a moment before he answered, "I have seen countless dead. A crime like this doesn't solely derive from a malicious intention to torture and kill. I believe there is more. I believe whoever did this had a greater purpose in mind. In fact, I am almost certain that this child lost his life not to a blade or fire, but to a bane far more vicious and powerful. Magic. Perhaps the vilest kind of sorcery we have ever known."

The last of his words chased through her mind, but whether they were her own thoughts or Bérètharomyr's, she couldn't have been certain.

"It took his soul long before his body," Bérètharomyr whispered, looking from her to the boy.

Yessenia stared at him until she dropped her glance to the dead in front of her.

What sort of magic or power could have done such a thing? And to what end?

Her skin tingled, and her brow furrowed as she pondered his words.

Yessenia let her eyes trace the cuts on the boy's skin once again, trying to determine if there was any sort of pattern or clue to what weapon had incurred them. As meager an improvement as it might be, perhaps it could help bring them yet one small step toward discovering who had done this.

Then, all at once, her chest tightened, and her gaze froze on one of the jagged lines. The marks weren't just wounds from a blade.

Her heart lurched, and she couldn't help but touch the boy's arm.

She heard Bérètharomyr gasp but refused to pay him any attention.

Before her, the lines and curves of the marks suddenly appeared as symbols. Yessenia's eyes locked onto them, and she felt their shape and design enthrall her.

Bérètharomyr started to warn her, but his words were muffled in the background, subdued by her own train of thought.

Yessenia pressed further through the confusion that settled over her mind, trying to decipher the meaning of the marks, when a sudden feeling of alarm overcame her. Something pricked at her neck, and she squinted at the sensation of another force touching her mind, almost like that of a living being.

It felt harmless at first, even peaceful as it stretched toward her, but then it changed.

Sensing a darkness and a malignity as if it were perspiring from the body, Yessenia let out a gasp, and her hands clutched the sides of the altar.

Tearing her eyes from the boy, she looked up at Bérètharomyr, who was watching her, noticeably disquieted by the alarm and the dark power he sensed she had felt.

This was precisely what he had meant when he had spoken of a foreign entity living within the body.

Yessenia held his gaze for a moment, and she noticed his magic reach toward her as he tried to pry the strange force from her and protect her from its effects.

But it was too late.

Involuntarily, her eyes snapped back onto the boy's frame, an insatiable curiosity consuming her mind for the power that enthralled her.

The elf's charred skin cast a violet glow, and before her eyes, it appeared as if the jagged lines and wounds transformed to runes that formed one phrase after the other. It was a language of its own, one she had never seen before, and nothing like the tongue of their ancestors.

The hostile power continued to beckon her, and the world around her vanished from existence just when she felt a pair of strong arms fold around her.

Yessenia heard Uryiel call out to her, but it was only after Bérètharomyr covered the body that she noticed the power lose its hold on her, and her knees buckled.

Catching her, Uryiel helped her to stand and pulled her close to himself, where she remained without speaking for a moment. She could feel the steady rise and fall of his chest while pressed up against him, and then he loosened his embrace.

Stepping back, he lifted her face to his and looked at her.

"Your eyes!" he exclaimed.

Yessenia's eyes shimmered gold and red like embers of a fire.

"Are you alright?" Uryiel asked, alarmed.

Yessenia stared at him as if unresponsive before she nodded and spoke. "Yes."

Blinking, she raised her hands to her temples. Her head felt heavy and her senses hazy, as if she had been exposed to some sort of poison.

Bérètharomyr approached them and laid a hand on Yessenia's shoulder, and at his touch, the pain in her head receded.

Looking at her for a moment and then turning to Uryiel, Bérètharomyr said, "I believe she is unharmed, but she should rest. You should go."

Staring at Bérètharomyr, Yessenia shook her head in protest against his instructions.

She could not leave. She couldn't give up; not when she had come so close!

She opened her mouth to speak, but then somehow found herself unable to form the words she had meant to say.

Uryiel reached for her and started to pull her away when she resisted.

Not letting go of her, he continued to speak to her calmly, reassuring her that everything was alright, that it was over, and that they were to leave, but his words were drowned out somewhere in the depths of her mind.

Then, finally, something caused her to stop struggling against his hold.

At last, tearing her gaze from Bérètharomyr, Yessenia let Uryiel lead her away.

When the cathedral's doors shut behind them, it was as if her thoughts cleared and the fog dissipated from her mind.

She abruptly stopped, yanking Uryiel backward.

He then turned to her and asked, "What is it? What did you see?"

Yessenia looked into his eyes, sensing his anger and his fear for her.

She hesitated at first, but then, bit by bit, the words carefully slipped past her lips. "Whoever did this is powerful; and their magic—it's unlike anything I have ever encountered."

She watched the color drain from his face as he looked back at her, listening to her intently.

Then Uryiel opened his mouth to speak but fell silent again.

"And there's more," she went on. "This was no ordinary fire that burned them; this was dragon's fire."

Chapter 16

Lord D'Arthragnan sat taciturn amidst the myriad of voices that reverberated throughout the council chamber.

"It is no longer mere superstition!" Lord Cenric yelled. "It is as our ancestors predicted. The dragons have returned to unleash the flame of their hatred and to destroy us once and for all!"

A fist slammed into the table before him, and Lord D'Arthragnan watched as Lord Tarquinius jolted from his seat, joining Lord Cenric, and growled, "The beasts are toying with us, manipulating their prey before they strike."

"Calm yourselves!" Lord Calaedorn interjected.

They had been discussing for hours as the morning bled into the afternoon, the warm summer light slowly vanishing from the room along with their poise.

THE RISE OF ISIGAR

Word had reached their council just this morning that the victims of the kidnappings had been burned with dragon's fire, and that a foreign sorcery had aided their gruesome demise.

Exhausted from listening, Lord D'Arthragnan grabbed hold of his cane and rose from his seat while the others continued undisturbed in their debate.

He circled the council chamber, making use of his invisibility to the other lords and advisors of the king when the unmistakable screech of Lord Yeva's voice stung his ears. "Certainly, the Dragon's Kin are aiding their cause. We must strike now and show force!"

His outburst only kindled the dispute as Lord Cenric chimed in again. "Indeed, Your Majesty, the Dragon's Kin are using the unrest in our kingdom to further weaken our position. We cannot hesitate to act."

"Neither can we afford to fight two wars," said Lord Calaedorn. "One against the rebellion and another against the fleets of the Dragon's Kin."

"Enough!" King Yevandrielle's voice boomed from across the chamber.

Everything stilled in the wake of his call, and yet the air sizzled from the broiling frustration that consumed the space between them. "This meeting is adjourned. Now get out. All of you!"

A tumult arose as chairs were shoved back, and the lords and advisors vacated the chamber, whispers and muttering following the echo of their steps as they left.

Lord D'Arthragnan started to move as well when the king spoke. "Not you, Gideon."

Stalling his steps, Lord D'Arthragnan looked at His Majesty, and he caught the unmistakable glare of Lord Calaedorn as he peered at him over his shoulder in passing.

A grin tugged at the corners of his mouth when Lord Calaedorn's stare vanished behind the double doors as the king's guards shut the entrance to the council chamber.

No amount of flattering words, gold or prestige would ever grant his fellow lords and council members the privileged standing he held with His Majesty.

He had something they didn't; he and Yevandrielle shared a childhood bond sealed in friendship from the age of seven. He knew the king better than any of the others did or ever would.

Redirecting his attention onto Yevandrielle, Lord D'Arthragnan eyed His Majesty, who had risen from his seat and stood bent over the table before him.

Having served Yevandrielle's father, the former king, from page to soldier, he had grown up alongside the elven prince.

He had watched a boy grow to a warrior and finally, to a king. He had witnessed Yevandrielle at both his weakest and his strongest.

King Yevandrielle did not speak, his eyes pressed shut. Lord D'Arthragnan held his silence, granting his friend a moment of solace and reprieve from the morning's turmoil.

His gaze dropped to his left hand that folded around the grip of his cane and lingered on the ring that decorated it.

His eyes slid from the smooth surface of the heirloom's polished ruby, retracing the fine lines of three crescent moons that formed a cross below it and wandered along the coil that wrapped around the middle of the cross before it curled around the hilt of a downcast sword.

A sigh broke the quiet that enveloped the room, and Lord D'Arthragnan glimpsed King Yevandrielle stir before he straightened and walked toward the tall windows on the opposite side of the chamber.

Following his lead, Lord D'Arthragnan circled the table.

His glance passed over the shelves of books that lined the walls, skimming the covers in various hues of leather. Their gold lettering stated the titles that ranged from works on military strategy to recordings of ancient elven battle history and tales of their past leaders' legacies.

The clicking of his cane slowed, the noise fading into silence as his feet stopped, and he took to the king's side.

Through the tall pair of windows before him and down below lay the beautiful city of Mòr Rhíoghain surrounded by plains of green and at last, by its borders, the lake, Diadéma.

"I can still see it," Yevandrielle began. "The tails of smoke rising into the heavens, the fire, the horrific shapes of the dragons… It will ever be unfathomable to me how we rebuilt after what the Eskhàra did. How something reduced to a heap of ashes could rise again to something so enchantingly beautiful."

"Is not light born of darkness and does not every light cast a shadow, my king?" Lord D'Arthragnan answered. Squinting at the glittering waters of Lake Diadéma, he drew a deep breath and added, "A day closes and a night begins; they are separable and yet there is not the one without the other."

He saw Yevandrielle turn toward him and met his gaze.

Lord D'Arthragnan could still see the youth Yevandrielle had once been. But the years had brought their fair share of cruel and unpredictable calamities, which had not left the young king unmarked. Looking at him now, he thought Yevandrielle looked older.

Gone was the mischievous spark in his gaze and the sly grin Lord D'Arthragnan remembered from their childhood days. Sorrowful lines ran across his forehead, his face was pale, and the otherwise vibrant bronze hue of his eyes seemed drained of its color.

King Yevandrielle nodded in silence and swallowed before he answered. "If only this reign were as simple as we imagined it as boys; every threat, every hardship felled by the single strike of a sword."

His jaw ticked, and Lord D'Arthragnan sensed his frustration.

Recollections of the battles they had fought side by side as comrades sped past his mind's eye, forcing the memory of his last battle to resurface when he had passed Yevandrielle's father's bloodied and battered frame onto the prince's back, hoping to get His Majesty to safety and ensure his survival.

Lord D'Arthragnan could still see the reflection of the soldier Yevandrielle had once been, the warrior prince too young to have had to bear the weight of the crown; and yet there he stood.

"What should I do, Gideon?" King Yevandrielle asked. His Majesty was the only one who called him by his childhood name. "Sometimes I wonder what my father would say, what he would do in times like these… I wonder if I have utterly failed his expectations."

Exhaling, Lord D'Arthragnan shook his head and steadied the grip on his cane before he answered, "It will not solve all our grievances, but for one, taking a stand against the rebellion will show the people that you are not the fearful and powerless king they mock you to be. The elves who made an attempt on your life and the lives of the lords at the banquet must be executed."

He heard Yevandrielle scoff as he spun away from the windows and toward the table behind them.

"If nothing is done against them, they will come for you again. They will only become bolder, and soon, there will be no kingdom for you to govern. You must prove to those who remain faithful and trust in your reign that the authority of the realm lies within your hands."

"If I execute the rebels, the people will make them martyrs. If I show force, they will only view me as a tyrant," said Yevandrielle, his gaze boring into him. "A cruel king who only adds to their suffering."

He stopped as if to collect himself, anger honing every angle and every shadow on his face.

"I cannot let them provoke me into becoming something I am not," said the king.

Weakness, Lord D'Arthragnan thought. His left hand clutched his cane, his thumb itching to brush the edges of his ring's band while he stayed silent.

He did his best not to flinch or grimace. He couldn't stand Yevandrielle's gentle temperament when so much was at stake. But he knew better than to press him further in his tired state.

Forcing himself to nod, feigning understanding, he responded calmly, "Forgive me, Your Majesty, I should not have spoken so boldly."

Yevandrielle shook his head and answered, "I'd rather you be honest with me than mask your true feelings with a cordial reply, Gideon."

Again, Lord D'Arthragnan nodded, but this time, he meant it.

"Tell me then," Yevandrielle began. "After all we have learned, do you think I should strike against the Dragon's Kin? Do you agree—do you think they have truly set out to destroy us?"

Lord D'Arthragnan shook his head before he took a step toward the king and replied, "Though I do not like to admit it, I must agree with Lord Calaedorn."

He hesitated and straightened, lifting his chin before he went on, "Truthfully, I believe it would be foolish to dismiss the possibility of a looming threat from the Dragon's Kin. However, it would be hubris to believe we could fight and win a battle against our enemy while we face another against our own people. This Liberator must be found. He must be seized and executed for his crimes, Your Majesty."

Holding Yevandrielle's gaze, Lord D'Arthragnan paused and then added, "Stop the bleeding by cauterizing its source. Treat the poison that is this Liberator and the kingdom will heal; when it does, we will face the Dragon's Kin as a strong and united force."

King Yevandrielle eyed him thoughtfully and then nodded. "Our spies have been working tirelessly to uncover his true identity. Every man I can spare has been ordered to take on the search for this traitor."

His Majesty shook his head, lowered his gaze, and sighed before continuing, "But we are no wiser than at the beginning. How do I—"

"Place a bounty on his head," Lord D'Arthragnan interrupted. He waited for the king to look up at him and then went on, "Yes, there are many who follow him with blind loyalty, but there are others who don't, subjects who choose not to forsake their king. Use his most powerful means against you; the very weapon he prides himself with—the people. Your people.

"He has no true power, Your Majesty. He is their commiserator, he has their sympathy, but what he does not have is authority over them. Pain and misery pass. Loyalty is a fickle thing. Offer a reward, and we shall see how his fortune changes at the dangle of riches before his devotees."

Chapter 17

With a gasp, Aleirya jolted upright, awoken from sleep. Drenched in sweat, her whole body stiffened, and her hands clutched the sheets of the bed beneath her.

Her eyes darted back and forth under the labored rise and fall of her chest and the stuttering beat of her heart that slowly calmed just as her mind eased, and she grasped where she was.

The familiar sight of her parents' cottage took shape before her eyes as she blinked, the colors warming from gray to soft browns, reds, greens and yellows, and she felt her muscles relax.

Her breath hitched, and her throat burned as she stifled a sob and rubbed her hands over her eyes. With a groan, she leaned forward and wrapped her arms around her knees.

A dull pain throbbed against her temples as she sat unmoving on the bed Zannia had prepared for her by the hearth in the living room of her childhood home.

The fire had gone out during the late hours of the night, and Aleirya shivered from the cold of the morning that seeped through the walls.

Swallowing, she pursed her dry lips and looked up at the rousing sound of footsteps when Zannia and Thoran entered the room.

"Oh, Aleirya," Zannia said softly as she rushed to her bedside.

Zannia's gentle hands swept over Aleirya's forehead and then draped around her shoulders before she pulled her into her arms and spoke. "You're shivering. Thoran, bring me the blankets, please."

Goosebumps ran down Aleirya's arms and back at the weight of the blankets against her skin and the sudden rush of warmth that spread through her body.

Thoran started to prepare another fire when she noticed the dark rings underneath his eyes.

Shrinking further into the wool covers, she glanced upward at Zannia's face, finding her expression bleeding with worry. She looked exhausted, and her eyes were red from crying.

"What's wrong? Did something happen?" Aleirya asked.

Zannia glanced at Thoran first, the two of them sharing a concerned look before she answered, "We're just worried about you."

Aleirya's stomach dropped. She had never intended to cause her parents any hardship, and it pained her to see them this way.

Her gaze moved back and forth between Zannia and Thoran, and she said, "I should go. I can stay at the academy."

Casting the blankets off her shoulders, she got to her feet when Thoran spoke. "No, you should stay here with us. You're safe here."

Aleirya stopped and looked at him.

Her brow furrowed, and she replied, confused, "Safe? What do you mean? I should be at the academy where I belong, training, instead of burdening the both of you."

She did not wait for an answer and began to gather her things when Zannia interjected, "You are no burden to us."

Shaking her head, Aleirya ignored her and continued to pack when Zannia blurted, "You wake up screaming, Aleirya."

"Zannia!" Thoran exclaimed.

Aleirya's hands stalled. She hesitated a moment before turning around to face her parents and asked, "I do what?"

Zannia had risen to her feet, standing an arm's length away from Thoran.

Her eyes glistened when she swallowed and spoke. "Ever since you have been home from the infirmary, we have heard you wake every night screaming."

Silence stole a moment between them while none of them moved.

Then Thoran sighed and added, "Whenever we try to soothe you, it's like you can't hear or see us. Though awake, it seems you aren't with us."

Aleirya grimaced and averted her gaze from her parents.

Her wounds had healed within days with no trace of a single injury from that night.

All had seemed fine when she had been released from the infirmary a fortnight ago.

Nevertheless, Aleirya had noticed a change in herself, one she couldn't explain and hadn't dared share with anyone, even Takhéa.

In truth, she felt nothing like herself.

A fiery, discordant tangle of emotions writhed within her. At times, she found herself struggling against a sense of fear she could not even name. Other times, she was grief stricken, as if she had lost a part of herself.

But most of all, there was a deeply rooted, unbridled anger that wrestled for control over her, a rage she could not explain that had made a home for itself somewhere in the depths of her heart.

Then there were the physical changes: the headaches, and the violent surges of energy that came and went as they pleased, interrupted by spells of exhaustion that kept her bedridden for large periods of time. Everything about her was amiss, and the lack of control over her physical and emotional state only angered her more.

The dreams had been part of it as well. They had started shortly after she had settled at the cottage with Thoran and Zannia.

THE RISE OF ISIGAR

Aleirya remembered having had nightmares as a child, but they were no match for the horrible scenes that haunted her whenever she closed her eyes.

Still, she couldn't remember awakening from them even once.

Aleirya blinked as if to jog her memory and stared down at her feet.

"I'm sorry," she said.

Thoran and Zannia both crossed the room to her, and Zannia pulled Aleirya back into her arms.

"You must not apologize for anything," Zannia answered.

"Just stay here," Thoran added, "at least until the trial is over."

Aleirya nodded silently.

The trial. Right...

She had tried her best not to think of it, as it only kindled the unnatural heat that slumbered in her chest and burned in her veins.

Shortly before she had been released from the infirmary, she had received word that she was to stand before the royal council and the king for them to discuss the happenings of that night at Killian's bar. Aleirya knew that there were several suspicious members of the council who wished to determine the true nature of her actions. The matter had seemed more than bizarre to her.

She had saved the life of a princess while endangering her own, and yet they questioned the circumstances and intent of her actions.

Aleirya forced herself not to think of what awaited her. She was not afraid.

"Izidora came to see you the other day," said Zannia, letting go of her.

Aleirya nodded but kept her eyes trained on the floor.

Her friends and even Sir Odynn had come to check on her regularly ever since her parents had taken her home from the infirmary. But Aleirya had had them sent away every time.

The thought of her closest friends and her mentor witnessing her in the state she found herself in, especially considering the transformation she sensed within herself, seemed unbearable. She didn't want them to worry.

However, befitting the princess she was, Izidora would not be ignored; and so, the letters began.

Aleirya received a message every couple of days through which the princess kept her informed of the royal council's dealings.

Zannia withdrew from her and crossed the room to the kitchen where she opened a drawer and added, "She left something for you."

Zannia held a folded piece of parchment in her hands, and studying Aleirya carefully, she handed it to her.

The rough surface of the letter's parchment rubbed against the tips of her fingers as Aleirya accepted it and unfolded it after a moment's pause.

Zannia and Thoran stepped aside, allowing her some privacy as she started to read.

Her chest tightened while her eyes raked over Izidora's message, and a flutter in her stomach grew to a burn at the mention of the trial.

Father and the council have been on edge ever since the attacks on the shelters, as they are now calling them.

Perhaps even more so than ever. They're afraid that whoever is behind them was aided by someone of our own, someone possibly unsympathetic toward the crown and my father. They fear that perhaps the shelter fires and Lord Varlam's death are connected, thinking that whoever is behind the one might be stirring distrust against the throne. But they still have no proof.

Aleirya swallowed, her throat having gone painfully dry, and she reminded herself to breathe.

All this to say, I do not know what awaits you, or what answers the council wishes to attain from you through this trial. But you should not fear. You are innocent. My father will make sure you will be treated well.

All my love,
Izidora

Her hands shook, and she clutched the letter, pinching it between her fingers so tightly that it made her skin prickle.

She was innocent. How could they think otherwise? How could they suspect her of being involved in a conspiracy against the crown?

Aleirya paced back and forth. Her pulse quickened, and a flame sparked in the core of her chest, making it impossible to stay calm.

Aleirya knew she needed to breathe, she needed to calm herself, but it felt like someone was holding her underwater.

An ache seized her whole body, and a scorching heat coursed through her as if her blood were boiling.

A shout tore through the room, and it wasn't until she felt someone grab hold of her shoulders that everything slowed, the pain subsided, her pulse decelerated, and a weight lifted from her chest.

Aleirya inhaled sharply. She let go of Izidora's letter and bent forward over her knees to steady herself.

Her vision swam from the tears that welled in her eyes, but she forced herself not to cry.

She could not break; she could not fall apart now.

"Water." She heard her own voice rise breathlessly and glimpsed Zannia rushing from her side to answer her request.

Her gaze trailed from her hands to the floor, and lastly to the parchment containing Izidora's message to her, and a shiver chased down her spine.

The letter was singed where her fingers had grasped it.

Panic clutched her.

Everything she touched, she burned.

Chapter 18

The palace halls were colder than Aleirya remembered. The drumming of the guards' joint footsteps echoed off the stone, the sound vanishing somewhere in the hollows of the endless corridor before her as the king's soldiers led her onward.

The hairs of her neck stood on end, and a chill swept over her skin as Aleirya worked against the stiffness in her gait and concentrated on placing one foot in front of the other.

Her eyes trailed the smooth tiles beneath her feet, polished to a state that she could see the rough contours of her face reflected in them.

Aleirya remembered the countless times she and Izidora had chased each other through these very hallways as children, played hide-and-seek or pretended to spy on the palace's staff. Her recollections of this place were fond ones, and yet, here, now, all their familiarity seemed lost, haunted by a bitter foreboding of what perhaps awaited her.

Daring to look up, Aleirya peered over her shoulder, catching sight of Thoran following closely behind the circle of armed men who escorted her.

He looked back at her and nodded while placing his right hand over his heart.

It was a gesture of his that she knew from her childhood.

Whenever she had been afraid, he had placed his hand on his chest and told her that just as he held her in his heart, she carried him in hers; wherever she was and whenever she was afraid, he would always be there with her.

Aleirya nodded back at him and held his comforting gaze for a moment before she turned once again to look ahead.

They came to a stop before a set of tall stone doors the color of charcoal.

The golden handles in the shape of two dragon heads, their jaws agape, glared at her just as the guards drove the ends of their spears into the ground three times. The ground shook, and the thundering sound reverberated through the soles of her feet.

For a moment, nothing happened. But then Aleirya saw the mighty doors draw open, and the throne room appeared before her.

Her eyes caught the gleam of the golden circlet molded around the king's head in a ring of flames that shone eerily bright against the dark throne just as King Ethuriel raised his scepter and permitted her to enter.

A silence enveloped her that made her skin crawl and pressed against her ears; for a moment, it seemed as if she had lost all sense of hearing until her first step ricocheted across the floor.

Aleirya could feel the weight of every footfall as she moved forward, leaving the guards and Thoran behind her.

The heavy doors of the throne room slammed shut, making her breath halt.

Cold trickled down the nape of her neck at the jolting realization that, at last, she was alone. Despite the steady and solid beat of her stride, she felt unanchored.

Aleirya swallowed and riveted her gaze on the sight ahead.

She refused to let her emotions cripple her. This was a test of her strength and her confidence. She had nothing to fear, and she would not let the sheer sight or presence of the king and his council daunt her.

The black marble of the throne room's floor, walls, and pillars fringed her vision as she advanced toward the dais. The stone's golden swirls and veins illuminated the path before her, struck by the only light in the throne room that shone from the open ceiling.

Lifting her chin, Aleirya set her eyes on the end of the Great Hall where four broad steps led up to the throne, a massive chair carved from out of a monolith of black opal.

A fierce-looking wing like that of a dragon's extended from each arm of the throne and descended the dais. The tip of each wing reached the base of the first step and then folded upward in an elegant curve.

Behind the throne was a raised platform on which lay the enormous form of a blue dragon. His name was Galàzios, the dragon of His Majesty, King Ethuriel.

The creature raised its mighty head when Aleirya approached the throne and watched her closely with his huge golden eyes just as she stopped at what seemed an appropriate distance.

Aleirya dragged her gaze from the creature to the king seated before her. She had only known Ethuriel as Izidora's father, generous and kind, one who had always treated her like a daughter. Now, standing before him, she suddenly became aware of herself as his subject.

To the left and the right of the throne sat the warlords and members of the royal council, eyeing Aleirya with obvious suspicion. As her gaze passed over them, she noticed an empty chair to her left, where she assumed Lord Varlam would have been seated.

No one spoke at first.

Then, breaking the silence, King Ethuriel looked at Aleirya and said, "Now that our assembly is complete, I, King Ethuriel of Tarragon, call this trial to begin."

Shifting his gaze from Aleirya to a tall figure to his right, he added, "Lord Acristus, you may proceed."

At the king's command, Lord Acristus arose from his seat and stepped forward, ascending the first two steps before coming to a stop before the king and facing Aleirya.

He wore a long black robe that covered his armor underneath, and his blond hair was pulled back behind his neck where it hung just above the center between his shoulder blades. A sword was sheathed at his side.

He looked down at Aleirya with ruthless scrutiny, examining her from head to toe in silence as if sizing up an enemy before he spoke. "State your full name for the council of the king."

His voice was grim and held a roughness befitting of his rather hostile manner.

Unperturbed, Aleirya nodded and answered, "My name is Aleirya Perèdur."

Lord Acristus fixed his gray eyes on her for a moment and then paced back and forth, unspeaking.

"Daughter of Thoran and Zannia Perèdur," said Lord Acristus while he continued to pace, the sound of his steps echoing powerfully through the throne room. "And if my inquiry is correct, you are attending your third year as a cadet of the Esdras Academy?"

"Actually, it is now the fourth year, my lord," Aleirya said and swallowed.

Lord Acristus stopped and looked at her, seemingly unpleased about the correction.

Then, turning toward her, he asked, "And what is your age?"

"Seventeen years, my lord," Aleirya replied.

"Hmm," said Lord Acristus. "Tell us, Miss Perèdur, what happened on the night of Lord Varlam's death?"

Lord Varlam's death? How about the assault on the princess?

Aleirya wanted to grit her teeth.

She started to feel that unfamiliarly strong anger form in the pit of her stomach; the odd furious sensation that never completely dissipated from her ever since the night of the assault and that was easily rekindled by the slightest provocation.

Her hands clenched into fists at her sides.

When she saw Lord Acristus notice them, she immediately released them, instantly regretting her lapse of control.

Forcing herself to move past what she assumed had been a mistake, Aleirya recited the course of the forenamed night.

She told of Lord Varlam's ranting against the king, the fight that had erupted inside the bar, forcing her and Izidora's escape, and her encounter with Lord Varlam.

"And then I awoke inside the infirmary," said Aleirya, finishing her recollection of the events that had taken place.

Silence followed as the king and his council, along with the warlords, considered her report.

"You told us you had taken a harsh fall toward the end of your fight and that you could not clearly identify Lord Varlam? And I understood correctly that you cannot recall releasing the chakram from your grasp nor are you able to state with certainty that you saw it strike Lord Varlam?" said Lord Acristus.

"Yes, that is correct. But the injury across my palm must prove that I reached for the chakram," Aleirya answered.

"Yet you are certain that you were alone and that no one else had come to the defense of the princess? No one followed you and Izidora?" Lord Acristus interrupted her loudly.

"Yes," Aleirya replied.

The throne room grew utterly still once again.

"Lord Acristus, if I may, I have spoken truthfully and left nothing hidden from my king, your lordship, or the council." Aleirya spoke cautiously.

Lord Acristus looked at her and then resumed pacing back and forth.

"Indeed, the account of the princess resembles that of your own, and we have no other witnesses to declare that you have withheld the truth from us. However, the council bears significant doubt that a youth like yourself, despite your training, could have brought Lord Varlam to his demise without any form of assistance," said Lord Acristus.

Aleirya felt her skin prickle as she listened, not daring to speak again.

"Furthermore, you yourself cannot clearly remember the circumstances of his death and the thrust of the chakram. Yet the lethal strike Lord Varlam suffered, apparently from your hands, requires a vast amount of precision and perhaps years of training," he added.

He continued to watch her closely while he went on, "This leads us to wonder how you, in your injured state as you have described to us, could have wielded the chakram so effectively and precisely that it led to Lord Varlam's immediate death."

Lord Acristus paused and stared down at her.

Aleirya did not shy away from his gaze, and though he kept his face still, she was certain he suppressed a grin. She wondered what it was he was waiting for her to do as he seemed to hesitate in his speech, an insatiable thrill in the dark pits of his eyes as if this were a game he intended to win by tricking her into making a mistake.

"We do not wish to declare you a liar before this council and, more importantly, before His Majesty, Miss Perèdur. However, this does still beckon us to question whether there wasn't perhaps someone there to aid your rescue of the princess after all. Perhaps some part of the night's events vanished from your memory?" he asked.

He paused as if expecting her objection, and when she did not speak, he went on, seemingly angered by her lack of response. "Or perhaps you are trying to protect someone, someone who truly wanted to see Lord Varlam dead and abused this incident to see their plot through instead of plainly arresting him for his crimes?"

Aleirya felt a jolt course through her at the rage simmering in her veins, instigated by Lord Acristus' words. But she compelled herself to stay calm.

"Tell us, how much experience have you gathered in the course of your training with the chakram? It is an unusual weapon to be wielded by a Dragon's Kin," said Lord Acristus.

Forcing herself to ignore his provocation, Aleirya answered carefully, "To be truthful, I have only little experience with it. Yet, as you know, my ancestors have forged weapons for the armies of Tarragon and once for the elves in the past; it is a weapon I have known and wielded before."

Lord Acristus stood still on the steps in front of her for a moment, as if to ponder his next move.

He eyed her suspiciously before he then raised his chin and spoke. "Should we believe your report to be true, down to its very detail, then it would appear to me you at your young age pose quite the danger. What example would we be setting for yours and that of the younger generations if we allow actions such as yours against the higher authorities of Tarragon to go unsanctioned?" Lord Acristus asked and then paused again to watch Aleirya's reaction.

When he found not even the slightest indication of a flinch in her expression at his provocative statement, he continued, "Yes, the princess was indeed rescued, and if you speak the truth, then your intentions are to be considered honorable. Nevertheless, according to your words, Lord Varlam, one of Tarragon's warlords, a protector of our people and subject to the king, was slain at your hands. There are no other witnesses to support your claim besides the princess, who herself admitted being beaten unconscious over larger periods during the assault.

"As leaders of Tarragon, we are charged to ensure justice and equality and uphold the statutes given to us by our law. This also means to practice discipline among the younger generations of our kin and protect them from potential danger," Lord Acristus added.

Aleirya's heart pounded violently against her chest as she listened, anticipating in horror what was about to be spoken over her.

Lord Acristus let his gaze pass over the gathered council and then glanced at the king before he spoke again. "Miss Perèdur, as an aspiring dragon warrior and defender of our people, you have been taught in our statutes, and you have vowed to adhere to them and honor them in your service to the throne. These very statues state that the unlawful taking of a life is punishable by death."

He paused, staring directly into her eyes, and then added, "Miss Perèdur, I say this to you in the utmost sincerity to demonstrate the gravity of this crime. However, in light of all the things discussed and since we do choose to acknowledge your willingness to risk your own life for that of the Princess Izidora, the council and I have considered the following verdict: Due to the murder of Lord Varlam, the council insists that there be a disciplinary action and a close observation of your further developments. You are, therefore, suspended from the Esdras Academy, effective immediately. This council will determine the duration and point of your reinstatement, depending on our observations of your improvement."

Aleirya's whole body stiffened, every muscle clenched, and with every breath she drew, she could feel her anger burn hotter. It was as if it began to turn into physical pain that coursed through her body from her head to the soles of her feet.

Her ears rang, and she wanted to raise her arms to cover them and shield them from the horrible sound, but she forced herself to remain still.

Lord Acristus looked to the king and said, "It is but for our king to consent to the verdict of his council."

Every fiber of her being wanted her to look away, but Aleirya made herself look at Ethuriel.

The king looked back at her. His expression was unreadable; then he spoke at last. "Aleirya, for your courage and for saving my daughter's life, I offer the utmost gratitude to you. However, according to the findings of this trial by my trusted council, I, King Ethuriel, consent to this verdict."

He paused but continued to study her as if he meant to convey his pity for her.

"I release you from this hearing. You are dismissed," said the king.

Aleirya felt as if the ground had been torn out from underneath her.

The ringing in her ears grew louder, and the pain inside her seemed to escalate, threatening to devour every last ounce of composure she had left like the flames of a fire. Resisting the urge to scream, she made herself bow, forcing her body to bend against its will.

Heat engulfed her chest as she straightened and turned to the entrance of the throne room. Every one of her steps echoed louder than when she had first entered the hall. When she was within arm's reach of the doors, she stretched out her hands to push them open.

She hadn't yet grabbed hold of the two dragonheads when the doors swung open with a loud crack, almost knocking the guards that stood behind them to the ground.

Aleirya didn't stop to determine what had happened in that instance. All she could think of was that she wanted to escape.

Crossing the threshold of the entrance to the throne room, she took off in a mad run, leaving the bewildered guards and Thoran behind her.

Chapter 19

"I cannot believe you!" Izidora yelled, cheeks flushed and her fists balled tightly at her sides.

Her voice carried through the royal hall, ricocheting off the marbled pillars that towered around them. "You lied to me! You promised that if Aleirya was innocent, that if it was true that she only meant to save me, no harm would come to her! You lied!"

Tearing her gaze from her father, she turned away and looked out over the rest of the throne room. Only a few guards stood along the sides of the hall, staring blankly into the large space, their faces as still as if carved out of stone. She could only imagine what they were thinking, observing her outburst from the sidelines.

"Izidora," King Ethuriel spoke softly, "I did not lie to you."

"You twisted the truth!" she shouted, whirling around to face him again. "You never intended to accept that she only did what she did to save me! You never intended to let her be, after all that happened! And worst of all, you never believed me, even when you promised you did."

Tears streamed down her face as she spoke and gasped for air.

Her glance shifted briefly to Kalithea, who stood across from her and looked at her with the same expression their mother wore whenever she meant to caution her to manage her emotions. Izidora couldn't help but recognize her mother's rebuke and the pity in her sister's eyes. It made her want to wince.

Pressing her hand against her lips, she shut her eyes and tried to calm herself.

Letting a moment of silence pass between them, Ethuriel hesitated before speaking again. "Izidora, it is only a temporary expulsion from the academy. Aleirya will be reinstated, and this will all soon be forgotten."

Shaking her head fiercely, Izidora answered, "You marred her as a rebel, a criminal, Father. Not a single warlord will instate her amongst their ranks, no matter with how many honors she graduates or how many glowing recommendations she presents herself with. You and your council have given her the reputation of a rule-breaker."

"Then I will personally call her into the service of my army," King Ethuriel replied firmly. "I give you my word."

Izidora scoffed and muttered under her breath, "Your word means little to me now."

She lowered her gaze to the floor, hugging her ribs.

"Izidora!" Ethuriel raised his voice, rising from the throne. "That is enough. I will not have my daughter speak to me in such a manner!"

Izidora's gaze shot upward to meet her father's face, and she abruptly pulled her arms back down to her sides.

Staring daggers at him, she spoke. "As you wish. After all, I no longer have any desire to speak to you."

She noticed his jaw tighten as he looked back at her; with that, she spun around on her heels and stalked away.

Clutching her skirts, she bit down on her lip, hoping he wouldn't say another word while she exited the hall. She knew she wouldn't be able to suppress her frustration should he speak to her again.

Ignoring any glances that followed her, Izidora fixed her gaze on the tall doors ahead that led out of the throne room.

She could hardly contain the guilt and the anger she felt after having assured Aleirya time upon time that all would be well and that her father would do what was right.

Not only had he made her believe he was on her side, he had also made her a liar.

If left up to her, they didn't have to share another conversation ever again.

* * *

With a long sigh, Ethuriel continued to pace before the throne.

"Perhaps your mother would have handled this better," he said, the weight of his crown pressing uncomfortably against his forehead.

Now more than ever, he resented the hard saying passed on to him that he would always be a king before a husband and a father.

"I mean no disrespect, Father, but I understand her," his eldest daughter's voice rose softly.

Stopping, Ethuriel looked at her and answered, "I know."

Nodding, he went on, "I know she feels as if I betrayed her trust. I wish I could undo the pain I've caused her."

He tried to smile at Kalithea comfortingly, and approaching her, he gently placed his right hand on her arm.

"Aleirya's expulsion will not last forever. She will be allowed to return and complete her training at the academy. If Tarragon's warlords should truly refuse to let her join their armies, then, as I have given Izidora my word, I will instate her," he added, looking deeply into Kalithea's eyes as if to seal the promise he had made.

"But she has done nothing wrong, Father," Kalithea said gently.

Lowering his hand from her, King Ethuriel answered, "I believe Aleirya meant to save Izidora's life, and as I have told Izidora, I say to you, I will always be grateful for her sacrifice. However, as presented before me by the council, the circumstances surrounding the incident were most peculiar. Aleirya was injured. Her perception and memories of that night were compromised. Aleirya was hardly a match for Lord Varlam, and yet he was killed. You yourself know that there were many who were unsympathetic toward him. The council could not and still cannot rule out a conspiracy against him with certainty. Whether I believe in Aleirya's innocence, in order to appease the council and salvage Aleirya's future, I consented to this measure of discipline," King Ethuriel answered.

He eyed Kalithea a while longer before stepping away and ascending the dais when she said nothing.

Before seating himself on the throne, he glanced at her again and said, "Sometimes the decisions we are forced to make aren't always fair, Kalithea."

They continued to dwell silently in each other's company until Kalithea approached him.

Wordlessly, she climbed the steps of the dais and then came to a stop before him.

Placing her hand over his, she looked up at him and replied, "I understand, Father."

Pursing her lips, she began to go on when the entrance of the royal hall burst open with a crack.

Both Ethuriel's and Kalithea's eyes darted toward the tall doors as a group of guards stormed inside.

Coming to a stop before him, one of them bowed and spoke. "Your Majesty, there is something you must see."

* * *

A horde of people flooded the square before the palace, obscuring the view as the guards accompanied Kalithea alongside her father.

Shouts rang out from the masses, and the people scattered to the sides upon the sight of the royal guard passing through the gates and toward the center of the commotion.

The soldiers drew closer to her sides as the volume rose around her, and she could feel the cool touch of their armor pressing up against her as they guided her along, making sure no one could get close to her or her father.

When they came to a stop, Kalithea lifted herself up onto her toes and peered over the shoulders of the guards in front of her.

A pair of men stood in the middle of the crowds, raising their voices anew. "War! We are at war!"

Terrified looks covered their faces that were smeared with dirt and blood.

They wore armor that looked scratched and bent, and their swords were blood-stained, proving that they had been in a fight.

An ugly gaping wound marred one of the men's cheeks who cried out, "They are coming!"

"The elves are coming! They will bring death upon us!" the other screamed even louder.

Both men continued to yell at the crowds, upsetting the people, when her father gave the order, "Seize them!"

The soldiers immediately followed his command and arrested the men, dragging them from the square.

"Have them cared for, and once their wounds have been tended to, have them brought before me at once," Kalithea overheard her father say to Lord Jarek.

Lord Jarek nodded and then hurried after the soldiers who had arrested the men.

Quickly, the royal guard urged them back toward the palace when Kalithea turned to her father and shouted above the commotion that arose around them once more, "What does this mean?"

Without stopping, King Ethuriel shook his head and answered, "We shall find out. But for the elves' sake, I pray that there is no truth to their words."

* * *

"They're all dead?" Ethuriel uttered, sinking back against the throne.

"Yes, that is all they spoke of once they were brought to the infirmary. They kept repeating it," said Lord Jarek.

Leaning forward, Ethuriel raised his left hand to his temple and rubbed the side of his forehead, closing his eyes for a moment.

"We weren't able to get anything else from them yet. I hope that perhaps once they have received proper care, they will be able to tell us more," Lord Jarek added. "Whatever happened to them was no small thing."

Straightening, King Ethuriel folded his hands over his lap and stared out ahead of him at the tall doors at the end of the Great Hall. The throne room lay completely still while they continued to wait in silence.

Then, waving his hand, Ethuriel signaled the servant to his left to bring him something to drink.

The swift steps of the boy were the only sound to be heard throughout the hall as he climbed the dais, and approaching Ethuriel's side, he handed him a chalice of wine.

Raising the cup to his lips, Ethuriel drank as Lord Jarek spoke. "Ethuriel, the men bore the mark of Gerlach's army. They served under Lord Varlam."

Lowering the chalice, Ethuriel exhaled and then turned to look at Lord Jarek and Kalithea, who stood quietly beside him.

"I warned you that something like this might happen," said Lord Jarek.

"We don't know what happened or what these men have done," Ethuriel interrupted.

Taking another sip of his wine, he paused and then exhaled before adding, "We shall hear what they have to say for themselves."

Just then, a rumbling sound echoed from beyond the doors of the throne room before they were opened.

Seeing the group of guards stand below the arch of the entrance, Ethuriel raised his scepter and signaled them to enter.

Watching them as they approached, he drew a deep breath and leaned back against the throne.

Night had fallen, and the moon shone from the starlit sky above, casting a silver glow upon one of the men's heads once they came to a stop.

Ethuriel heard Galàzios utter a low growl when, out of the corner of his eye, he saw his dragon's head appear at his left as the dragon's neck curled around the side of the throne from behind him. Eyeing the men closely, Galàzios bared his teeth and snorted.

Tearing his gaze from the great dragon, his body shaking, one of the soldiers began to speak. "Your Majesty."

Both men then bowed nervously to Ethuriel before the first went on, "I am Silas of Taran and this is Owen, my brother. We are most grateful for the care we have received at your mercy, my king."

"You have caused quite the uproar amongst the people," King Ethuriel interrupted him firmly.

Staring down at them, he went on, "Such grave tidings of a war with the elves should have been brought to me first and not proclaimed before the people. You have acted foolishly."

Taking a step forward, Silas lowered his head and said to the king, "Forgive us, Your Majesty. We only meant to speak the truth."

"Then it is the truth that you shall share with your king," Ethuriel said, cutting his words short. "I command you to tell me of this threat you claim to know of. What happened between you and the elves who I am told you encountered?"

There was a pause while Silas hesitated to answer him. The soldier's voice trembled when he finally spoke. "They were all killed, Your Majesty, every one of them slaughtered in a single night. Besides the both of us, not one survived, and how we stand before you at this very moment, I do not know."

He stopped and then added, "They must have mistaken us for dead. For when I awoke, they were gone and there was only blood."

Drawing another sharp breath, he continued, his lips quivering, "We had been journeying through the Dhaharran Forest and were only three days' travel from Erysméa when they attacked. It was an ambush. Cowards they were, they fell upon us during the night, having waited once our dragons had left our sides to hunt."

A moment of silence fell between them before Silas finally mustered the courage to meet Ethuriel's gaze. Raising his head, he spoke. "Your Majesty, they seemed far more powerful than ever. More than half of our forces had been slain before the dragons returned—and the elves were ready for them. Many were subdued by their magic and then injured, while those who could and who had lost their rider fled for their lives. The men who tried to escape were caught and then killed, ensuring that no word of the attack could be brought back to you, my king."

Ethuriel's jaw tightened, and his hands clenched into fists as he listened to Silas speak of what had happened.

Letting the words of his report linger in the air between them, Ethuriel stared out into the space in front of him.

After a while, Silas began shifting his weight nervously from one leg to the other while he stood before him.

He abruptly froze when Ethuriel spoke at last. "What were you doing in the forest? And who ordered you to do so?"

Silas looked up at him, and Ethuriel could see his fear plainly displayed all over his face.

Then, reaching up to touch the cut that ran along his left cheek, Silas turned to look at his brother who seemed just as terrified as he was.

Not willing to deny his king an answer, Silas looked back at Ethuriel, and nodding, he replied, "It was Lord Varlam who gave the order. He gathered a force of men, inviting any who would volunteer to support his cause of righting the wrongs that were done to us. He promised us gold, a fortune, and a better life for our families. We were to be rewarded for our loyalty."

Silas paused as he searched Ethuriel's expression and then went on, "We were to travel through the depths of the Dhaharran Forest until we reached its border into Inaesa of Erysméa. By night, we were to raid the villages closest to the border and set them ablaze. It was to be a warning to the elves to never again set foot in our kingdom and to receive vengeance for what we had lost at their hands in the shelter fires. But they must have already been sent on their way to strike at us again, Your Majesty."

Afraid of Ethuriel's response, he immediately took a step back from the throne and lowered his gaze to the ground.

"This is disastrous!" Lord Jarek exclaimed. "Not only have we lost a respectable force of able warriors to face this threat, but we have also increased the elves' confidence in their victory against us! What were you thinking?"

"Lord Jarek," Ethuriel cautioned.

Then, turning his attention back toward the men, Ethuriel asked, "The elves that attacked you, did they bear a mark, a sigil?"

Silas shook his head and answered, "It was dark, my king. I cannot be certain."

Eyeing him, Ethuriel nodded but said nothing as he contemplated the report the young man had given him.

Panic suddenly gripped the men, and breathing heavily, they both fell onto their knees before Ethuriel.

Trembling, Silas called out, "Please, Your Majesty! Please do not punish us! We were under the instruction of our lord. What we did, we did in service to the kingdom."

Staring down at the men, Ethuriel answered, "Rise."

Slowly, both scrambled to their feet and looked up at him.

"You shall receive no punishment from me this day," said Ethuriel.

The men gasped in astonishment as relief overcame them while he went on, "You are to be released and return home to your families."

Then he turned to the guards and nodded, signaling them to lead the men away.

Just before the guards took them, both men bowed before Ethuriel, and Silas exclaimed, "Merciful are you, our great king! Forever shall we be grateful to you, Your Majesty!"

Their shouts of gratitude continued to ring loudly through the hall until the heavy stone doors of the throne room fell shut with a crack.

But before another quiet could settle around them, Lord Jarek immediately began to pace angrily across the podium before the throne.

"Unbelievable," he kept on muttering.

Ethuriel could feel Kalithea's eyes on him while he continued to sit in silence, lost in thought over what they had just learned.

Taking a careful step toward him, she spoke up gently. "Father?"

Ethuriel turned to look at her when Lord Jarek abruptly interrupted his pacing and said, "So, then it is true? We are at war with the elves. I shall summon the council at the break of dawn. Our armies must be prepared and then there are, of course, strategies to discuss."

Rising from the throne, Ethuriel stared out into the distance before him and interrupted, "After all these years of peace."

Then he turned his head toward Kalithea and Lord Jarek, who, for the moment, had ceased from rambling on, and spoke. "If it is a war they desire, then a war they shall have."

Chapter 20

"A soldier is more than a strong body and the sharp edge of his weapon," Valeirys' voice roared above the heads of the recruits gathered before him. "A keen mind is just as essential to your survival as your physical capabilities."

The heels of his boots clicked against the floor and bounced off the walls of the arena as he traversed along the rows of soldiers in training, the youngest ones not a day older than fifteen years.

Their faces were still, their eyes riveted on him as they stood in formation, each gripping a battle ax in their hands.

The labyrinth rose on Valeirys' right and opposite the young elven soldiers.

Several passageways opened in the stone wall that made up its front, and inside, a series of combat trials awaited the recruits.

"Before we begin this challenge, look at the axe in your hand. Tell me, what do you see?"

The group hesitated a moment, carefully studying the make of the weapon before one of the elves raised his hand.

Nodding, Valeirys granted permission to speak, and the soldier answered, "Érètha vraelnynniae. The seven blessings, sir."

Valeirys dipped his head in approval of the answer and spoke. "Correct. You may elaborate for the rest of your unit."

The elf cleared his throat and began to speak. "The origin of the seven blessings lies in Erysméa's first founding of the seven leagues. Each league bestowed a blessing on every one of their warriors in the form of a mark that was magically traced onto their skin. The blessing demonstrated the faith the lord of the league had in the individual warrior. It was a blessing of strength and endurance for battle, but also, because of its magical origin, it was to protect the soldiers from growing bitter by the gruesomeness they witnessed in their service."

The recruit stopped and swallowed before adding, "After the Uprising of the Eskhàra, who had also received a mark upon their birth in celebration of their powerful nature, the tradition was forsaken. It proved too cruel a reminder of the devastation and suffering the hybrid warrior race brought upon Erysméa."

The arena fell silent before Valeirys raised his voice anew. "Notice the engraving on the blade of your ax. When you approach the labyrinth, one of the blessings will spark alight. Find the same mark etched into the stone of one of the entrances in front of you and enter by it. Inside the labyrinth, the ax shall be your guide, and it will lead you to the trials you are to face alongside your comrades. Work together, use your wit just as much as your weapon. The blades are sealed in magic. Any injury you incur will heal the moment the blade touches your skin. While you will not die, you will feel it. So, take this challenge seriously."

The thundering stomp of the soldiers' footfalls resounded through the arena while the recruits marched a few steps forward and then stopped, holding their axes in battle-ready position, the shaft raised in a diagonal cross over their chests. An ancient cry for battle bellowed from their lips just as Valeirys reached the end of the front row and turned to observe the soldiers split into groups and approach the labyrinth.

He watched as group by group, the young elves entered and disappeared from view when a voice rose from behind him. "Leadership certainly suits you."

Turning, Valeirys saw the prince and immediately stepped back and offered a bow before he spoke. "Your Highness."

With arms folded across his chest, Prince Malik stood beneath the grand arch of the arena's entrance, his personal guard positioned closely behind him.

Grinning smugly, he said, "Though I enjoy the sentiment, you need not bow. If at all, it is I who should grant you the honor after saving my life."

He released his arms to his sides and took a few steps into the large hall and toward Valeirys.

Looking at him, Valeirys thought he looked much like the king, though perhaps his eyes held a sharper reddish glint than the bronze hue of his father's. His silver hair was trimmed to his shoulders and brushed the black steel of his breastplate decorated with the king's sigil of the great sycamore tree, the seven sigils of the elven leagues entangled in its roots. The polished hilt of his sword peered out from beneath the crimson cape draped over his shoulders and back.

A stripe marred his cheek from the grazing of an arrow, most likely from the attack on the banquet. Why he had not let the healers remove it or healed it himself with his magic, Valeirys did not know. Some soldiers preferred to leave wounds and scars to harden their features.

"You have nothing to thank me for, Your Highness," said Valeirys. "After all, it is my sworn duty to protect and serve the throne—"

"Malik," he interrupted. "Please. Prince Malik if you must, but 'Your Majesty' is my father—and the sound of it makes me feel quite old."

"As you wish," Valeirys answered with a nod.

"Good," said the prince and smiled. "I have a proposition for you, Valeirys."

Barely glancing over his shoulder, he raised his right hand and formed a sign, ordering the pair of his guards to retreat.

A breath of silence followed as they did as their prince commanded before Malik continued, "You are leading your father's investigation of the rebellion and the efforts to unmask their leader, correct?"

Valeirys' brow furrowed, but he nodded and spoke. "That is correct."

Folding his hands behind his back, the prince began to stroll past him. His glance wandered throughout the hall and over the façade of the labyrinth before he stopped and replied, "You need not worry. This is not some misguided fascination of you as my rescuer. I merely like to do my due diligence towards those I intend to employ; besides, everyone knows your father. I am certain the apple does not fall far from the tree despite the both of you not sharing the same blood."

Instinctively, Valeirys' hands folded into fists at his sides, but he quickly unclenched them. He did his very best to fit the mold of his predecessors and worked hard to earn his place with the family who had taken him in despite his unknown heritage.

Turning toward Valeirys, a glint of the torchlight flitting across his breastplate, Malik went on, "As I am sure you have heard, my father has set a rather extravagant price on the head of this 'Liberator'. While it was a good idea, it has set off a witch hunt."

He sighed and shook his head before glancing at Valeirys and adding, "Of late, any fool with a fondness for a shiny coin finds their way into my father's court, claiming to have found the wanted. It has made my father's audiences, to which I have been privy, quite aggravating and frankly, a waste of time which we do not have.

"However, I have not been half as idle as the public might assume, sipping wine and sitting in my gilded chair while one crook after the other is cast before my father's feet. Like you, I have been intent on finding this fellow who fancies himself king of the people, and I believe I have found just the way to do it."

"Forgive me, Your—" Valeirys stopped and cleared his throat, "Malik, but why are you coming to me with this and not to your father or to his council?"

The prince grinned, and a mischievous spark lit his eyes when he answered, "Because the high-minded members of my father's council, and no doubt His Majesty himself, would fiercely object to the means of this undertaking."

Cocking his head to the side in a sly manner, he went on, "It is precisely where you come into play. I need someone I can trust, and someone who will join me and act as my shield and my right hand. I cannot rely on my guards since they are sworn to answer to my father, and though that technically accounts for you as well, he will not be looking to question you should he notice my absence or wish to inquire of my activities of late."

The hairs on Valeirys' neck stood on end, and a strange sense of excitement mingled with the warning voice of reason that urged him to reject the prince's offer due to its moral ambiguity.

When he hesitated to answer, Malik took a step closer and continued, "There is a Dragon's Kin who has garnered quite the reputation through his wealth of secrets. Supposedly, nothing happens in the kingdoms of both elves and Dragon's Kin that he does not know of. The only difficulty is finding him. But as prince, there are some perks to my position, one of which is the riches I own."

His grin deepened just as his left hand reached for the pouch attached to his weapons belt. Valeirys saw the glow of something bright shine from beneath the prince's cape as he drew his hand forward, pinching a coin in between his fingers and added, "This fellow, alike the avaricious elves slithering into my father's court, has a liking for gold."

A gentle clink bounced off the arena's walls as the prince flicked the coin into the air and watched it spin before him while he continued, "I managed to relay him an offer he could simply not refuse in exchange for a name, and I promised more if he could uncover the location of the rebellion's leader. I received a message this morning stating where and when we can meet."

Valeirys' jaw ticked, but he swallowed and loosed the tension built up in his muscles before asking, "And where is this meeting to take place?"

Malik held his gaze, delaying an answer until the coin plopped into his palm. The prince closed his fingers over it and replied, "The Black Market."

Valeirys' lips pursed, but he said nothing. He had heard rumors of the Black Market. No one knew exactly where it was except the few who dared dabble in its illicit affairs. If they were caught, they could be put to death, as it was forbidden for any elf to trespass into the realm of the Dragon's Kin or deal with the likes of their kind; not even the title of prince could save oneself from execution.

Valeirys' spine tingled, his blood running cold at the thought.

Instinctively, the word 'no' rushed to the tip of his tongue, but before he could speak it, Malik interrupted him. "While outside the lines of a proper investigation, I find that the necessity to catch this radical as soon as possible outweighs such perhaps dishonorable means."

He seemed to sense Valeirys' unease, and his expression changed, the roguish semblance in the quirk of his lips and the gleam of his bronze eyes dulled for the length of a heartbeat.

"Arrangements have already been made; an alibi made up for my absence at court, should anyone notice me leave in the dead of night," he said. "I, that is 'we,' leave in three days."

Once again, the prince tossed the coin in his hand, a flash of gold bouncing in his palm while he eyed Valeirys.

Then, taking another step toward him, he held it up before him and said, "I will see that it is a reward well worth the risk."

He then tucked the piece away and went on, "I'll even let you be the one to deliver the traitor's name to your father on a platter. So, what say you, Valeirys? I've heard it said that fortune favors the bold."

* * *

Yessenia stared down at the array of strange symbols scribbled across the parchment before her. Ever since she and Uryiel had returned from Aram after observing the body, she had hidden herself away in the small library of their home. Their cook checked on her regularly, serving her the most delicious-looking meals, but Yessenia could not bring herself to eat.

She hadn't been able to sleep either. Whenever exhaustion overtook her, she found herself trapped in dreams of chasing after something, only to wake up just before she discovered what it was.

Her mind yearned for answers, desperate for clarity over what had happened in Aram.

Yessenia exhaled heavily and leaned back against her chair.

Shivering, she lifted her arms to wrap them around herself when she stopped. Her hands were stained with ink.

Angered, she rose abruptly, shoving the chair back with a loud screech, and swept the pages off the desk. Stepping aside, she began to pace back and forth until something in the corner of her eye caught her attention.

Yessenia stopped and turned to look at the oval-shaped mirror that hung on the wall.

One half of its silver frame showed a band of interlocking thorns, while the other half was covered in a strand of vine and lilies. Carved at the top of the frame was an open eye.

Among the elves, thorns denoted evil and falsity, while lilies were a symbol of purity. The open eye represented life and truth.

Athrèmn di caelési ena onira, the mirror of good and evil was the name it had been given.

It had been a gift to King Izurion upon his coronation.

According to the rumors, the mirror was enchanted. The identity of its maker had never been revealed.

The common belief was that the mirror had been given to the king by a wealthy elven family. Others believed, however, that it had been crafted by one of the Metatari and presented to an elven servant for the king as an offering of peace, since both races had been estranged from one another.

Upon acquiring the unique piece for the king, the elf had been warned that the mirror would reveal the true nature of the one who gazed upon it. Once the beholder opened their mind to the mirror's power, it would unveil their deepest and darkest desires as well as the good within them.

It would expose both their weaknesses and their strengths. The mirror could be used to rule wisely if the one who possessed it was willing to humbly accept and understand their frailties and seek to overcome them. But it could also bring about the demise of its master by enticing them into giving in to the darkness inside of them. Whichever part was stronger would eventually assume control over the mind and soul while diminishing the other.

Many years ago, after receiving the mirror, King Izurion gave in to the evil of his own heart and eventually raised an army to destroy the good in their world.

Uryiel's family had been in possession of the mirror for decades now.

After Erysméa's victory over Izurion, the new king of the elves had desired to rid himself of the accursed piece. Uryiel had told her that his great-grandfather, a collector of such rare magical artifacts, had retrieved it from the king for it to serve as a reminder over his household never to underestimate the power of magic. Ever since then, it had hung on the wall in the library of the Altair manor.

Yessenia stepped closer to the mirror.

Tearing her gaze from the frame, she looked at the mirror's surface. She wore a white gown. Its sleeves, bodice, and the trim of its skirt were decorated with a fine golden design. Her thick raven hair lay cast over her shoulders. There were dark lines underneath her eyes.

Then, taking another step toward the mirror, Yessenia stared at her reflection. She raised her hand to its frame where it came to rest over the sharp points of the silver thorns.

Moments after her palm had touched the cool surface of the frame, the glass of the mirror rippled, and suddenly, Yessenia found herself looking back at a woman.

She wore the same dress as Yessenia, her hair and eyes bore the same color, but something was different about her manner.

The expression on the woman's face changed, and a sinister smile crept over her face.

Yessenia felt her stomach lurch.

The woman's eyes flashed gold-red, and she spoke. "Yessenia, my dear, don't look so surprised."

Yessenia stood frozen before the mirror, unable to remove her hand from its frame.

"Who are you?" she asked.

The woman in the mirror laughed aloud.

"My dear! You can't pretend to be ignorant. We are one. I am what you have always been," said the woman and tilted her head to the side as she eyed Yessenia.

Her voice sounded just like Yessenia's, but her laugh was nothing like her own.

"No," said Yessenia.

"Why, yes! You seek to know the truth about who it is that you are, or do you not? I have the answers you seek. I am what you are so desperately searching for," said the woman.

Yessenia shook her head.

"No, there is a deep darkness within you. I can feel it! I am nothing like you!" Yessenia shouted.

The woman laughed at her again and said, "Dearest, I am the revelation of your true self! I cannot lie."

She paused and then went on, "You want to know what happened to you in Aram?"

Goosebumps rushed down the skin of her arms, and Yessenia gasped.

"How do you know about Aram?" she asked.

The woman's eyes flashed again, and she grinned before answering, "It is as I said. I am the answer you seek."

There was a pause as their eyes locked onto each other for a moment. Helplessly, Yessenia searched for anything in the woman's appearance that differed from that of her own but found nothing. She was the unmistakable mirror-image of herself.

Then the woman continued to speak. "The reason your mind is restless, the reason your soul finds no peace is because you do not want to see who you are. You felt the power in Aram. You felt it, and it pleased you, and now you long for it. Your mind and soul lust after it. I can feel it," said the woman.

Her features had darkened. A sneer distorted her mouth, and an insatiable hunger lit her golden irises with a pulsating glow.

Then she laughed. The sound of it made Yessenia's skin tingle.

This cannot be true, she thought. How could this possibly be her true self? How could the mirror show her this? She was good. She had always been good.

The woman must have noticed the horror in her expression, for she grinned and shook her head at her.

"Oh, don't look so grim! Why do you think your magic has always been stronger than that of those around you? Just like your father has always told you, Yessenia, your magic is special. And not for just any reason. You have been born with a darkness inside of you, Yessenia. It festers within you! You were born for great things. But you fear yourself. You refuse to accept who you truly are and that limits you!" she exclaimed ecstatically.

Then it seemed as if she had stepped closer. Her smile disappeared for a moment while her eyes searched Yessenia's face.

Again, her expression changed, almost as if Yessenia had saddened her.

"You only have to embrace it, my dear. I can give you what you seek. I can satisfy your thirst and help you understand," said the woman, her voice as soft as silk.

"No! No, you know nothing of who I am!" shouted Yessenia, shaking her head.

Then she grabbed hold of the mirror and tore it from the wall.

Turning, Yessenia thrust it onto the ground. But to her surprise, the mirror's surface did not break.

It didn't even crack.

A cold shrouded her body, and she couldn't help but stare back at the woman in the mirror.

Smirking, the woman began to shake her head and laugh, the shrill noise growing louder and louder.

"You can't hide from yourself, Yessenia! You can't run from your calling. Someday you will accept who you are!" said the woman.

Yessenia raised her hands before her as if to protect herself from the reflection in the mirror.

"No! I will never become who you say I am!" she shouted back.

As the last words fell from her lips, she felt a surge of energy course through her body, over her arms and into her hands, before a flashing light, like lightning, shot forth and struck the glass surface of the mirror, shattering it into a thousand pieces.

At last, the woman disappeared, and the echo of her voice grew quieter and quieter until it was no longer to be heard.

Yessenia stood before the broken mirror with her arms still outstretched before her. Her breath hitched under the sobs that shook her body. Her hands trembled, and she felt tears stream down her face.

Slowly, Yessenia stepped backward until she hit the wall.

Then she sank to the ground, and burying her head in her knees, she let herself crumble.

Chapter 21

A shout escaped her lips as Aleirya swung the baton forcefully against the Pell, feeling a sharp pain jolt up her wrists and into her arms from the impact. Catching her breath, she stepped back and stared at the wooden stake in front of her.

Then, with a grunt, she charged at it again, thrusting the baton forward and striking at the head, shoulders, gut, and knees of her imaginary opponent. All the while, memories of the trial continued to torment her as she relived the moment standing before the king and his council over and over again.

Aleirya could still picture Lord Acristus' face as he questioned her.

It angered her how he had made her feel powerless, small, and ashamed, as if she was supposed to feel shame for having saved Izidora's life.

Aleirya seethed, and with a shout, she raised the baton over her shoulder, leaning her whole body into the strike, and hit the Pell as hard as she could.

A cracking sound, so loud that it hurt her ears, shot forth once the wooden sword met its target. Her palms burned, and her whole body ached when she tossed the baton aside. Panting, she turned and leaned against the Pell, sliding down onto the ground, and closed her eyes.

She could hear the mighty sound of her dragon's wings throbbing against the wind as Takhéa landed in the field close to her.

Without opening her eyes, Aleirya called out to her in a tired voice, "I'm not ready to talk about what happened."

The trial had ripped the ground out from underneath her. Nothing was as it should be. Bereft of her plans, her purpose, and her sense of justice, Aleirya felt as if she had been torn apart from the inside. Everything was distorted and wrong.

The king and his council had twisted the truth; they had made her out to be a conspirator, a murderer, a liar.

"It's been days, Aleirya," the dragon said gently, drawing her out of her thoughts. "Whatever happened, I should know; you should tell me."

"And I will," Aleirya replied harshly, getting to her feet.

She began to walk away when Takhéa moved in front of her and spread her wings wide, barring her path.

The dragon lowered her head toward Aleirya, forcing her to meet her gaze.

"You've been shutting me out," said Takhéa, "and for a time, I could understand. But it ends now."

Immediately, a wave of guilt overcame her.

She could feel her heart break at the thought of sharing the result of the trial with Takhéa.

Swallowing hard, she clenched her fists and pressed her lips to a line to prevent them from quivering.

Regardless of the council's sentence, Aleirya knew that what had happened was everything else but temporary. She was marked. Even if she returned to the academy and completed her training, Lord Acristus had made sure that any warlord would see her as trouble, volatile, and untrustworthy.

Though she didn't regret it, by saving Izidora's life, Aleirya knew she had ruined everything. She had damaged their prospects; worst of all, she had bound her dragon to a fate she knew she never wanted—bonded to a disgraced rider. The best thing she could do, the only way to make it right, was to set Takhéa free, release her dragon from her bond and relinquish the claim she had on her.

Aleirya's chest tightened, and her whole body ached as she pursed her lips to speak, but nothing came of it.

Sensing her struggle, Takhéa dipped her chin and pressed her snout to her heart, humming softly.

Aleirya felt the vibrations travel from her chest into the rest of her body, flooding her with warmth, and she rested her forehead against her dragon's scales.

As her fingers played across the smooth surface of her dragon's onyx hide, Aleirya let herself crumble in Takhéa's embrace, permitting her dragon's comforting presence to wash over her and tear down the walls she had built around herself.

Her brow furrowed, and she pinched her eyes shut, forsaking her fears and concerns and letting her hurt and emotions flow toward Takhéa through the bond.

A sense of ease overtook her, and she released a gasp.

But then, all at once, her dragon reared, and Takhéa's head tore skyward just before a terrifying roar broke over her.

The dragon's maw drew wide open before her chin dipped toward the ground again, and she released a gust of bluish flames that turned gold once they engulfed the tall grass.

Aleirya staggered backward as a fiery wall rose between them.

Not once did she take her eyes off Takhéa.

Crouched on all fours, her dragon's eyes gleamed silver and lilac through the black smoke that poured from her nostrils and rose upward from the ground.

"How could they do this to you?" the dragon asked before another low growl sounded from her throat.

Awestruck, Aleirya stood before her and replied, "How did you—"

Takhéa roared again before she dragged one of her enormous claws over the ground and answered her, "I saw image after image of you standing before the council. I could feel your emotions and hear your thoughts and how they questioned you. It must have been a memory of yours."

Aleirya blinked and stared at her incredulously. "Has—has this happened to you before?"

"No," Takhéa answered furiously.

She took a few steps back and eyed Aleirya from head to toe.

"Something about you has changed ever since the night you rescued Izidora… The emotions I sense in you are more powerful. A restlessness, an anger, a fire consumes you… body and soul," said the dragon.

Takhéa paced before her, beating her tail against the ground to extinguish the flames.

Another rumbled escaped her set jaw as she bared her teeth and then spoke again. "Our bond is not what it once was. A barrier has been removed from your mind, enabling me to see what your eyes have seen and hear what your ears have heard."

Swallowing hard, Aleirya lowered her gaze from Takhéa.

She couldn't stand to look at her. Her fears, her guilt, and pain surged into the pit of her stomach, making her want to buckle over, but she stood still.

"I don't know how to explain what you have told me," she replied breathlessly.

She heard the dragon's heavy footfalls as Takhéa approached and stopped in front of her once again.

Aleirya reached out to touch her.

She could feel a part of her dragon pull away.

"You should have told me," said Takhéa. "We should not keep secrets from each other."

Aleirya could no longer contain herself, and tears spilled over her cheeks while she looked up at her dragon.

Her shoulders shook involuntarily, and she wrapped her arms around herself.

"It scares me, Takhéa," she admitted. "The world is coming undone; it's crumbling to ashes around me. I can see everything slipping through my fingers. I can't lose you, Takhéa… I can't!"

Her eyes burned, and a dreadful hollowness formed in the pit of her stomach when, all at once, her dragon closed the distance between them, her head crashing against Aleirya's chest.

"Our bond was not made to be broken, Aleirya," said Takhéa. "This shall not change my promise to you. Together, we will fight this. But you must trust me. You must not hide."

Aleirya threw her arms around Takhéa's snout but failed to encircle its width, making Takhéa hum in amusement.

After a moment's pause, when it had grown quiet around them again, the dragon asked, "What do you want to do now? Hunt a draspith? Paint the sky black?"

With a sigh, Aleirya withdrew and looked up at her.

"I'm not sure," she answered.

Unintentionally, her hand traveled to the academy's pendant at her neck that held her tracking stone, and she heard her dragon speak. "For starters, get rid of that."

Aleirya grinned and nodded.

The dragon was right. The instructors of the Esdras Academy didn't need to know her whereabouts anymore.

"That sounds like a good plan… for starters," she replied.

Upon her response, Takhéa lowered her upper body to the ground, and with a wink, she said, "Then let us go."

Back at the academy, Aleirya tore the pendant holding the tracking stone from her neck and dropped it onto the bed.

Beside it lay the pin bearing the signet of the Esdras Academy. Aleirya stared down at the two objects.

They would not get rid of her that easily. She would return, and when she did, she'd be stronger than ever before.

An immature plan began to form in her mind. She would continue to train on her own. She would refine her skills and abilities. She would make herself irresistible for any warlord looking for new recruits. The king and his council would not change her future, her destiny. She would make sure of it.

If at all, it was hers to change and hers alone.

Aleirya averted her attention from the pendant, grinning slyly. Oddly, she felt free.

Taking one last spin around the modest space she had claimed as her own for a little over three years, Aleirya retrieved Ismené and Valdr. The familiar pressure of the pair of swords against her back felt good, comforting even.

Regardless of Lord Acristus' efforts, no one was going to make her feel small or weak. She was a warrior; not even the king himself could take that from her.

Aleirya headed toward the door of her room when her footsteps suddenly stalled, and she glimpsed her reflection in the mirror that hung on the wall to her right.

Retreating, she moved to stand before it.

Something about her appearance was different.

Tilting her head to the side, Aleirya searched her features, a map of lines and angles that seemed finer and perhaps more pointed than she remembered.

Lifting a hand to her face, she let her fingers trace her pale skin and run along the line of her cheekbone before she sighed and tucked a stray strand of hair behind her ear.

Straightening, her attention shifted back to her eyes which she imagined looked bluer than usual.

Not wanting to make more of it, she frowned and turned away.

She had just pulled the door to her room shut when a pair of footsteps rose to her left, and Aleirya looked up to see Nathanael approaching.

At the sight of him, her stomach lurched, and her hand clutched the handle of the door.

"Hey there," he said.

A weak smile broke across her face when he stopped beside her, but she said nothing.

"I was wondering when I'd see you again," Nathanael went on.

Aleirya nodded, lowering her gaze. They hadn't spoken in a while.

He had stopped by her parents' cottage several times after she had returned home from the infirmary, but she hadn't been able to muster up the strength to talk to him. At least that was what she told herself when, in truth, she hadn't really wanted to see him after watching him with Kara on the night of the fight.

"Izidora told me what happened. She convinced someone from the council to tell her all about the trial," he said.

Looking back up at him, Aleirya hesitated and bit down on her lip before she replied, "They called it a 'disciplinary action.'"

Scoffing, she let go of the door handle and shook her head. "I don't understand. I save the life of their princess, and this is what they do to me?"

Her words lingered between them for a while until Nathanael spoke. "You'll be back sooner than you know."

Aleirya knew he only meant to comfort her and glanced at him before she looked away again.

Perhaps she would be back soon; but perhaps she wouldn't.

Her mind still struggled to believe what had happened, and she sensed an anger stir inside her chest. It wasn't right. It wasn't fair.

Aleirya tried to relax, opening her hands that had balled into fists. She did not want to think about it anymore. After all, thinking about it wouldn't change what had happened. She needed to let it go.

"Is there anything I can do?" Nathanael asked, taking a step toward her and interrupting her thoughts.

His approach startled her, and she jumped.

Looking up at him, Aleirya searched his face. Sparks leaped across her fingertips, and she sensed an unfamiliar warmth rush to her cheeks.

To her relief, he seemed to pretend as if he hadn't noticed.

Then he smiled and spoke. "If you'd like, I thought perhaps you might enjoy one last sparring match. Just the two of us."

Grinning, he gestured at the two swords that hung crossed over his back.

"That sounds good," she answered, trying to come across calmer and more collected than she was.

One last time, Aleirya turned and glanced at the door to her room.

It didn't seem real. How could she be leaving when she was meant to be here?

"Come on," said Nathanael.

With a sigh, Aleirya nodded and then turned, finally walking away.

Aleirya followed Nathanael to the large open-roofed court where the dual wield competition of the tournament had taken place. Passing through the halls, she noticed many of the cadets staring at her.

At first, she thought they were all looking at Nathanael, especially the girls, since this was nothing unusual whenever she spent time with him. But when they neared a small group and one of the young men pointed at her, causing the others to turn and look, she realized that the curious stares and whispers had been directed at her.

They couldn't possibly have heard of the verdict, she thought to herself and tried to ignore the unwanted attention while they passed them.

The training site was just beginning to clear as a session had ended, and the cadets retreated from the court.

"Perfect," said Nathanael, "looks like we'll have the place to ourselves. I'll grab us some sparring swords. Be right back."

Aleirya nodded and tried to match his smile as he walked away. Nathanael had just turned the corner, vanishing from sight, when another pair came toward her.

Aleirya's arms went rigid at her sides, and she lifted her chin just as Damian came to a stop in front of her with Cassian at his heels.

"Still here, Perèdur?" Damian asked, a devilish grin stretching across his face. "I would have assumed they'd dragged you off to the dungeons by now. Killer instincts got the better of you in your last fight, didn't they?"

Aleirya clenched her teeth and took a step forward. A jolt coursed through her limbs, and a heat built up in her chest almost immediately after Damian had opened his mouth. *How dare he?*

"Where's Nathanael, your guardian? Is he off duty or simply questioning the morals of Tarragon's most notorious hellion?"

Damian chuckled maliciously, and Cassian joined him, leaning back against the stalagmites that surrounded the training court and enjoying the spectacle of Damain's taunt.

"Never mind him," said Damian, "I didn't take you for one in need of a protector anyway."

He came closer and sneered at her, undoubtedly taking pleasure in his cruelty.

Aleirya narrowed her eyes and bit her tongue, trying not to give in to the ire Damian roused within her.

"After all, you prefer to take care of the fighting yourself—or should I say, killing," said Damian.

His words pricked her skin like knives, and her chest tightened as if ready to burst, jolts darting along the bones of her ribs, making her want to scream in his face.

Damian leaned closer, and Aleirya fought the urge to flinch as they stood cheek to cheek, and he whispered into her ear, "Come to think of it, there is a rather nasty fellow I would like to rid myself of. You wouldn't mind taking care of that for me, would you? I'd even pay you for it."

He snickered when Aleirya pushed him backward.

"Get away from me," she said in a warning tone.

Her gaze pierced his as she watched him take a step back and heard him laugh.

"You're no soldier, Perèdur. You're a cold-hearted killer," he spat. "A killer disguised as a little girl."

A scorching heat shot through her limbs, and Aleirya's eyes sparked blue.

The space around her vanished in a haze of red, and before she knew it, her arm swung forward and her knuckles smashed against Damian's nose.

Damian doubled back with a yelp, blood pouring down his mouth and chin when Aleirya threw another punch with her left to his gut and drove her knee into his groin.

He made a choking sound and heaved a breath before he forced himself upright, his face vermilion; then he came for her.

Aleirya dodged his left strike to her ribs and caught his right fist before it hit her temple. With a strength unknown to her, she twisted his wrist until a grueling crack split the space between them, and Damian screamed.

His left heel plummeted into her gut, knocking the breath out of her for a second, but she managed to keep herself upright.

Hunched awkwardly over his injured arm, Damian spat blood and bared his teeth at her.

"You'll regret this!" he barked, and then he lunged at her.

Aleirya took a kick to her knee and leaned back just as he swung at her again with his left. His movements were laced with pain, impacting his aim, and his fist barely missed her chin before she hauled herself upright and swept her right leg upward, driving her heel into his side and against the bottom of his ribcage. Her left fist followed, planting a facer before Damian howled, and she watched him stagger backward. Aleirya moved toward him just as someone struck her from behind.

The hit sent sharp jolts down her spine and a shooting pain into her legs and arms.

Her head snapped backward as she crashed onto her knees, and her eyes tore wide open.

Aleirya felt a fire consume her from within, a burning sensation suddenly surging through her veins, and a scream lodged in her throat.

Her attacker didn't hesitate, and she felt something hard thrash against her side before he knocked her onto the ground.

Another hit followed before she glimpsed the shaft of the baton he continued to swing at her.

Blots darted across her vision, the taste of blood filled her mouth. Her throat burned as she gasped a breath, and her gaze locked onto Damian, who came marching toward her.

She had seconds to get to her feet.

Her fingers dug into the grooves of the stone beneath her; her jaw clenched and then tore open to a shout.

An unnatural force roared to life within her, and Aleirya felt her strength return tenfold.

Rolling onto her back, she grabbed hold of the baton, catching Cassian, who stood over her, by surprise. With a tug, she yanked him forward and onto the ground before she leaped to her feet and whirled. Aleirya struck a blow to Cassian's temple, knocking him out, and then dropped the baton just in time to seize Damian by the neck before he could snatch her.

A vengeful hiss slipped through her set teeth, and she heaved him up against one of the stalagmites that surrounded the training field.

Blood rushed into her limbs, flooding her arms and legs, and she felt the invigorating twitch of each muscle as they contracted, following her command. The overwhelming power stored within her body seemed to thrive off her anger, growing stronger the longer she held onto Damian.

A rush of awe overcame her, but Aleirya didn't stop to question the oddity of the power that overtook her like a being of its own. It didn't shock her as it should have or scare her enough to stop. Instead, she sensed her excitement grow, kindling the violent thrill.

Aleirya couldn't help herself.

Her eyes fixated on Damian. His terrified face transformed as the light around her extinguished, and her nightmares and memories blended into one cruel fantasy. Aleirya found herself standing in utter darkness behind Killian's bar. Lord Varlam's laughs rang in her ears, causing her skin to crawl, and then his ugly sneer rose before her eyes.

Panic clutched her, gnawing at her bones, and she sensed her grip around Damian's neck tighten even more before her fear turned to unbridled rage.

Once more, her eyes flashed blue.

A sense of delight overcame her as she watched him suffer at her hands.

Aleirya squeezed his neck harder, provoking a horrible scream that pierced the air and broke the mad spell that consumed her.

Her body froze, a cold seizing her grip, before she gasped and let Damian go.

Damian slumped to the ground, heaving for air as her surroundings cleared and sharpened around her.

Tremors painfully seized her hands, and Aleirya stepped back in shock.

What had she done?

Damian continued to wheeze and choke, trying to recover from her attack. The awful echo of the noises coming from his throat rose to her ears in an unnatural volume.

Terrified by what had just happened, Aleirya spun around on her heels.

"Aleirya," Nathanael called out. She could tell he was near, perhaps even coming toward her, but his voice was only a faint echo, vanishing somewhere in the depths of her mind.

Aleirya couldn't look up from her hands. She couldn't bear to face him, and instead, she ran.

Panic ravaged her, and once again, it felt as if her whole body was burning from the inside.

Aleirya burst through the doors of the academy and sprinted down the winding path of the hill before her, leaving everything she knew behind. Time rushed past her in a blur. Minutes seemed to pass like seconds, and she could no longer tell what was happening.

She kept going tirelessly at a blinding speed that made her dizzy, but she couldn't stop and lost all sense of time.

The sky grumbled and cracked, its pale blue obscured by swirls of thickening clouds, billowing and turning from dark gray to black.

Aleirya thought she would collapse as soon as she reached her parents' forge, but something forced her onward.

Thunder drummed as the light faded and the storm raged, releasing showers of rain.

Aleirya sprinted through the meadow on the outskirts of her father's lands, drenched within an instant by the relentless downpour, her clothes clinging to her like a second skin.

Unable to help herself, she kept on running, nearing the edge of a small forest just as a bolt of lightning struck the ground before her and finally forced her to a stop.

Aleirya stood before a row of tall dark trees, and bending over her knees, she gasped for air and then began to cry.

Her head pounded, and she raised her hands, placing them over her ears and screamed.

What is happening to me? she thought repeatedly until she could hear her own voice echoing inside her head, and she shouted the words into the darkness before her.

Aleirya looked up at the black sky and then down at her hands. They were white and shivering from the cold, but she felt nothing.

She stood hopelessly before the forest, unable to bring herself to move as the night crept along and surrounded her in utter darkness.

She was a monster, a killer, just as Damian had said.

Her chest rose and fell rapidly, anxiety drawing her breath in shallow puffs while tears stung her eyes.

This couldn't be happening. She gasped and choked back a sob.

Then, suddenly, a rustling sound erupted from somewhere out of the trees and caused her to stop, her head snapping upward.

A hum rose in her ears above her throbbing pulse, alertness sharpening her gaze and intensifying the scent of pine, damp moss, and mud gathered in her nose.

Wide-eyed, Aleirya stared out into the blackness when a pair of eyes appeared ahead from out of a thicket. She could make out no human form.

All she saw were the glowing pair of one golden and one silver eye staring back at her. For a brief moment, they vanished, and then, suddenly, the tall figure of a man appeared in front of her. Aleirya gasped and took a few steps back.

The Metatari stepped toward her and into the faint glow of the moonlight that struck the earth below the black sky. The white light gleamed off his dark skin.

Aleirya did not hesitate; her hands shot to the hilts of her swords which she drew to her sides.

Glaring at the strange creature, she warned, "Stop, turn back, and the king will never learn of your trespassing."

Looking at her with his wild shimmering gaze, he chuckled and spoke. "Your hospitality is overwhelming."

Tilting his head while watching her, he continued to move toward her, stopping just before the points of her blades.

"It is precisely your king to whom I wish to speak," said the shapeshifter.

Aleirya felt incredibly small beside his towering form that loomed over her.

Frowning, she narrowed her eyes and answered, "What business could your kind possibly have with the Dragon's Kin?"

"My business is my own," he replied.

He proceeded to eye her intently again, as if trying to read her thoughts off her mind.

Aleirya compelled herself to remain calm and not let his startling gaze unsettle her.

A grin broke over his lips and he spoke. "Try to stay out of trouble… Aleirya."

He then gave a nod and passed her without another word.

Aghast, Aleirya whirled after him and blurted, "Wait! How do you know my name?"

Once again, the Metatari stopped and turned to face her.

Observing her in silence, he smiled again before answering, "Go home. Your dragon will be with you shortly."

Speechless, Aleirya went rigid. Her lips twitched, and she moved her mouth to speak, to call after him, but found herself unable to utter a single word.

Bit by bit, her body unfroze while she watched the Metatari disappear into the darkness.

Her arms dropped to her sides, and she lowered her blades once the powerful stroke of Takhéa's wings sounded behind her. The dragon touched down beside her, just like he had promised.

"Who was that? His call chased through my thoughts. He told me to come get you," said Takhéa.

Aleirya shook her head and answered, "I don't know."

Chapter 22

Sheltered from the downpour, King Ethuriel stood eavesdropping on the incessant tapping sound of the rain beating against the stone floor of the throne room.

His eyes fixated on the golden veins running through the black marble that glowed beneath the flashes of lightning breaking across the heavens.

Standing at the bottom of the dais, his gaze wandered from the angled shape of the dragon's wing extending from the side of the throne and then down the steps and back up toward the open ceiling.

The roaring wind whistled past him, tossing the hem of his royal cloak as he continued to watch the droplets of rain drip from the frame of the roof like silver liquid.

Even as a child, he had loved storms.

First, it brought a cool to the otherwise relentless heat that was common in Tarragon; and second, for as long as he could remember, every great storm had filled him with a sense of wonder at the raw, magnificent power that slumbered in the nature of their world, unrivaled, untamable, and most importantly, not to be controlled by anyone.

Galàzios hummed beside him, lowering his enormous head to his hand.

Standing beneath the arc of his dragon's neck, Ethuriel rubbed Galàzios' chin while vibrations chased down his hand and arm, flowing into the rest of his body as the dragon purred in delight.

Suddenly, one of the creature's huge golden eyes blocked his view of the sky as the dragon curved its neck and turned its face toward him.

A low rumbling sound bubbled from Galàzios' throat, and he nudged Ethuriel's shoulder with his snout.

Suppressing a laugh, Ethuriel grinned and spoke. "You need not worry. We won't be flying out tonight."

Running his hand over his dragon's sapphire scales, he recalled the many evenings he had left the palace in secret as a youth to fly out into the storm, reckless and eager for an adventure. He hadn't cared about the trouble he could have gotten himself into if caught or how dangerous it had been. The thrill of the challenge of maneuvering through the fog and the darkness, mastering the unpredictable strength of the winds, and dodging the violent strikes of lightning had always subdued the voice of reason within him.

Resting his palm on one of the spear-shaped scales of Galàzios' neck, the king remembered the metallic sheen reflecting off his dragon's hide amidst the rain and under the glow of the moon's white light.

As a boy, Ethuriel had always imagined it looking like a comet was chasing across the sky whenever they had flown at full speed through the gale.

Smiling at the memory, the king looked back into the dragon's golden eye that seemed to watch him warily as if expecting him to request for them to take to the sky at any minute.

Although dragons avoided the storms and despised the water, Galàzios had never once refused his wish. Ethuriel never doubted that there wasn't a soul more loyal than his. It was a rare gift he would never dare to abuse.

Drawing closer to his dragon's head, the king rubbed Galàzios' chin again and said, "I promise, my friend, those days are over."

The dragon hummed again as if to convey his approval, batting his golden eye at him.

"Good." Ethuriel heard his dragon's rough voice thunder from his throat. "Your father would roll over in his crypt if he learned his son had not given up his reckless ways."

Ethuriel gave a chuckle and then replied, "You knew him well."

Galàzios dipped his chin and closed his eyes briefly.

Opening them again, the dragon answered, "A prudent king with a fierce heart. He needed both his wisdom and his iron will with a son like you."

Again, Ethuriel grinned at Galàzios' banter and nodded.

All of a sudden, a bolt of lightning struck the floor in the middle of the throne room, blinding him briefly.

Blinking, Ethuriel raised a hand to shield his eyes and stepped aside to determine what had happened.

Alarm roused the hairs on his neck and made him reach for the hilt of his sword secured at his left hip upon the sight of a tall cloaked shape standing in the midst of the royal hall.

Before he could belt out the command for his guards to seize the intruder, Galàzios' head whipped toward the lone figure.

The dragon growled fiercely while its long neck extended toward the unknown visitor, and the ground shook as his claws dug into the stone floor.

Ethuriel watched in amazement as the intruder simply raised a hand from beneath his cloak, seemingly unperturbed by the threatening approach of the dragon.

Like a trained hound, Galàzios stopped, his head hovering before the stranger.

His lips drew upward, baring his deadly set of teeth, but his growl softened to a low rumble as if the intruder had somehow calmed him.

A moment passed between them before the stranger lifted both hands from underneath his dark mantle and lowered his hood.

An icy shiver rippled down Ethuriel's spine as a set of cruel-looking eyes pierced through him, gleaming silver and gold.

It had been a long time since he had last seen one of this visitor's kind.

Ethuriel's jaw tightened while he fixed the shapeshifter with an equally unwavering gaze, cautious to mask his uneasiness the way he had been taught.

The Metatari can sense fear as easily as any beast catches the scent of their desired prey. Ethuriel recalled his father's warning.

Pursing his lips, he was about to address the shapeshifter when the creature spoke instead. "King Ethuriel Medina, son of Aristaeus, son of Kyros; I come in peace."

* * *

"It will be alright," said Izidora, "boys beat each other up all the time and get away with a slap on the wrist."

They sat on the floor in the hallway of the academy's director's office while Aleirya waited to be called in.

After the fight with Damian, Aleirya had received a summons ordering her to present herself before the academy's authorities to discuss the incident. Though the letter had stated no form of punishment for her actions, she was certain there would be consequences.

Staring at the portrait of one of the academy's founders that hung on the wall across from them, Aleirya let out a sigh and answered, "Even if it isn't, what more could they do when they've already suspended me?"

A part of her didn't even care what happened.

Listlessly, she fixed her eyes on the conspicuous golden frame that surrounded the man's image. It was far too gaudy for her taste.

Beside her, Izidora let out a huff and crossed her arms over her chest before sinking back against the wall.

"Who cares what happened... So what? Damian has a few bruises and a wounded pride. It's not any worse than if he had gotten himself into a fight at a bar during one of his crazy nights out on the town. It's not fair."

Aleirya didn't even shrug at her words.

She may have understated the extent of her attack on Damian, but Izidora was right. Nothing seemed fair anymore.

"I bet Leucippus Erebus never got in trouble for getting into a fight," said Izidora in a mocking tone as she read the founder's name off the plaque that hung beside his image.

"I was simply too much of a goody-goody to bring myself into such predicaments," Izidora added, mimicking the tone of the voice she imagined him to have had.

Aleirya snorted and then let out a laugh.

They continued to mock the unfortunate stranger for a while longer until she slumped back to catch her breath.

Turning toward Izidora, Aleirya waited until she met her eyes, and it grew quiet again.

"Thanks for being here, Iz," she said.

Izidora reached out and squeezed Aleirya's hand.

"Of course," she answered.

Aleirya returned her smile and then averted her gaze toward her lap, growing solemn once more.

"Hey, I almost forgot…" said Izidora, and she waited for Aleirya to look at her again.

When she did, Izidora continued, "Remember Cullen, one of the young soldiers who joined my father's guard?"

Aleirya nodded and answered, "You mean the helpless boy you bat your pretty eyes at in exchange for information on your father's meetings?"

Frowning, Izidora nudged her with her elbow and replied, "He is no helpless boy… He knows it's just a game, and he plays along with it. It's kind of our thing. We're friends."

"Mhmm," Aleirya muttered.

"Oh, stop! I never do anything naughty; just let me have this. Besides, it's not like you're any less curious than I am about my father's plans. This is the only way I can get us the information we both want," said Izidora.

"Fine," said Aleirya.

Raising an eyebrow while she fixed her gaze on Aleirya, Izidora went on, "Now do you want to know what he told me or not?"

"Yes, yes!" Aleirya answered.

Grinning from ear to ear, Izidora scooted away from the wall and sat up cross-legged beside her.

"Well, it turns out my father had the most peculiar visitor the other night. A shapeshifter came to see him. Apparently, it was on good terms. He came to warn my father of a threat," said Izidora, almost whispering.

Aleirya felt goosebumps immediately spread across her arms, thankful that her long sleeves covered them and hid her reaction.

Izidora seemed to pause for dramatic purposes and then looked up and down the hall, making sure they were alone.

Leaning closer to Aleirya, she added, "But that wasn't all. He explicitly warned my father not to strike against the elves."

Confused, Aleirya whispered back, "But what about the fight in the woods Kalithea told you about? How could he deny it was the elves who killed Lord Varlam's men?"

Shaking her head, she said quietly, "He didn't. But apparently, he believes they weren't acting on the orders of the elven king. For whatever reason, he doesn't believe that they came from Erysméa."

"That doesn't make any sense," said Aleirya. "Where else would they have come from?"

"I don't know. The shapeshifter didn't say," Izidora answered.

For a moment, none of them said a word.

Remembering her encounter with the Metatari at the edge of the woods a few days ago, an icy cold spread through Aleirya's chest.

She didn't like the sound of it. Something didn't feel right.

Was this some kind of trick?

"What does your father plan to do about it?" Aleirya asked Izidora.

Izidora shot her a brief glance and then replied, "I'm not sure. But the council is supposed to meet again within a few days. Unfortunately, I couldn't sneak into the first meeting my father held with them the morning after his strange encounter with the shapeshifter. But I already have a plan on how to get into this next one, and as soon as I know more, I'll tell you."

Aleirya nodded. "Thanks, Iz. I—"

The sudden creaking sound of a door drawn open caused Aleirya to fall silent, and she turned toward the source of the noise.

A little way down the hall to her left, she saw Sir Odynn standing in the doorway.

Nodding at her, he spoke. "Aleirya, you may come and see us now."

Swallowing hard, she nodded back and then rose to her feet.

Glancing behind her at Izidora who had followed her cue, she mouthed another thank you and walked toward Sir Odynn. Though she hadn't been nervous before, she felt her heart race as she made her way over to the room where they were awaiting her.

Stepping inside, she held her breath, her hand still clinging to the bronze handle of the door when she heard Sir Odynn's voice again. "You may shut the door now, Aleirya."

CHAPTER 23

"Miss Perèdur, I must admit, never has a name from amongst our students raised so much concern and interest at the same time. It is quite unlike you to cause trouble," said Sir Hallvard. The academy's lead director turned to face her, hands folded behind his back.

Aleirya had only met him in passing a few times and had never shared an actual conversation with him.

Unsure whether she was supposed to speak, she remained silent, standing as still and as upright as she could with her hands trained to her sides.

Though terribly uncomfortable, she let him observe her.

The room was painfully quiet even with the other two present; Sir Odynn, who stood beside the hearth to her right and Sir Bradan, the instructor who had approached her after the tournament to her left.

Aleirya forced herself not to glance in either direction and kept her attention fixed on Sir Hallvard.

"Due to the incident with Lord Varlam and the council's observation you have been placed under, I am forced to treat this… mishap… with greater consideration than I normally would."

Aleirya's skin crawled, sensing Lord Acristus' sly entanglement in the matter.

Compelling herself to remain as calm as ever, she forced herself not to flinch nor reveal the slightest flicker of frustration in her gaze while Sir Hallvard studied her.

"As of this moment, we are trying to avoid another hearing with the king's council, and we wish to plead on your behalf. You are an excellent student and show great promise. However, I'm afraid I cannot offer you any certainty that we will succeed," said Sir Hallvard.

Aleirya wanted to drive her fist into the wall or stomp her foot against the ground but willed herself not to move.

She doubted she had any fair chance of avoiding the hearing. Who knew whatever punishment would follow? Lord Acristus meant to torture her. He had been waiting for her to mess up, and now that she had, he was going to take full advantage of her misfortune.

Aleirya could feel a tremor coming on as anger stirred to life inside her.

"You know that your behavior of striking out against a fellow cadet was unacceptable," said Sir Hallvard.

This time, it seemed as if he expected her admittance.

Lips quivering, she opened her mouth and spoke. "I understand, Sir Hallvard, and I… I regret my actions."

Aleirya forced the words out despite the part within her that revolted against her confession.

Damian had had it coming.

Sir Hallvard didn't seem to notice the lack of conviction in her reply or at least ignored it and replied, "Good."

Then, seating himself inside the large chair behind his desk that stood between them, he added, "Sir Bradan, Sir Odynn, and I have discussed at length what should be done about this. We have come to the agreement that the current suspension you are under is punishment enough. However, this decision is only admissible under the premise that you promise to stay out of trouble in the future. Another incident like this and we will have to make it permanent. Do you understand, Cadet Perèdur?"

Aleirya stiffened at the possibility of an expulsion.

Willing the muscles in her neck to relax and her jaw to loosen, she nodded and answered, "Yes, Sir Hallvard."

Folding his hands before him, Sir Hallvard spoke. "Well then, that would be all on our part. Sir Odynn will show you out. Should the council demand a hearing and our efforts to move against the notion fail, I will have you informed promptly."

With a nod, Aleirya responded, "Thank you, Sir Hallvard."

She noticed Sir Odynn's hand gently come to rest on her arm as he urged her toward the entrance when her feet somehow refused to move.

Grateful for his presence, she followed him, trying not to reveal the concern she felt for her future.

Once they were outside the hall and Sir Odynn had shut the door behind them, he turned toward her and said, "Come with me."

Wordlessly, she followed him through the quiet halls, all the way to the opposite wing of the academy where they came to a stop before his quarters.

Aleirya listened to the sound of his keys clanking against the panels of the door while he unlocked the entrance and then bid her inside.

The room was warm and familiar, instilling an almost immediate comfort within her, and her shoulders slumped forward in relief while she let out a breath.

Upon passing her, Sir Odynn motioned for her to settle down onto a chaise longue beside the hearth while he wandered over to the winged chair across from her.

Plopping down onto the chaise longue's soft fabric, Aleirya stared at the flames, sighed, and spoke. "They won't be able to persuade the council to give up the hearing, will they?"

She didn't bother to look up at him, already suspecting the answer.

"I'm afraid not," he answered solemnly.

Aleirya took a deep breath, inhaling the scent of the fire and asked, "What will they do to me?"

This time, she looked up to face him and found him watching her.

He seemed to hesitate but then answered, "I cannot be sure, Aleirya."

"But you have your suspicions?" she asked without wasting a breath.

Again, he waited and studied her before he replied, "Yes."

Aleirya fell silent, holding his gaze.

She could feel her pulse painfully climb up her throat while her mind obsessed over every outcome the hearing could have.

Her fingers shook nervously, and she folded her hands in her lap to stop them, desperate for any shred of control.

Boldly, she then posed the question, "What do you think will happen?"

Leaning forward in his chair, he responded, "I'm not sure knowing will be of any help to you, Aleirya."

"Sir Odynn, please," she interrupted. "Please... I need to know."

Aleirya hated begging, but she would if she had to.

With a sigh, Sir Odynn clutched his cane and spoke. "I'm afraid Lord Acristus will order you into service of the realm's guard, stationing you permanently at the northeastern post of our borders. Since they cannot sever the bond between you and Takhéa, you will be forced to join the men there and serve as a patrolling guard on dragonback. You will be allowed to complete your training, but you will not be permitted to join any of Tarragon's armies as a dragon warrior. You will not rise in rank but indefinitely remain a guard of the kingdom's borders and only ever be called into battle as a last resort."

Aleirya felt her chest and throat tighten. She couldn't move; she couldn't breathe.

Her mind drifted, and she lost sense of where she was. All she could think was that this couldn't happen. She couldn't let this happen.

Blind terror seized control of her. Suddenly, a completely different concern pierced through her clouded mind at the prickling sensation that began at the tips of her fingers and flooded her arms.

She couldn't lose control.

Already she could sense the tremors begin and the restless anger build inside her.

She had to stop it. Sir Odynn couldn't know; nobody could see her like this. A hand came to rest on her shoulder, and she jumped to her feet.

Sir Odynn stood an arm's reach away and spoke. "Aleirya."

Aleirya pictured her dragon flying through the sky under the light of the sun. She imagined watching the even strokes of her wings, hearing the powerful rhythmic beating of her heart and Takhéa's steady and slow intake of breath.

Burying all of her focus into the image, she tried to unclench her fists, one finger at a time. With every flap of her dragon's wings, she envisioned pushing the anger aside. With every echo of Takhéa's heartbeats, she stilled the chaos that ruled her thoughts.

Taking a deep breath, she dragged her gaze from the floor to meet Sir Odynn's eyes once she slowly felt control return to her.

"Perhaps I should take you home," he said, watching her closely.

Shaking her head, she replied, "No. I mean, please, Sir Odynn. Not yet."

"Alright," he said and wandered over to his desk. "Then maybe we should find something else to talk about."

"The investigation," Aleirya blurted without thinking.

Sir Odynn stopped and then turned around to face her. "What did you just say?"

Aleirya blinked and shook her head before beginning to walk toward him.

"The attacks on the shelters, I heard, I—I mean, I assume you took part in the investigation. I was just wondering how things were progressing?" she added rather clumsily.

Eyeing her suspiciously, he hesitated for a moment before replying, "I knew you were up to something. You and Izidora have been spying on the council, haven't you?"

"No!" Aleirya answered. "We would never…"

Sir Odynn fixed her with a serious gaze until she gave in and said, "Alright, maybe a little."

Instead of scolding her, she noticed him grin.

"While I should be admonishing you for this, I must admit, I am not surprised," he then said.

Approaching the opposite side of the desk from where Sir Odynn stood, Aleirya perused the array of opened books and pages of scribblings that decorated its surface.

"So, what do you know about the investigation? Or rather, what do you not know?" he asked.

Daring to look up at him again, she answered, "Is there any news on the groundskeeper? Were you able to learn anything from the stable boys who survived? What about the magic that was used to destroy the shelters? Are there any more clues who did it?"

Sir Odynn let out a long sigh and then spoke. "These are all questions to which I am uncertain I should provide you with answers. But I assume that if I don't tell you, you will find your own ways to learn them."

Aleirya failed to suppress a grin and lowered her gaze to the piles of paper before her.

Settling down in the chair behind his desk, Sir Odynn began to share his insights with her. Aleirya learned the groundskeeper had still not been found, and the search had grown increasingly aggressive now that the council felt certain that he had been involved in the attacks.

With a heavy heart, he also disclosed the news to her that the stable boy they had questioned had taken his own life just a few days ago. Along with his body, they had found several scraps of scribblings and sketches no one could so far make sense of. Regrettably, no one could know if their efforts of trying to decipher them were a waste of time, since the boy appeared to have lost his mind. Sir Odynn mentioned one of the boy's notes in particular that seemed to bear the most promise of possibly having any meaning to the investigation. It was an odd set of words jotted sloppily onto a torn page. Aleirya read over them, guessing the one or the other as she studied the piece of parchment.

Shadow, eyes, midnight… stone, death shall ashes bring… sky a ruby fire… iron of purest black.

For a while, both of them mulled over the stable boy's words, trying to make sense of them before they moved on to the foreign magic that had been used in the fires.

Aleirya recalled his discovery of the strange plant that had been found on the grounds of each of the shelters. Catching sight of a drawing of the plant amongst the chaos of opened books and loose pages, she pointed at the schematic sketch and asked, "Silver tongue is what you called it, right?"

Sir Odynn stopped and looked up at her over his spectacles that had slid down to the tip of his nose.

Readjusting them, he eyed her and replied, "Yes, yes, it is."

Nodding, Aleirya went on, "Do you think whoever attacked us truly used it on the dragons?"

"The dragons or the stable boys… Yes, I believe so. Though I'm uncertain to what end. It could, however, explain the regrettable state the surviving stable boys were found in and why most of them have died. This sort of spell, if administered recklessly, it can destroy the mind to the point of death," said Sir Odynn.

The room quieted until only the faint crackling of the fading flames within the hearth could be heard.

"I managed to recreate the spell from the silver tongue which I suspect was used in these terrible crimes." Sir Odynn suddenly spoke up again, surprising her.

Their gazes locked for a moment before he rose from his seat and retreated to another corner of the room. Stopping before a shelf of books, he ran his fingers along the covers until they froze on one in particular.

Withdrawing it from the shelf, he returned to the desk, placing the book down between them.

Fixing her once more with an intense glare as if to warn her not to mention this to anyone, he lifted the cover.

Carved within the pages was a small space in which he had hidden a vial.

Picking it up, he held it before her and spoke. "In this state, the potion is harmless. But once activated by the right spell and given to the chosen victim, the wielder of the spell can compel them to do anything they desire. They can force them to commit any atrocious act or admit any truth they wish to uncover."

"And what is the spell?" Aleirya asked, completely mesmerized by the shimmering silver liquid that seemed to move on its own within the vial.

"That is far too dangerous for me to reveal," Sir Odynn replied pointedly, placing the vial back inside the book and slamming it shut.

Aleirya couldn't help but sense that something had angered him, but when he returned from placing the book back onto the shelf, his mood appeared to have softened again.

"Could the groundskeeper have been subdued under the silver tongue's spell?" she asked.

"It is possible," Sir Odynn replied. "But I will wager that he was the one who brought the silver tongue to Tarragon in the first place and then crafted the spell. The question then is: How did he retrieve and smuggle it into our kingdom from the valley lands of Nyradorn?"

"Nyradorn—as in one of Erysméa's regions?" Aleirya asked in amazement.

Sir Odynn nodded.

"It seems difficult to believe that no one ever heard or witnessed anything. Perhaps the conspiracy against His Majesty runs deeper than we suspected," he continued to speculate, muttering more to himself than to her.

"Perhaps they entered the kingdom through the Black Market?" said Aleirya.

The idea caused him to jerk upright in his chair, and he stared at her.

"Careful, Aleirya," Sir Odynn warned. "If anyone even heard you speak of that place you could find yourself in a world of trouble; trouble that could cost you your life!"

He tried to keep his voice down, but the irritation in his tone was unmistakable.

"But what if it's true? What if it's the key to how they truly found their way into our kingdom undiscovered?" Aleirya pressed on. "How can they dismiss the possibility solely for the purpose of trying to convince us that the Black Market doesn't exist?"

"Aleirya," Sir Odynn cautioned.

But she couldn't stop. "No one knows for sure how the elves enter the Black Market. Some say those who sell their goods there are banished from their own kingdom. They say they have lived in hiding between our kingdoms throughout centuries and have formed secret alliances with some of the Dragon's Kin, enabling them to enter and leave our kingdom whenever they please. Then there are other rumors of elves traveling to Tarragon's cliffs in fishermen's boats disguised by spells. The whispers mention the vessels are invisible. The elves that make it onto our shores unnoticed wander onto the market by secret tunnels through the cliffs that were supposedly sealed long ago…"

All at once, Aleirya stopped at her own words as if something about them alarmed her, but she failed to place it.

Her eyes narrowed, and she shook her head.

Before she could go on, a violent rush of images flashed before her mind's eye, so quickly that it dizzied her, and she clutched the edge of Sir Odynn's desk. Her scalp tingled, and a shower of ice trickled down the back of her skull along the nape of her neck and ran down her spine.

A memory, foggy, as if subdued, buried deep within her subconscious, tore itself to the surface of her thoughts and jostled her. The stranger who had ambushed her inside the cliff when she had hunted the draspith, the Metatari who had warned her about straying too close to their kingdom's borders all those weeks ago; all of it suddenly came back to her.

Her breath stalled in her throat, and she froze.

The silver tongue, mind invading forces, the tunnels in the cliffs… What if it wasn't just the elves? What if the Metatari were involved?

Then another image rose before her. She remembered the wooden charm she had found inside the cleft after the Metatari had attacked her.

The stag's head… It had been missing a piece… A piece like the other she found at the shelter site.

Her skin prickled all over as she placed it together in her mind.

This couldn't be a coincidence. The same Metatari who had attacked her in the cleft had been at the shelter.

Her thoughts raced.

What if the elves had allied themselves with the Metatari? What if the Metatari were trying to convince the king that the elves were not their enemy, luring the Dragon's Kin into false safety?

"Aleirya? Are you alright?" Sir Odynn asked.

It took her a while to notice he had spoken to her. Then, shaking her head, she replied, "I'm fine… I think I just may be exhausted. Perhaps I should go home. I'm sorry I kept you for so long."

He came around the desk and said, "Don't trouble yourself. It was quite alright."

Nodding, she began to make for the door, when she stopped. Turning to face him, she asked once more, "Are we truly certain that this threat against our kingdom stems solely from the elves? Was the magic—were the attacks on the shelters really their doing?"

"It seems likely, considering the evidence," said Sir Odynn.

"And what of the Metatari?" Aleirya asked. "Aren't they capable of wielding magic as well? Are we truly certain that they aren't somehow involved?"

His eyes narrowed as he pondered her question, but he quickly answered, "The elves have a much stronger cause for considering a war against our people. There is no animosity between our people and the Metatari, but I suppose it is not impossible."

Aleirya looked away, pondering his reply.

For now, all she knew was that neither the elves nor the Metatari could be trusted. If the Metatari were truly double-crossing them, she had to find out before it was too late.

Then, with a nod, she spoke. "Thank you, Sir Odynn."

Offering her a weak smile, he answered, "For what?"

Still standing inside the entrance to his quarters, she peered at him over her shoulder and said, "For everything."

The halls were dark and quiet while she made her way out of the academy.

Aleirya's head ached, her mind overflowing with concern over the events of the day. Clenching her fists, she trudged onward.

In just a matter of hours, she seemed to have been given a glimpse into the doom of her future and that of her kingdom.

Her jaw tightened, and she picked up her pace.

She would not give up so easily.

THE RISE OF ISIGAR

If she could prove that the Metatari were not the allies they claimed to be, if she could uncover their ruse and warn the king in time, perhaps she could protect her people and reclaim the right to the future she wanted most.

The only question left was: Could she save her kingdom and herself all on her own?

Chapter 24

The next morning, Aleirya awoke with a plan.

It had all seemed so simple, so easy, when she had put it all together. But now she struggled to remember the first step while she stood before the familiar wooden door.

Her palms were cold and clammy, the hairs of her neck stood on end, and the muscles in her legs stiffened with tension, begging her to turn and run.

Breathe, she told herself and inhaled deeply before letting the air out slowly.

Now, knock... Her own voice echoed in her ears.

Aleirya scowled.

She could do this. Why was she making this so hard?

Clearing her throat, she curled the fingers of her right hand to a fist and tapped the door twice.

A moment passed before she heard footsteps, and the lock clicked before the handle turned briskly.

Aleirya saw Sir Odynn's familiar face peer around the door.

His eyes narrowed briefly beneath the furrows of his brow, and he spoke. "Aleirya, what in the dragon's name are you doing here so early? Is everything alright?"

"Yes, yes," she began. "I needed to speak to you again, and I wanted to avoid being seen… I'm sorry it's so early."

Sir Odynn let out a tired breath and replied, "I—I'm sorry, Aleirya. I have a class starting soon, and I—"

"It will only take a minute," she interrupted.

Aleirya held her breath while Sir Odynn studied her.

She had to convince him to invite her inside, otherwise this plan of hers would be over before she even got started.

With a sigh, Sir Odynn drew the door wide open, at last permitting her to enter.

Good.

Aleirya cast a quick glance over her shoulder. Nodding a thanks, she stepped inside.

Sir Odynn shut the door behind her, and immediately, Aleirya spun around to face him.

Dropping her gaze from him to the floor, she folded her hands awkwardly in front of her, intending for him to think she wasn't feeling quite herself.

You're going to have to try harder, said her own admonishing voice.

Aleirya wanted to growl at the sound of it but refrained.

Shifting her weight from one side to the other, she let her shoulders slump forward and then fiddled with the strap of her satchel that hung over her shoulder.

Better.

Her jaw tightened.

"Are you sure you're alright?" Sir Odynn asked.

"Yes!" Aleirya answered quickly. She bit down on her lip and hesitated briefly before adding, "I just wanted to thank you. I—I felt like I didn't do so properly yesterday, and I—"

"You don't have to thank me," Sir Odynn said, beginning to eye her suspiciously.

"I do," she responded, nodding her head. "You're the one person at the academy here who seems to never lose faith in me. No matter what I do or how much trouble I cause. I don't know if I'd even stand a chance coming back here if it weren't for you."

Taking a step toward her, he smiled and said, "You are kind. But truly, you don't need to thank me, Aleirya."

"I want to," she said, holding his gaze.

For a moment, it grew quiet between them; then Sir Odynn nodded and spoke, "Alright... Thank you. I appreciate it."

Pausing, he eyed her while she lowered her glance to the floor once again.

This was hopeless.

"Are you sure there isn't anything else?" he asked.

Her heart skipped a beat at his question.

Now was her chance.

Aleirya raised a hand to rub the back of her neck. She didn't meet his eyes, and shaking her head, she replied, "I should be going. I'm sorry to have disturbed you so early this morning."

She began to make her way out when Sir Odynn spoke, "Just a moment now."

Aleirya turned to face him just as he added, "What is the matter, Aleirya?"

Playing nervously with her fingers, she stared down at her hands before looking back up at him and answering, "I'm not sure if it's anything, but I've been having dreams. Once I awake, I can't remember them anymore, but they still torment me in my sleep... And the headaches are back, plaguing me like they did during the nights in the infirmary after the fight with Lord Varlam. I tried to ask the academy's healers for help, but they won't tend to me without an official order."

"Say no more," Sir Odynn interrupted her.

Aleirya felt an instant sense of relief but made sure not to make it too obvious.

Her plan was working.

"I'll speak to them right away," he said. "If it's alright, why don't you wait here? It shouldn't take long."

Aleirya forced herself to hesitate, watching him warily.

Then nodding, she replied, "Alright. Thank you, Sir Odynn."

Smiling comfortingly, he waved a hand at her thanks and then turned toward the door.

Once he had left, Aleirya made herself count to ten before she sprang into action.

Her pulse raced, and her skin tickled as she ran her fingers over the countless book covers until they froze on the one she was looking for. Drawing it from the shelf, she quickly flipped it open.

Removing the vial from the small space carved out of the pages, Aleirya scrambled over to the desk.

She placed the opened book down and quickly snuck the silver tongue potion inside her satchel before drawing forth another glass vial of her own.

Carefully, she put it inside the book where Sir Odynn's silver tongue potion had been.

Inspecting it, she decided it looked similar enough.

Aleirya had crafted an imitation of the silver tongue potion out of a mix of paints from Thoran's forge, which they sometimes used to decorate the one or the other piece of weaponry. Her eyes passed over the shimmering silver liquid once more. It shared a close resemblance with the silver tongue, but it wasn't quite perfect.

Exhaling, Aleirya snapped the book shut.

It would have to do.

She hurried to return the book to the shelf, cautious to put it back in place exactly as it had been before.

Letting go and stepping back from it, she breathed again.

Now to the hard part.

Where would she find Sir Odynn's notation of the spell? He had to have written it down somewhere.

Returning to the desk, Aleirya scanned the disarray of parchment and opened books that drowned its surface while trying to memorize the scattered sight.

She had little time. Sir Odynn would be back soon.

Swiftly, Aleirya rifled through the mess of pages searching for anything related to the silver tongue.

Her eyes scoured over every note, every scrap of information she could find while the seconds ticked away in her head.

Aleirya studied one page after the other, reading over them as fast as she could until she combed through all of Sir Odynn's writings.

Her fist slammed into the desk as she cursed under her breath, knocking down a pair of quills and tossing some loose pages onto the floor.

With a huff, she dropped to her knees and picked up the notes, carefully putting them back where they had been.

Then she reached down and grabbed the quills, placing them back onto the desk just as her gaze halted on one of the two.

Squinting, she drew it closer to herself and studied its form.

Oddly, its shaft was wider than that of the others, and its tip was unstained as if it hadn't been used.

By a fluke, Aleirya shook it, causing something small to slide forth out of the hollow of its shaft.

Hurry! she told herself.

Gently, Aleirya pulled the object out of the quill's shaft.

It unraveled in her hands, revealing itself as a thin piece of parchment rolled together into a scroll.

Aleirya held her breath while she inspected it.

Once again, her heart lurched in her chest, and her fingers trembled.

This was it. She had found the spell!

Without wasting another second, she tore a strip of parchment from an unmarked page and jotted down the foreign words of the spell's incantation.

A set of approaching footsteps grew louder as someone neared the door.

Scribbling the last word, Aleirya quickly shoved the note inside her pocket and rolled Sir Odynn's recording of the spell back to a scroll.

The footfalls stopped just as she began to carefully shove the parchment back inside the hollow of the quill, but it stuck.

As much as she dared, she twisted and pushed at the scroll between her fingers. Heat rose to her head, and the skin of her neck prickled while she cursed silently. Then the handle of the door turned and Sir Odynn stepped inside.

"Ah, already bored, I see," he said with a wink and turned to secure the door shut behind him.

Aleirya used the moment. Returning the quill to the others with the flick of her wrist, she shoved the piece of parchment with the torn edge under a pile of pages and sank back into his chair.

When Sir Odynn faced her once again, she pretended to hide her smile and replied, "I couldn't help myself."

Then she rose and came around the desk.

Meeting her in the middle of the room, he stopped and spoke, staring at her. "Take a drop or two of this before you lie down to rest." He handed her the vial containing the medicine.

When she accepted, he lingered, folding his hand around hers.

Aleirya noticed the throbbing sensation of her galloping pulse travel up her neck, and she held her breath.

Had he guessed what she had done?

Her gaze locked onto his, and then he said, "If your condition doesn't improve, come and see me again."

As he released his hand from hers, she nodded, swallowing the lump that had formed in her throat.

Then he passed her and moved toward his desk.

Aleirya watched him, still struggling to breathe while he appeared to hesitate before it.

When he turned around to face her and smiled, she inhaled.

"It was good of you to come," he said.

Aleirya nodded, feeling something dreadful already gnawing at her stomach, and she walked over to the door.

"Stay out of trouble for me, alright?" he added.

Pausing, her hand already wrapped around the circular handle, she looked back at him once more.

He had settled down on the chair behind his desk, a book already cradled in his hands, and he grinned at her.

Concentrating on the all-too-familiar sight of him seated there immersed in his studies, she managed a genuine smile and answered, "I promise."

Chapter 25

Drops of rain crackled against the pane of the window of his room as Valeirys studied the darkening sky. It was almost time.

There were some of his people who claimed that a storm before a quest brought luck. If this were true, it would certainly bode well for them.

Streams of water ran down the glass he leaned against, and a grayish mist obscured the view over the gardens of the manor, illuminated by mage lights that blurred to specks of orange and gold in the storm.

His left hand felt for the hilt of the dagger sheathed below his hip, the cool of the blade bleeding through the leather of his trousers. Two more were hidden inside the heels of his boots, and he had placed a small chakram inside a hidden sheath in the vest of his leather armor just below the ribs on his right.

No one could save him from his fate should this night go awry.

Valeirys swallowed.

Perhaps it was foolish, reckless even to join the prince. But what choice did he have?

What if this was their only chance to stop the rebellion for good and bring the Liberator to justice?

He couldn't let this opportunity pass him by; he just couldn't.

All this time, they had kept to standard procedures, followed along with the rules; and all of it, only to come up empty.

Perhaps the rules had to be broken in order to claim the victory they needed. Perhaps this Dragon's Kin they were set to meet tonight was the answer.

The mage lights dimmed, marking the end of the guards' patrol.

Valeirys spun away from the window and snatched his cloak from his bed before tossing it over his shoulders.

The faint click of the door was the only sound audible as his shadow melded into the blanket of darkness that loomed over the halls of his home. He had but a few minutes before the guards' formation would change, rendering his secret escape through the manor's cellar impossible.

The winding staircase glowed silver at the end of the hall ahead, drowned in the moon's light that broke through the tall windows of the atrium.

Stopping and pressing his back against the wall, Valeirys listened for any footsteps, any sound that would betray a guard, servant, or resident nearby.

He was about to make for the stairs when someone grabbed his shoulder from behind him.

Valeirys whirled and pinned the culprit against the wall, his forearm pressed against his neck when he heard the elf's choked whisper. "It's me!"

His eyes widened and shivers ran down his arms, his whole body jolted at the soundless approach of his brother. Immediately, he let go, and a thud sounded as Eyvindr's bare feet hit the floor.

"That's what you get for thinking it'd still be fun to sneak up on your soldier brother," Eyvindr muttered and coughed.

"What are you doing up?" Valeirys asked through set teeth, trying to keep his voice down.

Eyvindr glared at him, narrowing his eyes, and replied, "I could ask you the same. Why are you dressed and armed as if you're heading into a fight?"

"Just go back to bed," Valeirys answered.

"Don't tell me what to do," Eyvindr grumbled. "What are you up to?"

When Valeirys didn't answer, he crossed his arms over his chest. Tilting his head back, he smirked and said, "I could alert the guards; say I was just on my way to the kitchen to fetch something to drink when I ran into an intruder who turned out to be you." He unclasped his arms from his chest and shrugged his shoulders. "Oops, my mistake."

"Keep your voice down," Valeirys hissed.

His brow furrowed in annoyance. With a sigh, he whispered, "Fine. If you must know, I may have a lead on finding the rebellion's leader."

Eyvindr's arms dropped to his sides, and his brow rose. "That's great. But why so secretive? Is Trajan going with you? Does Father know?"

"No," Valeirys muttered.

Checking the hall and peering over his shoulder to make sure they were alone, he glanced back at Eyvindr and spoke. "And they can't know about this. In fact." He stopped. "No one can know of this."

"Why?" Eyvindr questioned.

"I can't say," Valeirys answered. "I'll be back before sunrise. You shouldn't worry. Now, can you please go?"

"Where in all the realms are you going that you can't tell me?" Eyvindr probed, as if he hadn't listened. "I won't say a word, I—"

Suddenly, he froze. His eyes widened before he fixed Valeirys with a stern look and said, "I'm coming with you."

"No," Valeirys answered. "It's one thing to risk my life. I won't risk yours, too."

"Well, that's not up to you," Eyvindr countered. "And I could be of good use to you. My life isn't half as boring as you might think. I have friends. Friends that read, and occasionally, we swap the one or the other piece; and, well, not everything we read is… sanctioned by our rulership. I've delved into the one or the other banned recording of the Black Market. I know a thing or two about it, and more importantly, I've always wanted to see it. So, if you don't want me taking off on my own, I suggest you let me tag along."

"Eyvindr, you can't come," said Valeirys and shook his head. "I can't risk it. Father would be furious…"

"Father would be furious either way," Eyvindr interjected. "So, let's just make sure he doesn't find out."

When Valeirys hesitated to answer, his brother smirked and raised an eyebrow.

"Remember that thing I said earlier about alerting the guards? Unless you want to miss your chance of seizing the rebellion's leader, you'll take me with you."

There was no way he was going to talk his brother out of this and convince him to stay behind. Once Eyvindr had put his mind to something, he was like a dog with a bone.

"Fine," Valeirys grumbled.

"Good!" Eyvindr said. He almost clapped his hands together in excitement but stopped himself just in time. "Give me a moment to match your dress code and we'll be off."

"We don't have that kind of time," Valeirys grumbled.

"We have at least until the guards change formation," said Eyvindr. "We just missed our first window of opportunity. You know that as much as I do."

Valeirys gave an annoyed sigh.

He cast Eyvindr a sideways glance and then spoke. "Bring your bow."

Eyvindr smiled widely and nodded before he replied, "Sit tight, 'blend with the shadows,' or whatever it is they teach you soldiers to do. I'll be back just in time for us to leave without a soul noticing."

"The library," Valeirys mused to himself as they waited for the prince. Leaning against one of the enormous shelves that towered toward the dome of the royal library's rotunda, he passed a glance at Eyvindr who stood just below the center of the high ceiling.

His brother leaned back his head and moved in a circle, staring up at the largest collection of written works the two of them had ever seen.

"So many books and yet, the noble are so… simple. That's a mystery even I can't solve," said Eyvindr.

"That's because they don't have time to stick their noses in books all day," Valeirys countered.

Eyvindr lowered his gaze onto him and spoke. "Well, I'd rather sharpen my wit than the steel point that will very well kill me one day. And—we can't all be weapon-wielding brutes; some of us must be the smart ones. Otherwise, who would tell you guys what to do?"

Valeirys stifled a laugh and caught Eyvindr's grin. His brother was in a good mood.

Perhaps the thrill of danger enticed him just as much as it did himself.

Valeirys had found everything exactly the way Prince Malik had explained.

The healer had been waiting for him a half hour's travel from the palace. Disguised as his apprentice with Eyvindr hidden amongst the contents of his wagon, they had found their way into the palace on a mission to attend one of the king's cooks who had mysteriously fallen ill, his state worsening and requiring immediate attention despite the late hour. The rest was child's play, and it reminded Valeirys of the many times he and Eyvindr had practiced sneaking past the guards of their father's manor when they had been younger.

Valeirys' gaze flicked toward the scribe keeping watch at the library's entrance. Cast into an enchanted sleep, he lay hunched over a large mahogany desk, no doubt one of the prince's tricks. His hand was stained with ink from the quill between his fingers, having drifted off in the middle of writing something down.

Valeirys shook his head and redirected his attention to Eyvindr who had already snatched a book from the shelves and continued to read, his bright gaze moving along with the lines of the page he studied.

"Why the library?" Valeirys asked, still observing his brother.

Eyvindr snapped the book shut and glanced up at him, answering him simultaneously with the prince, who approached from his right. "Because it holds the key."

Straightening, Valeirys watched Malik slow his steps and join them. Another elf was at his side.

Valeirys had seen the prince's companion before. His name was Alcides, and he was the son of one of the king's royal councilmen.

Dressed in plain leathers and a black cloak, nothing but Malik's firm stride and the proud carriage of his head hinted at his royal heritage.

"I didn't know you were bringing your own bodyguard," the prince teased and eyed Eyvindr from head to toe.

The prince knew perfectly well who Valeirys' brother was as Uryiel Altair's true-born son.

"Who invited the weakling? Won't he snap like a twig if he runs too fast?" said Alcides and snickered.

Valeirys saw Eyvindr's jaw tick and his fingers twitch, his eyes narrowing on Alcides.

Before his brother could retort, Valeirys stepped in between them and spoke to Malik. "He won't be any trouble."

Lowering his voice, he glanced toward Alcides and then at Eyvindr, indicating the bow strapped to his brother's back and added, "And... he's unbeatable with the bow; better than the king's finest marksman."

At that, Prince Malik raised an eyebrow and grinned, his reddish-brown eyes gleaming from beneath his hood.

Imitating Valeirys, he peered over his shoulder at Alcides and Eyvindr. Before he returned his attention to Valeirys, he said with a smirk, "Good. Come with me."

Past the silent rows of shelves and through the aisles of tables spread throughout the library, the prince led them into a separate reading room adjacent to the library but only accessible through its hall.

A set of four pillars ranked toward the ceiling in the center of the room, each of them functioning as cylindrical shelves.

The warmly lit space was furnished with a desk, a pair of winged chairs on both sides of it, and a lounge set before the large fireplace. The stone floor was decorated with carvings of legends, stories, and folklore. The smell of ink, cedar, and lavender engulfed Valeirys' nose, the warmth of the air in the room enticing him to sit down. If it was so for him, he had no doubt Eyvindr wouldn't mind making this place his new home.

"What now?" Alcides asked, flopping down onto the lounge and stacking his heels on its arm. "Let me guess, the fireplace moves and behind it lies a tunnel we'll need to take."

Malik bolted the door shut behind them and moved toward the fireplace. He grinned as his hand swept over its mantel, and he pursed his lips to speak. "We look for—"

"Uridair's tale of the lost path," Eyvindr interrupted. "It truly exists…"

"Juridare's what?" Alcides blurted.

"It's an enchantment," Eyvindr answered, not bothering to hide the annoyance in his tone. "Legend has it that Tycharis, the god of fate and fortune, stripped Uridair of everything he held dear. The only way to get it all back was to travel the twelve spheres of Helvaeythica, each a world of its own, and to find a treasure that would appease Tycharis and make him return Uridair's family, his home, and restore his life to what it had once been.

"Uridair traveled to the different spheres and into the different worlds through the stories written about them. He used an enchantment that would mark the path he had taken from one book to the next like a red thread to prevent from drowning in the worlds he immersed himself in and getting lost forever."

An expression of both amusement and awe spread across the prince's face while he grinned, studying Eyvindr with curiosity.

Eyvindr's glance darted toward Alcides, and he added, "I might snap like a twig, but at least I'm not as dull as one."

He continued to hold Alcides' gaze before he meandered toward the shelves of books, beginning to peruse them for the mentioned title.

"So, all we have to do is find this old book and we're golden," said Alcides, swinging his legs onto the ground and rising to his feet.

"If only it were that simple." Eyvindr spoke again. Lifting himself onto his toes, he reached up and retrieved a book from one of the four pillars.

Crossing the room to Malik, he handed the prince the book and continued, "Rumor has it that the story is, in fact, true and that the secret of Uridair's enchantment was passed on from one king or queen to the next. So, indeed, only a king or those sharing royal blood should know the secret of the enchantment hidden in the written words of Uridair's tale."

Malik took the book from Eyvindr, and flashing a smile at Valeirys, he spoke. "I take it all back. It is nice having someone smart enough to do all the talking for me."

Valeirys couldn't have been certain, but he thought he had heard Alcides growl at the prince's remark.

Looking at Eyvindr and then back at Malik, he grinned and replied, "So, then finish what he started, and let's get this rebel's name."

With a nod, Malik opened the book and flipped through the pages. His lips moved silently, the flickering light of the flames reflecting in his eyes that darted along the lines of the written word in front of him. Then the corners of his lips tugged to a smile once again, and he proceeded to approach the four pillars in the center of the room.

Valeirys joined his side along with Eyvindr and Alcides. The three of them watched the prince nick the skin of his index finger on the edges of the book's page opened before them.

A drop of blood ran into the pool of his palm, and then he closed the book and placed his hand on the cover as the words of the incantation left his lips.

The phrase was inaudible to the rest of them, undoubtedly part of the secrecy surrounding the enchantment. But then the circular carving decorating the floor between the four pillars began to vibrate and at last, move. Half-moon-shaped lines shifted along the tiled stone before them, causing the floor to descend and form a spiral staircase that led downward into an unknown darkness—a secret passageway.

Delight filled every crevice and angle of the lines that formed across the prince's face as he placed the book back on the shelf and began his descent down the stairs, beckoning the rest of their group to follow.

As they continued down the steps, Alcides' voice rose from behind them. "How do the elves born of common blood reach the Black Market?"

"It takes days, if not weeks," Malik replied above the scraping sound of their boots that swept over the stone steps as they went. "The paths are apparently as many as they are mysterious. Though my favorite hearsay is that the elves travel by boats made invisible by magic and journey across the great waters that separate our realm from that of the Dragon's Kin."

The prince slowed his pace, and they all stopped, reaching the bottom of the staircase.

The four of them stood at what looked like the bottom of a tower. The only way out besides up was a single passageway leading into a dark nothingness.

Valeirys could hear a rushing sound like that of the sea echoing from out of the tunnel when the prince grabbed hold of a torch sconce from the wall to his right.

Uttering a spell to spark a flame, Malik set the torch alight and handed it to Alcides. "I almost forgot," he said, and then he pulled out a collection of masks each black as pitch. He handed one to each of them and then fastened his own before his face by tying a pair of silken strands behind his head before drawing his hood up and passing a glance at each of them.

"If anyone wishes to back out, now would be your last chance," he said.

None of them moved, and after a moment of silence had passed, Malik dipped his chin in a nod and led the way into the tunnel.

Valeirys followed, marking the last of the group. As his foot passed over the threshold of the tunnel's passageway, he heard a rumbling behind him and saw the staircase vanish from view within the blink of an eye.

There was indeed no turning back.

Chapter 26

In the dead of the night, Aleirya snuck out of the cottage, careful not to make a sound.

Already, Takhéa lay waiting for her, her body a large black shadow emerging out of the eerie gray sheet that covered the tall grasses.

"Are you sure about this?" the dragon asked upon her approach.

Pulling the leather strap of her satchel over her shoulders, Aleirya sighed and answered, "Yes."

The irritation in her voice was unmistakable.

The dragon fell silent at her reply. Her huge eyes followed Aleirya as she trudged over to her side.

"I need to be back by sunrise before anyone notices I was gone," she said, avoiding Takhéa's gaze.

Tugging the hood of her cape over her head, Aleirya raised her arms, preparing to pull herself up onto the dragon's back, when she stopped.

Glancing at Takhéa, who was still watching her, her chest tightened with guilt at the rather harsh tone of her voice.

Aleirya tried to speak, but the words stalled in her throat, and she pressed her lips against each other.

Averting her gaze from the dragon's and staring at Takhéa's black scales in front of her, she pinched her eyes shut, willing her frustration to abate before she made herself say, "I don't have a choice. I have to stop the Metatari before it's too late."

The dragon hummed softly.

Then she answered, "I know. But you don't have to do this on your own."

"Yes, I do," Aleirya interrupted and glared at Takhéa. "Even if I mentioned the Metatari I encountered in the cliffs before the shelter fires, no one would believe me. The king's council is against me; Lord Acristus wants to get rid of me. He would turn my testimony against me, make me out to be an accomplice and a traitor... No, I must first find proof of the Metatari's scheme."

The darkness had thickened around them, making it difficult to distinguish the exact outline of Takhéa's form from her surroundings.

Neither of them spoke, until Takhéa moved, lowering herself further toward the ground to make it easier for Aleirya to climb up her side.

"I don't like this," she let out with a grumble.

Swinging her leg over the slope at the base of her dragon's neck and dragging herself upright, Aleirya breathed another sigh and spoke. "I know. But this will all be over soon. I'll find the Metatari's kingdom, capture one of their kind, and with the help of the silver tongue, I will force them to reveal their true plans. Once I have proof and have uncovered the Metatari's deception, King Ethuriel will have no other choice but to lift the suspension and instate us in his army, and the Dragon's Kin will defeat the elves and the Metatari."

Spreading her wings to their full length, Takhéa readied herself to take off into the sky.

"And what if we fail?" the dragon asked.

Shaking her head, Aleirya felt for the hilt of her dagger at her hip, making sure it was properly secured and answered, "We won't fail. We can't."

Small specks of yellow light covered the ground below them as Takhéa soared through the sky under cover of the night. A twinge of sorrow overcame Aleirya as she stared down at the countless golden spots scattered below that mirrored the starlit canopy above them.

Usually, flying made her feel whole and invincible but nothing like she did now.

Like a rough sword that was tempered to strengthen it and to receive its desired form, Aleirya tried to convince herself that this hardship would only make her stronger. Would she bend or break? What if she never fit the mold or never took on the shape she needed to fulfill her purpose?

Leaning forward against Takhéa as if to hide from her doubts, Aleirya pressed her eyes shut, struggling to think of something else.

She couldn't let herself believe any part of them to be true. Even though she would never admit it, she worried sometimes. Aleirya knew that if she allowed them to take root within herself, she would fail. She would lose the fragile control she had over herself and her future.

Pitting all of her focus on Takhéa, Aleirya felt a completely different wave of emotions and doubt overwhelm her.

All this time, her dragon had remained faithful to her. Never once had she abandoned or disappointed her. She was willing to follow her despite her own disapproval of her dangerous plan, and in return, she had been unkind to her.

Opening her eyes once again, Aleirya stroked her dragon's scales and said, "I'm sorry… I'm sorry about before."

Takhéa hummed and then flapped her wings, rising further into the sky as they soared above a cluster of clouds.

"It's alright," she answered.

With a sigh, Aleirya spoke. "Actually, it's not." She hesitated briefly before adding, "I did something bad. I messed up, and I could have…"

Her breath caught, and she swallowed, forcing down the heavy lump that had formed in her throat.

Her gaze dropped to the earth below, and for a moment, she let the glittering sight distract her.

Although neither of them spoke, Aleirya felt a strange calm soothe her she could sense was coming from Takhéa.

Their bond had indeed changed over the past weeks. Aleirya did not know how to explain it, but it was as if it had somehow grown deeper and stronger.

The link between them was incredible. Not only had her sense of Takhéa's emotions intensified, but now, physical touch was no longer necessary for them to share their feelings with one another. What scared Aleirya the most was that she could tap into her dragon's thoughts and memories whenever their minds connected.

"The other day, Thoran offered to duel with me for practice. I think he meant to help distract me and raise my spirits after all that had happened and my suspension from the academy," said Aleirya.

Pausing, she let her eyes wander back to her hands that lay against Takhéa's scales and went on, "It was fun, at first, and I actually thought it was helping me. It was like old times. When I was little, Thoran and I used to pretend that I was a dragon warrior." She stopped and scoffed, "Tarragon's brave hero."

"He would invent quests for me to go on and act as the villain or the monster I was to contend against. He'd always let me win, no matter how easily he could have bested me," she said.

A weak smile formed over her lips as she recalled the memories.

But then it vanished.

The dragon hummed softly. Aleirya sensed the vibrations travel up her arm as a warmth filled her.

Knitting her brows, she continued, "I thought I had everything under control. My mind was clear, I was so focused… But then—"

Aleirya could see the memory of what had happened between herself and Thoran unfold before her mind's eye, and she felt Takhéa's consciousness brush against hers. Quickly forcing the images aside, she tried to hide them from Takhéa, ashamed of what she had done.

Aleirya sensed the dragon pull away from her slightly as she went on. "All at once, nothing mattered more to me than to win. All I wanted was to move faster, strike harder… I wanted to fight better than him. I wanted to win… I wanted to beat him, because I was stronger, better, and not because he let me."

Her eyes stung as she fought the urge to cry.

"Thoran called out to me to slow down, to stop, but I didn't hear him. I didn't want to stop until it was almost too late. My sword came down… and I heard him shout," she said.

Aleirya stopped to take a breath and bit down on her lip.

"When I realized what had happened, that I had hurt him, I let my sword go. I can still hear the ringing of the steel striking the earth after I let it slip from my hands… I remember how the skin of my palm burned, and the pain chased up my arm. It felt like I had severed a part of myself from me. It was like my body—my hands—yearned for me to hold the sword again, like they craved the excitement, the power I had held over Thoran during our fight."

It had grown awfully quiet between them while Takhéa listened to her.

"I've asked myself why so many times since that day. Why or how had I let it turn into a contest, a battle? Why would I want to fight and prevail over Thoran as if he was my enemy? Thoran who raised me and has always been a father to me?"

A part of her wished she could see her dragon's face.

"You want to know the worst part?" Aleirya asked, making herself continue. "In that moment, the moment I had lost myself in the fight, I didn't care what happened… It didn't matter to me because I felt more like myself than ever before."

"Aleirya," Takhéa began.

But Aleirya shook her head and quickly resumed speaking. "My powers have changed. I've grown stronger. I'm different, perhaps even transformed in a way… at least that is what it feels like most of the time. But I've never felt so alive, so invigorated, while wielding a weapon against someone else."

Aleirya felt a sudden chill around her. She wanted to pull her cloak tighter around her body, but she didn't dare let go of her dragon for fear of losing her grip as she trembled.

Pressing her eyes shut, as if to drown out everything around her, Aleirya said, almost whispering, "It scares me, Takhéa. How could I feel this way? How could I have acted so violently and thoughtlessly toward someone for whom I care so much? What kind of monster am I becoming?"

"You are not a monster, Aleirya," the dragon replied.

Staring down at her fingers that were still shaking, she said, "How do you know that?"

"Do you trust me?" Takhéa asked in return.

Nodding immediately, Aleirya said, "If there is anyone I trust, it's you."

She could sense her dragon's happiness over her response through their bond and it comforted her.

"In your heart, you mean to do what is good. That doesn't mean that you will always do well, Aleirya, but to me it signifies that you are no monster," said Takhéa.

Nodding silently, as if to convince herself that the dragon was right, she hesitated for a moment before going on, "I don't know what I would have done had something happened to Thoran."

"He will be alright," Takhéa replied.

Taking a deep breath, Aleirya's glance dropped to her hands.

Faint white scars dressed the face of her palms as a testament to her training and her skill with the blade. They gleamed under the moon's light while she stared down at them.

It used to fill her with pride to see them. For to her, scars were the marks of warriors.

However, looking closely at them now, Aleirya no longer felt pride, and she wondered. Maybe a scar was just what it was, an ugly blemish that disfigured something that had once been flawless, something that had once been innocent. Perhaps her scars had always heralded the abhorrent change she was now coming to notice in herself.

"Aleirya?" Takhéa asked, forcing Aleirya to stop and redirect her attention toward her dragon. "Look."

The dragon slowed her pace. Holding her wings steady, she gently tilted sideways, granting Aleirya an unobstructed view of the sight ahead.

The corners of Aleirya's lips curved upward into a smile as she took it in.

Before them lay the city of Ismir, a popular place for merchants and tradesmen and known for its bazaars, attractions, and highly praised taverns.

Unlike most villages and marketplaces of Tarragon, Ismir had been constructed overlaying the cleft that ran through the kingdom's center. It was built inside an enormous cliff near the realm's northern border, and its unique spiral-shaped outline was best admired from above and especially beautiful at night.

Eying it from where she sat perched on her dragon's back, it reminded her of an evolute shell.

The city was entered at the foot of the cliffs. One could pass through it by simply following along its main street that led visitors from the city's entrance all the way up to its viewpoint at the very top of the cliff.

The famous pathway was a broad, winding road lined by Ismir's various shops and taverns, purposely set up so close to the roadside so as to entice passersby to make a spontaneous purchase.

Aleirya knew Ismir well. It had served as a common place where she and her fellow cadets had often gone to amuse themselves whenever they could get away from the academy.

Takhéa circled above the city in search of a spot to land. Then, in one swift motion, she descended.

The commotion of the city grew louder as they neared the ground, and Takhéa glided along the outside walls, passing by the main entrance.

Aleirya noticed a few of the city's visitors stare up into the sky as they flew past the crowds entering the city below.

The beating of Takhéa's wings accelerated into rapid flaps before Aleirya heard stone crack as the dragon drove her talons into the rocky surface beside the mouth of an abandoned cave. Dust and bits of rock crumbled and rolled down the cliff as she crawled along the outside wall and at last, inside the dark opening, which appeared to have once been a dragon's nesting place. When she came to a stop, Aleirya carefully slipped off her back.

The cave was completely void of light, dissolving Takhéa's body in the darkness that surrounded them.

"I shouldn't be too long," said Aleirya.

THE RISE OF ISIGAR

Once more, she tightened the strap of her satchel over her shoulder and made sure that its clasp was shut securely. Takhéa had crept deeper inside the cave and lay down on her side. Her large head rested on the tip of her tail that curled around her body.

"I'll be waiting," she answered.

Aleirya nodded and began to leave when she heard Takhéa add, "Just try to stay out of trouble. I would hate to have to interrupt a perfectly peaceful nap."

Aleirya looked over her shoulder and smiled.

All she could see were Takhéa's eyes that glowed from within the dark corner of the cave, one bright silver and the other lilac.

"I'll try to be on my best behavior," said Aleirya.

She continued to look back at Takhéa until the dragon slowly closed her eyes, and the only light inside the cavern vanished.

It wasn't long before Aleirya reached the bottom of the cliff.

Tugging once more at the hood of her cape, making sure that it concealed most of her face, she proceeded toward Ismir's entrance.

Music rang from the city, and the voices and laughter of the people echoed louder as she neared Ismir's gates.

Aleirya swept through the masses, cleverly avoiding the crowds that huddled themselves around the shops and stands.

A plethora of vibrant colors, lights, and sounds brought the city to life. Merchants paraded through the masses, some shoving along their carts, while others raised tall wooden poles covered in beautiful fabrics and jewelry as they called out to the crowds to lay their eyes on the wares they offered.

Ismir's streets were filled with a mixture of the most delightful scents of expensive ointments and incense and the delicious foods that overwhelmed the senses of its visitors. Many stopped to clap and cheer at the music played by the countless musicians who sought to capture their audience's attention with their rhymes and tunes. It was a place meant to drown the mundane concerns and sorrows of their world, a purpose it served quite well.

An old storefront caught Aleirya's attention, and she withdrew from the main road toward the outskirts of the crowds.

She came to a stop before the corner of the small shop.

Unlike the other well-kept stores and boutiques that decorated Ismir's public roads, this one was empty and dismal. The red paint of its façade was faded and chipped; its windows were weathered and dusty, a few bore cracks and dents.

The lettering on the storefront was undecipherable, leaving no way to tell what sort of shop it had once been.

The old abandoned store stood at the opening of a blind and narrow cobblestone alley. At its end, there was a small wooden door crafted inside the stone wall. No windows dressed the façade framing the strange entrance.

The sign above the doorpost read, 'Phanuel's Bookshop.'

Casting a quick look over her shoulder, Aleirya turned into the alley, her footsteps barely echoing along the cobblestones of the narrow passage as she approached the door.

The iron was cold to the touch when she grabbed hold of the door's handle and pushed it open.

Stepping inside, the door cracked and squeaked below the sound of a small bell that announced her entrance.

The air inside was stale and warm, carrying a peculiar smell somewhat heavy with leather and cedar. The shop was cluttered with tall shelves, ranked with books and scrolls cast in dim light.

Aleirya continued onward, passing through the maze of shelves lined up before her.

The store seemed empty. The only sound that filled the cramped salesroom came from the wooden floor panels that creaked under the weight of her body as she made her way to the shop's counter.

It was unattended as well, and a small golden bell lay atop it.

Aleirya eyed it for a moment, catching her dark reflection in the golden surface.

For a while, nothing happened. The shop owner seemed not to have noticed her entry or perhaps he simply wasn't eager to attend to his customers' needs.

Impatient and annoyed by either possibility, Aleirya finally struck the bell a few times and not too gently.

Again, for what seemed to be an unnecessarily long time, nothing happened.

All the more irritated, Aleirya rang the bell for the salesman anew.

Then something rattled and clanked from a distant corner of the shop. Shortly thereafter, Aleirya heard the deep voice of the salesman muttering something unfriendly before the burgundy curtain behind the counter was tossed aside, and he stepped forward.

His black hair looked bedraggled. His long beard was unkept and had come loose from its braid. The salesman's clothes were wrinkled and smeared, and he reeked of strong drink.

"What can I do you for?" he asked in a hoarse voice.

Fixing him with an unwavering gaze, she answered, "I'm in search of the second volume of Uridair's tale of the lost path. I've been told I might find it here amongst your selection."

The man sniffed and rubbed his sweaty fist against his nose.

Shrugging his shoulders, he replied, "Never heard of it."

Raising her chin slightly, Aleirya unfastened the clasp of her satchel and reached inside. She pulled forth a small bag of silver coins, dropping it onto the counter in front of the salesman, and answered, "I've heard differently."

The salesman's eyes darted back and forth between the coins and her gaze.

"I would hate to have to take my business elsewhere," Aleirya added.

The corner of his lip twitched, and then he smiled, baring a rather unpleasant row of yellow teeth.

He nodded, and grabbing hold of the bag of silver, he said, "My collection is the finest in Ismir."

Clutching the coins, his grin deepened.

"Perhaps I may have overlooked this precious piece. I keep the most prized items in the back if you'd like to take a look, milady." The words came out slick, as if dripping from his mouth.

Aleirya did her best to hide her disgust and nodded in reply.

Reaching for a candle, he turned around and beckoned her to follow him behind the red curtain.

Befitting his shabby appearance, the back of the shop proved a disaster. Empty bottles, clothes, and crumpled up scraps of paper littered the ground. Dust covered the worn furniture, and the space smelled of must and sweat.

Forming a path through the mess, and occasionally kicking an empty bottle aside, the salesman swore under his breath as he led her to a small chamber.

Inside the room, there was a small desk covered with a pile of books and sheets of vellum, along with a quill and an inkpot. Other odds and ends had been stacked along the rest of the walls, and on the floor lay a pale rug.

The salesman stopped, and bending over, he pulled the carpet aside, revealing a trapdoor built in between the panels of the floor. He set the candle on the desk and undid the lock.

The sound of the trapdoor being opened echoed down the dark set of steps that appeared below. Then the salesman turned and opened one of the drawers belonging to the desk.

Aleirya had approached the trapdoor's entrance when he handed her a black mask.

Accepting it, she nodded silently and then lowered her hood.

Gently, she placed the mask over her face and fastened its black silken strands behind her head in a tight knot. Drawing the hood of her cape back over her head, she looked once more at the salesman, nodded, and then began her descent.

The salesman waited a short while before letting the trapdoor slam shut above her.

Stopping briefly, Aleirya heard the clicking sound of the trapdoor's lock being sealed. The noise traveled beyond along the stone walls and then vanished in depths of the blackness that lay before her.

A cold draft passed through the dark stairwell. The wind whistled ahead, and the soles of her shoes scraped against the steps while she carefully crept down the winding staircase.

No light guided her path while she continued to tread deeper inside the cliff, letting her hand glide along the cool surface of the rock. It all seemed to take much longer than she had remembered, and a sense of relief overcame her once she neared the bottom of the stairwell and sounds of a commotion echoed upward from below.

Reaching the end of the stone stairway, her footsteps slowed, and Aleirya finally passed over the last set of steps that had led her deep into the center of the mountain.

Turning the corner around a massive wall of rock, she stopped.

Spread out all over the enormous cavern that opened up before her eyes lay the familiar scene of the Black Market.

CHAPTER 27

Masses of dark hooded figures, each wearing a black mask like hers, flooded the grounds of the marketplace.

Instead of the vibrant colors and decorated storefronts of Ismir's public streets, rugged stalls and tents with the canvases patched and stained from use lined the beaten pathways of the Black Market.

There was no music, dance or laughter to be heard. Rather than stop to watch an attraction, the crowds that formed in these streets were mostly those that gathered around the few fireplaces spread out along the market to warm themselves.

Befitting its illicit establishment, the Black Market was known for its rather precarious scenery. Any dealings or even setting foot in the market were strictly forbidden for any of the known races and could lead to severe consequences if one were to be discovered.

Here, trust was a relative virtue, and it was wise to keep one's true identity a secret. For there was no telling if the whispers of royal spies infiltrating the market scene were true. This was why it had become a custom among those entering the Black Market to wear a mask.

Only a few of the merchants themselves proved brave enough to neglect this policy and would often commence their trades with their faces unhidden from their customers.

Aleirya slipped through the crowds, avoiding any eye contact as best she could. Signs and different colored flags signified the sort of merchandise or service one could purchase from the various booths and tents. Many offered charms of good luck and trinkets infused with magic, while others exchanged elven delicacies, medicines, rare spirits, and narcotics for a handsome price.

There were stands that sold and traded weaponry and armor, some of which had been fashioned from the scales and the bones of dragons, making them especially powerful. However, for some, the Black Market was also a popular place to gather for trading secrets and immersing themselves in the telling of each other's fortune.

Determined to spend as little time as possible at the market, Aleirya hurried her pace. She knew Takhéa would expect her to return soon.

As quickly as she could, she maneuvered her way through the crowds until she finally reached the familiar wooden cabin.

She could see yellow light spilling outside through its windows.

Having climbed the front steps that led up to the door, she stopped and drew a deep breath before shoving it open.

Upon entering, Aleirya let her eyes trace the inside of the cabin for a moment. Several sets of tables and chairs in the small tavern were occupied by guests engrossed in their own conversations by the weak candlelight. The indistinct murmurs continued as none seemed to notice or mind her entry.

The tavern was much quieter than one would expect from such an establishment. However, this was no ordinary place where the usual townspeople would gather to drown their sorrows in ale and good company. It certainly wasn't a place one would want to have been noticed visiting.

Her eyes caught on the bar. A tall man stood behind it, drying off a set of jugs. Aleirya crossed the room and pulled aside one of the surrounding stools to step closer to the counter.

Leaning forward, she spoke quietly. "I'm here to see Luther, Luther Fynn."

Without interrupting his task, the barman cast her a sharp look and answered, "Then you must be lost. I have not served anyone here by the name of this Sir Fynn."

She knew, of course, that it was a lie.

Luther Fynn made sure the secret of his trade was well kept. He was an overly suspicious man who didn't trust anyone but himself.

He was a smuggler of sorts. Ripe in age and rich in secrets. There was hardly anything that went on in all the realms that he did not know about. He had made good use of his knowledge over the years and could be persuaded to share some of it for the right price. Only a few knew how and where to find him.

Aleirya nodded. Then, swinging herself up onto the barstool, she replied, "I'll have myself the finest of the Dragon's Stone then."

She eyed him carefully while observing his response.

The barman stopped and looked back at her.

After a moment's hesitation, he tossed his rag down onto the counter and answered, "As you wish. However, I'll have to retrieve it for you… An excellent choice."

Tilting his head to the right, he beckoned her to follow him as he walked away from the bar. Aleirya accompanied him to a secluded part of the tavern where no guests were permitted.

A large tapestry bearing the Medina family's royal coat of arms hung over the center of a wall in the farthest corner of the tavern. The barman approached it, and after having cast a careful glance behind them, he lifted the side of the tapestry, revealing a secret door concealed amongst the wooden panels of the wall.

He knocked twice, then, quietly pushed the door open and stepped aside to allow Aleirya to enter first.

A bearded figure sat bent over a wooden desk, poring over a pile of loose pages. Some had fallen from the desk and covered the ground around him as well as his feet.

The man seemed awfully lost in thought as his lips moved silently along the lines he was reading. He didn't seem to notice their intrusion until the barman uttered a low grunt.

The man's head jerked up when he heard the noise.

A sly smile dressed his face, and he spoke. "Ahh, yes. I was wondering when I'd see you again. It has been a while since we last met, Deianira."

Deianira was the name she had called herself, unwilling to trust an unpredictable man such as Luther with her true identity.

He nodded at the barman, signaling that it was alright for him to leave them to their affairs.

In response, the barman walked over to a cabinet and retrieved a set of bottles before at last stepping outside of the chamber. Aleirya looked back and watched as he shut the door and then returned her attention to the man at the desk.

"As always, it's a pleasure to see you, Luther," said Aleirya.

Luther grinned and stroked the brown locks of his beard as he leaned back in his chair.

He had aged much since Aleirya had last seen him. The roots of his brown hair had grayed and the furrows along his brow seemed to have deepened.

Looking up at her with his dark eyes, he chuckled and said, "What is it you'd like me to do for you?"

Reaching for the satchel that hung at her side, Aleirya retrieved a small scroll. Then she stepped closer to the desk and unraveled it before him.

Intrigued, Luther straightened and bent forward to inspect it.

The scroll contained an ancient map of the different realms, including the uncharted regions of the Dhaharran Forest and the Forsaken Lands beyond its borders, also known as Isigar.

Once populated by human clans centuries ago, little was known of these areas since no one had dared travel that far after Isigar's destruction and the demise of the human race.

Placing her hands on both sides of the map spread out before them, Aleirya said, "The Metatari's kingdom… I need to find it."

Sinking back against his chair, Luther laughed and answered, "I should have known you're not one to make small requests."

But his smile faded when he realized she was serious.

"I know it is hidden somewhere deep inside the Dhaharran Forest. Some say it's even concealed by the Metatari's magic."

Pushing off the desk, Aleirya straightened and added, "I'll make it worth your while."

"I doubt that," said Luther, his eyes scaling the map once again.

Crossing her arms in front of her chest, Aleirya dipped her chin and spoke. "Hmm, not even if, say, I offered you an elven relic from the era of Izurion's reign?"

Aleirya noticed his body stiffen, but still he didn't meet her gaze.

She knew him to be a collector of artifacts and rare pieces of ancient elven history.

There was no way he could resist.

"I'm fairly certain it isn't something I don't already possess," said Luther.

Gradually lowering her arms to her sides, Aleirya nodded and began to pace before his desk.

"Selling secrets has been your trade for several decades now, hasn't it?" she began. "I hear the competition is growing fierce these days. Now, everyone claims to know something the rest of the world doesn't."

"But I am the best," said Luther. His voice was calm, but his jaw tightened.

Stopping, Aleirya cast him a glance and replied, "Indeed you are. For now."

His fingers twitched.

Inhaling, she continued, "What if I told you I had something that would enable you to know secrets no one else could? Something that would enable you, and you alone, to gather information your sources might not necessarily want to reveal?"

At that, his head snapped upward.

His eyes locked onto hers, and he uttered, "Aggyreidimos idiss."

Aleirya smirked and nodded.

She had him.

"Otherwise known as silver tongue. Yes," she answered, and approached the desk once more.

"It can't be," said Luther, his gaze riveted on her. "It was destroyed. The valley lands of Nyradorn were stripped of its existence after Izurion was defeated. The spell to create the potion was never discovered again. It's impossible... how did you—"

"You have your sources, I have mine," said Aleirya, and she grinned.

The chamber fell silent for a moment.

"Now, do we have a deal?" she asked.

Luther leaned back in his chair and raised a hand to his lips.

He pretended to be relaxed, taking his time as if to ponder if the trade was worth it.

He was a bargainer, after all; Aleirya knew he would try to make certain that he got more out of this agreement than she did. But she wasn't about to let him play her.

Reclining even further in his chair, he folded his hands in his lap and spoke. "You intrigue me, Deianira. There is a way I might help you enter the Metatari's kingdom. An acquaintance of mine can bring you to them, but it will take time. I can orchestrate a meeting within a few weeks perhaps, and then you will need to provide payment for their services as well."

There it was. His typical game. But she would not fall for it.

Shaking her head, Aleirya replied, "I prefer to travel alone."

Luther gave a chuckle and spoke. "That is far too dangerous."

Aleirya grinned and answered, "I've had worse. No, I believe you have all the information I need. After all, if the rumors are true, you were once a captive in the Metatari's kingdom. You've been there before. Someone with a gift of persuasion such as yours—surely, if anyone, you amassed quite a treasure of the shapeshifters' secrets."

Aleirya saw him grit his teeth as his demeanor changed.

"The Metatari have spells to make you forget," said Luther.

"And yet you seem to know so much about them," she interrupted, bending further over the desk and toward him.

"How do I know that the silver tongue potion you claim to have is truly what you say it is? How can I believe that this isn't some trick?" he asked.

"I would be happy to demonstrate. Are you volunteering?" Aleirya replied, grinning crookedly.

Amused, Luther chuckled at her suggestion but fell silent again.

They stared at each other for a while as she studied him.

Then, shaking her head, she spoke. "This is a waste of my time."

Clutching the map, she turned and walked away.

She had almost reached the hidden door that led outside of his quarters when she heard him call out, "Wait!"

Aleirya stopped, and with her back still facing him, she grinned.

Then she turned around.

Luther had risen from his chair and stood watching her.

"I'll tell you how you can find their kingdom," he said.

Aleirya eyed him. She did not twitch or reveal the slightest hint of satisfaction over the matter that she had driven him to do exactly as she wanted.

"One more thing," she said.

"No," Luther answered through gritted teeth.

Lifting her chin, Aleirya went on, "Yes. For your delay of answers, my price for the silver tongue just went up. You will not only tell me how to find the Metatari but also how best to subdue one of them."

Scoffing, Luther shook his head.

"You are out of your mind! The Metatari are a powerful people and fond of their secrets. I swore on my life not to tell a soul of the things I learned from them. I care not a jot about your life, but I do value mine," he retorted. "If I tell you anything of the sort, they will come for my head."

Aleirya's skin crawled at the frustration that sparked within her. She could feel her impatience slowly get the better of her.

This had to work. She could not and she would not let him refuse her request.

"Fine," she spat. "Have it your way. We'll see how long your business remains intact after I've spread the news that your word isn't worth a coin."

Slamming his fists into the desk, Luther scowled and shouted, "You wretched girl! How dare you slander my name! I will—"

But his threat choked in his mouth as Aleirya took him by surprise and seized him by the collar.

He tried to strike at her, but faster than he could blink, she grabbed his wrist and pinned it firmly against the desk.

The same odd power that had overtaken her when she had attacked Damian, the same rage that had seethed within her as she had stood last before the king and the council spread through her like a wildfire.

Aleirya noticed Luther's face turn white as her eyes flared bright blue. She continued to stare into his terrified gaze when an unfamiliar sensation rippled through her arm and ebbed from her body at the tips of her fingers.

The notion brought about an incomparable thrill as Luther's scream split the air. His eyes dropped to his wrist trapped under her grip.

Aleirya continued to hold him in place.

She would not loosen her grip until he gave in.

"Tell me what I want to know, and I'll stop," she said.

Sweat trickled down the side of his face from his brow, and his breathing grew labored.

A grunt sounded from his throat while he gritted his teeth and stared back at her. When he said nothing, Aleirya bit her lip and tugged forcefully at his collar, growing even more furious. She felt another jolt of power chase through her and leave her body through her hand that still held Luther's fist tightly against the desk.

Distorting the features of his face, Luther writhed in pain, and another choked scream resonated through the chamber.

"You wanted to know if the silver tongue potion I have truly works? Well, you're about to find out," Aleirya spat out.

Clutching his neck, she pinned his head against the desk. She was about to draw forth the silver tongue's vial when the door to the chamber burst open with a crack.

Four dark figures filed inside, gleams of silver catching Aleirya's eyes from the hilts of their weapons concealed beneath their cloaks.

Her gaze locked with the hooded stranger standing in the middle of the group just as he commanded, "Grab her."

Chapter 28

Valeirys watched the masked figure drag the Dragon's Kin, the ominous Luther Fynn, across the desk and press a dagger to his throat.

"If you still want a chance at talking to this one, you'd better call off your hounds," the stranger said to Malik. The voice was undoubtedly feminine.

Valeirys' gaze flitted between the girl and Luther who gurgled and gasped under her grip, his body arched backward at an awkward angle, the back of his head pressed against her collarbone.

Judging by her physical strength and the way she held her weapon, she was no commoner. She was a soldier, a fighter.

Valeirys glimpsed the leather armor beneath her cloak. The vest protecting her torso was stitched in a pattern that resembled something like a dragon's scales.

Her face was hidden behind a mask just like his own. Only the flint of her bright eyes showed through her guise, boring into him with relentless intensity as her gaze flicked between him and the prince.

Valeirys tensed and kept his hand steady on the hilt of his sword. The muscles in his jaw twitched as he watched Malik step forward from out of the corner of his eye.

"There's no reason we can't both get what we want," said Malik and clicked his tongue.

There was something off about his tone of voice, deceit lacing the cool resonant melody of his words.

"How about a trade?" the prince suggested. "He's yours to do with as you please once my business is concluded."

Valeirys shot the prince a look, but Malik did not meet his eyes. Unease bubbled in his stomach, and the hairs of his neck stood on end as he studied him, wondering what it was he could possibly offer as a trade.

"How about you wait your turn?" she threw back at him and gripped Luther harder.

Sweat dripped from the Dragon's Kin's brow, and his skin had taken on an icy pallor, suggesting the obvious fear he had for his life.

Valeirys hardly registered what happened next. A knife whizzed past the girl's head, boring into the wall behind her. Whether it had missed its mark or she had moved with an eerie speed to evade the blow, he couldn't have been certain. Malik must have signaled Alcides again, for he hurled another blade toward her.

She dodged the hit, ducking and losing control of Luther. But instead of watching her, Valeirys' glance shot toward the prince just as he gripped Eyvindr by the neck and shoved him toward the armed stranger.

The girl lunged for Luther, but when he rolled away, she grabbed hold of Eyvindr instead.

"No!" Valeirys shouted.

He had taken two steps toward her when he felt Alcides seize his arm, holding him back.

The girl's eyes darted from Valeirys to the prince and back again just as Valeirys wriggled himself free from Alcides' grasp.

Fire surged through his blood, anger coiling around his chest and limbs while he found his own fury mirrored in the seething glare from the girl's eyes as she riveted her attention on Malik and uttered, "Another one of your tricks and he's dead."

Malik simply chuckled. "There's no need for things to become uncivilized."

He held out a hand to Luther who had come scrambling toward them and fought to get to his feet.

Something cracked, an Eyvindr winced but otherwise kept silent and didn't struggle. Valeirys caught the strange look of concern or shock in the girl's fiery glance as she looked at Eyvindr and then back at Malik. She didn't lower her weapon, but she readjusted her grip to put less strain on Eyvindr's left shoulder, where she must have heard the bone crack.

Valeirys felt sick to his stomach. Heat rushed to his head, and his frustration fought to get the better of him while his focus leaped from the girl to Malik, and he spat out, "Get on with it, before she changes her mind."

He didn't care that it was the prince he was talking to. He had a bone to pick with him when all of this was over.

Malik didn't seem the least bit bothered by his tone and shrugged his shoulders before giving a sigh and turning toward Luther.

Drawing forth a ring that bore the king's signet, he grabbed the Dragon's Kin's shoulder and secured him in a sitting position on the desk before speaking in a low voice. "I gather you received the gold. Now—to your end of the deal."

Luther's focus moved back and forth between Malik and the ring the prince held in front of his nose. His chest still rose and fell at a rapid pace while he caught his breath.

His lip curled slightly as he narrowed his eyes and spoke to Malik. "I'm going to need a little more proof than that."

He gestured toward the ring.

Valeirys noticed Malik's fingers digging into the Dragon's Kin's shoulder, pinching him harder and provoking a wince from Luther before the prince released him, lowered his hood, and undid his mask.

Valeirys' throat tightened, and he wondered if it truly was about proof or if it was more about Luther having seen Malik's face for evidence of their meeting in case he was to be seized and his mind probed during questioning. His gaze flicked back to the stranger who held Eyvindr. His brother did not meet his eyes as both his and the girl's attention were riveted on the prince.

Valeirys reminded himself to breath. The fear for his brother's life was still driving his bounding pulse, and he knew in a matter of seconds everything could change.

"This enough proof for you?" Malik asked, and Valeirys' focus shifted to the prince.

The corner of Malik's mouth tugged upward to a crooked smile as if showing his face to the Dragon's Kin didn't make him the least bit concerned.

Luther let out a gasp and a choked laugh before he responded, "It's a pretty face, prince-like for sure, but no. I'm afraid I'm going to need proof by blood."

Without taking his eyes off Malik, Luther's hand fumbled beneath the desk. There was a click and the sound of a latch opening before the Dragon's Kin pulled forth a ballock dagger. The shaft was wooden, a carving of strange creatures, thorns, and vines dressing it.

Wriggling himself out from underneath Malik's grip, Luther stared at the prince with a twisted look on his face, and he spoke. "It's called Truthteller. One of the gems I've stumbled across throughout my years of many… transactions."

He raised it, point facing upward, ogling it with an unsettling fascination before he went on, "It's enchanted, as you might have already guessed."

He lowered it again and looked at Malik before he said, "If you are who you claim to be, then at the taste of your blood, the blade will grow to a bright ruby red. Should you have lied, the touch of its steel will have poisoned you, and you will die what I hear is quite a grueling death."

Malik didn't even flinch, almost as if impressed by Luther's bold scheme.

"You must understand," said Luther, "for the sake of my name and my business, I must ensure the information does not get into the wrong hands."

Malik smirked and pursed his lips to speak when Valeirys interrupted, "If that dagger so much as brushes his skin, I'll bury it in your throat."

At that, Luther glared at him and gave a snarl.

"How are we to know that the information we paid you for is, in fact, reliable? You could just as well be playing us for fools for an easy coin," said Valeirys.

He took a step toward Luther and then added, "The same rules should apply to you. Cut yourself first, and prove that it isn't all lies coming from your mouth."

Luther stiffened. His brow knitted together, and his nostrils flared before he huffed a breath and spat. "Fine."

He stood up from the desk holding the dagger in his left while he spoke. "I vow that my word is as true as the gold it comes by. The information you seek is indeed that which you are to receive."

There was a slicing sound that made Valeirys grimace behind his mask when the Dragon's Kin cut his palm and balled his hand to a fist. Blood dripped from his right as he raised it and glanced down at the blade that began to change its color.

Valeirys' brow rose at the flare of bright red that consumed the dagger's steel. When he met Luther's frigid gaze, he nodded.

Luther grimaced and shook out his fist just as Malik spoke up. "Well, doesn't that look like fun?"

Approaching Luther, he accepted the dagger from the Dragon's Kin and did as he had done, letting his blood color the steel red once more.

Eyeing the Dragon's Kin, Malik returned the weapon when all at once, he spun it in his grasp, clutched Luther by the collar with his bloodied hand, and pinned the dagger's point to his side while he spoke in low tones. "Question my honor again, and it'll be the last thing you do."

The Dragon's Kin blanched and nodded.

"Now give me what I paid you for," Malik growled through set teeth.

Luther's breath quickened, the tips of his boots scratching the floor as Malik lifted him higher and drew him closer so that they were almost nose to nose.

"Desk. Middle drawer. Scroll bound with the purple silk," Luther said, his voice strained and his face reddening under the prince's grip.

Tilting his head sideways, Malik indicated at Alcides who then moved around the desk and retrieved the scroll.

"A pleasure doing business with you," said Malik. He glanced over at the girl who held Eyvindr captive and then added to Luther, "I trust the rest of your evening will be just as pleasant."

The prince's grin deepened, and he released Luther to crumple to his feet.

But the Dragon's Kin didn't wait to see what happened next and staggered forward the moment his boots thudded against the panels of the floor.

He dove under the desk and toward the pair of shelves behind it.

Throwing his weight against them, the shelves moved like a revolving door and swallowed him whole.

Valeirys' breath caught, a prickling sensation jolting down his spine and limbs like shards of ice biting into his skin. His head snapped sideways, his gaze locking onto the girl who held Eyvindr captive, and he lunged, a metallic screech piercing his ears from his sword released from its sheath.

Eyvindr screamed and sank to his knees, blood running down his arm from the slash wound across his left shoulder just before the girl drew a sword from her hip and swung it toward Valeirys to parry his attack.

The air reverberated at the shrill song that echoed between the steel of their blades. Valeirys' vision threatened to blur from their pace, but he kept his attention riveted on her dark silhouette, interrupted only by the gleam of her sword and the flash of blue sparking from her eyes as she moved like a shadow fleeing the light.

The room seemed to have stilled as if they were alone, but Valeirys didn't dare stop to wonder where the rest of them were. His heart drummed in his chest, his bones humming from the weight of each thrust and each clash of their weapons.

As quick as he was, as precise and cunning as he attacked, she seemed to guess the plan hatching in his mind before it took shape, mirroring his movements, prepared for anything he threw at her.

A strange sense of excitement grew from out of the bind of their swords, mingling with the horror that any mistake he made would be his last.

A breath of wind roused the hairs on Valeirys' neck just before something whizzed past his ear. Goosebumps rushed down his arms as he ducked and noticed a flicker of silver dart through the space above him, the knife missing the girl as she crouched low and caught herself just in time to evade the blow.

His pulse leaped as he lost sight of her blade for the blink of an eye. Recovering faster than he did, she pivoted toward him.

Her sword moved in an arc around her and came down before he could block it. He felt the agonizing sting of its point slicing through his skin from his left collarbone down to his elbow.

A hiss burst from his mouth, and he bit down on his lip, tasting blood as he staggered out of reach. A flaming heat licked at his arm as he fought to maintain control over his weapon, the limb throbbing from his accelerated pulse that surged under the pain of his injury.

His palms burned, and sweat coated his brow as he bit back a groan and clenched his teeth, forcing himself to keep his sword raised before his body and jump back into the fight.

But before he could retaliate, another knife sailed through the air from behind him. Once again, it found no purchase, and Valeirys' gaze shot toward the girl just as she threw her dagger in answer to the attack, only barely missing Alcides' head as he ducked and then lunged for her.

Ignoring the crippling pain from the wound across his upper arm, Valeirys did not hesitate and moved.

The girl warded off the blow from Alcides' sword and followed her riposte with a kick to his groin that knocked him off balance.

She turned and caught sight of Valeirys coming at her, dragging her sword downward as she twisted and met his blade with a crack.

The impact sent an ache through his body and a searing, ripping sensation through the wound across his arm. But Valeirys did not loosen his hold on his weapon. The steel gave off an ear-splitting screech as her sword slid along the true edge of his own and caught at his cross-guard.

Without hesitation, Valeirys moved and closed the distance between them, pushing the pommel toward her and grasping the flat of her weapon with his right before disarming her in one swift motion.

Her sword clashed onto the floor, and he slammed her back against the wall behind them, trapping her beneath his forearm.

The tip of his sword rested against the bottom of her ribcage while the echo of their heavy breaths rose between them and the smoldering glare of their gazes locked.

To his right, he could hear Alcides heaving in between spits of blood.

Malik stood somewhere behind him, having apparently not moved the entire time, and clapped.

Both their hoods had fallen back, revealing the truth of their blood. Staring at her, Valeirys noticed the rounded shape of her ears hidden beneath the strands of her hair loosened from her braid. A Dragon's Kin.

"You owe me," she growled. Valeirys knew her words had been directed at Malik, but her eyes never left his.

The prince scoffed and replied, "I made no promises. Besides, look at where you are. The Black Market is no place for a girl like you. If you can't handle its ways, you shouldn't be here, and that's not my fault."

Valeirys noticed her eyes narrow through the slits of her mask as if she had flinched at his words. Her breathing steadied, and he imagined her chin to have lifted the slightest bit when she replied, "Even here, there is a code."

She seemed to look down at Valeirys, not taking her attention off him as she continued to speak to Malik, her voice rough with disdain. "But I guess, by the likes of you, I shouldn't be surprised. There is a reason dragons despise elvish blood. Deception is your second nature."

Valeirys heard Malik scoff behind him, followed by the pattering sound of his footsteps as he came up behind him, undoubtedly to look the girl straight in the eyes before he ordered, "Kill her."

"No!" Eyvindr shouted from behind him.

Valeirys did not move and continued to watch the girl who didn't even twitch and eyed him still.

"Leave her," said Eyvindr. "Don't do this, V—"

Valeirys withdrew his arm, letting her go, but immediately raised his sword to her chin.

Malik let out a long sigh, as if bored, and reattached his mask while he spoke. "Don't take too long. We will be waiting outside."

He then signaled Alcides, and the two of them strode outside the chamber. Eyvindr remained standing behind him, and Valeirys could feel his gaze boring into his back. The faint click of the door's latch falling shut echoed behind them, and the room froze before the girl spoke, "Well, what are you waiting for?"

Chapter 29

Panic entwined Aleirya's neck and numbed her body like a paralyzing venom seeping into her system as the elvish blade kissed her skin.

Her scalp prickled, and the breath in her lungs grew so hot she thought it might incinerate her from within.

She swallowed, compelling her chest to rise and fall evenly and fixed her eyes on the elf at the opposite end of the sword.

She would not grant him the satisfaction of trembling in the wake of the death he was about to cast her into.

Seconds felt like minutes as they all stood frozen in place, and she wondered if his lingering brought him some cruel form of pleasure, as if he enjoyed lording his power over her.

Aleirya clenched her teeth and grimaced behind her mask when he continued to hesitate, his blade nestled against her chin like a cold set of fingers forcing her to look up at him.

"I won't beg if that's what you're waiting for," she said.

She wasn't a gambler or much of a talker, and the thought of pleading for mercy made her stomach churn and her fingers spread to claws in revulsion. She was a warrior and prepared to die by the steel that gave her life and purpose.

"I will not kill you," he answered collectedly.

The other elf behind him blew out a breath, and Aleirya wondered if he had been holding it this entire time.

A sense of relief tickled her spine, and the tension in her shoulders lessened a bit as her body responded to his words.

She didn't know this stranger, and yet, oddly and against her every instinct, a part of her believed him.

There was something about him; his presence filling her with a mingling sense of awe, wariness, and somehow a connectedness, as if they were familiar to each other. Never had she fought anyone like him. The dance of their swords bringing about a tantalizing thrill and at the same time, an indescribable fright, as if she were playing with fire or sipping from a poisoned chalice.

"Your sword says differently," she replied.

Aleirya wondered if he cringed behind his mask.

The elf lowered his weapon, allowing her to step away from the wall, but still held it ready to plunge into her chest.

"Why have you sent your dragons to murder my people?" he asked.

Her brow furrowed, and she blurted, "What?"

Something in his green eyes seemed to flare at her response, as if her ignorance angered him.

Aleirya's hands curled into fists, and she spat, "Why have you sent spies into our kingdom to steal our dragons, burn their shelters, and kill innocents?"

Taking a step toward him so that the tip of his weapon pressed against her chest, she glared at him and added, "Whatever scheme you and the Metatari have wrought together, it shall fail. We have no interest in a war against your people, but we will avenge the dragons as our blood demands it."

Quicker than the blink of an eye, the elf dropped his sword and seized her.

The air was knocked from her lungs as he hurled her against the wall. Aleirya felt a dull pain reach her temples, spreading from the back of her skull as her head thudded against the wood.

His body pressed against hers, hand clutching the collar of her cloak while his gaze pierced her own.

Aleirya imagined his nostrils flaring behind his mask before he loosened his grip slightly as if not wanting to hurt her and spoke. "You call my kind deceitful, and yet the lies flow effortlessly from your lips."

The huffing of his breath was audible in the silence that settled between them before he continued, "You speak of vengeance—well, we do not see kindly to those spilling elvish blood without scruple. Rest assured, even fire is extinguished."

The blow of his fist sent blots across her vision, and she sank to the floor. A veil of darkness descended upon her while her mind drifted, two beacons of bright green the last thing she saw.

CHAPTER 30

A large hand clasped her shoulder as Aleirya awoke. Groggy, she forced herself up into a sitting position, her body screaming as she moved, her limbs bruised and rigid.

Prying her eyes open, she blinked through the fog that shrouded her vision until she caught sight of a familiar face staring back at her.

Goosebumps broke out over her arms at the flash of silver and gold gleaming from his eyes, and her hand flitted to the dagger at her left thigh, only to find the sheath empty.

A lump built in her throat, and her heart pounded against her chest as everything slowly came back to her.

"I'm not here to harm you," he said, his voice a low rumbling that had a strange comfort to it.

The Metatari she had encountered by the woods after her fight with Damian, the same one who had sought an audience with King Ethuriel, crouched before her and inspected her thoughtfully, as if assessing her injuries.

His piercing gaze moved over her, making her skin crawl and sending shivers down her spine.

"Can you stand?" he asked, searching her face once again.

It was then that she realized that she no longer wore her mask.

Aleirya nodded silently and swallowed, her throat dry and her tongue feeling swollen.

The Metatari helped her up, hooking an arm behind her back and under her shoulders.

Aleirya winced as she found her footing, her soles vibrating under the first few steps she took.

The shapeshifter held onto her for a moment longer before he let go, watching her closely, and spoke. "Let's get you out of here."

Again, she simply nodded and tugged the hood of her cloak over her head.

Any reluctance to follow him was made void by the strain of the effort to hold herself upright and process his words.

Aleirya followed him as they made for the exit of the tavern, passing by the guests as quickly and discreetly as they could. Once they found themselves outside, the Metatari reached for her hand.

Looking over his shoulder, he spoke. "Don't let go, and don't look back."

The sound of his voice was like thunder, causing a chill to settle over the skin of her arms while she let him lead her onward.

The Metatari steered them through the streets and past the stands and tents of the Black Market as if he knew the place like the back of his hand.

The movement and the brisk pace of their steps, though at first dizzying, seemed to help stabilize her senses, and she felt more like herself again.

Aleirya kept her head low and held onto the Metatari's hand as they maneuvered through the crowds, the notion as odd as it was reassuring.

Her thoughts still spun like a carousel as she recalled what had happened at the tavern, what she had done to Luther, the intrusion, the fight, and what the elf had said to her…

Had he told her the truth? Had the dragons truly been killing elves?

Her mind reeled in confusion, a haze settling over her so that she no longer felt certain what was true and what was false.

Then, all at once, a weight slammed against her chest. She felt her strength wane from her, and her legs wobbled beneath her.

Aleirya staggered and looked up, but all around her there was nothing.

For a moment, it appeared as if her surroundings had vanished, and she had forgotten where she was.

She could hear her own breath echoing in her ears and began to panic when everything blurred.

Enveloped in a bright light, she was no longer sure if they were moving forward or if they had stopped. Her vision swam, and nausea gripped her middle just as she pulled away from the shapeshifter, who instantly released her hand.

Then, all at once, everything eased.

Strength returned to her limbs, and the sickness abated; however, Aleirya still felt fatigued, and her head started to pound again.

It wasn't until she raised her hands to stroke her temples that she realized they were no longer in the Black Market.

Blinking, she tried to determine what had happened.

They must have portaled out of the mountain, she realized.

They stood atop a cliff, overlooking the ocean's waves below.

The sun was rising in the distance as the night ended, and a new day broke before them. A few steps ahead of her, at the edge of the cliff, stood the Metatari with his back toward her.

Aleirya watched him as the wind tossed the ends of his dark cloak, and he continued to gaze at the sun, unspeaking.

Taking a few steps back, Aleirya spun around, trying to guess where exactly he had taken her. Without her dragon, there was no escape from this height.

The hairs of her neck stood on end, and her stomach knotted as she whirled to face him once more.

Suddenly, the insanity of the situation and the uncertainty of the shapeshifter's intentions toward her struck her like a wave.

Aleirya's body went cold when she saw him slowly turn toward her.

She swallowed, and her arms stiffened beside her as she balled her hands into fists.

If he was going to kill her, at least she wouldn't go down without a fight.

The Metatari approached her; with every one of his long strides, she backed up a bit more, sharp jolts traveling up her legs from the soles of her feet.

Aleirya's breath quickened, and she cast a quick glance over her shoulder, making sure she wasn't about to walk off the cliff.

"Is this the part where you cast me to my death?" she asked.

Stopping, he studied her until she slowed her steps to a halt as well.

"I'm not here to hurt you," said the Metatari. "I thought I made that clear when I found you in the tavern."

She was about to go on when a familiar sound coming from behind her rose louder. There was a loud crushing noise, and the ground below them shook and cracked as Takhéa landed on the cliff side behind her. Lowering her large head as if to prowl, with her wings flapping loudly, Takhéa clawed angrily at the ground.

A low rumbling sounded from the depth of her throat before she roared and let out a burst of flames. The dragon's razor-sharp gaze fixated on the Metatari, who then spoke. "Do you think I'd invite your dragon to join us if I wanted to kill you?"

Shifting his gaze onto her dragon, he grinned and added, "It is good to see you, too, Takhéa."

The dragon's growling grew quieter, and with a snort, she raised her head and tucked her wings into her sides.

Slowly his glance wandered back to Aleirya, and he said, "We're not the enemy, Aleirya. I'm trying to help your people."

How did he know? Could he read her mind? Was he doing it now?

Her hands trembled, and her mouth went dry.

"I don't believe you," said Aleirya.

The sun blinded her, and she lifted a hand to shield her eyes.

He laughed and replied, "That's quite bold of you to say after I saved you from the elves."

Takhéa growled behind her, but Aleirya didn't look at her.

"I don't think you can call that 'saving me from the elves.' You simply found me after they left," said Aleirya.

"Who is to say they weren't about to come back?" said the Metatari.

He studied her intently for a moment before speaking again. "Tarragon is in danger, as is Erysméa, Aleirya. I believe a common enemy is trying to turn both of your kingdoms against each other. I know what you're thinking, but my people and I are trying to stop that from happening. We are not against you… and neither are the elves."

"How am I to know that you speak the truth?" Aleirya asked.

Nodding, the shapeshifter came closer to her. His footsteps seemed far too quiet for a man of his stature when he neared her.

Stopping, he held out a hand and said, "Let me show you."

Leaping backward so that she almost bumped into Takhéa, she answered, "No! No more mind tricks or mind reading, whatever it is you shapeshifters do… I've felt it before, I don't want it."

"The cliffs… You encountered one of my men," said the Metatari.

Speechless, Aleirya froze.

"How?" she asked.

"Did he harm you?" the shapeshifter asked in return, ignoring her question.

"I don't think so," she answered.

"Then trust me. Let me show you," he said.

But Aleirya shook her head.

The Metatari chuckled, and a bright smile spilled over his face, bearing a set of perfectly white teeth that shone against his dark skin.

"You are stubborn," he said.

"If by 'stubborn' you mean smart, then yes," Aleirya replied.

Still grinning, he gave a sigh and then spoke. "The silver tongue, do you still have it?"

"Yes," Aleirya said warily, unsettled by how much he knew.

"You planned to use it on Luther and perhaps one of my own... Use it on me," he said. "Like any other, I won't be able to resist its power."

Aleirya hesitated, studying him.

Was he truly so intent on proving her suspicions wrong, or was this some kind of trick?

The Metatari continued to stare back at her in silence.

Then slowly, Aleirya opened her satchel and folded her fingers around the vial, relief overcoming her that the elves hadn't robbed her after rendering her unconscious.

Withdrawing it from her bag, she eyed it thoughtfully for a moment as it lay inside her hand.

Peering upward at the shapeshifter again, she pursed her lips, about to speak, when he interrupted, "Irva néyum onithéa cave elypsem onithéa va ohntérun dinengea dinir pyridimos."

"You know the spell," Aleirya said, amazed.

He nodded and then replied, "And now its power is bound to you. Ask me anything, and I will have no choice but to reveal the truth."

For once, she took a step toward him.

This was what she had wanted to do all along; she wanted to uncover the truth. But why did she suddenly feel so cruel? Was he perhaps influencing the way she felt? Could he do that?

Squeezing the vial in her hand once more, she then extended her arm toward him and released her grip on it.

This sort of spell, if administered recklessly, can destroy the mind to the point of death.

Aleirya suppressed a flinch while remembering Sir Odynn's words.

Regardless of the silver tongue's dangerous power, she had to know.

Watching him take it from her hands, she spoke. "A drop will suffice."

Something about his calm and unquestioning gaze made her gut twist with guilt.

She had never wielded magic like this before. What if she did something wrong?

Nodding, he tilted his head back and brought the opened vial to his lips.

Once he had drunk from it, he straightened and placed it back inside her hands.

A moment passed while nothing happened.

Aleirya stared into his strange eyes. Warmth flooded her limbs and something tickled the nape of her neck as she sensed the magic within her thrum to life.

The sensation was tantalizing, enticing her to immerse herself deeper and deeper inside the power she held.

But then Aleirya felt the entire weight of his thoughts crash into her.

Wincing, she stepped back, lowering her head and raising her arms before her as if to shield herself from the ambush of his foreign consciousness. She could hear a choir of unfamiliar voices flood her ears in a painful volume as his memories came to life all around her.

Aleirya gave a shout and squeezed her eyes shut even harder, trying to gain control of the chaos.

Was this supposed to happen?

Her heart pounded forcefully in her chest while she tried to steady herself.

"Aleirya," said the shapeshifter, his voice crystal clear, breaking through the overwhelming noise. "Open your eyes. Look at me."

At first, she shook her head, wincing again at the sharp sounds that exploded all around her. But then she did as he said.

Her gaze locked onto his and all at once, it was as if a bond formed between them, tethering one mind to the other. Something about it unsettled her, but Aleirya compelled herself not to look away and held on, imagining she were grabbing onto a rope to pull herself out of a pit.

Her pulse steadied, and she noticed the voices around her soften to whispers.

"Very good." She heard the shapeshifter speak into her thoughts. "Now tell me what you want to know."

The first question fled her lips faster than she could think. "Do you, the Metatari, share any alliance with the enemy who has set themselves against my people, the Dragon's Kin?"

"We do not."

The muscles in her neck began to spasm and Aleirya felt a crippling pain rise to her head. A dizziness settled over her as she tried to maintain the bond between them and subdue the ongoing flow of the shapeshifter's thoughts.

Drawing in a sharp breath, she went on, "Is it true that you and your people are innocent of any evil committed or devised against us and the dragons?"

"Yes, as I stand here before you, I speak the truth that we have not set ourselves against you, the Dragon's Kin, or the dragons."

Aleirya felt her knees buckle, but she caught herself, placing her right foot forward. Her strength was failing her. The spell was more powerful than she had thought. She couldn't maintain it for much longer.

Dedicating all her focus on keeping the link between them intact, she didn't notice the Metatari reach for her until she felt his hand fold over her own.

She didn't know how, but somehow it seemed as if he were steadying her, enabling her to hold on.

Staring back at him, the part of her that had wanted to blame his people for all the wrong that had been done to the Dragon's Kin, the part that wanted to prove the Metatari's deceit and ill will against them, abated.

Instead of interrogating him further on his intentions toward her kingdom, Aleirya grew conscious of another question that lingered on the tip of her tongue.

Slowly, but surely, she could sense the connection between them break, unraveling like the strands of a rope.

Something within made her hesitate, but then at last, just before her mind separated from his, she spoke. "When we first met, you knew my name… How?"

A tiny thread of the once powerful link remained when she heard his answer.

"I once knew your true father, Aleirya."

Aleirya felt a jolt and then the cloud of voices rose and fell, rushing past her ears before they vanished once and for all.

Blinking, she pushed herself onto her feet, having sunk to her knees at the release of the spell.

The shapeshifter stood at the edge of the cliff again and eyed her thoughtfully.

Nodding at her as if to say goodbye, he then turned away when she shouted, "Wait!"

Running toward him, she suddenly stopped, unsure how close she should dare to tread.

"Will I see you again?" she asked.

Peering at her over his shoulder, he caught her gaze with his silver eye and grinned but said nothing.

Then she watched in awe as a dark cluster of something that reminded her of feathers spread outward from the middle of his back and along his spine, slowly dissolving the form of his body. The feathers turned into flocks of black birds that cawed and screeched as they dispersed from the dark center in disarray.

Aleirya stepped back, a blend of both horror and awe consuming her from within.

At last, the flock disappeared, and the view ahead cleared, and Aleirya saw the mighty form of a great eagle soar into the morning sky as it flew toward the light of the risen sun.

Chapter 31

"The Liberator's name is Alessander Melquart." Valeirys' voice echoed through his father's study as the doors swung wide open, and he stormed inside. "His true name is Alessander Melquart."

Squaring his shoulders, he willed his bounding pulse to calm and ignored the wave of panic that instantly washed over him.

The chamber was dead silent.

As if time had suddenly ceased, the guards had gone rigid in an active stance, uncertain whether they should remove him from the room.

Valeirys could feel the weight of everyone's stares on him, but he compelled himself to pay attention to the only one that mattered.

His father's sharp gaze bored into him, pinning him in place. No matter how well Valeirys knew him, it was impossible to read him. Nothing, not a single muscle in Uryiel's face twitched to betray his thoughts or his reaction.

Valeirys hated that about him, probably foremost because it was something he envied.

Not daring to untether his gaze from his father's, he mentally pieced the picture of the rest of the chamber together, noting the members positioned throughout the room.

Lord Rhaegalisron stood bent over the rectangular table to his left, his hands resting on its edges.

Lord Zelathiel leaned against the tall window behind his father, arms crossed over his chest, his fingers paused from tracing the sigil of the chakram stitched onto the right arm of his black doublet. Without even looking in his direction, Valeirys sensed the sting of the lord's scrutiny ebbing from the ruthless pits of his eyes.

Trajan flanked his father's left, opposite Lord Zelathiel. The commander's arms were strung taut at his sides, undoubtedly revealing his concern for Valeirys, considering how he had just barged into the room without any thought for the consequences.

Lastly, to Valeirys' right, and veiled in the shadows of the shelves surrounding him, was Lord Councilor D'Arthragnan, acting representative of His Majesty, King Yevandrielle.

Uryiel straightened, taking a step back from the table, and spoke in a matter-of-fact tone. "Explain yourself, soldier."

A chill ran up Valeirys' spine, and his jaw tightened. His nerves were still jolted from the night, his head throbbed, and a dull ache still tugged at his arm where he had healed the wound he had suffered from the fight at the tavern.

He had stomped into his father's study, interrupting what appeared to be a strategic gathering of Erysméa's northwestern rulers with only a half-fledged plan, anger over what had happened to Eyvindr prompting his steps.

Or was it perhaps something else entirely that festered the rage and the unease stirring in his chest?

The question rose unbidden to the forefront of his mind, and an image of the Dragon's Kin, the girl he had left unconscious, flashed before him, but he forced it aside. He couldn't allow himself to get distracted by whatever it was about her that still haunted him.

Swallowing, he nodded. A jumble of words and phrases organized itself to a tolerable speech in his mind, and he began. "I received word that an informant connected to our spies had a name and a location of the rebellion's leader. Last night, I spoke with them myself. The meeting was carefully orchestrated, the terms including that the informant remain anonymous."

Valeirys spoke swiftly, concentrating on getting the words out without overthinking.

Then, boldly, he willed his rigid legs to move and approached his father's table. His boots clicked obnoxiously loud against the stillness that overtook the chamber while he drew forth the scroll they had received from Luther.

Extending it toward Uryiel, he held his breath.

There was no way to tell how he had acquired it or where it had come from; Valeirys had made sure of it.

The parchment was of the same matter as any other elven document. There was no signature or seal revealing its author, and the handwriting had been glamoured to match the traditionally taught elven script; even so, Valeirys couldn't shake the fear of his father's discerning eyes.

Uryiel studied him with an unwavering look before he accepted the scroll as if he waited to see if Valeirys' arm might start to tremble.

When his father took it and began to unravel it, Valeirys continued, "There is a tavern in Phera by the coast of Lyrr."

He watched Uryiel's eyes flick upward at him while he interrupted his reading.

"According to the intel, the Liberator, Alessander Melquart, has a supporter there by the name of Ganymedes. He owns a tavern called the 'Tempest' where he has offered Melquart shelter. Melquart is to arrive there within a fortnight," said Valeirys.

His chest tightened under the grueling silence that settled between them, the tension as palpable to him as the temperature of the air.

Uryiel had to believe him.

Valeirys swallowed, ignoring the violent surge of his pulse. He had no explanation why Melquart would journey to Phera should his father question him further. Luther had precisely delivered the information he had been paid for, no more, no less.

"It coincides with what my spies have already been speculating." Lord Rhaegalisron spoke, and immediately, Valeirys felt a weight lift off his chest.

"A week ago, the sketch of the serpent started resurfacing again. But this time, it wasn't printed. My soldiers found images of it all throughout Alaisdair's villages; painted on the walls of houses, storefronts, even banners; charcoal drawings smeared onto the cobblestone of the public streets, carriages, homes… and every few days, the sketch changes again…

"I wasn't certain that it meant anything until I received word from Lord Yeva, Lord Cenric, Lord Fearghail… and just yesterday from Nyradorn of the same occurrences." He glanced at Lord Zelathiel, who offered him a grim nod, confirming his words, before he went on, "I have no doubt the same will begin soon in Inaesa. The Liberator is rallying his forces and, no doubt, he intends to convince more to join his cause. The serpent's image, the details added to it, bit by bit… it's a code. The rebellion's unique language and their way of communicating throughout the realm, and this time, he's telling them where to gather."

Valeirys met Lord Rhaegalisron's gaze, and the lord dipped his chin in his direction before he turned toward Uryiel and added, "They're planning something, and they're making fools of us as they do it."

"They're going to strike against the crown, attempt the assassination of His Majesty again," Lord Zelathiel chimed in, drawing all attention onto himself.

Staring at Valeirys, he added, "If the boy is to be believed, we could end this coup before it begins. The only question is how? We most certainly cannot move into Lyrr with an army if we wish to catch him off guard."

"Exploit the mess the rebellion recently caused," said Lord D'Arthragnan.

He stood far off in the chamber's corner to Valeirys' right, as if he were only meant to be a silent participant.

"The lumber shortage in Lyrr," he began and paused, waiting for the rest of them to catch on. "Due to the protesters' recent arson in Alaisdair and Eihbir and the destruction of their forest lands, the lumber supplies have been depleted for weeks now. It has become nigh impossible to replenish their stores ever since this loss."

His cane clicked against the tiled floor of the room as he approached the table bearing the map of Erysméa's realm.

Setting his eyes on the aforementioned regions and paying little attention to the others who stared at him, Lord D'Arthragnan continued, "With the situation as it is, Lyrr would normally rely on the cedar shipments coming from Nyradorn over the Adeyhi rivers, but this, too, has been made impossible due to the rebellion's work of damming those waters. Lyrr needs the lumber to resume the construction of our naval ships to prepare for a war against the Dragon's Kin, and the parts of the villages that were destroyed by the rebels must be rebuilt."

"So, what do you suggest we do?" Lord Rhaegalisron asked. "If he's summoning those loyal to him to Lyrr, there's no telling what kind of a force we're up against."

"We send a unit of fourteen soldiers disguised into Lyrr in an attempt to catch him off guard and arrest him," said Trajan. "If all fails, they'll have the support of Lord Tarquinius' league, and the soldiers stationed in Phera."

He stepped closer to Uryiel's side and went on, "The unit can depart in small separate groups every couple of days. The largest can pose as merchants and laborers bringing cedar from Nyradorn; others could travel into the city of Phera as roofers and carpenters in search of work after their homes and livelihoods have been destroyed. Under their cover, local inns will take them in."

"And Lyrr's garrison will provide the unit with any necessary armor and weaponry for the arrest, enabling our men to travel inconspicuously," said Uryiel, staring down at the map before him.

It grew quiet again until Lord Zelathiel interrupted the peace. "You are certain your informant can be trusted? Alessander Melquart is indeed the Liberator's true name, boy?"

Valeirys kept his expression still despite Lord Zelathiel's demeaning tone and answered, "Yes. I am certain."

"The kingdom would be in your debt, young soldier," said Lord D'Arthragnan, eyeing him with a strange curiosity. "You will have proved yourself quite useful."

"Useful indeed," said Uryiel.

Valeirys' attention darted back toward his father. The dryness in his tone gave away his lack of conviction.

"If this information proves to be false, this will fall on your head, soldier," Uryiel added.

Valeirys did not let his gaze wither under his father's. He could not risk appearing insecure. It was a weakness his father would forgive even less than the embarrassment he would bring upon him and the family's name should Luther's word mislead them.

Nodding, he lifted his chin and replied, "Understood."

Uryiel continued to observe him when Valeirys noticed Lord Zelathiel approach and lay a hand on his father's shoulder, a devilish smirk on his face as he spoke in a low tone. "Seems like the need to overachieve runs in the family."

He stepped back and distanced himself from the rest of the gathering when he gave a bow and said, "I shall take my leave. My forces will be prepared and ready to join this endeavor of yours."

He strolled outside the room just as the guards drew open the doors and Lord D'Arthragnan spoke. "I shall relay all that has been discussed to His Majesty. No doubt he will be intrigued. Let us only hope that this plan does not go awry."

Valeirys exhaled once the doors fell shut behind him and closed his eyes.

Opening them again, he turned the corner and headed down the hall when he almost ran into Eyvindr.

"So, did they believe you?" his brother asked.

"What are you doing lurking around like that?" Valeirys asked, startled.

Eyvindr grimaced and replied, "I live here. I'm not lurking."

Valeirys grinned slightly and studied his brother. "Are you alright? How's the shoulder?"

THE RISE OF ISIGAR

Eyvindr shrugged and responded, "I'm fine. Questioning my choice of friends, you know, but I'm fine… It's just a shame I couldn't let the wound scar. Would have made an interesting story, and it would have made my rugged good looks even more enticing."

He grinned foolishly, mirroring Valeirys' own smile.

"I'm glad you're alright," said Valeirys. "I don't know what twisted idea was running through Malik's head when he did that, but he'll regret it."

"Because you'll do what exactly?" said Eyvindr, crossing his arms over his chest. "He's a prince, *the prince*, and the son of our king. Unless you want to get all of us executed, you cannot tell His Majesty of his son's dealings, and you can't simply walk up to him and punch him in the face."

"Unless he invites me to do so," Valeirys replied sarcastically.

Eyvindr straightened and unclasped his arms from his chest. "I don't need you to protect me or pretend that I'm some weakling in need of you carrying out my revenge."

His tone had darkened, his brows furrowed while he stared back at Valeirys.

"I'm no soldier. But I can fight for myself."

His brother seemed more unnerved by what had happened than he had at first let on.

Valeirys looked at him, and his expression softened before he spoke. "That's not what I meant. You are far more capable than you let yourself believe… I—"

"Don't explain yourself to me," Eyvindr interrupted. "Just make sure you actually find and seize this Melquart fellow. It would be a shame if everything had been for nothing."

With that, he walked away, brushing Valeirys' shoulder while he passed him.

Chapter 32

Thoran's knuckles broke against the wall with a crack.

Aleirya noticed every line of his familiar face deepen while he closed his eyes, lips pressed to a hard line as if trying to keep himself from saying anything further.

The council's summons was now crumpled up in his tightly balled fist that hung at his side. When he turned to look at her again, the color of his eyes matched the black of his beard and hair.

"This is not you, Aleirya," said Thoran.

She could tell he was doing his best not to yell at her.

His broad chest rose and fell under his audible breath.

He shook his head, dropping his gaze from her and expelled a gasp. "Another hearing…" he muttered and paced back and forth. "Do you not realize what this means for you? You are risking your entire future, Aleirya!"

His eyes bored into her once again.

Grabbing the summons from his fist, he raised it before her with his other hand and spoke. "You are not violent. You have never attacked your peers or tried to harm anyone intentionally before… I do not understand, Aleirya. This is not how Zannia and I have raised you!"

"I know…" was all she managed to say.

Aleirya stood in the middle of the small kitchen of her parents' cottage, unable to move.

"I cannot believe you tried to hide this from us," said Thoran.

Aleirya said nothing and stared down at her feet.

Just this morning, they had found the summons for the council's hearing she had hidden amongst her belongings. She had received it shortly after she had returned from the Black Market and couldn't bring herself to mention it to them. She had no plan, not the faintest idea of how to make things right again, and she couldn't bear to confess it aloud to anyone.

She had spent the last days, if not weeks, trying to put everything behind her, forget everything that had happened as if that would somehow make it disappear for good and dissolve her problems. She had thrown herself into the task of assisting Thoran and working at the forge, pretending to be taking some time away from the academy when, in truth, she knew she was hiding, hiding from the king's council, hiding from reality.

The fight at the tavern in the Black Market, the Metatari, the elves, the thought of dragons killing elves… it haunted her. The entire world was turned upside down, and she was as lost as she had ever been, uncertain how to navigate amongst it.

Swallowing, Aleirya lifted her gaze from the floor and drew back her shoulders, feigning confidence when she spoke. "I didn't tell you, because I didn't want you to worry. I can take care of this myself."

Thoran's features distorted again, almost to a scowl, and his voice rose louder. "No, you can't, and this is proof of the matter!"

He clutched the summons again and then smacked it onto the table. Letting go of it, he spun around in frustration, turning his back toward her.

Aleirya's jaw tightened, and she clenched her fists.

How could he go on treating her like a child when she wasn't? Even if she was left without a plan, she didn't need his help. She could fight for herself.

With a sigh, Thoran's shoulders dropped, and he lowered his voice. "The hearing is tomorrow. We will prepare you, and then you will go, you will apologize for your actions, and from now on, you will do better."

"No," said Aleirya.

She paused when Thoran whirled around to face her, his cheeks flushed with anger.

"I won't go. I won't give them the chance to take everything from me." Her voice broke at the end.

"This is foolishness!" Thoran shouted at her. "And then what, Aleirya? They could turn it into another trial. You could be charged with resistance against the royal council's authority! For wings and talons, why do you have to be so stubborn?"

"Thoran," Zannia interrupted gently. She stepped between them as if to keep them from each other's throats.

Glancing back and forth between Thoran and Aleirya, she went on calmly, "Aleirya, we worry for you."

Her eyes lingered on her for a moment, and then she added, "Perhaps it wouldn't be the worst thing if the council made the suspension permanent and if you returned home. You would have a fresh start; you could forget all these horrible things that happened to you."

"No." Aleirya stopped her, shaking her head fervently.

"Yes," Thoran interrupted. "Zannia is right."

Aleirya glared at him.

His words stung, and she bit down on her lip, struggling to believe what he had just said.

"Look at you, Aleirya. You haven't been yourself ever since the night Lord Varlam harmed Izidora. I know you've wanted nothing more than to be a warrior, but you took one life, and look at what it's done to you," said Thoran.

THE RISE OF ISIGAR

Aleirya felt a sharp pain cut through her chest. He had never said it that way before… He had never accused her of killing anyone.

"I was protecting my friend. I wasn't trying to kill him," she said, correcting him. Tears welled in her eyes, but she forced them back.

Thoran just shook his head, interrupting her again. "Aleirya, if you were to become a warrior, countless more would die on the battlefield at the strike of your sword. If one death did this to you, what would the other thousands do that are yet to come?"

"I can't—I can't believe you," Aleirya replied, choking on her own words as her throat tightened. Her eyes burned, and the pain in her chest intensified, making it hard to breathe.

How could they? How could they say these things?

Her hands trembled at her sides.

"Aleirya," Zannia said softly and approached her.

Gently, she reached for Aleirya's wrists with her hands.

Every part of her wanted to resist the closeness of Zannia.

She didn't want to listen to them. She didn't want to be here.

How could they agree with the council? How could they try to convince her to give up everything she had ever wanted?

A lump swelled in her throat.

Then, all at once, Aleirya's gaze dropped from Zannia's face to where a searing pain crawled up her arms from where she touched her. Zannia's grip physically hurt so much that Aleirya gasped.

The unchecked force that stirred within her whenever her emotions boiled, whenever her anger sparked alive, began to grow.

Pinching her eyes shut, she told herself it was all just her imagination and that Zannia would never hurt her. But then an unbidden voice inside her grew louder.

But they had—they had hurt her. They thought she wasn't good enough, not strong enough to be a warrior. They didn't believe in her and who she could be.

Zannia's hands seemed to tighten around her like a noose.

No! Aleirya thought, gritting her teeth.

They were wrong. She would prove it to them.

Aleirya's fingers shook violently under the agony that tore through her body, and she sensed the new and yet familiar power demanding its release.

Sharp jolts chased up her arms as if someone had cut her skin with a blade, and she screamed.

Seizing Zannia by the shoulders as if to shove her away, Aleirya felt her fingers dig into her skin.

Her gaze fixated on Zannia's horrified face while she held her in place.

Aleirya's eyes brightened under the fury that surged inside her, and then she heard a terrible shrieking sound pierce her ears.

Warmth tickled Aleirya's palms just as Zannia's body began to twist and convulse under her grasp, and something sizzled and snapped under her cries like firewood burning in a hearth.

Thoran's roar split the air, and moments later, Aleirya felt his hand plummet into her chest as he tried to pry them apart.

At first, her grip on Zannia tightened even more, provoking a crippling noise to erupt from her throat while the fighting spirit within Aleirya bellowed.

She would prove that she was strong enough.

Blind rage obscured her senses, and Aleirya stood her ground.

Her strength outdid Thoran's as he tried to separate them, and she didn't relent.

Zannia crumbled before her, and Aleirya heard Thoran's aching cry. "Aleirya, please!"

Suddenly, the weight of their screams crashed into her, knocking the breath from her lungs, and she let go.

Tripping, she stumbled backward as the strange flow of power she had released stopped.

Dread and a different sort of agony gripped her, replacing the pit her fury had carved out inside her.

Aleirya stared down at her open palms. Her eyes narrowed as she tried to comprehend what had happened, and then they squeezed shut under Zannia's whimpering.

Swallowing hard, Aleirya forced herself to look up to see what she had done.

Zannia lay curled up on the ground, shaking. Thoran kneeled at her side, propping her head up on his lap, the torment of his anguish written all over his face.

Aleirya's blood ran cold at the sight of Zannia's burned arms where she had held her.

What in the dragon's name had she done?

Aleirya's whole body stiffened in horror.

She had lost control. She had hurt Zannia.

Whatever magic she'd wielded under the spell of her anger, whatever force had taken over her, it was too strong. She could not control it; she could not bend it to her will.

She was powerless.

Aleirya's lips quivered. Shaking her head, she came toward them, her hands still extended before her as if they were a vile curse she wanted to keep as far from her as she could.

"No!" Thoran belted.

His eyes pinned her in place so that she stopped.

Looking at him, Aleirya felt as if her heart might shatter into a thousand pieces. Ridden with guilt, she wanted to break, to crumble to ashes for what she had done to Zannia.

Though she knew she shouldn't, her mouth opened, and she spoke. "Thoran, I never wanted—"

"Leave!" he shouted.

Tears streamed down his face, and he rose to his feet.

"Thoran." Zannia's weak voice rose as she struggled to prop herself up onto her side.

Aleirya's gaze immediately darted toward her, and she gasped in relief.

Zannia didn't meet her eyes and continued to look up at Thoran.

"I should have known…" said Thoran through gritted teeth, still staring at Aleirya.

A tingle raced down her spine. Whatever did he mean?

But the thought seemed of little importance now, and Aleirya shoved it aside.

Breathing hard, Thoran tore the door of the cottage's entrance open, drawing Aleirya's attention back onto him, and he yelled, "Get out!"

Aleirya jumped at his outraged cry.

All her strength, her spirit, seemed to have drained from her, leaving her frightened and weak.

She struggled to move, and when he warned her again, she lurched into motion. Her legs wobbled beneath her as she hurried outside, and when the door slammed shut behind her, the impact seemed strong enough to thrust her to the ground.

Aleirya forced herself to move, and she stumbled forward into the fields until her feet stopped, and she crashed onto her knees.

Catching herself with her hands, she broke into sobs.

Her gut twisted painfully, and she clutched her sides, bending forward until her forehead rested against the ground, and she screamed into it.

What had she done?

Chapter 33

Valeirys let his fingers glide over the smooth iron of the breastplate that hung on the wall before him.

The armory of Lyrr's garrison lay completely still. In fact, it was so quiet it reminded him of a tomb.

As far as the eye could see, mounds of steel forged into plated armor and every weapon known to the elven warrior consumed its space. Though it was smaller than the royal armory of Mòr Rhíoghaìn his father had taken him to see several years ago, its assortment was quite impressive.

Ever since he had been a child and strong enough to swing a sword, Valeirys had held a deep fascination for the history and craftsmanship of armor and weaponry. Had he not been given the rare opportunities and quality of training his family's name had granted him, he might have even fancied himself a blacksmith someday, forging himself and his kingdom the most lethal works of art.

Stepping closer, he admired the design that embellished the breastplate.

The sigil embossed over its polished center showed the anchor of Lord Tarquinius and gleamed faintly beneath the rays of light that broke through the windows above him. Along the anchor's shank stood a phrase: *Irvèn agrennon nír éva tios irvèn donoveiam arwa paromir nír thyouna.*

"Fierce is the one who is not moved when the storm comes," he whispered to himself as he read the words.

The corners of his lips twitched upward slightly while his hand lingered on the armor, the crispness of its touch against his skin a balm to his troubled mind.

If all were to go to plan, in two days Melquart would be arrested and on his way to Mòr Rhíoghain to face his trial by His Majesty.

In two days, it would all be over.

But what if something went wrong? What if Melquart escaped them again?

With a sigh, Valeirys let his fingers slide off the breastplate, pinching his eyes shut for a moment to compel his racing thoughts to cease.

He could not dwell on the possibility of failure.

He would do everything in his might to make sure Melquart found his way to the capital, bound in chains.

Opening his eyes again, he continued to stroll through the rest of the armory.

To his left and right, endless rows of helmets, shields, and gauntlets stocked the walls, each a welcome distraction that lured him deeper inside Lyrr's arsenal.

His feet finally slowed before a set of steps that led up to a stone altar.

The walls surrounding it showed scenes of some of the oldest tales of elven battle history, including one of Erysméa's victory over Izurion.

The image portrayed the elven heroine standing over King Izurion, who kneeled at her feet with her sword thrust through him. An arrow protruded from Erysméa's chest, having pierced her heart.

Valeirys had seen similar variations of this scene before.

According to the reports on Erysméa's death, their heroine had indeed suffered a deadly strike by an arrow. However, whether the arrow had truly struck her heart had never been clearly recorded. Nevertheless, the artists who had designed these images preferred to depict her death in this way, intending to demonstrate the great love she had felt for her people.

Far more intriguing to Valeirys than the displayed recordings of their military history, however, was an ebony chest that lay upon the stone altar.

Its strange form reminded him much of a coffin, though its size was too small for it to be so.

Valeirys peered over his shoulder, making sure he was alone, and then climbed the steps to the altar.

Inlaid on the lid of the chest was a silver circlet.

Its centerpiece held an oval-shaped stone, the color of gold, and along its center ran a black line that looked like a slit pupil.

The curves of the circlet's sides resembled the shape of outspread wings, like those of a dragon.

Curious what lay inside the chest, he reached for the clasp of the lock, unsurprised to find it secured shut.

Casting a quick glance over his shoulder, he riveted his eyes on the lock, his entire focus narrowing on it while he let his mind reach for the magic that encompassed the silver seal.

Adeptly, he began to decipher each piece of the spell, much like pulling apart strands of a rope, until he had disassembled and understood each component of its design.

He hadn't realized he had been holding his breath the entire time until the lock snapped open at the release of the command that left his lips in a faint whisper. "Theros ta irven yeun."

Grinning, Valeirys drew a breath and carefully opened the lid, trying not to make a sound.

His eyes grew wide as they settled on the sword that lay inside the chest.

It was unlike any other he had seen before.

This was no elven blade, of that he was sure. Its unique appearance and the unmistakable quality of its craftsmanship gave its origin away.

This was a weapon forged by the Dragon's Kin.

Sparks danced along the tips of Valeirys' fingers, and without a second thought, he reached inside the chest.

He began to trace the intricate design that decorated its cross-guard and blade, showing a battle scene.

A few of the warriors' forms had been overlaid with gold, while others had been left silver.

Embossed onto the center of the cross-guard and the forte of the blade was another larger golden image of a warrior. The armed figure had drawn his sword and raised it over his head, and by his feet lay the ones who had fallen at his hand.

Wrapped around the warrior's ankle was the tip of a dragon's tail.

The creature crouched on all fours before the warrior, like a hound before his master; its body extended along the fuller of the sword. While its scaly form was silver, its eyes and the gust of flames that emerged from its open mouth appeared golden.

Entranced by the sight of it, Valeirys couldn't help himself, and his fingers curled around the hilt.

The stitching of its leather had been made to look like dragon scales, and the touch of it felt enticingly smooth and cool against his palm.

Valeirys backed away from the altar, sword in hand.

His wrist flexed and extended in soothing dips and curves as his mind eased under the flow of his movements that melded gracefully from one familiar stance to the next.

The sword was beautiful, dazzling in the torchlight that illuminated the armory's space, like a rare gem.

Placing his left foot forward, Valeirys tilted the pommel upward, letting the blade glide behind his head and past his right shoulder in a descending arc.

The notion sent a jolt piercing through his chest.

Suddenly, the shadow of a girl darted before him, and his memories of the Black Market rose to the forefront of his mind. The hairs of his neck stood an end, a shiver sending goosebumps down his arms.

Drawing the sword to himself, he turned the flat of it toward him, his eyes catching the reflection of a face across its radiant surface. But it wasn't his own.

The Dragon's Kin girl, the spine-chilling blue of her eyes, stared back at him, and Valeirys froze.

All at once, his arm burned where her sword had pierced him, and the steel of the weapon in his hands grew scalding hot. But Valeirys would not, he could not let go. He gritted his teeth and stared back at her, drawing up the defenses in his mind while wondering if this was some sort of trick, some strange sorcery, until he blinked, and she vanished.

Valeirys drew in a deep breath. Before he could give it any more thought, he heard someone approach.

"I thought I might find you here," said Trajan.

Valeirys turned to face him, just when he added, "And from the looks of it doing something you're not supposed to."

The commander raised an eyebrow, and his mouth formed a half smile while he joined Valeirys beside the altar.

Like him, Trajan was still dressed in the ragged clothes he had worn when they arrived in Lyrr early that morning, disguised as day workers. It was strange seeing him like this.

"You know, that was locked for a reason. You shouldn't have been able to open it in the first place. It's protected by a complicated blend of spells," said the commander.

"I, I… I was just looking," Valeirys began, carefully returning the sword to the chest.

"Hmm, sure you were," said Trajan. "Then you know what it is?"

He crossed his arms over his chest and observed him with a stern expression, as if ready to lecture him.

Valeirys looked from the commander to the sword, concentrating on the details of the weapon and trying not to let himself get distracted once again by its brilliance.

Swallowing, he answered, "It was fashioned for one of the Eskhàra… Or at least that is what I assumed, since traditional elven weaponry isn't embellished by the image of a dragon."

He glanced at Trajan and saw him nod silently before he looked back at the sword and added, "I thought everything was destroyed after the Uprising?"

"Some things were kept to serve as a reminder and a warning of what had once been," Trajan answered.

Resting his hands on either side of the altar, the commander leaned forward and went on, "I was fortunate to have been too young to remember the Eskhàra myself. But I know from my brother's stories and my father's memories that nothing was ever the same after the Uprising.

"They thought they were more powerful than any other being. They thought they were invincible, undefeatable, even more powerful than a dragon. That is why the dragon was placed below the warrior with its tail wrapped around his ankle. They depended on the dragon to increase their power, and yet they grew so conceited, they even assumed that the dragons were inferior to them."

Listening to him, Valeirys swallowed. His glance swept over the dragon's open maw, its fiery eyes, and down the spiked ridge of its spine.

"This sword belonged to an Eskhàra. It was crafted before the final battle of the Uprising when they were convinced that nothing could withstand their might. It was discovered after they had fallen."

As Valeirys looked down at the blade, it saddened him to think that a sword of such beauty could have wrought so much destruction.

A sword was meant to serve justice and to protect the good in a fallen world such as theirs.

"Did any of the Eskhàra survive the Uprising?"

"A few," said Trajan, "but after they fled, they were found, arrested, and then executed."

Valeirys fell silent again. Another question lingered on the tip of his tongue, one he wasn't sure he wanted to know the answer to.

"Were there children?" he asked, not looking up at the commander.

Trajan hesitated but then answered him. "Yes. But there could be no mercy, not for a race such as theirs."

Valeirys nodded. He couldn't bring himself to speak after hearing Trajan's reply.

"So," Trajan began, pushing off the altar and straightening beside him. "Are you ready to tell me how you got the rebel's name? Thanks to you, this will all be over soon."

When Valeirys hesitated to answer, Trajan went on, "You might have convinced everyone in Inaesa; by the blade, you might have even fooled your father; but I taught you to be the soldier you are… There never was an informant, was there? At least, not one connected to our spies. Where did you get this information?"

Valeirys stiffened, and the hairs of his neck rose. Did he know?

Tension gripped his body under the leap of his pulse at the commander's question, but he compelled himself to relax and made his lips curve into a smile before looking up at Trajan and answering, "You flatter me if you consider me capable of fooling my father. If my report came across as disingenuous, then I have my nerves to blame.

"In truth, I did not know if the meeting would even take place until it did, and then when it was over, to actually have a name… It seemed unbelievable."

It wasn't much of a lie. After all, the meeting with Luther, the Black Market, the fight… Valeirys had been rattled, and a part of him had struggled to believe they would ever meet this odd figure of a Dragon's Kin who had credible knowledge they could use.

Trajan studied him wordlessly for a moment, as if weighing his answer. Then he pursed his lips, drawing in a breath, and was about to speak when a whistled tune and footsteps rose behind them.

"There you are!" Malik exclaimed, sauntering toward them. He seemed to have fully embraced his commoner's disguise from their journey and was hardly recognizable with his disheveled hair and smudged face, dressed in his plain tunic and hose that lacked any sort of embellishment or royal sigil signifying his station.

Valeirys fought the urge to cringe at the sight of him, his fingers itching to form fists.

They hadn't spoken since the night of their visit to the Black Market.

Valeirys had tried to keep his distance all throughout their journey to Lyrr out of consideration for both of their safety.

If the truth of where they had been was to come to light, they'd be inhabiting neighboring cells to Melquart and awaiting their deaths upon their return home.

The prince grinned widely and spoke. "While I always enjoy a game of hide-and-seek, it is rather unfortunate not to have my servants around to look for whomever I desire to speak with."

"Shall I offer you something to drink, Your Highness, and perhaps some place to sit down to replenish your spirit after such an exhausting task?" Trajan asked, making no effort to hide the sarcastic tone in his voice.

Simply watching them converse with one another, made it seem absurd that Trajan addressed him as royalty when they both looked like two peasants one could have plucked from the streets.

"Oh, no, there is no need for you to trouble yourself, Sir Rheiavirn. I only wish to ask Valeirys to accompany me if you have nothing more to discuss," said Malik. "Some of our comrades and I were hoping to meet in the city. I thought Valeirys might like to join us."

"And how many wish to partake in this gathering of yours?" Trajan asked in return.

"Only Alcides, son of Lord Councilor Velior, and Eris, one of the new recruits, commander," said Malik. "I realize that a larger group could draw suspicion."

"Hmm," Trajan responded. He cast a glance at Valeirys and spoke. "I believe Valeirys and I have concluded our business. He is free to join you if he wishes."

Valeirys had no desire to spend a minute with the prince after what he had done to Eyvindr, but he couldn't reject the invitation so blatantly in front of Trajan.

Loosening the tension in his jaw, he offered Trajan a respectful nod and then followed Malik, who gleefully spun around on his heels and began heading toward the entrance of the armory.

"Be careful," Trajan called out after them, making them both stop and hesitate. "You are foreigners in this place. There will be eyes watching you. Be mindful of your conduct."

Nodding, Valeirys swallowed and held the commander's gaze for just a moment, catching the unspoken message embedded in his expression that their previous conversation was far from over.

***

"What makes you think that I could possibly want to join you after our last little trip?" Valeirys hissed.

They had trod deeper inside the underbelly of Phera's city, making their way down the narrow and meandering streets, when he stopped in his tracks and waited for the prince to face him.

Malik let out a long sigh, letting his head fall back before he turned around and looked at him.

"I knew this would come up," he said. "Look."

He came a step closer and went on, "I had everything under control. I was never going to let anything happen to your brother."

"It's rather convenient of you to say that, considering how things turned out," Valeirys replied, his eyes narrowing on the prince.

It grew still between them, the night's growing shadows looming above and darkening the alley they found themselves in.

Malik's expression had grown solemn, his reddish gaze for once serious and not glowing with mischief.

"Eyvindr could have died. She could have slit his throat." The words came out pointedly, and Valeirys' mouth went dry at the thought of his brother's near murder.

"But she didn't," said Malik. The usual provocative candor of his voice was gone.

Malik drew a breath and added, "Despite what you think, I'm quite good at reading people. I knew she wasn't going to harm him; that is, at least, lethally—"

"You didn't know," Valeirys interrupted. A needle-like sensation pricked his skin, and he felt the heat of his frustration rush to his head. "Let's make at least one thing clear. You gambled. You—"

"Yes! Fine," Malik yelled, making Valeirys stop.

The prince tossed his hands up into the air and went on, "I may have cruelly tempted fate in your brother's case. But I am not the villain you make me out to be."

They stood across from each other, chests puffed out, hands balled into fists, each glowering at the other from beneath the hoods of their cloaks.

Malik licked his lips, his brow softening, and he spoke. "If anything had happened to Eyvindr, if that wretched girl had killed him, you must know, I would have thrust her through with my very own sword and, as a matter of fact, anyone else who would have tried to defend her. That is how far I go for my friends," he said.

"Oh, we're friends now?" Valeirys asked. The harshness had not left his tone, but his shoulders fell.

Valeirys wasn't certain any apology would ever be enough for what the prince had done. He didn't know if he truly trusted the words coming from his mouth, and yet a part of him believed that, in some misguided way, Malik had considered his plan a good one and had never intended to get Eyvindr killed.

"I thought so," Malik replied. "After all, I'm trying to invite you out for a drink. What else can I do?"

Valeirys studied him, and then, narrowing his eyes, he said, "I've never had a prince apologize to me. You could start there."

Malik laughed and then nodded. "Fine."

He grinned and then gave a rather exaggerated bow before speaking. "Most excellent, Lord Valeirys Altair. I humbly beg your forgiveness for my reckless act and plead for your mercy to not shun me from your presence forever."

Valeirys waited for him to straighten and then raised a brow.

"A little much, don't you think?" he said, unenthused.

The prince smiled before letting his features grow solemn and spoke. "I am sorry, Valeirys. I'm glad Eyvindr is alright."

Valeirys nodded silently and then started to move.

The prince followed before once again leading the way.

The muddied and steep paths reeked of fish and the waste that lay scattered across the ground. The further they descended into Phera's underworld, the more the streets grew crowded with groups of ominous figures who watched their steps with baleful looks lurking beneath their hoods from the shadows. Other roads seemed abandoned, hollowed out by a silence that made Valeirys' spine tingle.

A draft passed through the dark alley they had turned onto, causing his nose to wrinkle at the overwhelming stench of dung that rose before him, and he grimaced.

"How long have you known Trajan Rheiavirn?" Malik asked, not stopping or glancing back at him.

"He's served my father for as long as I can remember, and he's been my mentor for years now," said Valeirys. "Why do you ask?"

Swerving left and moving past a pair of beggars huddled on the ground in front of them, the prince replied, "Just curious."

He cast a glance over his shoulder at Valeirys and then proceeded to lead them down another dark road when he went on, "He is quite the intense fellow… The two of you seemed more like good friends than a mentor and a student."

"He has been nothing but faithful to my father and my family. It's difficult not to appreciate that," said Valeirys.

He almost stumbled over a pile of garbage, following the prince, and nearly colliding with Malik, who had stopped at a crossing before a larger road and seemed to search for something. Valeirys wondered if he knew where he was going or if he was simply guessing which direction they were to turn next.

The streets had grown louder and far busier than the alleyways they had previously passed through.

Down along the wider road before them, Valeirys could see rows of taverns, inns, and ragged-looking shop houses. Dim light and noises rang out onto the crammed street through the run-down storefronts, partly broken windows and doors opening and closing at the revolving flood of patrons entering and exiting the various establishments.

"Indeed, he bears quite the noble reputation as one of the youngest commanders amongst the ranks of our military; he has quite the skill. You are truly fortunate to have one like him committed to you and your family. Such loyalty is rare," said Malik.

He didn't turn to look at Valeirys while he spoke, still preoccupied by his search for something or someone.

Valeirys followed his gaze, scanning the crowds ahead.

It wasn't long before he recognized a pair of familiar faces joined by four others he quickly identified as their fellow soldiers.

His gut twisted, and he remembered Trajan's warning to avoid any suspicion. Turning toward Malik, he was about to speak up when the prince grabbed his arm. "Come on," he said.

Pulling away, Valeirys spoke. "You said only Eris and Alcides were joining us. A group of eight foreigners wandering the streets is conspicuous."

Waving him off, the prince replied, "Oh, live a little, Valeirys! It's one night of fun. Besides, aren't we celebrating? Within days, Melquart will be in chains, and all because of you. Now, are you coming or not?"

Chapter 34

The clanking of beakers, laughter, and swearing hushed at the sound of the lute that broke through the commotion.

Like the rest of the tavern's patrons, Valeirys' attention briefly turned toward the entryway as a troubadour began his song and wandered around the stifling space.

Louder and louder, his voice rose as the guests resumed their talk and others joined the young elf in the recital of an ancient folklore tune.

The tavern smelled unpleasantly of musk and fish, and the air felt hot, almost suffocating.

While the rest of their group continued in their jokes and conversation rather heartily, indulging in the spiced ale they couldn't seem to get enough of, Valeirys scanned the masses of figures huddled around tables, crowding the bar, or openly indulging in the company of a maiden settled on their laps.

These were definitely simpler folk than he was used to back in Inaesa. Their villages had taverns, too, but the people's demeanor there seemed less primitive in comparison.

However great the realm's suffering was over the murdered elves and the growing violence throughout the kingdom, here, none of that seemed to matter. It was as if they had wandered into a different world for a moment.

Perhaps that was precisely why the streets and the taverns here were packed to the brim. Perhaps the people wanted nothing more than to forget; for that, Valeirys couldn't blame them.

A group of drunk patrons, hanging on to each other's arms, circled the bar, traipsing after the troubadour who made his rounds. They tripped over their own feet and laughed while they slurred the lyrics as best they could.

Valeirys stared after them for lack of anything better to do, failing to find interest in the conversations held by his comrades.

Inebriated, some men began to throw coins after the troubadour as if sowing seeds over the ground, breaking into boisterous laughter whenever the silver hit the troubadour's head.

Sipping the ale from his goblet, Valeirys watched the young artist adeptly evade their blows by leaping up onto one of the less crammed tables just as the crescendo of the song invited him to do so.

Along with the thud of the elf's boots landing on the table, Valeirys jerked and tore his attention to the waitress before them, who set down a platter of herring and several bowls of stew before their group.

She turned to leave when Alcides, seated opposite him and at the end of their table, snatched her hand and drew her close to whisper something into her ear.

Valeirys watched his comrade closely, clenching his fists at the brazen behavior.

The girl smiled and gave a nod before she disappeared once more. Alcides looked after her.

"What are you thinking?" Valeirys muttered through gritted teeth at him. "We're supposed to blend in, not attract unnecessary attention."

"Oh, give it a rest, Valeirys! Malik, help him to another. Maybe some more of that ale will shut him up!" Eris teased.

He chuckled, and the others joined just as Malik shoved a bowl of stew wordlessly in front of Valeirys and spoke. "Relax… Let him have some fun. It's not like he has enough brain power left after his indulgence to share our entire mission with the girl. He'll be passed out before he can mention a thing."

He smirked without a shred of concern and raised his beaker to his lips just as the waitress returned and let Alcides hoist her onto his lap. Two of the others whistled at the sight, grinning foolishly while the rest returned to their jokes and looked out over the tavern's crowded space.

It wasn't long before Alcides rose with the girl, letting her grab his hand and pull him toward the middle of the bar where others had gathered to dance to the troubadour's new song.

Valeirys' hands clutched the table, and he wanted to follow and drag Alcides outside to catch a breath of fresh air and come to his senses when he felt Malik's hand beat against his chest, pushing him back down onto his seat.

"Calm yourself," he said, "or you'll be the one giving us away."

Valeirys glanced at him, straining his jaw, and fixed him with a glare but then nodded silently and sat back down.

"This can't be good," he muttered again.

"He'll be fine," Malik replied.

But Valeirys knew it wasn't. Heeding Malik's warning, he let himself grow distracted by the rest of the happenings inside the tavern and forced the rest of the stew down his throat.

It wasn't until Alcides had long disappeared with the waitress before he began to search the tavern for the pair again.

Jabbing his elbow into the prince's side, Valeirys spoke. "Malik!"

"Ouch! What in all the realms is the matter with you?" the prince responded, rubbing his side.

"They're gone," said Valeirys, nodding his head toward the center of the tavern where the two had been dancing. "Alcides and the girl."

"So?" Malik asked, as if oblivious. "He'll be right back. Don't you worry… Or are you getting jealous?" he grinned, teasing him.

Valeirys' eyes narrowed. He fixed the prince with an annoyed look, pausing a moment before he rose, shoving his chair back and spoke. "I'm leaving, as should you."

Mouth open, and with a sigh and the rolling of his eyes, Malik slapped his hands on the table and pushed himself to his feet after Valeirys.

"Come on," he said to the rest of the group, "this one here can't do without his beauty sleep."

The other soldiers laughed but followed without grudging, and the seven of them made for the entrance, leaving behind a bag of coins for the drinks and the meal.

Pushing through the crowds, Valeirys continued to search for Alcides amongst the fray but without success. Finally reaching the doors, he shoved them open while the rest of the group stumbled after him, still engrossed in their talk and laughing at each other's drunken clumsiness.

Once outside, Valeirys scanned the dark street for any sign of his comrade or the girl.

Malik came up behind him, slapping him on the shoulder while hanging onto him, the effects of his indulgence clearly having gotten to him, and he said, "He knows the way to the inn. Let him be. With any luck, we'll have a good story to hear in the morning."

He laughed and tugged at Valeirys as if trying to get him to loosen up, but Valeirys could only flinch.

He began to run strategies through his mind of how best to search for and find Alcides when, to his relief, the entrance of the tavern slammed open loudly, and a drunken holler bellowed from behind him.

"Alcides!" the others called out cheerfully.

Valeirys turned just as the elf rejoined the group and caught his gaze with a glare.

"Uh oh," Alcides said and laughed, tripping forward and into the arms of his comrades while he giggled and added, "Fellows, I thought we left our annoying commanders behind. It seems Valeirys has some desperate need to lick their boots and make sure we stay in line."

The group exploded in laughter.

Valeirys' fists tightened, and he swallowed, not taking his eyes off the elf.

He forced himself to refrain from entertaining his banter and only muttered to Malik, "Come on, let's make sure they don't get lost."

The others still howled behind him, dragging their feet as they meandered through the sunken streets, following Valeirys, who offered Malik his shoulder to lean on whenever the need overcame the prince to steady himself.

The inn's entrance held nearly no light as, one by one, their group entered, each of them unavoidably encountering the grim stare of the keeper. No one dared speak above the sound of a whisper as they passed him by.

Guided by the faint light of a candle, Malik and Valeirys made their way toward the east wing of the humble establishment.

Reaching the narrow staircase that led up to the sleeping quarters they had been assigned to, their group came to a halt.

Valeirys and Malik waited, and then silently followed the others, who struggled up the stairs that creaked underneath their weight with every step.

Standing at the top of the staircase, and when they were outside the purview of anyone else, Valeirys spoke quietly to Malik. "Perhaps we should speak to one of the commanders about tonight's events. I wouldn't be so certain we weren't noticed."

"Are you out of your mind?" Malik whispered back at him, blinking and shaking his head. "You would place Alcides in a world of trouble and possible banishment from service and for what? The faintest possibility that he might have blabbed. Don't be such a snitch, Valeirys. Everything will be fine!"

Valeirys gritted his teeth. If this mission failed, they might lose their chance at capturing Melquart for good.

But besides making a fool of himself, he had no proof that Alcides had let anything about their intentions here in Lyrr slip. He would need something more convincing than a hunch to convince the leading commanders to advance the timeline of their undertaking.

So, despite the fact that he couldn't shake the strange feeling that something wasn't right, Valeirys nodded at Malik and said, "Let us hope for the best."

Grinning, Malik clasped a hand around his shoulder and replied, "Lighten up, Valeirys."

He started down the hallway when he suddenly hesitated and turned to face him again.

"I've been dying to ask," he began. "What was it like when you killed her? The Dragon's Kin. I imagine after all they've done to our own, it must have been... satisfying."

Valeirys felt his chest tighten, and his stomach dropped. He was thankful for the darkness that concealed at least parts of his face and his reaction to the prince's question. He hadn't told Malik the truth that he let her live. Perhaps her people had truly orchestrated the deaths of the young elves, but there was no evidence proving that she had been involved in the killings. He wasn't an executioner, and he couldn't kill her for something she may not have done. Besides, she could have ended Eyvindr's life right before his eyes when she had the chance. The fact that she hadn't made him think she wasn't a murderer.

Valeirys' eyes narrowed, and he swallowed before answering, "I think you've had a lot to drink. You should get some rest."

He watched the candle's light flicker across Malik's features, his expression holding an odd curiosity, before he smirked and headed onward toward his room.

Valeirys watched his form disappear in the shadows of the hall and then found his way to his own chamber.

Stepping inside, he blindly fumbled for the bed and dropped onto his back.

It was far from the comfort he was used to from his own home, but it didn't bother him. His mind whirled, but not from his concerns about Melquart's arrest and what had happened at the tavern earlier.

Instead, all he could see before him were the piercing blue eyes of the Dragon's Kin girl staring back at him from the gleaming blade of the Eskhàra sword.

A loud pounding at the door roused Valeirys from his sleep.

It had only been a few hours since he had drifted off.

He groaned, unwilling to get up, and remained lying on his back, pretending to ignore what he had just heard. However, after a momentary pause, the pounding resounded again, and this time, seemingly more aggressive than before.

Groaning, Valeirys rolled over onto his side and covered his ears, hoping the intruder would give up and leave.

Then he heard his name being shouted, followed by another forceful knock that rattled the wooden panels of the door.

Valeirys bolted upright and scrambled for his clothes just as the lock turned and clicked, and the door swung open.

Casting a quick glance at the entrance of his room while hastening to dress, he saw Trajan come in, armed and visibly irritated.

"Your explanation better be that you're a deep sleeper," said Trajan. "Grab your things and come with me. We must get you armed."

From the hallway behind him, Valeirys could hear footsteps pounding up and down the old paneled floor as a commotion arose.

"What happened?" he asked while hurrying to retrieve his boots.

"Somehow, the word got out to Melquart of our plans to arrest him. We have little time before he disappears again. Our best chance is to seize him now," said Trajan.

Valeirys felt his stomach twist awkwardly. *Alcides.*

Quickly lacing his boots, he didn't dare look up at Trajan for fear of him sensing he had known something was off.

Pulling the strings as tight as he could, he leaped upright and met the gaze of the commander, who then nodded and spoke. "Follow the commands closely, do not stray from the rest of the unit and most importantly, if things go awry, don't play the hero… You'll get yourself killed; understand?"

Valeirys nodded wordlessly and then lowered his eyes from his face.

He took a step forward, beginning to walk outside the room when Trajan stopped him once more with the words, "When this is over, we'll talk about what's been up with you lately and what happened last night."

Valeirys glanced up at him past his shoulder and swallowed, clenching his fists.

His jaw tightened briefly, and he answered, "Yes, sir."

"Good," said Trajan, "now let's go."

CHAPTER 35

Darkness blanketed the streets of Phera as Valeirys and Trajan found their way through the city to the Tempest.

The unit had already surrounded the tavern in five groups when they approached and joined their leading commander. He was crouched against the wall of a house and observed the tavern.

His glance briefly strayed to them, and he nodded in their direction as their steps slowed to a stop behind him.

No one moved, and a deathly silence encompassed the grounds before the seedy establishment, veiled in a thin layer of fog as Valeirys took in the sight before him.

The unit's soldiers were hidden in the shadowed alleys. Two squatted atop the roof of a shop, ducked behind its chimney that overlooked the square to

Valeirys' right. The rest had taken up position inside the remaining houses and stores that bordered the cobblestone square ahead.

There was no sight of Malik, and Valeirys wondered where he stood watching, waiting for events to unfold. A part of him hoped that the prince felt guilty for his rebuke of his concerns. There was no doubt in his mind that Alcides had let something slip. It had to be.

But they couldn't fail.

They couldn't let the Liberator, Alessander Melquart, escape. Not when they were so close to seizing him.

The crisp, damp air nipped at his skin. The scent of it was heavy with the stench of something rotten mixed with the smell of salt and seaweed that betrayed their proximity to the sea. Valeirys was certain he could taste it if he stretched out his tongue, and the thought alone brought a taste of bile to his mouth.

The soles of his feet burned, impatience exacerbating the tension in his limbs that had gone cold despite the heat burning in his chest.

Gritting his teeth, Valeirys steeled his attention once again on the sight ahead, his spine tingling from the unnatural quiet.

His gaze sharpened on the silhouettes of a horse and a cart stationed in front of the tavern and beside a large well.

"They're expecting us," he overheard the commander whisper to Trajan. "When we arrived, the cart was already here. They're trying to get Melquart out and could be hiding him amongst the freight. I've sent one of our soldiers back to alert the garrison for reinforcements. But I dare say we'll have to act before they arrive."

Valeirys' lips pursed. He narrowed his eyes as if trying to spy a hint of movement from the wagon when the squeal of a door traveled toward them. A hunched, hooded figure emerged out of the tavern. The stranger whistled a tune and proceeded to ensure that the tarp covering the cart was secured.

"That's him," said the commander, keeping his voice low. "Ganymedes, the traitor and keeper of this wretched establishment."

Valeirys glanced at the commander and noticed his nose wrinkle at the sight of the tavern owner.

Ganymedes had come full circle around the cart and began to pull himself up onto its seat when the commander spoke to Trajan and Valeirys. "Now. Come with me."

Stepping out of their cover, the three of them strode toward the taverner, Valeirys and Trajan following a stone's throw behind their unit's leader.

The ground felt slick beneath Valeirys' measured steps as if it had just rained.

"It's a bit late for a trip," the commander called out.

Ganymedes stopped and looked down at them. Valeirys glimpsed the right half of the taverner's face from beneath his hood.

His leathery skin bore a ghostly pallor, accentuating the dark pit of his right eye that glowered at them.

"My business is my own," the elf muttered under the sneer that disfigured his lips.

He reached for the reigns, feigning ignorance of the commander's authority, just as the unit's leader spoke. "Not tonight."

Valeirys then noticed the commander sweep the edge of his cloak back past the pommel of the sword that was strapped to his hip and that bore the king's sigil.

Ganymedes flinched. His lips curled to a snarl, but then he climbed down the cart begrudgingly and turned to face them.

The hairs of Valeirys' neck stood on end, and his skin crawled once the moon illuminated the other half of the elf's face and revealed a patch of scarred tissue where his left eye had once been.

The jagged line of a scar ran from the left corner of his lip along his cheek and up toward his left ear.

"My carrier has taken ill, so it has fallen upon me to make the delivery. The cargo has been weighed and taxed. I can present proof of it, if that's what you're out for?"

He thrust his hands up, underlining his annoyance.

The commander raised his chin and said, "Your cooperation is noted. Raise the tarp. I want to inspect the shipment first."

Ganymedes hesitated.

The air thickened between them, the stiffness of it palpable against Valeirys' skin and enough to stall his breath.

The tavern keeper cocked his head to the side, studying the commander before he asked, "Is that really necessary, my lord? I am but a humble subject looking to make ends meet."

A shudder coursed down Valeirys' spine at the sudden shift in the sound of the elf's voice. It was soft, as smooth as oil and unbefitting of his horrid appearance.

The commander stiffened, and his grip tightened around the pommel of his sword just as he replied, "I will not ask again, Ganymedes."

Ganymedes grimaced but then nodded and led the commander closer to the cart.

Valeirys' hand itched for the hilt of his sword, but he compelled himself not to move. His eyes widened, and he scrutinized every movement of the tavern keeper as he set to undoing the tarp.

The covering gave off a slapping noise as Ganymedes lifted it and tossed it over the edge of the cart, baring stacks of wooden crates, sacks of grain, and barrels loaded inside it.

But there was no sight of Melquart or his followers.

Ganymedes turned once again to face them, a condescending smile marring his features before he said, "Does that satisfy your curiosity?"

The commander glared at him and then raised his right arm to point out the closest barrel.

"Unseal the barrel. Now," he demanded.

Ganymedes growled, setting his teeth.

He did not move at first, as if to test the commander's patience. But then, finally, he nodded and made to follow the order.

Climbing up onto the bed of the cart, he retrieved a hammer and chisel and started loosening the rings at the barrel's head.

Valeirys' heart lurched at every second clink and clatter as the tavern keeper removed the rings.

Finally, the lid of the barrel creaked just as Ganymedes shook at the staves, removing the head and bared its inner contents.

There was a splashing noise just as the elf jumped down from the cart and indicated toward the opened barrel.

"The finest from the vineyards of Eihbir," Ganymedes muttered. "I planned to deliver it to the garrison upon my return. A show of gratitude for your unwavering service."

The last of his words were unmistakably meant as a mockery, laced with spite.

The commander peered inside the barrel before glancing back at him.

He nodded and then spoke. "Unload the cart. I want everything searched."

Ganymedes hissed, the lines deepening across his aged face and disfiguring the grueling scar that replaced his left eye.

"You expect me, one twice your age, to undo a day's work? All to satisfy your curiosity?" he spat.

At his remark, the commander clutched Ganymedes' collar and yanked him away from the cart before hauling him against the wall of the Tempest.

"It's a small price considering His Majesty is willing to forgo the investigation of your traitorous actions," he said. He raised his voice ever so slightly, his temper simmering beneath the surface of his unflinching expression.

"We know you've been aiding the Liberator. Granting him a place of hiding in this forsaken establishment of yours."

The taverner said nothing, but his body stiffened in the commander's grasp.

"Where is he? Where is Melquart?" the commander growled.

Ganymedes' hands clenched to fists at his sides just before the commander released him.

"I do not know what you speak of!" he spat back at him. "You can search my belongings. You can search the Tempest. But you shall find nothing. This wretched quest of yours shall fail."

He sidestepped and trudged toward the cart, adhering to the command. Then he reached for a crate, pulling it toward himself.

His dark cloak moved under the motion of his arms now hidden from view.

Valeirys heard the gruff loud rant of his voice as he called out at an unnecessary volume, "Long live the king. Long may he—"

The last word never left his lips.

Valeirys watched in horror as Ganymedes whirled at the commander, his movements unexpectedly agile. A flash of silver split the space above Ganymedes' head as the elf seized and yanked the commander forward.

He pulled him to himself and, having drawn forth a dagger from beneath his cloak, he drove the weapon into the commander's neck.

The commander sank to his knees. Blood surged and trickled from his mouth down his chin, and at last, he fell face forward.

A scream died in Valeirys' throat as the tavern door burst wide with a thunderous crack that split the midnight sky. A blur of shadows, two, three, then six figures clad in black leathers and commoners' garb stormed toward him and Trajan.

Valeirys' peripheral vision blurred, his throat tightened, and the rush of his own blood engulfed his ears. The muscles in his legs seized, but he forced himself to work against the rigidness in his limbs.

Valeirys barely caught a glimpse of Trajan severing Ganymedes' head from his body under the screech of a blade drawn forth from its sheath as he dove toward the first of the enemy's force that lunged for him.

A sharp hiss cut the space above him as a flight of arrows from the unit's soldiers stationed atop the roof killed two of Melquart's rebels that followed his attacker.

Valeirys' left hand freed the dagger at his hip, and he plunged it into the neck of the elf who fisted a knife in his right.

A hot splatter of blood coated his skin. The taste of metal spread over his lips, and the smell of copper filled his nose as he thrust the writhing body off him.

Valeirys recognized the black inky streaks that marked the rebel's face. The sight of the smeared lines yanked the attack on the banquet to the forefront of his mind. The horrid cries of the people from his memories melded with the blur of shouts and the clicking of boots that ricocheted off the cobblestone behind him while the rest of his unit charged out of their posts and toward the ambush of Melquart's forces.

Valeirys drew his sword just as the squeal of the mount hitched to the cart shot through the air, and the wagon lurched into motion.

But the next of Melquart's followers was already upon him.

Valeirys retreated and met the elf's blow, blocking the hit before his body. He could see the horse and cart barreling toward them from his right.

His pulse thundered. He clenched his teeth, and then he gave a shout, willing all his strength into his arms before he shoved against the bind of their weapons and propelled the rebel backward.

Valeirys leapt back in the nick of time, nearly losing his footing but evaded the frenzied creature. A grueling crack of bones rose in his ears along with the stifled scream as his enemy was pulled under the cart.

With his chest heaving, Valeirys straightened and secured his stance.

His arms burned, and blood and grime stuck to his face while he scoured the battle grounds and tried to grasp the rebels' numbers.

Jagged lines of silver streaked the overcast sky like lightning bolts.

The heavens trembled under the wake of morning, a storm brewing above the choked screams, shouts, and the clatter of steel that pierced his ears.

The fight unfurled as Melquart's follower took up arms against them. Valeirys caught sight of eight of his unit's soldiers including Trajan and fifteen rebels with still more of them spilling out onto the square from seemingly every direction.

Melquart's army was a mob of commoners. Honed axes, knives, pikes, and goedendags lodged in their hands. Only a few held battered swords.

Valeirys' unit was outnumbered. This was a trap.

Rather than run, the Liberator, Melquart, had lain in wait for them.

Valeirys grit his teeth, fury fueling the roar that left his lips as he sprinted toward a pair of rebels that had singled him out of the chaos of the fight and ran at him.

The first held an axe raised above his head, the other a shortsword.

Valeirys had almost reached them when something exploded to his right.

His body collided with stone as he was knocked to the ground by the blast, and his sword slipped from his hand.

For the length of a heartbeat, a blinding flash of light robbed him of sight. A red-hot blaze stole over him and provoked an agonizing scream from his lips.

His body felt as if it was on fire, and he rolled over sideways, grasping for his weapon that lay past his head. A piercing noise rang in his hears, and his skin vibrated under the numbness that set in from his fall.

His eyes watered and stung from the fumes as he glimpsed his surroundings. Bodies of the fallen lay scattered in the wake of the explosion. Valeirys caught sight of four rebels and two of his fellow soldiers. His throat constricted, and ice surged through his veins as he recognized one of the dead.

Alcides.

The soldier lay still, trapped under the wreckage of the shophouse that stood engulfed in flames.

A cry burst from Valeirys' mouth, fury flooding his chest.

Sword in hand, he clenched his teeth and compelled himself to stand under the searing pain that consumed his limbs.

He had barely made it onto his feet when someone plowed into him from behind. Something scraped over the backplate of his armor before he was knocked to the ground anew.

A crippling jolt of pain chased up and down his back, and he slammed onto his stomach. If not for his armor, Valeirys was certain the blow would have incapacitated him.

Valeirys lost control of his blade. He clutched for it, but his hand came up empty as the weapon spun and skidded across the stone beyond his reach.

Realizing he had seconds left, he rolled onto his back, raised his hands, and shouted a spell.

The magical shield took form and deflected the brunt force of his enemy's ax just in time.

Blinding veins of blueish-silver light darted along the shield's translucent surface, accumulating where the blade of the ax struck it.

He heard his attacker grunt and shout in between heaves of breath, but he did not relent and continued to bring his weapon down against him.

Valeirys felt every hit reverberate in his bones. Spasms darted up and down the lines of his jaw as he gritted his teeth and pitted all of his strength into the shield.

Time seemed to pass gruelingly slowly as Valeirys hauled himself into a sitting position and then worked himself up onto his knees. His arms were still extended and raised above his body, rigid as if turned to stone, and his muscles screamed from the strain that coiled them.

The elf's blows came more quickly now, almost desperate. But just as Valeirys knew that his enemy's strength was fading, so was his own.

Valeirys shut his eyes. He thought of Alcides lying dead amongst the wreckage, the commander who had been murdered at the hands of Ganymedes, and the dwindling chances of Trajan's and Malik's survival as well as that of every other soldier belonging to their unit.

Something he could not name sparked inside him. He felt it grow from a flame to a blaze that overtook his entire being. The force had a mind of its own. It drew on his pride, his fear, his hatred, and his will to survive, forbidding him to give up or weaken in the face of the enemy. And then it compelled him to move.

Something tore between his hands. The sensation sparked a wave of panic in him, and Valeirys' eyes snapped back open. He caught sight of a fraction of the sharp point of the ax that had broken through his shield, and he cursed.

He couldn't hold it much longer.

Valeirys' arms trembled.

He shifted his weight onto his left knee and then set his right foot before him. The unfamiliar strength stirring inside him spurred him onward despite the sense of fatigue that weighed him down, as powerful and as a deadly as a current ready to pull him under at any moment.

Valeirys waited for the elf to raise the ax above his shoulders before he collapsed the shield and leaped.

His left heel plummeted into his attacker's middle, knocking him off balance before Valeirys drew the bloodied dagger at his hip and lunged.

The blade sliced into the elf's chest as Valeirys threw himself onto him, and they crashed onto the ground.

The elf's grip loosened on his weapon, and finally, Valeirys wrenched it from his grasp before getting to his feet.

His enemy stilled.

Valeirys' entire frame shook and thrummed under the blend of exhilaration and horror that coursed through his blood while he stared down at his fallen opponent.

Then he yanked his dagger from out of the elf's body, sheathed it, and rid himself of the ax to retrieve his sword.

His hand wound around its familiar hilt when he suddenly froze as a violent shriek and a movement in his periphery caught his attention.

His gaze snapped toward the well where he noticed a cloaked figure, a rebel, bury a knife into the side of one of his unit's soldiers and toss the limp body over its edge.

Valeirys shouted, and the rebel looked up, a malicious smile spreading over his face from beneath his hood.

Valeirys' blood ran cold as a pair of silver eyes gleamed back at him, and he recognized the elf as no one other than Melquart himself.

Heat surged through his legs as he prepared to bound toward him when, all at once, the blare of a horn sounded, paired with the rumble of hooves beating the ground. Valeirys' focus snapped to his left and he caught sight of a platoon charging toward the square, the soldiers bearing the sigil of Lord Tarquinius embossed upon their chests.

A choir of shouts rang through the air, as the rebels began to scatter at the sight of the reinforcements, the tides suddenly turned.

Valeirys' gaze darted back to Melquart, who smirked, spun on his heels, and fled.

There was no time to waste, no time to think. Valeirys' choice had been made.

He could not let Melquart escape.

Valeirys sheathed his sword, and with the world around him forgotten, he ran.

CHAPTER 36

The chase continued as Melquart deserted the scene of the fight, running straight for the center of the city. Valeirys followed him while they raced past houses and shops, down the tight winding streets, reaping angry shouts and insults from those they sped by.

Whenever he could, Melquart would try to grab hold of objects such as small wagons and baskets from the local merchants and tip them over, hoping to slow down Valeirys, who was gradually closing in on him.

The loud clicking of their footsteps echoed along the cobblestones as Valeirys pursued him through the seemingly endless maze of alleys.

With every turn, the passages seemed to grow darker and narrower.

Just when Valeirys was prepared to leap forward and grab hold of him, Melquart quickly took a sharp right and then another before he disappeared.

Valeirys quickly doubled back and sprinted down the street Melquart had turned onto, only to haul to a stop at the end of a road behind a line of houses.

Before him lay a dock surrounded by a group of fishing boats.

As Valeirys looked left and right, there was no sign of Melquart. In fact, the place was utterly still, void of any sounds but the peaceful sloshing of the water that struck the piles of the dock.

Minutes passed with no indication of where Melquart could have run off to or where he could be hiding.

Valeirys began to quietly pass along the side of the house beside him, Trajan's words playing through his mind over and over again.

If things go awry, don't play the hero... You'll get yourself killed.

It was a warning he chose to ignore; an order he knew he couldn't possibly heed.

It was as if the earth had swallowed Melquart whole.

But Valeirys wasn't about to give up. How could he?

Melquart's wicked smile loomed before his mind's eye, as detailed and clear as if he were standing before the elf's portrait.

His nails dug into his palms with a jolt at the reminder, stinging his calloused skin and sharpening his senses.

The faintest echo of a creak rose from somewhere behind him, disappearing as quickly as it came.

Valeirys' feet froze, his breath stalled, and then someone crashed onto him from above.

Strong arms wrapped around his neck, and like a noose, his attacker's grip squeezed tighter and tighter as Valeirys struggled for air.

The sight of the alley before him blurred as dark blots obscured his vision. Then the stranger suddenly loosened his grip, holding only one arm pressed up against Valeirys' throat.

Valeirys could only assume that he was reaching for a weapon, so he launched himself forward, dragging both of them onto the ground.

Pain thundered through his skull and his limbs once he struck the stone beneath him, and he thought he had heard cracks echo along his spine.

His ears blared with a shrill sound, and a numbness prickled his skin as he released a gasp and rolled over onto his stomach.

With his fingers sprawled like claws, Valeirys gripped at the cobblestones and forced himself to his feet when his head snapped sideways at the blow of a fist colliding with his temple.

Valeirys rolled sideways, and his vision failed him. His eyes were drawn wide open, but he saw only blackness. His surroundings tilted, vertigo pinning him onto his hands and knees.

Valeirys pinched his eyes shut and pressed his forehead against the cool surface of the cobblestones as he compelled himself to try to get to his feet.

Under the haze that obscured his senses, it seemed as if the ground vibrated beneath him under the thud of footsteps treading toward him.

He blinked, recognizing only a rough shape of lines merging to a silhouette of a large frame that loomed over him. He thought he heard a snicker escape Melquart's lips just before the elf drove the heel of his boot into his side.

Valeirys' lungs seized, and a searing pain shot up his throat as he gasped, heaving for air, but nothing came.

A strong hand gripped his collar, and he felt his body being dragged along the gangway of the dock.

Bile stirred in his stomach, his head swam, and a high-pitched noise rang in his ears.

If things go awry, don't play the hero…You'll get yourself killed.

Again, Trajan's words echoed from somewhere out of the depths of his mind. But Valeirys no longer recalled their meaning, his consciousness fading, his body numbing.

Then a weight was released from his hip, and he felt his back hit something hard.

Blinking, he watched as the world slowly came back into focus. His surroundings sharpened, and he recognized Melquart standing before him, Valeirys' own sword tucked beneath his chin. The cold sensation of the steel was an odd relief to the searing pain that throbbed at his temples and seized his limbs.

Sitting and perched against a pile at the end of the gangway, Valeirys could once again hear the sloshing against the dock beneath him.

His gaze traveled up the figure standing in front of him. He noticed a trickle of blood running down his right leg from his hip and side where the leather of his vest was torn and the pale fabric of his tunic was stained red.

Valeirys licked his dry lips and raised his voice between his shallow breaths. "You're injured."

Melquart shrugged his shoulders. "Not any worse than you."

But Valeirys could tell by the labored rise and fall of his chest that his strength was dwindling.

"At least, I'll live," the elf added, and a wry smile broke across his face.

Valeirys swallowed and lifted his chin, refusing to look away from Melquart.

"Tell me why you're doing this?" he asked. "Turning against your own people. Your king."

Laughter shook the elf's frame, and the sword inched a bit lower toward Valeirys' chest.

Melquart glowered at him and scoffed, "You think I'm in a confessing mood all because it no longer matters what you know? I'm about to end your life, boy. If at all, it is you who might want to confess."

"But it's precisely what you want," said Valeirys. "Regardless of whether I die, you want to prove that yours is an honorable cause. You fight for the people. You are their true voice, their defender… nothing like their craven king."

A bitter taste filled his mouth, but Valeirys noticed a flicker of movement in Melquart's face, his eyes sparking under his words.

"Only something truly gruesome," Valeirys went on, and shook his head, "an abhorrent injustice or perhaps a series of wrongs that needed to be righted could force someone like you to take to such measures."

He paused, watching a look of curiosity pass over Melquart's features. The elf seemed to study him, and Valeirys noticed beads of sweat coat his brow and run down the side of his face.

A warm rush of blood surged into Valeirys' limbs, and he felt the skin of his soles and palms tingle. Again, the unfamiliar force he had sensed in the heat of battle stirred to life inside him as a fire kindled his spirit and sharpened his mind.

Valeirys began to feel more like himself, forgetting the pain that had rendered him helpless under Melquart's clutches.

"Surely, the people will not forget your sacrifice," Valeirys spoke.

Melquart squinted. His brow furrowed as if he mulled over what Valeirys had said, and the sword grasped in his hands trembled ever so slightly.

Valeirys did not hesitate.

Jaw clenched and with every ounce of strength he could muster, he raised his forearms and batted the edge of the sword aside, rolling to the left before he drove his foot against Melquart's knee and made him buckle. The point of Valeirys' sword scraped over the gangway as Melquart tried to steady himself, but Valeirys had already sprung to his feet and kicked at him again, pitting the full weight of the hit into Melquart's injured side.

Melquart screamed and whirled to retaliate, but Valeirys was faster, landing a punch to his throat, He disarmed him, wrenching the sword from his grasp and thrust him onto the gangway.

Melquart coughed and sputtered.

Valeirys placed his right foot over his wounded side and nestled the edge of his blade in the crook of Melquart's neck.

A grin tugged at the corner of his lip under the heave of his breath, but he suppressed it.

A moment passed while he held Melquart's stare, and the muscles in his jaw bulged before he spoke. "Surrender and I'll make sure your cooperation is noted."

Melquart's tongue clicked, and smiling, he let his head loll against the gangway of the dock.

"You amuse me, boy… You're a good fighter; strong, brave, but perhaps not as smart as I thought. What makes you think I would do as you say?" he asked.

The elf's breath was labored, drawn deeper and heavier than before.

His wound was draining him, eating away at his strength.

Eyeing him from above, he noticed Melquart's complexion worsen, and Valeirys began to guess how much time he had left before the elf fainted before his eyes.

The taste of victory spilled over his tongue, but he ignored it.

Overconfidence could cost him. Even wounded, Melquart was not to be underestimated.

Valeirys' eyes narrowed, and he fixed the elf with a glare. His sword did not move a hair's width from Melquart's neck when he replied, "You will go with me. You will stand before our king, and you will answer to your crimes."

The peremptory tone of his voice seemed to have captured Melquart's attention as his grin vanished. He stared back at him, the uncanny silver of his eyes boring into Valeirys like a shard of ice.

"You care about honor. But you don't see the failure of your own attempt to practice it," said Melquart.

Another cough rasped from his throat before he spat, "You think you're doing an honorable thing, fighting for a just cause, for the good of your people... You're wrong."

Valeirys did not answer. Instead, he hesitated and continued to stare at the elf trapped under the tip of his blade.

The notion only seemed to further infuriate Melquart, and he growled, "Our people, the ones you so apparently pledge yourself to protect, are left to die. Captured, tortured, and murdered with no one to fight for them. You and the rest of Erysméa's soldiers deceive yourselves, believing that you are good; that you fight for the weak and the vulnerable..." He paused and scoffed. "You're all liars and cowards, and your king is no better."

Then he smirked and added, "But I'm simply repeating your words."

"You would be wise to watch your tongue," Valeirys warned, cutting him off.

His nose wrinkled under the surge of his anger that rose within.

Ignoring him, Melquart laughed and answered, "You can drag me before your king, you and the rest of your corrupt army, but I have done nothing wrong... I have fought, and I will keep fighting for the good of my people."

He stopped and then leaned forward, propping himself up onto his elbows so that his neck pressed against Valeirys' sword and cut the skin of his throat beneath his chin.

Valeirys watched a bead of the elf's blood run down toward the edge of his collar where it bled into the neck of his cloak.

"You could kill me right here, right now." Melquart's voice rose again.

It was soft and calm, coaxing even.

Valeirys swallowed.

A part of him wanted to drive his sword through Melquart's neck and end the misery his treason had caused. After all, he had him. There was no way for him to escape.

"You would return home a hero… the boy who defeated his king's enemy," Melquart added and chuckled. "Now, wouldn't that be something?"

Valeirys bit down on his lip and spoke firmly. "Get up."

When he didn't move, he dug his right heel into Melquart's wound, and a choked shriek pierced the air. Melquart panted, sweat now pouring from his brow, and he glared at Valeirys before he forced himself up onto his feet.

All the while Valeirys' blade never lost contact with the elf's frame. When Melquart stood, Valeirys grabbed him by the collar and spun him in the opposite direction.

A whisper fled his lips, and the incantation took effect, drawing Melquart's arms behind his back and binding his wrists.

The elf winced but then grunted and forced out a laugh.

"Ah, aren't we Sir Chivalry! You can't kill me, boy, can you? Not only does the realm's poison run deep within your veins, you're also weak."

Despite his mockery, Valeirys heard a hiss sweep past Melquart's lips.

Lowering his sword to the elf's ribs and bending forward, Valeirys spoke at last. "The only poison I must fear are the words coming from your mouth. Save your breath for your trial. Now move."

The streets were much calmer when Valeirys traveled through them on his way back to the Tempest where the battle had taken place.

Most of Phera's citizens seemed to have retreated indoors, and only a few passed him by while none even dared look at him as he led Melquart onward and bound before him.

The elf didn't speak a word as they walked, staring at the ground and occasionally meeting the glances of the people, nodding as if he meant to assure them that all would be well.

As if he was their hero.

Valeirys pressed his lips to a hard line and did his best to ignore Melquart and the manner of those they passed by.

As he neared the place where his unit had fought against the rebels, there were no more sounds of a fight to be heard. Instead, he saw thin clouds of smoke beginning to rise into the sky.

A lump formed in his throat once he came to a stop, and his eyes froze on the burning pyres stacked with the fallen.

Soldiers of the platoon that had come to their aid were spread out over the square, some standing in groups close to the pyres while others tended to the wounded.

Valeirys' whole body stiffened, his mind dragged back to the scenes of the battle.

Someone called out his name as several soldiers came rushing toward him, recognizing Melquart.

Valeirys didn't bother to explain or look at them as they approached and took Melquart from him. He didn't hear a word they said until he felt a comforting hand come to rest on his shoulder.

Finally, he tore his gaze from the pyres and turned around.

Trajan stood at his side. His face was scratched and bloodied, but otherwise he appeared unharmed.

"Looks like you decided to play the hero after all," he said.

Valeirys only nodded.

Then, turning and skimming the battlefield once again, he asked dryly, "How many did we lose?"

Trajan eyed him thoughtfully and then answered, "More than we should have. But you mustn't concern yourself with that now."

Valeirys swallowed, not knowing what to say. He began to lower his gaze when he noticed Trajan start to speak but then immediately fall silent again.

When nothing more followed and he sensed something strange, he asked, "There's something else, isn't there?"

Trajan's lips formed a hard line, and he drew a deep breath.

Then he nodded and replied, "Having gathered our forces, the surviving members of our unit and counted the dead and the wounded…" The commander paused suddenly as if contemplating whether he could confide in him.

Without warning, Valeirys' stomach lurched, and he blurted, "What is it?"

He grew more anxious as the commander hesitated to continue.

Finally, Trajan stepped closer, as if intending to prevent anyone else from overhearing them.

Meeting Valeirys' gaze, he spoke. "Some of our soldiers are missing without a trace. We don't understand why or how they disappeared, but they're gone—and so is Malik."

Chapter 37

Aleirya awoke to the pattering of raindrops and the faint squealing of rats scurrying over the ground across from her makeshift bed. Light broke through the arrow slit of the quiet tower, falling over her in a sheet of pale gray.

Lying on her side, she imagined listening to the crackling sound of a fire in a hearth while she pulled the rough blanket tighter around her body and shut her eyes, longing for the familiar comfort.

Aleirya had lost all sense of time, uncertain how long she had been here in this tower in one of the palace's ancient abandoned wings.

With the help of her handmaiden, Izidora had kept Aleirya's presence a secret and created a small space for her to hide until she had figured out a plan.

Sighing, Aleirya dragged herself upward into a sitting position.

Hugging her legs, she rested her chin on her knees for a moment and listened to the interplay between the rain beating against the tower's wall and the squeaking and scratching noises coming from the only four-legged company she had.

A small voice spoke up inside her.

Somehow everything would work itself out, wouldn't it?

Staring at her bare feet tucked under the covers, she wiggled her toes against the fabric; a weak smile formed along her lips at the odd comfort it brought her.

The sudden creaking sound of the tower door's hinges caused her head to perk up as someone shoved it open.

Izidora peered past its old wooden panels and smiled, stepping inside.

She was carrying a small tray of food with her, making Aleirya's stomach grumble at the sight of it.

She hadn't even noticed how hungry she was until she had taken in the wonderful scent of freshly baked bread and cheese Izidora had brought her.

Aleirya drew the covers aside and rose from her bed, meeting Izidora by a set of worn stools and a barrel they used as a table.

"I thought you might be hungry," said Izidora, placing the tray down before her.

Nodding a thanks, Aleirya settled down on the stool and eagerly took a bite of the fresh bread that still held a bit of warmth.

Gathering some of the fruit and cheese in her hand, and after swallowing the first few bites, she asked, "Is there any news?"

Drawing her heels up onto the top of the stool and hugging her legs, Izidora looked at her and replied, "Still, no one knows where you are. With your arrest having been ordered two weeks ago after failing to attend the hearing, Lord Acristus is furious that his men haven't found you yet."

Aleirya couldn't help but smirk at the idea.

Izidora caught her grin and said, "It's not funny."

Aleirya's smile stole away, and she answered, "I know… Believe me, I do."

Izidora eyed her for a moment as if to decide whether she believed she was being sincere and then added, "Kalithea tried to plead for you. She spoke to my father and begged him to let this go, but it didn't work. He won't dare upset the council now that he needs their support and advice. They are still contemplating whether to strike against the elves, and Kalithea says he's been questioning the Metatari's advice. He's even taken it upon himself to search for the vanished groundskeeper."

"They still haven't found him?" Aleirya asked, taking the last bite of the meal Izidora had brought her.

Izidora shook her head and replied, "No. But my father believes the groundskeeper is the key to unveiling this enemy."

When she had finished speaking, it grew quiet between them.

Outside, the rain came down in showers.

Pondering what had been spoken, Aleirya looked over her shoulder at the arrow slit behind her and inhaled deeply as the incomparable scent of the storm filled her nose.

A cool draft passed through the tower's space and brushed past her face before she returned her attention back to Izidora who eyed her warily.

"What is it?" Aleirya asked.

"I'm scared, scared of what Lord Acristus will do if he finds you," said Izidora.

Aleirya wanted to nod. Even though she wouldn't admit it, she was too.

Shaking her head, she answered, "You don't have to be afraid."

"There are whispers he plans to tie you to the shelter fires and the attacks on Tarragon. One of his guards was overheard bragging about how he plans to convince the council of his theory that the murder of Lord Varlam was a part of this plot by the enemy. He plans to portray you as an accomplice in a conspiracy against the kingdom; a rebel who killed the only warlord ready to strike at the elves and who even bravely led his men into the Dhaharran Forest to seek out the enemy, but tragically failed. He's even started rumors that perhaps you know more than they assume and that you might even know where the groundskeeper fled to."

Staring down at her feet, she sucked in a breath and went on, "If he succeeds, he'll paint you as a traitor and then who knows what they will do to you."

She looked up at Aleirya with tears in her eyes.

Pushing herself onto her feet, Aleirya approached and threw her arms around Izidora.

Hugging her, she shut her eyes and willed herself not to let her own doubts or fears of what could happen get the better of her.

She had to be strong.

The thought made her think of Takhéa, and her heart ached. She hadn't seen her dragon in so long, having sent her away to hide as well.

Izidora gasped, sobbing as she held onto her.

Aleirya hugged her a while longer before slowly releasing her and meeting her eyes.

"It'll be alright," she said and nodded.

She waited until Izidora calmed and nodded back at her silently as if she had convinced her.

Looking into her friend's eyes, Aleirya went on, "However, I think I should leave."

"What? No! Where would you even go?" Izidora asked, alarmed. "You can't!"

A new set of tears welled up in her eyes, and she breathed in deeply, trying to force them away. "I mean, what is your plan?"

Aleirya hesitated briefly but then answered, "I need to leave Tarragon. At least until this all calms down a bit or you and Kalithea can somehow clear my name."

"B-b-but we can't..." she said and gasped. "That could mean you'd have to stay away until the war is over?"

Aleirya lowered her gaze to the floor and nodded. "I know. But if I stay, they will find me and then who knows how we could... if we could stop them."

Aleirya could tell by her expression that Izidora was trying her best to remain calm, but she struggled.

Shutting her eyes, she inhaled deeply again and then opened them.

"Okay," she said.

"Okay? You never say 'okay,'" Aleirya teased, provoking her to smile.

Izidora let out a laugh and then answered, "Not the time for jokes, Aleirya."

Her eyes glistened, and Aleirya noticed that a bit of color had returned to her face.

"What can I do to help?" Izidora asked.

Despite everything, Aleirya felt a grin coming on, and she answered, "Do you still talk to that young soldier from your father's guard? Cullen?"

"Yes, he's the one who told me about Lord Acristus' schemes," said Izidora. "What about him?"

Narrowing her eyes, Aleirya went on, "I need him to retrieve something for me before I go."

The plan was for them to meet again an hour before sunrise.

Aleirya's heart pounded in her chest as she paced through the room. Her breath came in quick shallow puffs while she watched the door tirelessly, trying not to let her mind run wild with fear.

Something was wrong.

Aleirya clutched her elbows, hugging her ribs even harder.

It was already past noon, and still Izidora hadn't shown up.

Perhaps Lord Acristus had discovered that she had been helping her. Maybe he was questioning her right now…

All Aleirya knew was that she had to come up with another plan—just in case.

The floor scratched beneath the soles of her boots as she continued to walk up and down the tower's space.

She tried to picture the palace's exact outline, constructing a visual map inside her head as she carried on.

If no one came for her, perhaps it would be best if she waited until nightfall to attempt her escape.

Then she stopped.

But what if that was too late? What if they found her before she could leave?

She couldn't wait for that to happen; she had to at least make it out of the palace before Lord Acristus came looking for her here.

Aleirya expelled a sigh.

If Izidora had been caught, wasn't everything lost?

Rubbing her hands over her face, she shook her head. She couldn't lose hope now. Part of winning any fight or battle was keeping a strong mind.

If she let her doubts rule her, she didn't stand a chance.

Even though it seemed impossible, she would beat the odds; she always had.

Footsteps...

Aleirya froze. Had she only imagined it?

Her body went rigid, and she held her breath, listening carefully.

Minutes went by in a torturous manner while her eyes locked on the handle of the tower's door, and she waited for someone to draw it open at any moment.

Aleirya heard the sound of her own pulse beating in her ears as her chest tightened, and her lungs beckoned for a fresh intake of breath.

The seconds dragged on; when nothing happened and she couldn't stand it any longer, she heaved a breath.

She began to move again until something made her stop in her tracks.

There was someone out there. She had heard something.

Or was she losing her mind?

Her gaze froze on the door once again. This time, she was certain.

A light tapping sound slithered through the cracks of the door.

Aleirya's heart felt as if it might jump out of her chest, but she willed herself not to panic.

Clenching her fists, she prepared herself to fight whatever came through that entrance and ground her teeth just as the door opened.

Aleirya's knees buckled, and she almost sank to the floor when Izidora slipped inside and carefully shut the door behind her.

Relief came over her in cool waves, and she let out a sigh.

"Are you alright?" Izidora asked, hurrying to her side.

Two swords hung across her back, and she rushed to throw her arms around Aleirya.

"I'm so sorry! I couldn't make it to you any sooner. Father positioned a new pair of guards in front of my rooms. I couldn't risk trusting that they would keep silent and had to wait for them to rotate their watch. I left as soon as I could," she said.

Aleirya expelled another deep breath and released her.

"I'm glad you're alright. I was afraid Lord Acristus might have figured out that you were hiding me and took you in for questioning," Aleirya replied.

She held onto Izidora's arms and eyed her for a moment before a grin swept across her lips, and she went on, "I see you and Cullen were able to retrieve my swords?"

Izidora nodded, returning her smile. "Yes. It wasn't easy, but we managed. Lord Acristus made sure they were well guarded after he had had them seized."

"How did you do it?" Aleirya asked, unable to help herself.

Averting her gaze, Izidora blushed and replied, "That's a story for another time."

Both Aleirya and Izidora laughed, and for a second, it felt as if nothing of the past weeks had happened.

"And... the other thing?" Aleirya asked, breaking the silence that had followed their laughter.

Izidora smiled and nodded.

Reaching inside a hidden pocket in the skirt of her dress, she pulled out the familiarly shaped object wrapped in brown leather and handed it to her.

Aleirya felt a spark of hope return to her once her hands folded around her grandfather's chakram. Pulling it closer to herself, she beheld it, resisting the urge to hug it to her chest.

Her grandfather's chakram... The only heirloom she had. At last, it was hers again.

The royal council had taken everything from her. But finally, as she held her grandfather's weapon in her grasp, though to anyone else it might have seemed meaningless, to her it felt like a small victory; a small piece of revenge.

Clutching it briefly, Aleirya sighed and then tucked it away in the pocket of her trousers just above her right knee.

"Thank you," she told Izidora.

Then Izidora removed the swords from her back and helped Aleirya strap them onto her own.

They didn't speak to each other for a while, as if both wanted to ignore the reality that this meant farewell.

Pretending to adjust the satchel at her side once more, trying to delay the moment, Aleirya slowly dragged her gaze upward to meet Izidora's.

Both nodded, agreeing silently that neither of them wanted to even so much as speak the word goodbye, and then Aleirya embraced her once more.

She could hear Izidora's breath catch as she suppressed a sob and bit down on her lip to prevent herself from joining her.

Finally releasing Izidora, Aleirya asked, "Were you able to speak with Nathanael? Will he... will he..."

"He will," said Izidora. "He'll meet you before you go. I told him where to find you."

Aleirya nodded.

There was so much more she felt she should say.

This shouldn't be goodbye, she told herself. It wasn't fair.

The muscles in her neck tightened, and she readied herself to speak once more. Her lips pursed, and she lifted her face.

The tower door suddenly burst open, crashing against the stone wall with a crack that made her ears hurt.

Aleirya ducked and squinted at the noise just as Izidora spun around in front of her to determine what had happened.

"Detain the princess, seize the rebel!" Lord Acristus' voice chased through the tower's chamber.

"No!" Izidora screamed.

Spreading her arms wide, she stood in front of Aleirya, guarding her like a shield, until one of the two soldiers standing beside Lord Acristus, who blocked the only escape from the tower, came toward them.

Izidora shouted and tried to ward him off, but he grabbed her and dragged her aside.

Izidora twisted around in his grasp to face Aleirya.

"No!" she yelled, tears rolling down her cheeks.

Aleirya's attention darted from Izidora to Lord Acristus who fixed her with a triumphant look.

The other guard had already moved toward her, and when he was close enough, Aleirya swung a fist at him.

The soldier stopped her and struck her in return.

Aleirya felt her head whip sideways as the burn chased across her cheek, and she stumbled backward, tasting her own blood in her mouth.

Forcing herself upright, she aimed to retaliate but was hit again.

Her head spun and her vision blurred as her back crashed against a wall.

Izidora's awful screams were muffled in the background.

Aleirya spat blood and dragged her gaze toward the guard, struggling to decipher his exact outline when he grabbed her by the collar.

With no time to think, she drove her right foot into his groin as hard as she could. He buckled and let go of her, and she saw her chance.

Swinging her left arm at him, she feigned a strike, and when he seized her hand, she buried her right fist in his temple.

The soldier staggered, and before he could stop himself, Aleirya stretched out both her arms toward his chest. Her open palms had almost reached his body when she felt a flow of energy leave her sending the guard sailing through the air.

He slammed into the opposite wall and immediately sank to the ground, unconscious.

Aleirya heaved a breath. She heard Izidora's warning shout, but it was too late.

Aleirya felt another set of strong hands fold around her, and then she was shoved back.

Cold seeped through her body as she struck the wall again.

Another hit to her side knocked the breath from her lungs, and she felt the bone of a rib crack beneath Lord Acristus' blow.

Her stomach convulsed, and she resisted the urge to vomit just as he seized her by the jaw and pinned her head back against the wall.

Forcing her to look into his face, she saw his lips twist, and the lines around his eyes deepened to a sneer.

Aleirya could feel his fingernails dig into her skin, sending knife-like jolts upward along the sides of her head and down her neck, following the course of her bone. She wanted to shriek with pain, but the cry stalled in her throat at the force of her will, and she made herself glare into the malicious glint of his dark gaze.

"I always knew there was something wrong about you," he said and gave a chuckle. "You've made it so easy to destroy you; I almost wished you'd tried harder."

Bringing his face closer to hers, he smirked and added, "It will be a pleasure to watch your head fall from your neck when you die at my command."

"You monster!" Izidora screamed.

Aleirya could hear Izidora struggle in the distance, but she did not look away from Lord Acristus.

Her mind continued to race and then slowly drift under the waves of doubt and the crushing reality that she had lost.

It was over.

Blood trickled down the side of her face, and she noticed the tension in her limbs give way. The sound of her own labored breath filled her ears, and fatigue began to overwhelm her.

Her eyes rolled backward as her consciousness started to fade.

"Aleirya!" someone cried. "Aleirya!" the voice screeched again.

Aleirya knew it by heart but failed to recognize whom it belonged to.

Then, all at once, an overwhelming force tore through her. Her whole body shook, and she gasped. Her eyes widened and stung from the brightness that flared around her before they froze once again on Lord Acristus.

"Back for more, it seems," he jested and snickered.

Then Aleirya heard Izidora yell, "Now, Aleirya!"

There was a thump as the guard who had held Izidora dropped to the ground, rendered unconscious by a wooden stool she held raised above her shoulders.

Lord Acristus glared in Izidora's direction, losing his focus on Aleirya long enough for her to yank herself free from his grasp and fold her hands around his neck.

She sensed the same incredible power she had used earlier to propel his guard off her demand its control over her, and for once, she didn't fight it.

With an unbelievable strength, Aleirya hauled Lord Acristus backward and onto the ground.

Still at his throat, the memory of what had happened with Zannia resurfaced in her mind. She thought of Zannia's cry and her scorched arms, and though the thought pained her, this time she willed the surging heat of her anger to take physical form.

The skin of her palms tickled, and she sensed the power rush through her and onto Lord Acristus. His face contorted, and he let out a deafening scream, his hands clawing at her wrists while he tried to make her stop.

Then he choked, and Aleirya let go.

A sizzling noise sounded, and the smell of burned flesh reached her nose when she leaped to her feet and sprinted toward the door.

Halting once, she cast a glance toward Izidora who shook her head and shouted, "Go!"

Nodding, Aleirya did not hesitate, and she ran.

Bursting out of the tower's door, she heard the echo of Lord Acristus' hoarse voice chase after her as he called, "Eskhàra!"

Chapter 38

Killian's bar had never looked the same to her after the night she had slain Lord Varlam.

The ghosts of that very evening haunted the tavern. The memories had soaked themselves into the stained floors and seeped into the old wooden walls, leaving behind their unmistakable scent, and all so that she may never be allowed to forget.

Aleirya could still see the incorporeal spirits of the drunken soldiers like white shadows dispersed throughout the room. Some hung in each other's arms, belting out tunes of ancient folklore, while others gathered closely together around the tables.

Their voices were raised to shouts as they shared their jokes and conversations, laughing, cheering, and raising their goblets.

She could still recall Lord Varlam climbing up onto the counter of the bar and lifting the large jugs of ale, trapped in each of his hands, high above his head as the crowds chanted his name louder and louder. She remembered the disgusting sight of his long sweaty hair that fell past his shoulders, the soaked beard framing his large smile, and the bright red flush of his cheeks.

One, two, three… Aleirya counted silently, watching the scene play out in front of her as Lord Varlam released the beakers.

Clank! A loud thump shook the table where she sat when someone approached and set a goblet of ale down before her.

"Drink something," he said, tossing a rag over his shoulder.

Aleirya looked up at Killian who rested his hands on the edge of the table and fixed his eyes on her.

"They won't find you here. You don't have to worry," he added.

Aleirya nodded, but even she knew it wasn't very convincing.

With a sigh, Killian let his head slump forward. Then, lifting his chin to look into her eyes, he went on, "The group behind me to the right, you see them?"

Aleirya nodded.

"They come here every other night, angry about everything, complaining about how kings shouldn't be kings, and the real power should belong to the people… a bunch of grumbling old men. They may use big words, but they wouldn't harm a fly. I doubt they've even paid enough attention to notice you here," he said.

He paused, holding her gaze before he lowered his again.

Subtly tilting his head left, backward, and then to the right, he went on, "The loners at the tables to my left, behind me, and to my right have been coming here for as long as I can remember."

Tilting left again, he spoke. "The smith," tilting right, "the baker," and then leaning backward, he added, "the butcher… The last two I have to make certain to keep apart at times. Life has been cruel to all of them. They come here to drown their sorrows and escape their demons with my ale, and by the time the sun rises, they've forgotten who they are… Even if they recognized you, they won't say a word about you."

Studying her, he grinned, trying to cheer her up. "And lastly… the booth across from yours, that's Hallam. He brings in different girls every night, hoping to win their affections. He claims they're respectable townswomen."

He shook his head and added, "They're only interested in the coin he can offer, and he's too much of a fool to notice. They're not concerned about what else goes on in this place, trust me."

Aleirya couldn't help herself, and a faint grin broke over her lips.

Killian had been more than kind to her, letting her hide here after she had fled the palace.

When soldiers had come looking for her, he had loyally covered for her, concealing her inside an empty barrel in his storage while they searched his place.

Neither of them had known it would work, but she had trusted him.

Once it was safe, he had let her out.

"Thank you," she mumbled quietly.

Killian nodded, his gaze lingering on her, but he remained silent, and for that, she was grateful.

Aleirya could not take it anymore. She could not hear another person tell her that all was going to be alright, and that, in time, all would go back to normal; life would be as it was before. Those empty phrases, they were all lies.

Nothing would ever be the same. Her life, her future, would never be what she had imagined it would become. The king and his council had made sure of that.

Aleirya clenched her jaw and swallowed the bitter aftertaste of the sip of ale she had just taken.

"Can I get you anything else?" he asked.

Aleirya shook her head and then took another big sip from her goblet. The cool ale surged down her throat while she tried to wash away the memory of the last several days and weeks.

Her dreams, her purpose, had all gone up in smoke.

Once she left Tarragon tonight, she didn't know what would happen or if she'd ever return home… if she'd ever see her friends or Thoran and Zannia again.

"Aleirya?" she heard Killian ask.

Aleirya clenched the stem of her goblet so tightly, she felt her wrists ache.

Shaking her head, she met his gaze and answered, "Thanks... for the drink, I mean."

"Sure," he answered and then hesitated with a curious expression on his face, as if he had expected her to say something else. "Wait here. I have something for you."

Furrows formed across her brow, and she looked after him in bewilderment once he turned around and walked away from the table.

Waiting for him to return, her eyes scanned the familiar space of the bar, grazing over the handful of guests Killian had described to her earlier and who had wandered inside the modest establishment that night.

The air was stale and far too warm. She felt as if she might suffocate underneath her cloak if she were to remain as she was for much longer. But she refused to lower or remove her hood, unwilling to give up the privacy or lose the morsel of anonymity she wanted to believe it gave her.

Finally, she saw Killian turn the corner around the bar and come toward her.

Reaching her table, he carefully set a small box down in front of her.

It was just large enough to fit inside the width of her palm. Without touching it, she asked, "You got me a gift?"

Awkwardly wagging his head from side to side, he replied, "I've had it for a while now and have been meaning to give it to you."

Aleirya skeptically eyed the small box on the table, studying the color of its wooden surface and the small clasp of its lock.

It looked like the sort of box that would hold something valuable, a personal treasure like a ring or a brooch passed down from mother to daughter or some sort of keepsake from a lost beloved one.

Shaking her head, Aleirya answered, "I can't accept this. Whatever it is, it must be special to you. I couldn't take it as my own—"

"Just open it," he interrupted her.

Hesitantly, Aleirya stared at him for a while before she looked back down at the small chest and reached for it.

Glancing once more at Killian, she fumbled at the lock and waited for the click of its opening sound. The lid snapped upward just a crack, and Aleirya studied it, wondering what it was she was about to discover inside.

Holding her breath, she flipped the top of the box open.

With a rather confused expression on her face, Aleirya looked down at the strange object. For a moment, she stared at its shape, trying to discern what it was.

Then, reaching inside, she took it out to inspect it more closely.

"A piece of metal?" she asked and turned once again to look at Killian.

Grinning, Killian shook his head and replied, "It's not just any piece of metal."

He paused, watching her inspect it, before he went on, "I found it outside the morning after what happened with Lord Varlam. At first, I didn't know what it was, but then I found one of the blood-smeared torch sconces broken and a part of its crown was missing," he added.

Aleirya froze, listening to him speak.

She didn't know what to say and continued to run her thumb over the metal fragment in her hand. Its pointed shape reminded her of an arrowhead.

"I don't know what happened during the fight or how the sconce came to break like that, but what I do know is that you survived; not only that, but you saved the princess's life. If it weren't for you, we would be mourning her death," said Killian.

Aleirya held his gaze, forcing herself not to reveal the struggle she felt within to remain calm.

"I thought maybe you should keep this with you. It will remind you that you did a brave thing that day, no matter what anyone says or thinks of you," he added.

When not one of them spoke again, Killian sighed and then gently tapped her shoulder.

"If there's anything else on your mind you'd like to talk about, you know where to find me," he said when she didn't respond.

Then he turned and started to leave.

"I don't know what I should do," Aleirya spoke up.

Stopping, Killian peered at her over his shoulder and then returned to her table.

Smiling weakly, he replied, "Well, for now you need to get yourself someplace safe where the soldiers won't find you."

"And then what?" said Aleirya. She glanced up at him and then, shrugging her shoulders, she went on, "I don't know how to fight this. Killian, I... I don't even really know who I am."

Her gaze dropped to her hands, and her brows narrowed when she spoke. "Sometimes I think that if I knew where I came from, if I knew more about my parents and their past, maybe I'd know how to fight this. Sometimes I think that would make me stronger…

"I don't know who I am supposed to be in a world where I don't know the ones who brought me into it; I can't help but think that there's something missing from the truth, something I ought to know."

Killian continued to look at her. His expression seemed full of empathy but equally full of concern.

"Maybe you don't know where you come from, who your parents were or what you are meant to do in this world… And I don't mean to pretend that I know you better than you know yourself, but I do know something about you. You are fierce. There is a fighting spirit within you that can beat all the odds that might be stacked against you," he said and smiled at her. "You must have gotten that strength from somewhere; or someone."

Swallowing hard, Aleirya just nodded at him, appreciative of his kind words.

All grew quiet again while she forced the lump downward that had formed inside her throat and thought about what he had told her and the gift he had given her.

"I'll be right over there if you need me. Alright?" he said, sensing she was all talked out for now.

Aleirya clutched tightly at the metal shard in her hand and replied, "Thank you, Killian."

He winked at her and then returned to the bar.

The metal had grown warm in the tight grasp of her hand, and when she was alone, she relaxed and let her fingers unfold.

Just then, the door of the tavern swung open, and a familiar figure walked inside.

Aleirya quickly tucked away Killian's gift.

She had just gotten up from where she sat when Nathanael approached her, and she draped her arms around his neck. Nathanael held her for a moment before letting go and sliding inside the booth across from her.

An awkward silence enveloped them at first while neither of them spoke.

"I'm sorry... for everything," was all she managed to say.

Shaking his head, Nathanael replied, "You don't have to apologize for anything."

Somehow, the way he spoke made her question whether he had really meant it.

Bending forward on his elbows, he stared down at the table and went on, "Izidora told me what happened. I know you're scared. I know you think you have a plan... but I don't think you should leave."

He looked up at her when he had finished speaking, and she felt her heart lurch when their eyes met.

Hesitating, she pursed her lips and then replied, "What do you mean? I—I don't have a choice."

"You do," he interrupted. He licked his lips and then went on, "We can find a place to hide you here. We'll figure out a way to clear your name. We can help you. Out there, you're all on your own."

Izidora clearly hadn't mentioned all that had happened, Aleirya thought, relieved.

If he had witnessed what she had done, what had happened back in that tower with Lord Acristus, he wouldn't be here. After all, who would want to be around her after having watched that happen, after having seen her like that?

Studying him, Aleirya hesitated.

Back at the tower, Lord Acristus had called her an Eskhàra.

The thought made her sick to her stomach.

It couldn't be true... It wasn't true.

Aleirya willed aside the memory of Lord Acristus' hoarse cry that still haunted her.

Looking at Nathanael, she shook her head and answered, "Nathanael, I can't. I'd be putting you and Iz in danger. If the council ever found out that you were helping me... I couldn't forgive myself. I—"

"I don't care," he said. He jerked as if he had wanted to grab her hand but didn't.

Her eyes dropped to his fingers, and she caught herself wondering what it would be like if he had. Warmth spread to her face, and she swallowed.

"What if something happened to you? What if you never come back?" he went on. Then he sank back against the booth and let out a sigh. "I don't…"

His gaze dropped to his lap, and he paused.

She watched him, noticing her pulse accelerate while she waited for him to speak again.

"I don't want you to go," he finally said and slowly looked back up at her.

Aleirya's mouth went dry, and something stirred in her stomach.

Their gazes locked for a moment, and then she dared to ask, "What do you mean?"

Nathanael expelled a breath. He straightened, and leaning toward her again, he answered, "It means that I want you to stay… here. With me."

He looked at her. Their hands lay close but didn't touch.

Aleirya felt warm all over, and her heart continued to pound.

Did he feel for her as she did for him? She wanted to say "Yes," she wanted to stay if that was truly what he wanted. But…

Her thoughts were suddenly interrupted, brought to a screeching halt, when she noticed one of the tavern's guests looking at her from a distance. She was certain he wasn't one of the guests Killian had mentioned earlier.

Or had he been sitting there all this time and she simply hadn't noticed?

The stranger continued to peer at her sideways from underneath the hood of his cloak, silently nursing his goblet.

A prickling sensation crawled upward along the ridges of her spine. After glaring back at him for a while longer, she simply forced herself to look away, ignoring him as if it were nothing.

Panic clutched at her.

What if he was one of Lord Acristus' men? What if they had found her, after all?

Trying to stay calm, she returned her attention back to Nathanael.

"Is everything alright?" he asked her.

Aleirya swallowed and then nodded her head. "Yes."

Taking in a breath, she added, "I want to stay, I—I want to…"

She stopped. Her eyes were on him, and she had absentmindedly reached for his hand.

Her cheeks flushed, and she felt a tingling sensation rush up her arms from where they touched.

For a moment, neither of them moved as they stared at each other. But then Aleirya quickly withdrew her hand, and shaking her head, she said, "But I can't. I have to go."

She slipped out of her booth and began to walk away when Nathanael stopped her, gently grabbing her arm.

Rising to his feet and stepping in front of her, he replied, "Wait."

Casting a quick, careful glance toward the stranger who had not moved and continued to sit at his table, seemingly oblivious to her departure, she looked back up at Nathanael.

Her chest tightened and hurt, and she felt the same tingling sensation from before spread all over her while his hand remained on her arm.

Lowering her gaze, she pressed her eyes shut and spoke. "I can't. I'm sorry." Then she pushed past him and made her way out of the bar.

Exiting the tavern, Aleirya gasped.

She wanted to wince or scream at the agony that this entire evening, these last weeks, had caused her. Doubling over, she pressed her hands against her stomach while she tried to push away the awful tugging she felt within. It was as if someone were wrenching something out of her.

Straightening, her mind raced back to Nathanael, and she fought the urge to run back inside and find him.

Shaking her head at only herself, she pulled at the edges of her hood and prepared to march off into the darkness.

Everything was falling apart. There was nothing she could do to stop it. Whatever had happened to her after that night, the fight with Lord Varlam, had destroyed her.

Taking the first few steps forward, she went on convincing herself that leaving was her only option.

THE RISE OF ISIGAR

It was a good thing she had forced herself to walk away from Nathanael. If Lord Acristus was right, if Nathanael found out who she really was, what she was… He couldn't save her; and he certainly could never love her.

Then she heard the tavern's door behind her swing open.

"Aleirya." Nathanael's voice rose in her ears.

Please, she thought and bit her lip. *I can't do this…*

Shutting her eyes, she heard him draw a breath.

He was about to say something when she whirled toward him and blurted, "Why didn't you tell me about Kara?"

"Kara?" he asked, clearly taken aback.

He sighed and then shook his head. "Aleirya, if you think that—"

"I thought we were friends!" she interrupted him. "I thought we told each other everything; good or bad. Do you know how much it hurt?" She stopped herself and tried to catch her breath.

This was stupid. How could she have been such a fool?

She shook her head and stirred, ready to spin around on her heels and leave when he spoke. "Aleirya, I didn't tell you about Kara, because there wasn't anything to tell."

She scoffed at that and replied, "Right."

"There wasn't—there isn't. Kara is and always was just a friend; at least for me. But you and me… we—"

"Are what?" she asked harshly.

"We're not friends, Aleirya!" Nathanael yelled, having raised his voice.

The words cut like a knife, and she shrank back, feeling as if something had shattered within her.

Raising his hands to his head, he stirred as well, and then he approached her so quickly her breath stalled.

He was so close that she thought she could hear his heart thundering inside his chest.

Aleirya froze, confused, and all at once uncertain of what was happening.

Holding her breath, she felt as if everything was coming undone within her. She no longer had any control of the storm that weathered inside, spinning a strange chaos of emotions. Hurt mixed with a bliss and a comfort she could not describe, and then there was a longing, an inexplicable, irrational desire for this moment to never end.

Aleirya froze under his spell. She could not move, and when her eyes met his, she could not look away.

They stood just inches apart, with only the sound of their shallow breaths between them.

His left hand cupped the side of her face, nestling his palm against the line of her jawbone.

Her eyes moved back and forth between his eyes and lips, and she noticed him gently draw her face closer to his just when his other hand found her waist and he pulled her in, closing the space between them.

Aleirya's mind spun. She could no longer form a clear thought while a warm and comforting haze overcame her.

She didn't want to move; she didn't want this to end.

Oddly, for once, nothing that had happened mattered. Aleirya even struggled to remember how she had gotten here and why she had told herself that she had to leave.

No more running. She heard her own voice ring through her mind.

Nathanael's nose brushed against hers. The warmth of his breath sweeping over her skin sent ripples of warmth down her spine, and her cheeks flushed.

The sensation was tantalizing, and she wanted to lean into it.

The lids of her eyes fluttered shut.

Was this real?

She wanted to know what he was thinking.

Did he feel the same? Was it just like this for him?

"Aleirya." She heard his voice.

Listening to him speak her name had never sounded better.

"Stay," he whispered. "Don't go, please…"

Suddenly, the spell around them broke. She felt the magic of the moment fade, swept away from underneath her, as the illusion of what she could never have vanished, and the reality of their world reared back into existence.

Although everything in her wanted to resist, Aleirya pulled away from him.

She could barely breathe, and she felt a cold immediately consume her the moment she withdrew from him.

Her eyes stung as she forced herself to look at him. Then, dragging her feet, she compelled herself to move and spoke. "I can't…"

Aleirya couldn't stand to watch him disappear before her eyes, but she couldn't wait for him to try to stop her again. So, whirling around, she ran.

Chapter 39

Aleirya kept on going, staggering forward through the darkness, letting her feet carry her blindly down one street after the other. She didn't slow down; she didn't stop.

Shadows of the figures who passed her as she ran looked like blots of paint through her blurred vision, and the cool wind bit at the skin of her dampened cheeks.

Aleirya forced herself to concentrate on moving forward, fighting every attempt of her mind to stray to what had happened with Nathanael.

An incomprehensible call rang out from somewhere behind her, and then all at once, she remembered him standing in front of her.

Her foot caught on the stone beneath her, and she tripped. Catching herself on the wall of a house, she slid into the shadow of its overhanging roof and let her back slam against the stone façade.

Drawing steady breaths, she allowed herself to rest for a moment and leaned her head back, shutting her eyes.

The nape of her neck tickled when she realized she had not once thought to look out for soldiers patrolling the streets while she had chased down them like a mad person. The odds weren't low that Lord Acristus still had men out searching for her, even at this hour.

Shaking herself, she regathered her senses.

She had to focus on getting out of here without being discovered. Distractions could cost her dearly.

Peering up and down the path before her, she made sure it was safe to move again and then stepped back onto the road.

Aleirya dodged any larger or busier streets, careful not to attract any attention.

Besides the few people that crossed ways with her, most of them being merchants putting up their stands at the end of a day's work, or farmers lugging their heavy carts before them as they returned from the fields, the roads she wandered were quiet.

The houses and the shops that lined the streets lay still. Aleirya could see dim lights spilling out from only a few of them onto the moonlit cobblestones.

Peering inside as she walked on by, she spied a seamstress bent forward in an uncomfortable-looking position over the hem of a dress the value of which alone surely trumped a year's worth of the poor woman's salary. In another, she glimpsed a carpenter laboring over a set of chairs, and in the one after that, she caught sight of a maid sweeping the floors before a hearth that gleamed from the embers of a dying fire.

The town appeared to have embraced the fall of night, and a hush swept through the roads that lay ahead along with the gentle wind.

The heels of her boots clicked against the ground, and the edge of her cloak whipped at her legs as she moved on at a brisk pace.

A sudden sense of alarm frightened her to a stop, and she cast a careful glance over her shoulder.

But nothing had changed.

No one seemed to have noticed her or cared to look in her direction.

Feeling ridiculous, Aleirya shook her head and continued her course.

Occasionally, she sensed the same disquieting sensation swell within her, crawling up her limbs and causing her chest to tighten. But she forced herself to ignore it.

Reaching a crossing, she turned onto a narrow street that led her toward the outskirts of the town and the fields where she knew Takhéa would be awaiting her.

She had just turned the corner of a house when someone seized her.

Quicker than in the blink of an eye, she felt the sharp edge of a dagger press up against her throat; her back crashed into the chest of another as the attacker yanked her off the road and dragged her into a nearby alley.

She could feel the stranger's breath against her ear, and the skin of her neck tingled at its warmth.

Aleirya tried to remain calm while her heart throbbed ferociously, and her mind spun into a panic.

For a moment, her vision blurred, and she heard a voice. "Faelyn, control yourself! She is not to be harmed."

Its depth gave away its male speaker, and Aleirya thought that something about it sounded familiar, but she couldn't place it.

Her gaze sharpened, adjusting to the darkness, and she felt her stomach lurch when she recognized the stranger from the bar standing across from her.

This time, she could see his face from underneath his hood, and her body shivered when she noticed his eyes.

Two bright rings of silver and green glared at her, and a sneer crept over his mouth as the corners of his lips twitched and curved upward.

Tousled strands of silver hair fell over his forehead and framed the sides of his face, glowing below the moon's light.

"Let her go, Faelyn," he said with a voice as slick as oil.

Immediately, his accomplice lowered the dagger from her neck and withdrew to join his side.

Silently cursing herself for not having her swords with her, Aleirya carefully turned her body and fumbled for the pocket on her trousers to retrieve the chakram. All the while, she kept her eyes on the two shapeshifters standing side by side.

"I wouldn't do that," said the Metatari.

Aleirya flinched involuntarily when he spoke. Had they met before?

"Faelyn can throw a dagger quicker than you can blink. If you don't want her to hurt you, I suggest you keep your hands where we can see them," he added, tilting his head tauntingly to the side with a smirk.

Aleirya glimpsed at the shorter Metatari at his side. Her auburn hair was pulled back into a tight braid that trailed down her body all the way down to the backs of her knees. Her eyes radiated in both violet and silver, and when she bared her teeth, Aleirya thought she had noticed a pair of fangs.

Shifting her gaze back toward the male shapeshifter, Aleirya spoke boldly. "What do you want from me?"

Somehow, she knew him, but she couldn't remember.

His eyes seemed to flash at her in amusement, and grinning, he approached her.

Standing uncomfortably close to her, he eyed her quietly for a while.

The Metatari was a head taller than she was, and his muscular torso suggested he could easily overpower her should she attempt to fight him.

"Go, find the dragon," he said, speaking to his accomplice.

No, Aleirya thought, panicking; and immediately, her arm twitched as she tried to raise it to punch him. But the Metatari was faster and had already seized both of her wrists, hardly moving his body.

His hands fastened around her, but his grip was not firm; instead, it felt almost gentle.

She felt a jolt as if her body recalled the sense of his grasp on her.

Aleirya looked up into his wild eyes, and instantly, she stopped resisting against his hold.

He seemed to eye her with an odd fascination and a pleasure, almost as if...

No, Aleirya wondered. Was he flirting with her?

The possibility made her stomach churn, and she drove the notion aside.

"You are quite the rebel," the shapeshifter said, grinning at her. "Tamar warned me you had spirit, but I wasn't expecting this."

His voice caused her skin to crawl, and she could feel her heart leap within her.

Gritting her teeth, Aleirya spoke. "You've messed with the wrong Dragon's Kin. I don't know this Tamar—"

"Sure you do," he interrupted her, and cocking his head to the side, he added, "The big scary guy with the gold and silver eyes… wings, too, when he shifts…"

Aleirya's brow furrowed at first, but then her eyes widened in understanding, and she watched the Metatari's grin deepen before he nodded and spoke. "Ah, see, I thought so."

Vexed by his nonchalant manner, Aleirya frowned, and staring back into his eyes with relentless ambition, she asked, "What do you—what does Tamar want from me?"

She paused, intending to give him a chance to answer; but then, driven by her concern for Takhéa, she spat out fiercely, "I swear to you, if you so much as raise a finger against my dragon, I will hunt you down to the ends of this world and feed your body to the dragons of the Unbound… and believe me, I am not afraid to crawl down into the darkest depths of the forsaken hole you crept out of."

Her answer seemed to achieve the exact opposite of what she had hoped.

The Metatari's smile grew even wider with delight while he continued to eye her.

Then, raising one of his hands to her chin, he lifted it slightly as if to gaze upon her face and replied with a smug expression, "I like you, dragon girl."

There it was.

Her eyes widened while the rest of her body went rigid.

He had called her that before… He was the shapeshifter from the cliffs.

The Metatari was about to say something else when he suddenly spun around and let go of her.

Aghast, Aleirya watched as he turned toward a familiar face, and his hands jerked upward before his body.

A scream stifled in her throat when she saw Nathanael standing at the end of the alley, swords raised and ready to attack.

But it was too late.

All of a sudden, the ground shook, and the winds howled and whistled around them as if they stood amidst a gale.

Gusts of the storm the Metatari had summoned from nothing scattered the dust from the ground into the air. Tiles of the roofs of the surrounding houses shook and creaked, and the shutters of the windows rattled and crashed against the stony façades of the homes that lined the alley.

Aleirya covered her ears with her hands and bent forward while her eyes searched for Nathanael.

A cold shock seized her when she noticed the winds were gathering in a circle around his throat like a noose tightening around his neck.

Aleirya screamed, her voice carrying above the raging torrent of the storm; and then it suddenly stopped.

Crumpling to her knees, Aleirya's head snapped upright, and her gaze darted toward Nathanael and past the shapeshifter who stood an arm's length away, looking back at her.

Nathanael lay bent over on all fours, heaving for air.

Jumping to her feet, Aleirya ran toward him when the Metatari called out behind her, "Leave him. He'll be alright as long as he stays put."

Aleirya stopped dead in her tracks, afraid to take another step, not knowing what the shapeshifter would do if she disobeyed him.

As if a sword had been thrust into her chest, Aleirya felt a ravenous ache cut through her, and a warmth flooded her torso as if she bled from within while she looked at Nathanael.

Her chest tightened, and it hurt to breathe when he met her gaze.

Staring back at him, she saw herself standing in front of Killian's bar, wrapped up in his embrace.

There was plenty she had wished to tell him, and yet not a word sounded between them now.

Nathanael shook his head and called out to her, "Aleirya, don't!"

Her eyes burned, and she swallowed, trying to subdue her desire to cry.

She wanted to run to him. She wanted to promise him she would stay if he asked, but her feet would not move.

Say something! she heard herself scream from within.

Nathanael continued to meet her gaze and opened his mouth to speak but then stopped himself.

Aleirya watched the look on his face change while he tried to drag himself onto his feet.

"Come now," she heard the Metatari say.

He must have come closer to her, for she felt the warmth of his body radiate onto hers from behind.

Wrapping his hand around her wrist, he tugged at her, beckoning her to follow. She saw Nathanael's eyes fall from her face to where the Metatari held onto her, and his jaw tightened.

A weakness settled in her knees, and breathless as she was, she did not resist the shapeshifter's touch as he pulled her away.

"Aleirya!" Nathanael's shout ricocheted down the alley.

Stumbling backward, her eyes still riveted on Nathanael, she let her feet guide her further into the depths of the darkness after the shapeshifter; and this time, there was no more holding back her tears.

Aleirya did not feel the ground beneath her as they went.

Her mind appeared as if trapped under a haze. Her heart ached from a devilish blend of anger, fear, and sorrow, and she no longer felt in control of her body.

She had no idea how much longer they wandered through the streets until she noticed the ground soften beneath her feet. Blinking, she found that they now stood amidst the fields that lay beyond the town they had passed through.

The shapeshifter let go of her and stood beside her just as a familiar rumbling arose from out of the blackness ahead.

When she looked up, she saw Takhéa's enormous head looming over them.

Her dragon's eyes glistened brighter than any starlit sky, and she could sense a rage boil in Takhéa's gut while the dragon lowered her head before the Metatari and tore open her mouth.

An earth-shattering roar blared from Takhéa's throat, and columns of black smoke poured forth from her nostrils.

Her growl caused the air to quiver around them while she stood proudly before the Metatari, staring down at the creature with obvious displeasure.

Aleirya crossed through the tall grass and joined her dragon's side.

Sensing a surge of strength and bravery replenishing her weary soul upon resting her hand on Takhéa's scales, she looked back at the Metatari and asked again, "What do you want from me?"

The Metatari's gaze slowly drifted from Takhéa to her, and he answered, "You are to come with me. Tamar sent me to retrieve you."

When she glared back at him but said nothing, he went on, "We could travel on foot, but I would prefer to ride dragonback."

He then eyed Takhéa, and an eerie thrill flared in his eyes.

Unsure if she even had a choice and oddly curious about the shapeshifter, she replied, "Fine."

Casting a glance behind her, she crossed through the field and headed toward a log that lay in the deep grass.

"Where's your friend?" She asked.

Crouching low, she then rolled the old trunk back a bit to reveal a hole she had dug. Inside lay the pair of sheathed swords she had hidden after her escape from the palace, and she pulled them out.

"You don't need to worry about her. She can find her own way," he answered.

Aleirya could feel the Metatari's eyes boring into her back while she strapped on her swords.

Returning to Takhéa's side, she fixed him with an equally penetrating stare.

The shapeshifter drew closer and brushed her shoulder with his own as he walked on past her and ran a hand over her dragon's scales.

Takhéa growled in return and swung her head toward him.

A familiar sly grin dressed the shapeshifter's lips while he looked at her and then back at Aleirya.

He was far too eager to climb up onto her dragon's back for her taste.

Aleirya stared at him, contemplating whether she should trust the words coming from his mouth.

How was she to know if Tamar had truly sent him or if this wasn't some cruel trick one of his bored men intended to play on her?

Lifting her chin, she approached him and closed the space between them. Standing toe to toe, she leaned forward, her cheek lightly touching his, and she spoke into his ear. "Watch your step; she bites."

Chapter 40

The prison of Mòr Rhíoghaìn was perhaps the darkest of places Trajan had ever been.

Surely, as a soldier, he had come by many unpleasant establishments, but none had been quite like this one.

Guided by the yellow light of the torch in his hand, he followed the assembly of lords and the royal guard ahead of him keeping a close pace with Uryiel.

It had been a little over two weeks since the unit had returned from Lyrr. The days following their arrival had been filled with meetings, interrogations, and the array of tasks that came with the close of a mission.

With no time to rest and recover from the journey and the battle, he was weary. The physical exertion and the repercussions of the past events clung to him like a sickness he couldn't shake.

A dampness settled over his skin. It grew colder, and the smell of mold wafting on the air increased as they descended further inside the tower that led them downward into the dungeon.

The torchlight in his right hand blazed ahead of him, almost blinding him, and Trajan squinted against the darkness that fell upon them like a heavy shroud, his feet slowing to a snail's pace as they neared the bottom of the staircase.

Coming to a stop, it seemed as if for a moment everyone held their breath, waiting for their eyes to adjust to the blackness.

Faint mournful howls echoed from somewhere in the depths of the unknown darkness before them joined by the sound of the moisture dripping from the ceilings as Trajan raised his torch higher to survey the space around them.

His eyes wandered along the walls, now slowly sharpening under the dim light of the flames, and he watched shadows come to life, playing across the stone surface.

Several archways opened up in front of them, each marking the entry into a dark corridor that led to a different part of the prison.

Even if one was seeing it for the first time and hadn't heard of the rumors and the history of this place, to Trajan, it was obvious that this was no ordinary dungeon.

It was said that not one passageway was like the other. Each had a unique course and was part of the complex design the crafters of the prison had so shrewdly devised.

Mòr Rhíoghain's prison was a labyrinth, making it impossible for any captive to flee without the help of someone who knew its outline.

He had been told once that those who had built the prison had created hidden traps amidst the maze-like halls to further ensure the failure of an attempted escape.

The guards were strictly ordered to blindfold any prisoner who was to be transported in and out of their cell. This was to make sure that none of them could tell with certainty in which part of the prison they were being held.

Additionally, any food or water offered to the prisoners was poisoned. They contained concoctions that would numb and confuse their senses, making it impossible to navigate with a clear mind or use magic to find a way out in the event they should somehow break out of the confinement of their cell.

"This way, Your Majesty," said the jailer, drawing Trajan's attention to the king who led the procession.

Orange light flickered across King Yevandrielle's features, intensifying the shadows that filled the hollows of his face. Certainly, even the most obtuse had noticed the king's transformation ever since the news of Prince Malik's disappearance had reached him.

Trajan had witnessed him change, even from a distance.

From one council meeting to the next, the subtle yet noticeable grief-begotten lines deepened around each corner of his face. The angles of his chin and cheekbones sharpened as one fruitless report followed the next; and his complexion seemed to pale more with each day his son was not found.

The crowd moved again as the prison warden led them into one of the northern passages.

Trajan followed, the scene before him changing, swallowed by the gloom of this forlorn place.

He could not rid himself of his concern for the king's worsening state.

The hardships of the past months had hardened as well as crippled him in a manner that seemed disingenuous to the king's character. Yes, in the eyes of many, he was a rather gentle-hearted ruler, but he was not fragile, not ill-tempered nor weak of spirit as he had recently presented himself.

The kingdom's peril had taken its toll on him. Trajan had heard the whispers and like many members of King Yevandrielle's council, he wondered how much longer the king could withstand the multiplying tragedies suffocating the realm.

Messengers had traveled the kingdom distributing search warrants for the missing prince and the young soldiers with the promise of an exorbitant amount of gold as reward for finding the lost and escorting them safely to the capital. Military reinforcements had been sent to every known border dividing Erysméa's regions with the command to guard, restrict crossing, and to thoroughly examine anyone who pleaded passage. Entire cities had been sealed shut and searched with not a stone left unturned, but to no avail.

The count of civilian deaths had tripled in the last days as the people resisted and revolted against the king's soldiers scouring one village after the other, tearing through various establishments and the homes of both the wealthy and the poor. The people's hatred toward him was growing by the day, and still, there was not the faintest indication of progress in sight. The kingdom remained in uproar, teetering on the brink of utter chaos.

The shrill clanking of the keys fastened to the jailer's belt tore Trajan out of his thoughts, the present reclaiming his focus.

The halls seemed to grow narrower and narrower the further they journeyed inside the prison, and the worsening foul odor brought a taste of bile to his mouth.

The passageways were arduous and with each bend, they became more convoluted than before. The cobblestones they trod upon were slick and uneven. Some of them had become loose, a few had been removed, leaving behind large holes that made it difficult to trek along the path ahead.

Mindful of his steps and keeping a careful eye on the ground, Trajan continued onward along with the rest of the crowd.

They came to another stop when they reached a crossing.

The jailer halted briefly and then took a left turn.

As Trajan looked up, he noticed some of the expressions on the other soldiers' faces.

Several of them seemed perturbed, and he wondered if they feared finding themselves lost somewhere amongst these halls, cursed to roam them for all eternity.

There was a sound of chains being dragged across a stone floor that grew louder just before the jailer led them down a right turn into another corridor where the first cells appeared.

The insides of the prison cells were pitch black, and although the enclosed spaces seemed to extend deep inside the rock, with no sight of an end, they were barely wide enough for an average-shaped body to pass through.

Flanked on both sides of the barred doors stood armed guards.

Not once did they so much as shift in their stance as the assembly walked on by.

Many of the prisoners had stepped forward out of the shadows, their hands clinging to the barred doors while they watched them. Their wrists and necks were strapped in chains as they stared out blankly into the hall.

Trajan hadn't intended to look. Yet, somehow, whether out of curiosity or pity, he found himself compelled to glance back at them.

As he eyed their desolate gazes, the weight of their despair clutched at his heart. It seemed that each set of iron bars did not merely separate the free from the condemned, but instead signified an impenetrable barrier between their two worlds.

His body couldn't help but shudder at the sight of the prisoners who wore the telling of their doomed fates like a mask over their faces.

They looked like ghosts. Their skin had turned ashen from the lack of sunlight with parts of it scarred and bruised. Their bodies looked frail and cachectic. This was most likely because of the self-imposed starvation they had inflicted upon themselves to not fall victim to the effects of the magic with which their food and drink was laced.

One of the prisoners caught his gaze, an old haggard-looking elf who suddenly threw himself against the bars of his cell, rattling them violently with his clenched fists and sputtering something incomprehensible.

A guard immediately responded by jabbing the dull end of his spear into his gut through the iron gate to silence him and forced him backward.

However, it only seemed to further upset the old elf who undoubtedly was no longer in control of his mind. He began to wail and scream over the jangling sound of his chains as he pressed his hands against his ears. Trajan quickly looked away just before the guard shouted at the crazed prisoner to fall silent and threatened a punishment should he not heed the order.

Their group continued down the hall as the shouts and cries grew quieter until they at last vanished somewhere in the distance behind them.

More cells lined the dismal halls left and right on their path, but no longer did Trajan allow his eyes to stray from the course ahead.

It wasn't long before they came to another stop, having finally reached Melquart's prison cell.

Unlike the others they had passed by, this one stood alone at the end of a long, secluded hall.

The entrance was a windowless metal door.

There was a silence while the jailer fumbled for the keys, and then the loud clicking sound of the locks being opened rang through the air.

Trajan stepped forward, joining the guard that surrounded the king, just as the heavy door was drawn open and secured for them to pass through.

The prison cell had more similarity with a pit than a chamber, and it seemed much darker than the others they had already seen.

Before them, a narrow set of steps descended into the depths of the cell where, somewhere in the darkness, Melquart lay shackled.

The scraping sound of gravel and dust being swept from the steps echoed as they crept down the stone staircase.

When they had reached the bottom of the pit, Trajan watched the king take a torch from the hand of the guard beside him and step forward, raising it as he went.

At last, the light fell on the prisoner who sat propped up in the far corner of the cell with his outstretched arms secured in chains against the wall.

The king stopped in front of him and waited until Melquart slowly raised his slumped head to look up at him.

His long dark hair fell over his face, and for a moment, the two of them only looked at each other without saying a word.

"If you have come to remind me that I am to die, then you have troubled yourself unnecessarily," said Melquart in a coarse voice.

A guard stepped forward to strike Melquart for his words, but the king stopped him, pressing his hand against the guard's chest.

"Most assuredly you do not need a reminder of the fate that awaits you; neither have I come to taunt you so cruelly... even if some might consider it justified given the gravity of your crimes," said the king.

A faint ringing sound echoed throughout the dark while Melquart shifted slightly in his chains.

"Then what is it you desire from me in my final hours?" he asked the king.

"I have come to offer you mercy, perhaps even lessen your sentence and spare your life, should you be willing to provide the answers I seek," the king answered.

"Mercy," Melquart scoffed, interrupting him.

It sounded like a whisper, and then he lowered his head, shaking it incredulously.

The king seemed to ignore his mockery, and after a moment's pause, he went on, "You had quite the force of loyal men at your disposal; a force large enough to fend off the arrest and perhaps carry out an ulterior mission."

He took another step toward him and then crouched down on his knees.

Upon the king's approach, the shackled elf slowly raised his head to meet his eyes.

Looking straight at Melquart, King Yevandrielle continued, "You are no fool; that much was clearly demonstrated in your trial. You knew that someday you would be brought before me and be forced to suffer the consequences for what you had done. You needed to ensure yourself leverage for when that day came, something that would convince me to spare your life."

He paused and then added, "Your reach was quite great. Just like us, you had spies bringing you bits and pieces of our plans to stop you. A web of conspirators I will most assuredly be spending a vast number of months uncovering long after you are gone."

The expression on Melquart's face was rigid and void of any emotion while he stared back at the king.

Not once did he move nor did he twitch. It was as if his face had turned to stone.

Then something changed in the king's tone of voice when he spoke again.

It sounded strangely calm and resigned, Trajan thought while he listened.

"Truth be told, Melquart, you were right; and I would be a liar to deny that you have succeeded."

The king tilted his head to the side as if to observe him from a different angle and went on, "You have something of immense value to me. Something so great, it is powerful enough to persuade me to let you live, regardless of whether you are deserving of such mercy."

Straightening, he waited for Melquart to react, to say something, anything.

The cold air seemed to freeze between them while all remained silent as Melquart refused to answer, and the pair stared at each other with disdain.

"You have the power to save yourself. All I ask for is the truth. All I want is an answer," said the king.

Again, not a word passed between them after he had spoken, and the stillness returned.

The king sighed audibly, and then, almost leisurely, he rose to his feet and paced back and forth as if to convey that his time and patience were endless.

But none of it seemed to provoke this prisoner enough to speak.

Trajan couldn't see the expression on the king's face, but he was sure it must have been just as callous as Melquart's.

Though outwardly, the king seemed calm, the tension in his voice gave away his angered mood when it rose again. "Somewhere, hidden away, your men hold innocent young lives, daughters, and sons of countless families captive, including my son, as you well know. You have the power to save them. You alone can return them to their homes, their parents. All you must do is tell me where we can find them."

Still, Melquart continued to say nothing. Instead, he just stared at the king, letting his request linger in the ears of those present without hope that it would be met by an answer.

Then, slowly, the motionless features of his face changed into a frown, and he replied in a low voice, "That is quite a theory you and your council have construed. While it flatters me that you think me so keen, I'm afraid I have yet again to disappoint you. I cannot give you the answers you seek."

There was a pause as the king halted before him.

Then, as if to calm his temper, he stepped away and turned his back toward Melquart.

Once more, Trajan heard the king repeat himself. "Where are the young soldiers? Where is my son? Where did you take them?"

Finally, Melquart himself seemed to lose his composure over the king's interrogation and replied bitterly, "I have nothing more to say to you than what I have already told you. I do not know of what you speak."

THE RISE OF ISIGAR

At his answer, the king spun around and shouted, "This is your last chance! Do not toy with me, Melquart! I will ask but once more, and I caution you to be wise, for your answer shall seal your fate. What have you done? Where are they?"

Glowering at the king, the elf answered through his gritted teeth, "I did not ask for your feigned mercy nor do I want your pity."

The king held his hands clenched angrily into fists at his sides, and finally releasing them, he spoke firmly. "Then at last you shall receive your due for the crimes you have committed and die as the traitor you are!"

With no further hesitation, he turned away from him and marched toward the steps to exit the cell, a horde of guards following him.

Watching the king turn away from him, Melquart thrust his body forward against the pull of the chains that held him confined as if to attack him, and shouted, "I did not harm your precious son!"

Eyeing him closely, Trajan thought he had noticed more than rage in Melquart's voice. There was something else.

Perhaps it was the slight quiver in his exclamation no one else seemed to have noticed that reminded him of the grief a suffering voice carried.

But what could have possibly driven him this far? What must he have suffered that it had seemed worth risking a fate such as this?

Melquart continued to shout and yank at his chains as the king and his guards disappeared, one by one, and only Trajan remained at the bottom of the pit.

Slowly, Melquart's shouting ceased. Trajan knew he ought to follow the rest of the soldiers, but something caused him to delay.

The rattling sound of Melquart's chains quieted, and having fallen silent at last, he dropped to his knees. His head hung low before his body like it had when they had first approached him in this dark cell. He didn't seem to care that Trajan was still there watching him.

Trajan turned and made for the stairs, but then stopped and paused. He looked back at Melquart once more, as if he had something to say to him, but found no words.

Confused as to why he had hesitated to leave the cell in the first place, Trajan forced himself to look away and started to climb the steps when he heard Melquart speak softly. "You must think me a monster."

The cell was silent as Trajan paused and stared back at him in surprise.

"After all that I've done, after all that has happened, surely, you see me as the wretched traitor they call me. But I am not who they say I am," he added.

Trajan waited a while for Melquart to continue, and when he didn't speak, he asked in return, "Then who are you?"

Melquart looked up at him. Shadows danced across his solemn face under the flickering light of the torch in Trajan's hand.

"I only did what I believed to be right," he answered.

Trajan exhaled audibly and turned away, shaking his head.

"I had a son," Melquart said suddenly.

Again, Trajan stopped in his tracks at his words.

Melquart's breathing seemed to speed up, and his voice shook.

"When I saw his body, I didn't recognize him... my own son. Can you imagine what that's like for a father?" he asked.

His voice rose higher as he posed the question, and then it broke. He inhaled sharply before going on, "Half of his form was scorched. He had been tortured... And as if that wasn't enough, those demons had carved the symbols of their witchcraft into his skin for whatever wretched purpose of their own," he went on furiously.

Trajan felt his skin prickle while he stood there frozen, listening to him.

Tears streamed down Melquart's face, and his body convulsed as he lamented the murder of his son.

Tossing his head backward, he drew a deep breath and tried to steady himself before he spoke again. "And then I had to watch one family, one father after the other, suffer the same horror, over and over again. And all the while, nothing was being done. Nothing! Nothing was changing. Instead of a rescue, instead of vengeance for the children that were taken from us, all we got were words... mere words that our king was doing his utmost to find the monsters that had done this."

He stopped to catch his breath for a moment and calm himself.

"The months went by without proof of his support. The dead multiplied and multiplied without sight of an end, without hope that help would ever come," said Melquart.

Once again, he looked up at Trajan and added, "Look at me and tell me now that I was wrong to fight back. Look at me and tell me I was wrong for giving the people a voice, for fighting for a leader that would protect us after all we had lost. Look me in the eye and tell me that any other father in my place wouldn't have done the same."

Then he yelled, "Look at me, and tell me you wouldn't have done the same if it had been your son!"

Swallowing hard, Trajan pondered his next words as a brief silence settled between them.

He couldn't help but see that Melquart had been broken, truly broken. All that had mattered to him had been stripped away.

Looking directly at him, Trajan answered, "Surely, what you have suffered I do not wish upon my worst enemy. But no matter how great the weight of our grievances, we are all given a choice. A choice whether to repay and return the evil that has been done to us in the same manner. I do not wish to judge you, but if you ask my opinion, it is this: The pain we suffer in this world does not justify the acts of vengeance we carry out upon one another."

He paused and then added carefully, "We are all subject to one king who is burdened with the responsibility to rule wisely for us. It is his task to protect his people, the very people who bestowed on him the crown as their ruler not because of his blood or their favor, but because of his actions proving his integrity. So then, as he has been called to rule, we shall let him rule and neither question nor set ourselves above his sovereignty."

Tears continued to stream down Melquart's face as he listened to Trajan.

Sobbing, he replied, "I did it for my son."

Then he shook his head and let it sink while he continued to cry.

Before Trajan turned to leave him, he spoke once more. "Regardless of what has happened, I promise you, justice will be done for the lives that were taken, including that of your son."

Melquart raised his head to look up at him when he had finished speaking.

For one last time, Trajan held his gaze as if to seal the promise he had just made to him before turning away and leaving Melquart behind in his final hours of darkness.

Chapter 41

"I dreamed," Valeirys whispered to no one other than himself. His eyelids fluttered. His gaze riveted on the ruffled sheets before him while he cleared his throat, and his voice steadied. "I dreamed of a darkness. Clash after clash broke over my head, screeches pierced my ears from the sides, as if I were caught—no—trapped in a cage, the bars humming around me upon every strike."

Valeirys' hands pressed against his temples, elbows digging into his knees, and he drew a deep breath before he muttered on, "I know my body is weary, my feet ache, but I cannot feel it... and suddenly, I'm surrounded by thousands, thousands of soldiers ready to slay me. I am alone, and at first, I think, defenseless against them until I move. My feet barely touch the ground, my armor shines underneath a bright red sun… I twist, I whirl, I run somewhere, but the world around me has blurred."

Valeirys squeezed his eyes shut and grimaced.

This is ridiculous, he thought and shook his head.

But speaking of his dreams aloud was the only way he could convince himself that that was precisely what they were—just dreams.

With a sigh, he opened his eyes anew, assuring himself once again that he was awake and continued, "I can hear cries of men falling to their deaths. I feel the ground shake, roars and shrieks tear through the sky above me so loudly I know the beasts are not far, but they do not scare me. Not a sword pierces my side, not a cut mars my cheek. My limbs are as steady and strong as two unbreakable pillars. I cannot fall…"

Pausing, he licked his lips.

"I smile and then the chaos vanishes. I fight a single warrior with only the sound of my even heartbeat drumming in my ears. We move opposite each other as if contending against our mirrored images. Each step, each slash of our blades the same—and then it stops. There is blood on my hands. I clutch the hilt of my sword, glowing gold and silver, a dragon's emerald eyes gleaming at me… The edge of it is bathed in crimson, but I do not know whose life I have taken or if it is my own that I have lost…"

Valeirys drew another breath and sat upright, releasing his shins and letting his hands sink to his sides.

His body was drenched, and he shivered as a breeze swept through the open window of his room.

His hands grabbed at the sheets beneath him, fingers clawing into the soft fabric as he reminded himself that it was over.

It was just a dream, another bad dream, he told himself when a knock sounded, and his gaze darted toward the entrance of his room.

A pale hand folded around the door as it was gently shoved open, and he saw Eyvindr poke his head inside.

Neither of them said a word at first.

Then Eyvindr gingerly stepped inside and neared his bed.

They had not spoken much since his return from Lyrr, and there seemed to be some sort of tension between the two of them despite Eyvindr having voiced his gratefulness over his return.

"Should I call for Mother?" Eyvindr asked, glancing up through the dark curls that hung before his eyes. "I can have the servants find her if you need anything."

Valeirys shook his head and loosed his grip on the sheets beneath him.

Eyvindr carefully sat down on the edge of his bed, and Valeirys scooted forward to sit beside him.

"I'm alright," he answered.

The silence returned as they sat awkwardly beside each other.

"Was it the dreams again?" Eyvindr suddenly asked.

His brother wasn't looking at him when he posed the question, studying the floor in front of them.

Incredulously, Valeirys stared at him for a moment.

He opened his mouth to reply, but the words stuck in his throat.

"They're getting worse, aren't they?" Eyvindr went on. "Ever since you've returned from Lyrr, you wake violently from your sleep. The servants are afraid to approach you."

Casting a sideways glance at him, Eyvindr finally met Valeirys' eyes and fell silent.

"What happened to you?" he finally asked.

Valeirys' jaw clenched, and he dug his fingers once again into the side of his bed.

"Nothing," he answered dryly.

He knew his brother only meant well, but he didn't want to speak of what he had witnessed in Lyrr, Melquart, or the battle at the tavern.

Nightmares had haunted him every night ever since he had returned home. His senses seemed constantly alert as if he were expecting an imminent attack. His body felt rigid, strained, and had been subject to odd seizures that would come and go as they pleased.

All that was enough to make him want to forget what he had experienced.

Yessenia and Eyvindr had both been uneasy around him. They were worried about him.

So, what good would it do to share any of it with them?

It would only unsettle them further. More importantly, he feared that even speaking of it would keep him from letting his own dreaded memories rot in the past.

Valeirys swallowed and then spoke up. "Where's Father?"

The moment the question had left his lips, he could see the impervious wall between himself and Eyvindr rise up as his brother's manner changed. His tone cooled, and he seemed to withdraw from him.

Staring at the floor again, Eyvindr answered, "He left for Mòr Rhíoghain yesterday. He wanted to join Melquart's final interrogation before the execution."

Valeirys watched the muscles along Eyvindr's neck tighten while he paused and swallowed.

"Something arrived for you this morning," his brother said and pushed himself off the bed.

He disappeared momentarily into the hall before returning with a chest that ran the length of both his arms.

Setting it down on the desk across from Valeirys, he went on, "I believe it came from the palace."

Valeirys eyed the oaken chest on the opposite side of the room, already guessing what lay inside it when Eyvindr rejoined his side and handed him a small piece of parchment.

"This came with it," his brother said, watching him as Valeirys broke the royal seal and read.

"The king thanks me for my service to the crown and the arrest of Melquart. Apparently, he intends to honor me before the eyes of the people after the execution," Valeirys said and gave a sigh.

His gaze dropped to the floor before he forced himself to his feet and trudged across the room.

Eyvindr followed and replied, "You don't seem pleased."

It didn't sound like his brother was at all perplexed by his reaction, and for a brief moment, Valeirys' lips twitched upward.

Their brotherly bond was unbreakable despite the tension between them and their differences. His brother understood him better than anyone.

Valeirys stopped before the chest and expelled another breath.

"No," he answered. "It just doesn't seem right to thank me after everything this small triumph has cost us."

A silence draped over them as they stood beside each other staring at the chest.

"Well," Eyvindr spoke up, interrupting the peace, "Are you going to open it?"

Valeirys' expression remained solemn, and he replied, "I guess I cannot refrain from doing so… It would be rude; and I imagine His Majesty will expect a letter stating my humble gratitude upon his generosity… at the very least."

With a shrug of his shoulders, Valeirys took another step closer and undid the chest's hasp.

It didn't come as a surprise to him to find the prized weapon lying inside it, and yet he felt his heartbeat quicken at the sight while an image of the Eskhàra's sword consumed his mind's eye.

Valeirys sucked in a breath and concealed his reaction by clearing his throat before he reached inside to take a closer look.

The elvish steel sang once released from its sheath, and he raised the well-fashioned weapon before him, turning it from side to side to admire it and dipping it into the morning light that poured through the windows of his room.

Valeirys' fingers curved adeptly around its grip, finding their position. It was a spectacular blade, made from only the finest materials. Any soldier would envy him for it.

The hilt was a finely polished black and decorated with an emerald stone set inside the center of the pommel. A symmetrical design of silver veins, resembling the tangled roots of a tree, circled the emerald gem and climbed up along the shaft of the hilt before they expanded into a crown that unfolded and bloomed over the cross-guard.

Several of the tree's delicate bows had been etched onto the fuller, visible only when the light touched it from a single angle.

"The tree and the emerald," Eyvindr began. "It bears the mark of the crown. All who see it shall know that you carry the king's favor. It seems you'll have to think of something grander than a simple letter to thank the king for his gift, brother."

Valeirys swallowed and continued to study the sword silently.

His brow furrowed as he squinted while eyeing the blade from point to pommel. He tried to make sense of the inexplicable notion stirring within him that this sword wasn't meant for him to bear.

"If it helps, I hear the king is determined to join the efforts to find the prince and the rest of the missing soldiers. He is to leave Mòr Rhíoghain after the execution if the rumors are to be believed. That should keep him away for a while and give you enough time to think of something better than a… well… 'thank you for my new toy,'" Eyvindr said, interrupting his thoughts.

Valeirys couldn't help but grin. Tearing his eyes from the blade, he looked at his brother.

"Since when do you listen to gossip?" he asked. "I doubt such whispers are carousing around the villages… Where did you hear that?"

Eyvindr grinned boyishly and replied, "I may have persuaded Father into letting me accompany him to the palace and bribed a scribe to let me peek into the records of the council's recent meetings… It is also how I know that Melquart and his followers were more than simply 'interrogated'. Apparently, there were more violent methods of persuasion to get them to talk, but none of it led to anything conclusive."

Both were quiet for a moment before Valeirys smirked and said, "If Father only knew how cunning you are. He would be ashamed if he knew how easily you maneuvered around him."

Eyvindr shrugged his shoulders and replied, "Well, just because I am not considered fit to be a soldier doesn't mean that our politics don't interest me. Besides, it's easy to outsmart someone whose attention you do not hold… There are advantages to being invisible; people tend to underestimate you."

His brother's expression had grown solemn again, and he looked away from Valeirys.

At a loss for words, Valeirys hesitated. Buried deep beneath the meaning of Eyvindr's quick-witted reply was an unamended wound their father had caused that would not disappear by any pretty words he might offer him.

"I'm going to petition before the king to join him and his guard on their search for Malik and the recruits. I believe it is the best way to thank him for this gift and prove my loyalty and devotion to the crown once again," he said instead.

Eyvindr shot him a sideways glance, raising his gaze to meet his and held it for a moment before he answered, "You want to leave again so soon? I don't mean to discourage you, but you don't seem to have fully recovered from your last assignment."

Valeirys sighed and began to speak when his brother interrupted him. "You've changed. I know it should not come as a surprise after what you went through. Whatever happened in Lyrr, I'm sure it was horrible, but this change… It's different."

All at once, Valeirys could not bear the weight of Eyvindr's discerning gaze anymore and lowered his head.

His guard slipped and for a moment, he ignored the warning voices in his head and answered, "The battle… being a part of so much bloodshed; I don't know how to describe it, Eyvindr. I don't think—"

"You don't think someone like me could understand… Someone who isn't a soldier," his brother interrupted him again.

"No, that is not what…" Valeirys started, but fell silent when Eyvindr added, "It's alright."

Valeirys looked up again to see that his eyes were still trained on him.

Despite Eyvindr's terse response, he guessed there was much more his brother had perhaps wished to say but had left unspoken. Eyvindr was not one to speak bitterly out of spite nor to be driven by jealously over differences between them that neither could be held accountable for.

"You are a soldier. It is your duty to serve the kingdom when it needs you, not when it suits you," he said and attempted to smile. "You should get yourself cleaned up. You reek. Let me know when you wish to leave for Mòr Rhíoghain. I promised Mother I wouldn't let you out of my sight."

The thought of the execution and of Melquart caused an indescribable blend of emotions to rise within him.

Valeirys felt an odd sensation of both satisfaction and an insurmountable anger stir within him. His palms prickled at the tantalizing sense of victory, and he found himself wishing he were the one to carry out Melquart's sentence.

"Valeirys?" Eyvindr's voice rose through his cloud of thoughts.

Valeirys shook his head and then nodded, replying, "Yes. I'll let you know when I'm ready."

Eyvindr dipped his chin in return and left, but Valeirys hardly noticed.

His hands clenched at his sides while he remembered Melquart's words to him.

You could kill me right here, right now… Now, wouldn't that be something?

Chapter 42

Click, click, click… the slight sharp sounds of Princess Kalithea's heels beating against the stone floor vanished in the quiet mutterings of the council.

It was a habit of hers her mother had tenaciously tried to break. Kalithea remembered her words well.

Princesses and queens do not tap their feet. It is rude, and it shows a lack of patience and composure. Qualities you are to exude as a good ruler.

But patience wasn't her strong suit. As much as it was a part of ruling, it was torturous.

They had been waiting for the king for at least an hour now, and something was beginning to feel wrong.

THE RISE OF ISIGAR

Subtly, Kalithea gave a sigh and straightened in her chair, reminded by her mother's training to always keep an upright and impeccable posture.

Eyeing the members of the council who were far more invested in their grumblings than to pay attention to her, she turned her head toward Lord Jarek beside her.

"Where is he?" she whispered.

He didn't look at her directly, watching the men seated around the large stone table as well and answered, "I couldn't say, Princess. He left the palace early this morning. Perhaps he went to investigate a new lead on the groundskeeper."

"A new lead," Kalithea scoffed quietly. "Hasn't he been doing this for weeks now without any progress? Can't he send someone else?"

Lord Jarek lowered his gaze and raised his brow. Nodding, he replied quietly, "I agree. But he is your father. He's grown impatient."

Kalithea sighed and returned her attention to the councilmen whose voices grew louder as they conversed with one another.

"This boyish behavior must end! The king cannot be out chasing after every useless tip," said Lord Amiyas or 'Flap Maw' as she secretly preferred to call him.

The balding fellow was one of the council's more obnoxious members. He had the tendency to run his mouth without thought, especially whenever her father was not present.

"Perhaps it is nostalgia for his youthful years of hunting and hawking or running off and chasing after young beautiful maidens and fleeing his lessons," Flap Maw added, hoping to reap some laughter from the other men around him.

Kalithea's fingers curled at the chuckling that traveled through the council at the comment.

Pretending not to hear them and trying her best to distract herself from their gossip, she let her eyes drift across the room.

Though she hadn't intended to, her gaze halted on Lord Acristus who sat at the very end of the long table. Dark rims lined his eyes, accentuating his pale complexion, and his expression was grim. He sat slumped against the back of his chair staring into the empty space before him as if his mind were elsewhere. The longer she studied him, the more his head seemed to sink deeper inside the oddly decorative high collar of his doublet. One of his hands lingered around the knot of his scarf as if he had intended to adjust it but had forgotten what he had meant to do, lost in thought.

Perhaps this ridiculous crusade of his against Aleirya was finally driving him mad, she wondered.

One of the other council members suddenly rose to his feet and spoke. "I believe our patience has been exhausted enough. Perhaps we should adjourn this meeting until His Majesty returns?"

Lord Jarek clutched the arms of his chair and had almost sprung upward from his seat when the doors of the throne room burst open.

All heads snapped toward the entrance when King Ethuriel marched inside, armed and flanked by his personal guard. Behind him, several other soldiers followed.

"Good, you're all here," he said.

Kalithea recognized the unmistakable tension in his voice as he approached the cupbearer whose hands fumbled as he immediately filled the king's chalice.

Taking the cup from the boy, King Ethuriel drank from it.

"Your Majesty." The royal title slithered off Flap Maw's lips, and he bowed before him.

The rest of the council imitated his behavior just as he went on, "We were growing concerned. Your expeditions have become quite venturesome…"

"And what would you prefer?" King Ethuriel answered, handing the chalice back to the cupbearer. "That I drink, feast, and sit in my marbled chair? That I grow old and fat until I am nothing but a figurehead under your government up to my long-awaited demise? I'd rather die a king who never forgot how to properly use a sword than grow feeble in my golden cage."

At that, he snapped his fingers and motioned to his guards.

Immediately, they moved.

Along with the rest of the council, Kalithea's head turned toward the line of soldiers before the entrance of the throne room. They cleared a path for a group of four of them to march forward, lugging something draped in a thick wool covering between them.

Kalithea held her breath as they approached the table.

Out of the corner of her eye, she noticed her father ascend the dais just as the soldiers heaved the large and seemingly heavy object onto the council's table.

Gasps and shrieks shot through the hall as part of the covering slipped, revealing the head of the corpse that now lay before them.

Kalithea stiffened and clutched the arms of her chair, feeling her stomach twist at the grueling sight.

Many of the council members had leaped to their feet, covering their noses and mouths with their hands, the color drained from their faces.

One by one, each turned to look at the king who had seated himself on the throne.

The groundskeeper... *they had found him*, Kalithea thought in horror, unable to look away from the body.

The groundskeeper's face looked swollen and distorted; his features were hardly recognizable, as if he had been mutilated. The sides of his head bore cuts and marks. Even parts of his ears had been severed.

Staring at the corpse and then redirecting his attention onto Flap Maw, King Ethuriel spoke. "The result of a useless tip... the hounds from a group of hunters found him at the edge of the forest in Megaera. Unfortunately, no one saw who killed him or how it was done."

Casting one glance at the cupbearer, Ethuriel stretched out his arm toward him, silently requesting more wine.

As the cupbearer filled his chalice, he added, "Though it was not easy, the shelter master confirmed it is the groundskeeper he hired before the attacks."

He took a sip and paused. Lowering his gaze to the inside of the chalice, he said, "Perhaps if you had treated every report with the same thoroughness, Lord Amiyas, we would have found him alive."

"Your Majesty," Flap Maw began, still aghast by the news and the dead body before them.

King Ethuriel raised a hand, silencing him at once. Then he lifted his voice again. "Sir Odynn."

Kalithea hadn't even noticed that Sir Odynn had accompanied her father and watched him step forward as bid.

"Cut the wretched creature. Now!" Ethuriel spoke through gritted teeth.

"Father!" Kalithea shouted, along with the gasps and the shocked voices that arose around them from the others.

Ethuriel immediately glared at her, warning her not to speak another word.

"Your Majesty, with all due respect, this is not the adequate place for me to perform this task, I—" said Sir Odynn.

But Ethuriel raised his hand, snapping his fingers, and immediately, two servants stepped forward.

Fixing a stern gaze on them, the king spoke. "You are to heed to his every word. Bring him everything he needs, and do not dawdle. Go!"

Murmurs chased through the rows while Sir Odynn quickly gave orders.

Then the king rose and descended the dais.

Having approached Sir Odynn, he pulled a dagger from the back of his boot and handed it to him, blade cast downward.

With a nod, he spoke. "Do it now."

Sir Odynn accepted the weapon gingerly and locked eyes with the king before Ethuriel turned toward the throne once again and added, "Those who cannot stomach the sight should best leave."

With one arm draped around the stone pillar, Kalithea kept her eyes shut, trying not to concentrate on the noises coming from behind her.

She could hear slicing, tearing, splashing, and clinging sounds while Sir Odynn continued to perform the autopsy.

She couldn't remember how long she had stood there, holding on to the pillar with her back toward them. Her legs had gone stiff and cold from tension and immobility, much like the body that lay on Sir Odynn's table.

The smells and noises were nauseating, and she silently wished her heightened senses away, a gift from her dragon's blood that definitely had its drawbacks.

Releasing a long-measured breath, she opened her eyes.

She took a few steps forward around the pillar, stopping once she had disappeared from the rest of the room's view.

Peeking past the marbled stone, she dared a glance at her father who had not moved since he had ordered the autopsy.

She had rarely seen him so angry before.

His fingers tapped against the arms of the throne while he stared down the dais watching Sir Odynn.

The cold and haunted look on his face frightened her, and she wished she knew what he was thinking.

Besides Sir Odynn and her father, only she and Lord Jarek had stayed. Lord Jarek stood beside her father's throne with his back toward the hall, equally sullen.

Though it seemed terribly unfitting, Kalithea almost wished for music to be played to distract from the awful silence of their joined waiting while Sir Odynn completed his task.

Studying them from where she stood in the shadows, Kalithea felt as invisible as a ghost. She wondered if her father even remembered that she had stayed behind.

A heavy sigh and the clinging noise of Sir Odynn releasing his utensils drew her attention toward the table again.

Kalithea tried her best not to look at the sickening sight of the corpse's chest that lay open.

"It was poison that took him," he said. "Whoever killed him must have wanted to make sure he would not be arrested and questioned. The trace of the silver tongue is unmistakable. From what I could determine, at this quantity, the amount administered to him was lethal. They probed his mind before they destroyed it, and with it, the rest of his body."

He eyed the dead man a moment longer before turning toward a wash basin, submerging his hands in the water. He then removed the blood-smeared covering he had worn over his clothes.

"Killed by his own poison," Ethuriel muttered, staring blankly into the distance.

Sir Odynn nodded while he finished cleansing himself.

Kalithea felt her throat run dry as she listened to them.

Still, no one seemed to have noticed that she was still there.

She swallowed and watched as Sir Odynn then stepped closer to the dais.

"There's more," he said.

The statement captured her father's attention and tore him from his mind's wanderings.

Fixing his eyes on Sir Odynn, she heard the king speak. "Go on."

"He was elven. His disfigurement makes it difficult to recognize, but blood does not lie," Sir Odynn answered.

Kalithea held her breath and noticed the furrows on her father's brow deepen.

Then his hands wrapped into tight fists, and he slammed his right against the arm of the throne.

"The Metatari assured us it wasn't King Yevandrielle who orchestrated the attack on our kingdom," Ethuriel grumbled angrily.

"Perhaps he lied," said Lord Jarek and turned to face them.

Sir Odynn shook his head.

"I don't believe this elf came from Erysméa," he said, earning both confused and fierce looks from the king and Lord Jarek.

"What could you possibly intend to mean by that?" Lord Jarek snarled.

King Ethuriel cast him a warning glance and then returned his attention to Sir Odynn.

"Explain yourself," said the king.

Nodding, Sir Odynn folded his hands before him and continued, "There was a mark. It was hidden well beneath the scarring of a few older wounds, most likely inflicted upon him in order to conceal it before he arrived in Tarragon… a mark from the age of the elven King Izurion's reign."

King Ethuriel's lips pursed, and he asked, "How is that possible? How is he still alive? Izurion's reign over the elven realm began longer than a century ago."

"Magic," said Sir Odynn. "Elves age differently than our kind, Your Majesty. It is nothing unusual for them to outlive the most venerable of our own; however, I believe there is some sort of darker, stronger magic at play here."

He cast a sideways glance at Kalithea, seemingly the only one still aware of her presence.

Meeting his gaze, she froze.

When she remained silent, he nodded as if to convey that whatever was said now must remain within these halls.

Kalithea returned the gesture as if to promise that she would not utter a word to another soul.

Sir Odynn dipped his chin toward her and then returned his attention back to the king.

"Your Majesty, did your father ever share with you what happened after the elven realm was reclaimed by Erysméa and what was done to those surviving and loyal to King Izurion after he fell?"

Ethuriel answered, "They were drawn before the court of law and most of them were sentenced to death, including their families. Others were banished and only very few pardoned and ordered into menial service."

"Yes," said Sir Odynn. "Did your father also mention the mark that was placed upon the banished?"

The king shook his head.

"The banished were given a mark crafted from a secret spell that was to rid these elves of their magic. However, unfortunately, an elf's magical ability cannot be completely stripped from their being since they are creatures of magic. But the spell limited and slowly stole away their strength to wield it, so that the rest of their power is nearly useless."

He paused to take a breath and then continued, "I would assume that this groundskeeper, along with whoever else of his kind survived, found a way to limit or stop the mark's effect and somehow reclaim a portion of their once held power. It would explain why he remained alive to this day and how he was able to use the silver tongue in the shelter attacks."

"So, they seek revenge over their former kingdom… Why does this mark trouble you so greatly?" asked Ethuriel.

Sir Odynn hesitated, but then replied, "The mark was not simply a punishment. It was an act of revenge by the new elven rulership after Erysméa's victory. After all the suffering afflicted upon the people under Izurion's orders, there were a few of the new royal court who considered banishment too merciful. They wanted to see the banished punished in a grueling manner that would make them wish they had been executed… And thus, after much convincing of the new elven king, the mark was created.

"Its spell derived from a dark, one might even say, sinister form of magic experts described as blood magic. It was once created by perhaps the most talented and powerful elves to ever wield magic… A surreptitious group who served King Izurion and belonged to the so-called Ring of Edrador. These elves murdered, tortured, and threatened any enemy or known adversary of Izurion as mercenaries. But not only that… They experimented with magic, sometimes through measures and at costs that are far too atrocious to even speak of. This magic, this power, not only changed and evolved their abilities, it altered their beings. It took possession of who they were and transformed them into vessels of evil.

"Supposedly, this blood magic vanished along with the execution of every surviving member of the Ring of Edrador and the demise of King Izurion. The crafting of the mark was meant to be the very last use of this power in all history of elven magic. There are rumors that say that the Erysméan government forced the last remaining members of the Ring to design the mark before they were executed. This was to ensure that the magic died with them. After the marks were placed on the banished, any remnant, written document or anything that bore so much as an essence of blood magic was destroyed."

He sighed and then added, "If these once banished elves found a way to alter the mark or its effect, that would mean that they were able to resurrect at least some form of this power. For a magic as such to return to our world—if someone has managed to understand, wield, and perhaps even alter it—it could put us all in danger."

"But why turn against the Dragon's Kin if it is revenge that they seek against their own?" Lord Jarek asked.

Sir Odynn shook his head and replied, "I cannot be certain. Perhaps there is something greater at play, perhaps an even greater power that has risen that somehow involves the dragons' magic. Or it is as the Metatari warned, Your Majesty, and this enemy is trying to use our forces to weaken Erysméa before they reveal themselves. But then I would dare say that it would be folly to believe that Tarragon would be left in peace once the banished have triumphed over Erysméa."

"So, what do you suggest we do?" said Lord Jarek.

"We fly to Mòr Rhíoghain," King Ethuriel interrupted.

Without looking at any of them, he rose from the throne.

THE RISE OF ISIGAR

Standing atop the dais, he looked to Lord Jarek and spoke. "It is time King Yevandrielle and I break the silence between our people. We leave at first light."

Lord Jarek and Sir Odynn bowed before the king.

Sir Odynn then began to retreat from the dais when Ethuriel said, "Sir Odynn, how long has it been since you've ridden on dragonback?"

Sir Odynn froze and turned to face the king.

He seemed confused and hesitated before answering. "I believe it has been far longer than any proud Dragon's Kin would like to admit, Your Majesty."

Kalithea noticed her father grin at his reply. The sight of it seemed to lift the pressing weight off her heart and filled her with relief.

Watching him, she heard his response to Sir Odynn. "Good. Then it is about time we changed that."

Chapter 43

Yessenia's feet glided over the tiled floor as she slipped inside the library and shut the door behind her.

Her back pressed against the wooden panels, and a long breath whistled past her lips as she exhaled and shut her eyes.

A cold seeped into her through the bare soles of her feet as if she were standing on frozen ground in the dead of winter, and a shiver shook her frame.

Bit by bit, she opened her eyes, the palms of her hands still pressed flat against the door, steadying her from behind; for a moment, her gaze halted on the evanescent drapes that drifted in the cool breeze in the morning's wake.

Her attention steered blankly through the open entrance of the balcony and out over the colorless sky, and she let herself breathe in the freshness of the newborn day.

Streaks of gray light broke over her golden gaze, washing over her face with a silken touch, and transformed the space around her to a dusty blue.

She had not set foot in this room ever since the woman in the mirror had appeared to her. Its broken frame and shattered surface still lay exactly where she had left it.

Her jaw clenched, and she swallowed, willing herself to look at its destruction.

Argent shards littered the floor like a mosaic image. But the pieces would not blend to a work of art before her eyes. Instead, Yessenia only saw the jagged edges, the sharp angles, and points sticking out with a piercing brightness that reminded her of the harsh gleam of a deadly blade.

There was a rottenness, an evil, lurking behind the sheen of glittering silver that covered the floor.

Her fingers curled inward, and her nails dug into the softness of her palms as she jerked away from the door.

In six measured strides, Yessenia approached the remains of the broken mirror and stooped down on one knee.

Her own image flitted across the sliver of a broken piece that her fingers stretched toward, and she winced.

Unbidden, her recollection of the woman's devilish smile that had lit her amber eyes consumed the reflection Yessenia glimpsed in front of her just as her own hand brushed the lines of her lips.

The woman's unmistakable laugh rang in Yessenia's ears, rousing an ire that brought a flush to her cheeks and flooded her chest.

With a scream, Yessenia's hands snatched one shard after the other, scattering them while she whirled, pelting the sharp fragments like arrows released from a bow.

Jolts darted across her palms, the sensation both burning and freezing cold, as hiss after hiss left her lips until she stopped.

With her arms extended from her sides, Yessenia wrestled for control over her reeling mind, the stubborn pounding of her heart and the aching rise and fall of her chest.

Her damp lashes swept against the blur of her vision.

Crimson blots dotted the stone tiles and stained the skirt of her dress with blood dripping from her cut palms.

Yessenia pinched her eyes shut and gasped before she dropped on her hands and knees.

She let her head sink, but then raised it again, and her gaze locked on the mirror's broken frame.

Three ugly cracks severed its once immaculate oval form, the largest tearing through the eye at the center of its top.

The corners of Yessenia's lips distorted into a frown, and she crawled forward.

Her bloodied left hand seized and tightened around the tangle of thorns that dressed half of its frame.

Pain shot up her arm from the prickling sensation of the iron digging into her injury, but she gritted her teeth and stifled a yelp.

Her right hand clutched the opposite side which was decorated with a blissful arrangement of lilies and wild vine as she hunched her body over the ruined piece to look upon its cracked eye.

Yessenia's gaze narrowed, a guttural sound like a growl rose in her throat as she summoned the strength to wrench the mirror's broken frame apart. All at once, her whole body went cold, and ice shot through her veins just as a violet light flashed before her, igniting at the center of the mirror's split eye.

A raw terror burrowed into her abdomen, and it was as if for a moment, everything ceased.

Paralyzed, her limbs clung rigidly to the mirror's frame. Her heart did not beat, she did not breathe; her mind enthralled by the sight in front of her, caught in the trance of the purple light that moved and swirled along the silver thorns and twisted vines.

As the symbols danced before her eyes, Yessenia remembered the chapel in Aram and the elven boy's body. His tortured frame rose before her once again, making her stomach lurch.

The boy's cuts and marks had looked the same, but now they were no longer confusing.

THE RISE OF ISIGAR

Yessenia blinked, a part of her trying to force the memory aside when, suddenly, black lines fringed in violet took form along the mirror's silver gilding like ink strokes from a quill, merging to runes and then words that made up a tongue unlike her own and yet familiar all at once.

Yessenia's lips moved as she read, whispers coating and swirling her lips before they left them like wisps of smoke, and she heard her own voice rise in a quiet echo. "Power forged in blood not even death shall break."

A thrill kindled at the tips of her fingers upon her utterance of the magical phrase. A subtle throbbing rose from the depth of her chest, and the relief of a vitalizing breath soared into her lungs at the surge of energy she felt tickling her palms where she grasped the mirror.

Her focus centered once again on the eye of the mirror, where embers of the violet light seemed to pulsate.

Mesmerized, Yessenia stared at it until she noticed a design glowing inside the pupil of the eye.

Three crescent shapes formed a cross, interlocking at the apex of their curves where they formed a knot. Above the knot, the violet light she had seen now gathered to a small oval that glowed red as a ruby gem. Sprouting from the precious stone, a scaly body like that of a snake wound its way downward, wrapping around the center of the strange cross before it coiled around the hilt of a downcast sword.

Yessenia's hands trembled as the sight evoked a searing pain that pierced her heart.

She gasped and threw her head back as a river of images obscured her vision. Glimpses of faces she did not recognize, scenes of unfounded darkness and power, a beast with a pair of glowing eyes, each a different color, and a fiery gale that sent flashes of heat down her spine broke over her.

Yessenia cried out, tearing her hands from the mirror's silver frame just as it burst.

Shielding herself from the blast, her arms snapped upward to guard her head, and she curled herself into a ball.

The shrill clatter drowned out behind her, and in the wake of her sobs and heaving breath, she slowly lowered her forearms and ran her hands over her face.

Her lips quivered, goosebumps covered her skin, and sweat lined the nape of her neck as a rush of adrenaline swept over her.

She had seen that symbol before.

Yessenia scrambled to her feet and over to the wall across from her that was lined with shelves.

Her fingers fumbled behind a row of books until they bumped against the object she was searching for, and she drew it out from its hiding place.

Setting it down on the desk, her eyes raked the lid of the small wooden chest in front of her. Fear and anger gnawed at her from the inside while her gaze passed over the familiar inscription: Samyiel Trageian.

A lump formed in her throat, and she forced it down as her fingers grappled for the lock.

The lid of the chest opened and revealed an array of contents before her, but Yessenia saw only one of its objects: a ring.

A strange cross of three crescent bows, a coil of scales, a sword, and a ruby stole across the ring's centerpiece and gleamed at her from below.

Unable to resist, Yessenia took the bejeweled piece out of the chest.

Pinching her father's ring between her fingers, a bitter taste filled her mouth and coated her throat, souring her stomach. What had he been hiding from her all these years? Who had he really been?

Tethered to the symbol decorating the ring's centerpiece was an untold power, a magic. It was the same force she had encountered in the body of the dead in Aram. Yessenia knew it without a shred of doubt.

A shudder coursed through her as realization dawned. This force, this power, it not only resonated with her; it lived within her.

Your magic is special, Yessenia. A gruesome blend of both her father's voice and that of the woman in the mirror rang in her ears.

Finally, Yessenia knew why.

It wasn't simply her magic that was special; it was her blood, her father's blood.

It was the key—the key to the peril that had yet to unleash itself upon them.

* * *

THE RISE OF ISIGAR

Ripples of a thundering beat broke through the clamor of the crowds and entered Valeirys' body through the soles of his boots as the guards drummed their spears against the stone of the palace's perron.

Dusk had broken and streaks of bright gold and cerise stretched across the darkening heavens like the veins of a lightning bolt.

Thousands had come to witness the execution, their bodies crowding the streets in a mass of gray and brown dots that faded into the cobblestones.

It wouldn't be long now before the prisoners would be brought out before them.

Another wave of shouts and jeers crashed over him, and Valeirys cursed, drawing his hood upward to shield himself from the noise.

Squinting, his eyes passed over the scene before him. Wisps of smoke flickered across his line of vision from the torches, trailing toward the heavens and mingling with the emerald banners bearing the king's sigil.

As far as the eye could see, bodies crowded the roads, crammed against each other all the way up to the line of barricades that curved around the enormous scaffold manned by plenty of soldiers.

Like a hideous statue, the structure's horrific image stretched toward the sky, causing Valeirys' chest to tighten and stalled the breath in his lungs.

Swallowing against the knot in his throat, Valeirys fought the urge to reach for the hilt of his sword as he noticed a body of onlookers surge against the barricade, flinging various items over its barrier and littering the ground with waste and scraps of wood and metal.

His jaw clenched; with every muscle in his body strung taut, he compelled himself to stay put atop the platform amongst the rest of the king's guests and watched the soldiers repel the violent culprits.

Eyvindr stood beside him, as still and inconspicuous as his own shadow. Valeirys glanced at him, and their gazes locked just as a pair of trumpets blared, announcing His Royal Highness.

Loosening the tight ball of his hands that had gone bone white, Valeirys' eyes dragged over the heads of the unruly throng and up toward the balcony of the tower across from him where King Yevandrielle stepped forward.

A glint flashed from above as the king's gauntlet-covered hands grasped the banister catching the sky's dying light.

The king wore no crown.

Instead, a palisade of sharp points like flaming arrows encircled the bowl of his bascinet. The sides of his helmet molded around his face, imitating the structure of his jaw and cheekbones and sharpening their lines.

His onyx robes were trimmed in tyrian purple and flowed down his back from his pauldrons, the left embellished with the image of the seven sigils of the elven leagues interlocking, while the right bore the image of a white-blossomed tree and the signet of the crown.

The masterfully crafted steel of King Yevandrielle's armor folded around his body, accentuating his strong frame. His chest was a glow of polished steel. Seven gems had been set inside the breastplate, representing the components of the royal oath he had taken.

His Majesty's appearance was meant to convey the very picture of strength and dedication; yet, at the sight of him, the people stirred in uproar.

Valeirys' gaze dropped from the king down to the endless rows of elves shouting and imprecating His Majesty, and something within him convulsed.

His frustration continued to build inside him at the sight of the grief- and rage-stricken faces of the people before him. An uncomfortable sensation wrapped itself around his limbs like a coil that seemed to grow tighter and tighter with every passing minute.

This was a people bereft of their love and their faith in their king, poisoned by lies from a traitor.

A flash of heat rose to his head, and Valeirys tore his attention from the crowds and glanced once again at the king.

His Majesty's complexion was as crisp as a winter's white, peeking out from the layers of steel and glowing almost ghostlike against his piercing bronze eyes that swept over the surging masses below him, the flame of their hatred reflected in his gaze.

King Yevandrielle's face remained motionless. He drummed his fingers twice against the banister of the balcony he stood upon, at once igniting a pair of braziers to his left and right and so giving the signal for the execution to begin.

THE RISE OF ISIGAR

Raucous cries bellowed across the square, and several elves pointed at the palace as all attention turned toward its gates where a lone figure draped in black emerged.

The tall elf wore a mask of blackened steel akin to the visage of a beast, and the long shaft of an ax, its blade the shape of a crescent moon, rested upon his shoulder.

A cold, needle-like sensation swept down the skin of Valeirys' arms and legs while his gaze locked on the executioner, shadows exaggerating the elf's horrid appearance as he descended the staircase that led down to the King's Square.

The guards lining the palace's steps drove their spears against the stone once more in a steady rhythm. The ground throbbed, and the people's voices reached an ear-splitting volume as the executioner claimed his position atop the scaffold.

A sharp whistle pierced his ears, boring through Valeirys' skull, and he winced just as the commotion suddenly ceased. Everything went still, and a hush swept over the crowds.

Not a soul moved, every breath caught, and every gaze froze upon the sight ahead while all hearkened to one sound, the chilling echo of clink after clink as a single-file line of prisoners crept down the stone steps.

The bodies of the condemned were concealed in white, their faces hidden below cloths that had been draped over their heads; their hands were folded before them, shackled in chains that bound them together.

Without warning, the people's cries exploded again, and a chant rose in a crescendo from their midst as they shouted, "Eleftherai," again and again.

Liberator. The meaning of the word roared through Valeirys' thoughts, and he flinched at the sound of it.

Tearing his attention from the prisoners who were forced onto the scaffold and on their knees, his glance snapped back toward the palace's gates.

Melquart's steel-colored eyes and his venomous smile flared up before Valeirys' mind's eye.

His head ached from the overwhelming noise around him, his hands shook, and he folded them into fists while his eyes narrowed on the group of soldiers treading down the palace's staircase surrounding Melquart.

An untamable fury tore at Valeirys from within. It surged forth from his heart into the rest of his body as if it was no longer blood that flowed through his veins but an insatiable ire.

Melquart's neck, wrists, and ankles were cuffed in chains. His feet were bare, and he wore a white rough-spun tunic just like the others. But his face was not hidden from sight.

His dark bedraggled hair hung in loose tangles down to his shoulders and past his lifted chin, bearing a stark contrast and enhancing the ferocity of his gaze that was riveted on the sea of people before him.

Valeirys bit back a snarl at the smirk he imagined spreading across Melquart's lips and the elf's complexion that seemed far too rosy for one who had been locked away in a dungeon.

Melquart's expression was stoic, fearless, even proud, void of the slightest twitch or quiver in his features even as the soldiers escorted him up onto the scaffold's platform.

Unable to look away, Valeirys glowered at him while he climbed each step with an unfathomable confidence.

Sensing the king's eyes on him, Melquart turned and looked upward at the tower where King Yevandrielle stood.

Valeirys felt something grip and claw at him with a force strong enough to crush his bones. His body trembled, and he wanted to scream but managed to force himself not to.

Finally, a guard shoved Melquart forward and struck the backs of his knees, making him drop onto the platform before the executioner's block.

"Alessander Melquart, subject of King Yevandrielle," the headsman's voice rose. "You have been found guilty of high treason against His Majesty and are, therefore, this day, sentenced to death."

The elf went on, naming the charges against Melquart and his followers in further detail. Once he had finished speaking, the hoods were removed from the other prisoners, and he proceeded to take his position.

Screams echoed across the square. A grapple began somewhere along the front lines behind the barricade, but Valeirys did not avert his eyes from Melquart or the executioner.

The headsman looked up at the king, awaiting permission to cast the deadly strike.

When he continued to hesitate, Valeirys glanced upward as well.

King Yevandrielle stared down at Melquart as if to torture him with the suspense of when he would, at last, give the command to end his life.

Valeirys could feel his own bounding pulse throbbing in his neck and temples while his gaze darted back and forth between Melquart and His Majesty.

The tension between them was palpable; so much that the skin of his body started to sting.

Watching, waiting for the king to give the command, Valeirys sensed the endless scorn and pain lingering between them, vitiating the air they both breathed like the noxious fumes of a fire.

Finally, redirecting his attention toward the scaffold, Valeirys' eyes locked on the blade of the ax.

He thought he had caught a glimpse of a large shadow floating across the square in the sky above, but was so entrapped by the scene unfolding ahead that he couldn't be certain.

The king must have given the headsman the signal to carry out Melquart's sentence, for the crowds burst into violent screams, and Valeirys saw the executioner grab hold of the ax's shaft.

All at once, all movement slowed, and his peripheral vision blurred as the center of his gaze froze on Melquart and the executioner.

Indistinct motion erupted all around him as the guards rushed toward the crowds.

The masses pushed against the barricade, intending to overturn it, while others struck out against the king's men with any object they could get their hands on.

The soldiers struggled to hold them back, yelling across the square. The flames of the torches surrounding the scaffold flickered and flared, and tongues of gold, orange, and red licked at the sky.

Something cracked and thundered in the heavens above. The darkening clouds gathered together, but Valeirys didn't look up.

Instead, he watched how the headsman folded each finger around the helve, one by one, in expert fashion.

Like a memorized pattern, an act of habit he had performed countless times before, he secured his grasp on the weapon.

His fists, wrapped in leather gloves, clutched at the wooden shaft several times. His outstretched arms grew stiff as his muscles contracted, and it seemed as if for a moment, he stopped and held his breath.

There was no way of telling who the elf was. His face was obscured from view, hidden behind the mask that concealed his features, and draped under the dark hood of his mantle.

Valeirys wondered what was running through the headsman's mind at that very moment, unable to look away from his chilling image. He then noticed the elf's back and shoulders lift beneath his cloak as he drew a deep breath before he began to propel the deadly device upward.

The shrill echo of the weapon's edge shot through the air, quelling every other sound in Valeirys' ears. Its sharp noise festered around him while his eyes locked onto its blade, and a bright light pierced his vision as the metal surface caught the last glow of light that lingered in the sky above.

The ax swung forward in a seemingly effortless motion, soaring above the executioner's head as it followed its set course directed at Melquart's neck.

Valeirys' body went rigid while he stood motionless in place as it sliced through the air, cutting through it effortlessly like a thin veil of cloth.

Knowing what was about to happen, he gripped the banister ahead of him and fought against the urge to shut his eyes which burned from the dry and charred-smelling air.

Valeirys noticed someone grab onto him; their hands wrapped around the sides of his shoulders, and shook his body firmly.

Even without glancing in his direction, Valeirys knew it was Eyvindr who was calling out to him, intending to make sure he was alright.

But he couldn't look away, he couldn't relent from staring at Melquart.

Then, suddenly, just before the blade's sharp edge could pierce the skin of Melquart's neck, a lightning bolt struck the scaffold.

THE RISE OF ISIGAR

The headsman's body was flung backward, and the ax slipped from his hands as the sky turned black and loud screeching pierced the air.

Valeirys saw Melquart crash onto his side and then roll over onto his knees just before his head jerked upward.

The wooden panels of the scaffold's platform caught fire, and all around him, fearful screams erupted from the crowds and the people scattered from the square in a frenzy.

Tearing his gaze from Melquart, Valeirys looked upward.

Soaring all across the heavens above them were the largest winged creatures he had ever seen. Like beasts, their size was triple that of any elf's. Their cries deafened those below and seemed to shake the earth as they drew near the ground.

Some guards fell back at the terror that filled the obsidian sky above, while others aligned themselves before the lords and the king's guests, drawing their weapons.

Then another ear-splitting screech blared ahead as one of the horrendous creatures swooped down from above them, plummeting toward the scaffold.

Valeirys crouched down to his knees at the sound, and his eyes immediately darted toward Melquart and the executioner who quickly retrieved the ax and raised it before his body.

Spreading its wings wide to slow its flight, the beast extended its legs and seized hold of the ax with its talons, tearing it from the executioner's grasp and knocking him to the ground anew.

Its eyes glowed, the one bright gold, the other silver, and its appearance resembled that of a wild eagle while it hovered above the scaffold, holding the ax tightly clenched in its monstrous grasp.

It cawed and then released the headsman's weapon, letting it fall onto the square while some of the soldiers grabbed hold of Melquart and the prisoners and scrambled off the platform.

The beast seemed to let them escape, glaring down at them until every one of them had deserted the scaffold that now began to give way.

The structure creaked and snapped, and piece by piece, it collapsed to the ground.

Valeirys couldn't help but stare at the creature ahead that landed in the center of the crumbling scaffold, unfrightened by the flames surrounding it that continued to climb higher and higher.

Its fiendish eyes seemed to bore into him just when he noticed something dark begin to dissipate from the tips of its wings.

Within seconds, a black swarm formed around the scaffold, twisting around the entire structure like a whirlwind and making it impossible to spy what was happening beyond it.

More high-pitched cries shot through the air as Valeirys eyed the mysterious shape ahead more closely and then noticed that it was a flock of small black birds circling around something much larger that mirrored the eagle's shape at the center.

Bit by bit, the creature disappeared behind the black mass, and the flock gradually dispersed into the air, finally leaving behind a single hominine form.

The shouts and cries of the people still rang out over the square as the frightened crowds fled the scene. More soldiers gathered in defense of the lords and the king's guests along with Valeirys and Eyvindr who had not yet escaped before the strange intruder.

There he stood amidst the wreckage of the fallen scaffold. Flames licked at his feet. A long dark cloak lay draped over his leather armor, and a strange-looking sword hung at his side while his eyes radiated in gold and silver.

Valeirys looked straight at the Metatari's face just when a smile broke over his lips, and he spoke in a voice like thunder. "A thousand years and, at last, we meet again."

Chapter 44

The throne room was utterly silent when King Yevandrielle stepped inside the familiar royal hall, hearing only the heavy doors fall shut behind him.

At first, there was no sign of the Metatari, and it seemed he was alone.

Yevandrielle expelled a breath, letting the air sail slowly past his lips and ignoring the throbbing sense of his pulse against his temple.

Despite his council's many warnings, he had chosen to grant the shapeshifter his request; though it seemed foolish to abandon his guards for a private audience with a stranger he knew nothing about, a creature harboring powers he hadn't yet begun to understand, he was curious.

His eyes searched the blueish veil of darkness that had fallen over the throne room and the trunks of the ebony trees that lined the walkway all the way up to the dais.

The royal hall was to remind any who entered it of an enchanted garden. However, surveying it now, it had more in common with the deepest parts of a forest no one dared tread into for fear of the evil that haunted its woods.

Drawing another breath, Yevandrielle's shoulders lowered, and he stepped forward.

This was his kingdom. The Metatari had trespassed into his realm of power. He had nothing to fear.

His feet swept over the opalescent tiles of the floor, reminiscent of a river's current, and while his glance skimmed their shimmering surface, he recalled the blood-curdling fables of the creatures roaming the Dhaharran Forrest, half man, half beast.

What could they possibly want from him?

His feet slowed before the dais, and he looked toward the throne. The dark silhouette of the royal seat loomed over him, carved from the ebony trunk of an enormous lone-standing tree that emerged from the podium. Its crown opened wide below the glass dome of the tower, and the white blossoms adorning its powerful boughs shone silver now under the light of the moon that broke above him.

Yevandrielle's lips drew back to a snarl, and his brow furrowed.

How dare the creature make him wait? Perhaps he'd have him seized and caged like the proper beast he was...

Then, all at once, Yevandrielle's eyes widened, the bronze rings almost vanishing behind his pupils, and he whirled.

A trickle as cold as ice and as hot as burning coals ran down his neck from the crown of his head when the large shape of a man stepped out from between a pair of trees at the end of the hall.

At first, the Metatari stopped, his face hidden beneath the hood of his mantle, as if he meant to make his presence known without even speaking a word.

An unnatural cool seemed to seep through the walls of the tower, chilling Yevandrielle to his bones while he stared at the strange creature who had invited himself into his court.

Something rustled the crowns of the trees that lined the walkway, drawing the white blossoms up into the air, and then the Metatari moved. The petals began to gather and twirl in spirals before him while he walked, as if carried by a wind that obeyed his command.

Yevandrielle clenched and then unclenched his fists while he kept his attention riveted on the shapeshifter who came to a stop a little more than six paces away from him.

He couldn't help but notice the white blossoms slowly sail to the ground, coating it like snow once the Metatari halted before him.

The shapeshifter lowered the hood of his cloak when Yevandrielle's glance darted to the stranger's face, locking onto his feral eyes which shone gold and silver against his dark skin.

Though every hair of his body stood on end, and the soles of his feet itched for him to turn and run, Yevandrielle made himself stand still in front of the creature.

Squaring his shoulders, he lifted his chin and spoke. "As you have asked, so I have come. What is it you so urgently wish to tell me?"

Yevandrielle did his best to keep his face still. He resisted even the smallest flicker of movement, so not to betray the odd sense of alarm that flared inside him while he watched the Metatari stroll across the path before him, his footsteps making no sound.

Without speaking, the stranger eyed him and then continued to survey the space surrounding them, seemingly not in a hurry to reply to his question.

For a moment, Yevandrielle wondered if he was making sure they were alone.

When the shapeshifter continued to keep his silence, he spoke. "You must forgive the suspicions of my council and their distrust against you and your kind. A vast mystery surrounds your people, and it is quite unlike the Metatari to present themselves so openly as you have on this day. It would be foolish not to consider this a dangerous encounter."

Yevandrielle found himself turning to follow the shapeshifter's movements, and he clenched his teeth, briefly averting his attention from him. Inwardly, his whole body wriggled with frustration; the Metatari's persistent silence only angered him further.

Yevandrielle felt the sting of the shapeshifter's dishonor pique his pride, but he chose to wait and see just how far the creature would go to test him.

Turning around to face the Metatari, his eyes narrowed and his skin crawled at the sight of the shapeshifter standing atop the dais and before the throne.

Was he mad?

But just before he could speak, a bright light that spilled from the center of the shapeshifter's palm seized his attention; he watched as the Metatari reached down to trace the course of one of the winding roots that surrounded the royal seat and draped down the dais's steps.

Leisurely, his fingers ran along the bark of the tree, and the root shimmered gold where he had touched it. Then, slowly withdrawing his hand, he finally answered, "You have nothing to fear from me, King Yevandrielle."

His mighty voice echoed throughout the throne room like the rumbling of the heavens during a storm, sending a tingle down Yevandrielle's spine.

The Metatari's eyes flashed from the tree's roots to Yevandrielle's face unsettlingly quickly, and he went on, "I have come to warn you of an evil that I fear has already risen against you and your kingdom."

Yevandrielle held his gaze and said nothing at first, stifling a laugh that threatened to burst from his mouth.

The corners of his lips twitched into a crooked grin, and he answered, "As long as there is light and darkness in our world, there will always be an enemy lurking in the shadows, awaiting their chance to overthrow me. Surely, you did not come to warn me of a simple threat."

There was a pause while each examined the other closely, and Yevandrielle contemplated what the shapeshifter could mean.

Then, with a suspicion lingering in his mind, he spoke again. "You amuse me, shapeshifter. Trespassing into my kingdom with no care for the consequences it might bring, feigning a concern for the well-being of my people. Tell me, do you wish to dishonor me by conveying that I am unable to protect my own?"

His voice had almost risen to a shout, and Yevandrielle paused, bridling his temper before he added, "I am well aware of the atrocities committed against us, and I fully intend to bring the perpetrators of these vile crimes to justice."

Stopping, he studied the Metatari carefully, watching for the slightest hint of a reaction before he said at last, "Even if it requires entering a war against the Dragon's Kin. Or against you."

"They are not your enemy," said the shapeshifter.

His voice resonated in Yevandrielle's ears with a power and an authority the king had not yet witnessed, and his reply had shot forth more quickly than Yevandrielle could have ever thought possible.

It was almost as if the Metatari's lips hadn't even moved and that he had instead spoken to him with his mind.

With teeth bared, Yevandrielle responded, "My people mourn the dead; loved ones whose bodies were found tortured and burned by the flames of dragon's fire. How can you stand before me and claim that they had no part in this?"

The Metatari eyed him calmly, and with a scoff, Yevandrielle turned away when the creature spoke. "I am not here to question your ability to defend your kingdom, Your Majesty."

He stood perfectly still on the podium, looking down at him as he went on, "I come with the sole intention of preventing the outbreak of an unnecessary war and the bloodshed of more innocents. Something much greater than a threat from the Dragon's Kin is coming, and I am afraid that even the strength of your armies will not withstand the power that has set itself against you."

Yevandrielle looked back at him and snickered.

"I was unaware that the Metatari shared alliances with those of the other races," he replied bitterly.

"We do not," the Metatari countered firmly.

Yevandrielle's smirk vanished from his face as the shapeshifter's eyes pierced through him almost painfully, and he added, "And most assuredly, not with the elves."

The Metatari's reply left a bitter taste in his mouth, and his jaw tightened.

Then, glaring at him, Yevandrielle asked, "Then how is it you believe I would trust you?"

The shapeshifter cocked his head to the side, and seemingly evading the question, he said instead, "Did you or did you not order the strike against the Dragon's Kin a month ago?"

"What?" Yevandrielle blurted.

His mouth had run dry, and he stared back at the Metatari, who continued to study him as if to determine whether he was lying.

"There was a battle in the Dhaharran Forest just a few days' travel from Inaesa's borders. The soldiers of the Dragon's Kin were slaughtered. Not one of them appeared to have survived," said the shapeshifter.

He paused briefly and then carried on, "We arrived too late to have witnessed the attack; but amongst the fallen, there were also those of your kind. However, their dead were far less in number than those of the Dragon's Kin, and not one of them bore a sigil belonging to one of Erysméa's leagues."

Yevandrielle's pulse drummed in his ears, and he balled his hands into fists while answering, "Those elves were not acting under my command. This was not my doing."

"As I suspected, Your Majesty," the Metatari replied quickly, almost interrupting him.

The shapeshifter descended the steps of the dais, and his strange eyes settled onto Yevandrielle's face while he joined him on the walkway and continued, "The Dragon's Kin have fallen victim to crimes I believe stem from the same enemy you face. Their dragon shelters were destroyed, their dragons taken or injured, some murdered, along with many of their people. They, too, have come to know loss and misery. It is why they encountered the elves in the forest. A rogue army of Dragon's Kin intended to retaliate for the attacks on the dragon shelters they assumed were your doing, without the knowledge or the blessing of their king. Had I not intervened and spoken with King Ethuriel, your kingdom would already be at war with the Dragon's Kin after what happened in the forest."

The Metatari stopped as if giving him a moment to take it all in.

His form well exceeded that of Yevandrielle's as he stood just an arm's reach away from him.

Dragging his gaze from him, Yevandrielle shook his head and walked past him.

Having ascended the steps of the dais, he turned and then seated himself on the throne.

"I know you are angry and that you seek justice for what has been done to those under your care, and rightfully so," said the Metatari. "But I warn you not to let yourself be deceived into battle against your greatest ally."

"Ally," Yevandrielle scoffed. "What understanding could you possibly have of an ally—you who choose to live separated from the rest of our world, hidden in the shadows of your forest?"

Leaning forward, his nails digging into the arms of the throne, Yevandrielle added, "Even if I were to listen to you—to trust you—the Dragon's Kin will never agree to fight alongside us. We took a vow to never again find ourselves face to face unless in war against each other—and this for good reason. Surely even you haven't forgotten the rise and fall of the Eskhàra."

"I do not need a reminder of what your pride and the dragon's greed for power wrought together," said the shapeshifter.

He let his response linger in the space between them for a moment before he spoke again. "I mean no offense by my words to you, Your Majesty. The Metatari do not meddle in the affairs between elves and the Dragon's Kin. And in truth, neither do we wish or care to settle your battles for you. However, this threat does not stem from any of your grievances with the Dragon's Kin. They, too, have been deceived and turned against you; were it merely a dispute between your kingdoms, I would not have come before you."

Yevandrielle said nothing, marveling at the shapeshifter's boldness and how he could stand before him and speak to him in such a manner.

"King Yevandrielle," the Metatari's voice rumbled in his ears. "This evil knows that separately the both of you are defeatable. A united force is what it fears; it seeks to turn you both against each other, even weaken your forces in an unnecessary war." He paused and then added, at last, "You will have destroyed yourselves before it has even brought its full force upon you."

"And what of you?" Yevandrielle asked suddenly. "What of your people? Do not tell me that, all at once, you suddenly share a fondness for elvish blood."

The shapeshifter dipped his chin ever so slightly and responded, "My people will not be spared the same fate as yours once this enemy has succeeded in their plot against you, Your Majesty. Indeed, we share no fondness with your kind; but even I, a beast—as you prefer to call me—know when pride is ill-placed and the good of my people takes precedence."

Yevandrielle's hands twitched, and he clutched the arms of the throne, suppressing a flinch.

A long silence fell between them as he contemplated the words that had been spoken; resting his back against the throne, he eyed the Metatari and answered, "Be that as it may, how am I to trust you? For, do not be mistaken, shapeshifter, I will not be frightened into an alliance with you or persuaded to join forces with your kind by some well-constructed tale."

Nodding as if having expected his response, the Metatari replied, "It began several months ago."

He started to stroll across the walkway before the throne as he spoke. "I received word of violent trespasses into our territory. Many of my people had been killed. Regions of the forest and our kingdom had been destroyed; some parts burned to ashes by fledgling dragons.

"Our wards that have been in place for centuries and that have protected my kind, concealing our kingdom from the rest of the world, failed. The Metatari who survived were forced to desert their homes."

The shapeshifter stopped and seemed to hesitate for the first time before he went on, "We began to prepare ourselves for what we thought could be the beginning of a war against the dragons of the Unbound. My men and I chased after each sighting for weeks. But what we discovered was everything other than what we had expected. These dragons weren't seeking a war against us."

Yevandrielle perceived a twinge of sorrow in the Metatari's voice as if it pained him to speak.

"The young dragons we encountered were injured and had sought refuge in the depths of the forest," said the shapeshifter. "Besides their injuries, they seemed crazed, as if tortured under a dark force that drove them insane. Ridden with fear and confused, they viewed any soul they encountered as hostile. As magic forms the essential part of their being, and in their deranged state of mind, my people's magic drew them to our kingdom. They sensed our power even beyond our wards. It gave them a sense of orientation and the only strand of hope to survive."

THE RISE OF ISIGAR

The Metatari paused, and then his eyes seemed to flare with anger when he spoke again. "At times, instead of a dragon, we would find a trail of their blood, one we would follow, but not once did it ever lead us to the injured. Somehow, somewhere, they disappeared, and the trail always ended in the same place. Something or someone was driving them out of the forest and into the Forsaken Lands of Isigar."

"The human realm?" Yevandrielle asked in bewilderment.

The shapeshifter nodded and replied, "The trail went cold shortly past the border of the Dhaharran Forest into Gothwin of Isigar. This continued for several months until it suddenly stopped. And just when we thought that whatever had befallen those dragons had ceased, a body was discovered. It was elven and had been left behind deep inside the forest. Dragon's fire had scorched large sections of its frame; other parts were covered with the strange symbols of a spell I did not recognize. Its essence was of a dark kind, one I have not yet come across and similar to the magic used to torture the young dragons."

The tips of Yevandrielle's fingers pricked, and his limbs froze while recollections of the dead scattered throughout Erysméa's regions surged to the forefront of his mind.

He hadn't said a word, and yet, when he met the shapeshifter's gaze, the Metatari nodded as if he knew his thoughts.

"Throughout the weeks that followed, more bodies, each of them elven, continued to appear in various places of the forest between Isigar and Erysméa. Every one of them bore the same injuries and strange symbols. The peculiarity of these horrific occurrences had seized my attention, and I could no longer ignore what we had discovered. So, I sent my people into both of your kingdoms," said the shapeshifter. "It was then that we learned of the unrest that was troubling your kingdoms, your search for those who had committed the kidnappings and murders, and the attacks on the dragon shelters in Tarragon."

Fixing his gaze on Yevandrielle, he added, finally, "After the battle in the Dhaharran Forrest, I knew it was time to act, and so I sought an audience with King Ethuriel. It was then that he told me that the fires weren't coincidental tragedies."

Still eyeing Yevandrielle as if to examine his reaction, the shapeshifter hesitated until the king nodded, motioning for him to continue.

"King Ethuriel's investigators discovered that the shelters had been breached and set ablaze by magic, a magic of a likewise dark nature and one the Dragon's Kin aren't known to master. Furthermore, they discovered a seedling by the name of Aggyreidimos idiss."

"Silver tongue," Yevandrielle interrupted breathlessly. "It can't be. The valley lands of Nyradorn were stripped of it…"

The Metatari nodded.

"Naturally, when this was made known to him, an involvement from those of your kind was suspected by his council. They feared that a war was imminent. However, the king was hesitant to act against you. It was only when he learned of the battle in the Dhaharran Forest that his mind changed."

There was a silence once he finished speaking.

The shapeshifter stood still before Yevandrielle as if waiting for a reply. When none followed, he continued, "If it is definite proof of a common enemy that you desire, then indeed, you will find me lacking such. But I believe both your kingdoms have suffered too much to just watch these tragic events unfold any further."

"And what would you have me do, shapeshifter?" Yevandrielle asked. "How do you suggest we proceed? How are we to defend ourselves against a malevolent power such as this?"

"Join forces with my people and the Dragon's Kin," the Metatari answered. "I believe your people's skill of magic and the Dragon's Kin's knowledge and bond with the dragons will aid us in the unveiling of the ones responsible for this evil and the source of its power."

"And then?" Yevandrielle asked. "The Forsaken Lands are a harsh and vast terrain unknown to our kind. Without knowledge of where the enemy resides, we would search for them for weeks, squandering resources and wasting the little time we might have left."

The Metatari's eyes narrowed, and the trace of a smile dressed his lips when he answered, "That is where our role in this endeavor begins. As you might recall, there lies a fortress in Strongard, once governed by the greatest of the human clans, a few days' travel from Gothwin. It is the only fortress large enough to harbor a force mighty enough to stand against yourself and the Dragon's Kin. My people know the Forsaken Lands of Isigar. With our magic, we can conceal your armies as you travel and provide safe passage through the Dhaharran Forrest. The enemy will not know you are coming. Once we pass the forest's borders and journey into Isigar, the Metatari will guide your soldiers where they may camp safely and where to replenish their supplies, for the land is not what it once was."

Yevandrielle smirked and spoke. "So, am I to understand you'll leave the actual fighting to us?"

"Not at all, Your Majesty," the shapeshifter answered. "I intend to attack with my men before yours have even lifted a finger."

Yevandrielle bit back a rather snide remark and continued to look the Metatari in the eyes as if unprovoked by his words.

Then, after a moment's pause, he spoke. "You mean to draw the enemy out of Strongard's fortress? You're suggesting an ambush?"

The shapeshifter nodded and answered, "Yes. The Metatari will strike first, fooling the enemy into believing that the odds are on their side. They will not know the full force of the power against them until it is too late."

His eyes seemed to gleam against the darkness, as if the notion of an unexpected attack delighted him.

Straightening, Yevandrielle lifted a hand to his lips.

"Alas, should I consent to this mission of yours, persuading my council will be a feat in itself, but I am not sure that I will find any elven soldier willing to join in arms with you out of their free will."

At that, the Metatari grinned and replied, "Is it not the great power of the elves to assume control over the mind and alter the will of another? Or so I hear you pride yourselves."

All at once everything went still between them, and then Yevandrielle answered, "Indeed, we are granted a great gift, as you have so boldly declared."

For a brief moment, the shapeshifter smiled rather charmingly.

But then the lightheartedness of his expression faded, and he spoke. "Persuade them, Your Majesty, or don't. However, this evil is coming. The fate of your kingdom lies within your hands. With or without us, it is up to you to decide what shall be done about it."

Yevandrielle gritted his teeth behind the hand that still hovered before his lips and hesitated.

The Metatari's gold and silver gaze never wavered, pinning him against the back of the throne while awaiting his answer, and Yevandrielle felt the angles of his shoulder blades press up uncomfortably against its cool wooden surface.

Indeed, a choice was to be made.

Studying the shapeshifter while he contemplated his answer, the king wondered for a moment what it would take to overpower a creature such as he was if it came to it.

Then, leaning forward, a reply ready on the tip of his tongue, he fixed the Metatari with an equally sharp gaze and pursed his lips to speak.

Chapter 45

The muffled sounds of the people's cries, the guards' shouts, and the shapeshifters' awful screeching rang in Valeirys' ears, the room reverberating from the dreadful noise as if time had not moved.

His clothes smelled like the smoke from the fire that had consumed the scaffold, and his head ached.

His throat was parched, his eyes still burned, and though they were opened, it was as if he saw nothing while he stared out blankly at the wall across from him.

A part of Valeirys' mind understood perfectly well where he was and what had happened while the rest drowned in his pool of thoughts.

His muscles felt stiff and hurt from inactivity as they waited in one of the palace's rooms for the news that it was safe for them to return home.

Valeirys couldn't recall having left the King's Square or even moving from where he had stood watching the events unfold that had surrounded the execution.

A thousand years and at last, we meet again... The Metatari's words still rumbled in the depths of his memory.

Though utterly terrifying, at the same time, there had been something magnificent about the creature.

The Metatari's presence alone had conveyed an incredible power, an unrivaled authority, and Valeirys knew he couldn't have been the only one who had sensed it.

Growing up, he had learned to view the shapeshifters as the enemy they were. He had been trained to fight their kind.

But the older he grew and the more he had been told of them, the more their existence had seemed a myth to him and his peers.

But now he understood.

Watching the Metatari stand there amidst the flames of the burning ruins of the scaffold, demanding a private audience with the king... He was fearless; one could have thought even perfectly comfortable in his position.

He did not tremble at the strength of the elven soldiers who stood before him nor did he seem afraid of the king's wrath, which he was most likely to bring upon himself. In a way, he had proven himself far too brave for his own good.

Were his confidence not foolish, Valeirys would have admired the shapeshifter for his bold spirit.

As if he were still standing before the scaffold, Valeirys could see the shapeshifter turn away, bit by bit, transforming back into the beastly creature he was.

With his body covered in layers of black and brown feathers, his arms exchanged for a set of powerful wings, feet for a pair of deadly talons, and a long, pointed beak protruding from a once human face, the Metatari had readied himself to take flight.

There was a gentle nudge at Valeirys' shoulder, and he heard Eyvindr speak. "Are you alright?"

Valeirys blinked and then nodded, replying, "Yes."

Eyvindr waited for him to glance in his direction before he added, "It shouldn't be much longer before we are released to return home."

Nodding once again in agreement, Valeirys said nothing and let his gaze drop to his hands that lay folded in his lap.

He could feel Eyvindr's gaze on him but didn't look up.

Just then, the door swung open, and one of the king's advisors entered, accompanied by his personal guard.

After what appeared to be a well-rehearsed explanation of the situation at hand, the elf declared that all was well and that they were safe. He then proceeded to extend the king's invitation to each of the guests to remain at the palace for as long as they wished and mentioned that proper accommodations were being prepared as he spoke.

A sigh of relief seemed to pass through the gathering of guests, who stirred and then slowly vacated the room, speaking in low murmurs.

Rising to his feet, Eyvindr extended his hand to Valeirys, helping him up from the ground before they both followed the hushed voices of the others exiting the chamber.

Passing over the threshold of the doorway, Eyvindr strayed from Valeirys' side and approached the king's advisor.

Politely declining the generous offer to stay, he then conveyed their desire to take their leave and return to their father's estate.

Valeirys barely overheard the conversation, lost in his own thoughts. He only became aware of his surroundings once again when Eyvindr offered a bow before the advisor and then followed the soldiers that had been ordered to escort them to the palace's main entrance.

Simply paying attention to keeping in stride beside his brother as they sought their leave of the palace, he continued to mull over the strange encounter with the Metatari.

Valeirys had hardly felt the scene around him change from the warmly lit palace halls to the bleak and abandoned sight of the King's Square where they had been just hours before.

A comfortable breeze swept past them while they stood side by side under cover of the night's darkness, waiting for their horses to be brought up from the stables.

The sky was perfectly clear. Not a single cloud hovered above them, and there was not the slightest trace left of the storm that had broken across the heavens when the Metatari had appeared and interrupted the execution.

Valeirys eyes wandered from the night sky down to the heap of the scorched remains of the scaffold.

The tall structure that had once stood proudly erect over the square was now unrecognizable, reduced to a pile of ashes and scraps of wood.

Most of the scaffold's fragments had already been carried off.

For a while, he continued to watch several servants dragging piece after piece from the wreckage and lugging it onto a cart under the dim torchlight that surrounded them.

His gaze then swept from their restless activity to a smaller figure crouched on the ground and scrubbing the grime and ashes from the palace's steps.

The scullion did not dare glance in their direction and continued to brush over each step until it was clean.

It was quite a cruel task to demand of him at this hour when there was hardly any light, Valeirys thought.

Tossing the brush into a large bucket, the scullion climbed the stairs, hauling the heavy wooden pail after him.

Valeirys kept on watching, noticing the elf stop and inch aside when a group of guards drew near.

Though it was dark and he could not see the guards' faces, it seemed as if they had slowed simply to stare down at the elf in disgust.

As if eager to escape their arrogant glances, the scullion leaped up the stairs in a hurry, just when one of the guards tripped him up, pretending to walk on past him.

The scullion fell, losing hold of his bucket that toppled down the steps and crashed onto the square.

The guards' boots and the stairs were now flooded in lye, and the unpleasant smell rose into the air.

A flash of anger overcame Valeirys. Raising the back of his hand to his nose, he grimaced and walked toward them.

He could hear the guards cursing angrily while quickly descending the remaining steps, treading onto the square and out of the mess.

Only one stayed behind, and voicing his displeasure, the guard reached out and forcefully grabbed hold of the scullion.

The elf shrieked and grasped for the brush that lay by his side, raising it above his head as if it were a weapon he could use to protect himself.

Clutching the collar of the scullion's tunic, the guard shook and hollered at him.

Frightened, the scullion dropped the brush and cried out, apologizing and begging for mercy.

Valeirys had almost reached the bottom of the staircase, feeling as if he could hardly contain his anger upon observing the guard's injustice.

He was prepared to leap up the stairs, placing his left foot on the first step, when he noticed someone catch up to him.

Eyvindr held his outstretched arm to Valeirys' chest and pushed him backward.

Valeirys did not once relent from glaring up at the guard who still held the scullion seized within his grasp.

The guard spat in the elf's face, and pulling him close, he readied himself to thrust the scullion back onto the stairs.

"That's quite enough," Valeirys heard Eyvindr shout firmly.

Without letting go of the scullion and rather slowly, the guard turned his head to face them.

"I can state with certainty that it was not the scullion's intention to cause this mess," Eyvindr went on.

He had climbed the first few steps and stood tall before the guard, fixing him with an unwavering stare.

"Let him go," Eyvindr said at last.

Hesitating, the guard looked back at him in contempt but then let the scullion go, tossing him aside, not too gently.

The elf then spat at the ground before Eyvindr's feet, and with a grunt, he stalked down the staircase.

Standing close by, Valeirys bit down on his lip, trying to stay calm. It was all he could do to keep himself from storming at the guard.

The elf's shoulder brushed up against Eyvindr's, and immediately, Eyvindr planted his open palm against the guard's breastplate, prohibiting him from moving any further.

Looking him directly in the eyes, Eyvindr leaned a bit forward and spoke in a low voice, "Such behavior must not be found in one of your station. Your standing does not empower you to show cruelty. Yours is a calling that is to exude courage, honor, and protection of those weaker than yourself."

He paused briefly and then continued, "Should I ever have to witness such misconduct on your behalf, rest assured, you will learn what it means to respect the boundaries of your position or else you will no longer enjoy the privilege of holding it."

With a snarl, the guard pushed past him, shooting Valeirys a rather haughty glance before rejoining his group on the square.

Valeirys could hear them muttering and snickering in the distance.

Then the guard turned around again, and walking back toward Eyvindr, he said, "What makes you think I would fear a command coming from your lips?"

From the moment he had spoken, Valeirys had balled his hands into fists, sensing his anger boil inside him.

Eyvindr turned around to face the guard when he went on, "Do you really believe that you have any authority, any power? You—the frail son of the Lord Altair? The laughingstock to your family's name? You are no soldier; no lord. You are but a fortunate misfit fed with a silver spoon ever since you drew your first breath."

The elf's words had barely rolled off the tip of his tongue when Valeirys felt a power unlike anything he had ever known surge through him.

A jolt coursed through his veins and into his legs, and he spun around and sprinted toward the guard at a speed he would have never thought possible.

But Valeirys did not care about what was happening to him.

All he could feel was the rage he had so vehemently tried to contain and that he could no longer bind to himself.

All he wanted was to silence the half-witted elf. He wanted to avenge the scullion the guard had mistreated and punish him for his insolence and the slander he had uttered against his brother.

So he lunged.

His right hand had barely fastened around the guard's neck before Valeirys drove him backward, causing the elf to lose his footing and driving him harshly to the ground.

The elf's back crashed onto the cobblestones with an unnatural force that seemed to shake the earth beneath them.

Protected by his helmet, the guard's head swung backward, sending forth a screeching sound as the steel clashed against the stone.

The elf screamed just as Valeirys swung his left arm forward and tore off his helmet, flinging it into the air as if it weighed nothing.

The incessant drumming of his own pulse and the rush of his own blood were the only sounds that resonated in his ears.

He did not hear the shouts of the other soldiers or the shrill echo of the weapons they released from their scabbards. He did not pick up the sound of Eyvindr's voice calling out for him to stop or the groaning noise coming from the guard trapped under his grip.

Staring back into the guard's terrified face, Valeirys knew he had seconds before the rest of his company was about to fall upon him.

Without intending to, he felt a sneer form over his lips just before he threw a punch, hurling his left fist at the elf's temple.

The guard's eyes rolled back, and at once, his body went limp.

Not an ounce of strength seemed to have left Valeirys when he jumped to his feet and darted toward the soldiers that came charging at him.

Instead, it was as if his strike against the guard had given him power, rewarding him with a surge of energy that made his heart beat stronger and his body move even swifter than it had before.

In fact, the sheer act of violence seemed to fill him with an unmeasured satisfaction that fueled his every movement.

Though any sane bystander would have clearly recognized that the odds were against him as the five soldiers bolted toward him, Valeirys only felt his ambition grow.

Instead of feeling beaten by the constant agony and the tremors that had wrought control over him throughout the past weeks, every part of his body felt strong and invincible. Finally, his untamable anger seemed to have a place and a purpose.

Driven by an impulse he could not explain, and while running, Valeirys stretched out his arms and shouted, "Ispèiron!"

Erupting from the palms of his hands, a rippling force surged forward and struck the line of guards before him.

Only one managed to stand his ground while the rest let out a scream as their bodies were flung backward, propelled in various directions, and disappeared into the depths of the darkness around them.

The elf had lost his weapon and raised his fists, prepared to strike a blow when Valeirys came at him. But the soldier's movements were too slow.

Valeirys caught the swing of the guard's right arm and plunged his left fist against the elf's jaw. He could feel the bone burst beneath his knuckles as the soldier's face contorted in agony, and he screamed.

Blood welled in the elf's mouth, and he spat out a pair of teeth as his knees buckled, and he lunged, trying to reach the hilt of his sword that lay on the ground. Valeirys watched the guard's hand scratch and claw at the cobblestones as he grappled for his weapon. Without hesitation, he drew his own blade and severed the elf's hand from his arm.

It was an unnecessary cruelty, but he didn't seem to care.

The elf screamed a curse and then fainted before his feet.

Valeirys dodged the drop of his head against the ground just as another pair of soldiers came running at him.

"In the name of His Majesty, I order you to surrender!" one of them shouted.

Valeirys ignored the warning. Snagging a dagger from his boot, he propelled the blade forward.

A horrible cry rang through the air as the dagger plummeted into the soldier's right leg, burying itself into the bone as it bore its way through the crevice between the soldier's greave and cuisse.

Valeirys watched the elf collapse onto the ground and then raised his sword before him as the other guard advanced onto him.

Their weapons locked; pressing hard against his enemy's blade, Valeirys shoved his adversary backward.

With feet gliding over the cobblestones, they moved swiftly against each other, their bodies a blurred dance of shadows against the darkness, the only light coming from the sparks that flew from the clashing edges of their swords.

Drawing his weapon upward before him, the guard swung his blade, aiming for Valeirys' neck, but his movements were slowing, his strength was fading while Valeirys' thrived instead.

Parrying the strike just above the height of his shoulders and grasping his weapon with both hands like his opponent, Valeirys held steady.

The soldier's whole body seemed to tremble, and he grunted, trying to hold his own against Valeirys.

Then, with a grin and the flick of his wrist, Valeirys rotated the hilt of his sword, making the guard face upward before pushing and jabbing the tip of his weapon into the elf's collarbone.

Shrinking back in pain, the guard lost control of his sword and dropped his arm.

Instantly, Valeirys withdrew, and then with the powerful thrust of his right hand, he drove the pommel against the guard's temple.

But just as the elf's head swung sideways, and the soldier fell unconscious to the ground, all at once, something sharp cut into Valeirys' left side from behind him.

Without even looking down, he knew something was wrong. He felt it.

A scream lodged in his throat, his breath was knocked out of him, and his heart lurched in his chest.

He could feel the iron blade of his enemy tear its way through him, ripping apart fiber after fiber of his flesh; where its point and edge had pierced him, a smoldering heat spread forth, consuming everything in its wake.

Time seemed to have stopped as if cruelly letting him linger in the agony that seized him, and Valeirys gasped.

He waited for his mind to faint and for his body to weaken under the extent of his injury, but none of that seemed to happen.

Instead, his pain dissipated as something much stronger claimed its control over him.

He could hear the elf's labored breath behind him, and furious over what the soldier had done to him, Valeirys erupted with an ire that seemed to feed on his agony and spun around.

His strength returned tenfold, his mind cleared, and his hands tightened around the hilt of his sword.

The guard had withdrawn his weapon from Valeirys' side and leaped back, awkwardly catching himself on his left leg while blood dripped from his right where Valeirys' dagger still protruded from above his knee.

Valeirys clenched his teeth with a snarl and moved toward him.

A boiling anger roared from within, accompanied by a single thought that continued to resound repeatedly in his mind.

At my hands, they shall all fall. Against my power, their defense shall crumble. Victory shall be mine and mine alone.

The tips of his fingers stung, and he could feel his body yearn to release the power that built up inside him.

But instead of coercing him to lift his sword and advance at his opponent, something compelled him to raise his weaponless hand.

The corners of Valeirys' lips twitched upward, and then his lips moved of their own accord. "Naflégon seis pyrakàiam."

Riveting his gaze on the soldier, Valeirys watched the blunt horror displayed in the elf's eyes as his sword glowed orange red.

Smoke rose from the hilt of the guard's weapon, along with the smell of burned flesh, as he screamed and released the blade before staring down at his burned hands.

Making use of the elf's distraction, Valeirys closed the distance between them and seized the guard by the collar.

With his sword still in his left hand, Valeirys dragged the soldier after him, approaching the wreckage of the scaffold.

Driving him up against a heap of its ruins, Valeirys raised the edge of his blade to the elf's neck.

At my hands, they shall all fall. Against my power, their defense shall crumble. Victory shall be mine and mine alone.

His own voice roared in his ears without ceasing.

The guard continued to beg for mercy, pleading for him to stop while he twitched and trembled in his grasp. But Valeirys didn't hear him, neither did he care to listen to the commotion rising behind him as another voice screamed for him to stop.

Gritting his teeth together, Valeirys tightened his grip around the elf's throat and began to drag his sword across his neck, watching the blood begin to pour from where his weapon had pierced the elf's skin.

The guard struggled and kicked against him, trying to wring himself free.

There was a yelp and a choke before another sound swept past Valeirys' ear, so quickly, he couldn't discern what it was until he saw the head of an arrow bury itself into the back of his left hand.

Valeirys froze.

Then, dropping his sword from the guard's throat, he let the elf go.

His hand writhed but clung vigorously to the hilt of his weapon, as if to deny his weakness and refuse defeat.

Before he could determine what had happened, someone spun him around, grabbing him fiercely by his shoulders and shouting something at him he didn't comprehend.

Staring him in the eyes, Trajan continued to speak to him. But Valeirys just gaped back at him as if his mind were adrift.

Then, all of a sudden, his knees buckled, and he crashed onto the ground.

Catching him, Trajan steadied his body, holding onto Valeirys' arms so that he could see his face.

But Valeirys' glance drifted past Trajan's shoulder and stopped on a familiar figure standing on the palace's steps, a bow tightly drawn in his hands with another arrow notched.

Their gazes met, and for a while, Valeirys just looked at him, staring into the striking blue of his brother's eyes before his sight grew weary, and his head fell forward.

At last, Valeirys saw the sword still clutched within his grasp and Eyvindr's arrow protruding from the wound across the back of his left hand.

As if prying each finger from the hilt of his weapon, Valeirys released the blade and watched it fall to the ground with a clatter that silenced the voice inside his head.

At my hands, they shall all fall. Against my power, their defense shall crumble. Victory shall be mine and mine alone.

Chapter 46

Aleirya awoke to a gentle rustling above her. Blots of various shades of green filled her vision when she opened her eyes, staring at the crowns of trees that stretched out above her and obscured the view of the sky.

For the first time in a while, she had slept peacefully.

Still studying the shapes of the countless green dots that loomed over her, she watched their color change as faint rays of sunlight illuminated them and others trickled through the verdurous canopy.

For a moment, she couldn't even remember where she was or how she had come to this place.

Her back lay against the cool ground, bedded in the soft mosses and leaves of the forest. She could hear the first birdsong whistle through the rows of trees that surrounded her and smiled weakly, willing herself not to move and linger in the moment for as long as she could.

But the lingering ceased quickly once she thought of Takhéa. The dragon had been by her side when she had fallen asleep the previous night. Now she had disappeared.

She's most likely out to hunt, Aleirya told herself, propping herself up onto her elbows.

Sitting up, she blinked and then rubbed her hands over her face, shrugging off the remaining haze of her sleep.

She began to look around when she heard his voice, "… And she awakes."

Aleirya's head whirled toward the sound, and she caught sight of the shapeshifter reclining against the enormous trunk of a tree not far away.

Her hands tightened around her knees, but she tried her best not to reveal the unnerving sensation she felt in his presence.

He grinned smugly, studying her.

His right arm was perched atop his right knee that was bent before him while his other leg lay stretched out over the tree's roots.

In a way, his shape fit perfectly into the curve of its trunk.

"I was wondering when you'd join me again. Are all Dragon's Kin long sleepers?" he said.

Aleirya's brow furrowed, and she answered, "Have you been watching me all this time?"

His smile deepened even more, revealing a glimpse of his perfect white teeth.

Her gaze froze on his strange pair of eyes that shimmered. The sight was mesmerizing, almost as if the forest somehow made their colors even more vibrant and… beautiful.

Aleirya shook herself and looked away from him. What was she thinking?

"Were you hoping I was?" he responded.

At that, she shot him a glare and pursed her lips to retort when he interrupted, "No worries, you're not that fascinating."

Aleirya felt her stomach twitch, and she gritted her teeth.

With a slow exhale of breath, he got to his feet, moving so quietly and smoothly that it sent a shower of goosebumps down her arms.

She watched him as he approached and then stretched out his hand toward her to help her up.

Aleirya hesitated, letting her eyes leap from his face to his open palm and back.

The color of his hair was different in the day's light, looking less silver and instead, more a pale gold. The longer strands of his otherwise short hair were tousled and hung over his forehead and the sides of his face, accentuating his bold cheekbones and sharp jawline. His thick, dark brows matched his overall wild appearance, contrasting his unblemished, almost regal-looking complexion.

Her gaze halted briefly on the angled lines of his lips until she noticed their form change as his smile deepened.

His slightly upturned eyes glistened even more, aware that she was still studying his face.

Aleirya's fingers dug into her shins while she suppressed a grunt.

She hated that she seemed to amuse him.

Wishing that she hadn't stared at him for so long, she scowled; ignoring his hand, she got up from the ground.

He let her pass by him, still grinning smugly, and only turned his head to watch after her.

Aleirya tried her best to pretend that his haughty manner didn't bother her.

The leaves rustled under the flow of her step as she meandered deeper into the woods, aware that the shapeshifter was keeping his eyes on her.

She stopped and stared upward, wondering what it was about this place that made her feel so strange.

The wind whistled past her ears and tossed a pile of leaves into the air, and all at once, the Metatari stood before her.

He was so close it made her spine tingle and stalled her breath.

Her body went cold at his looming presence and the twisted smile that spread over his lips. His eyes sparked, and she bit back the blend of awe and fear that rose within her.

Aleirya forced herself to stare into his wild gaze, ignoring every instinct of hers that screamed for her to run. How she could have ever assumed that there was something trustworthy about him baffled her.

He was feral; an unpredictable creature she knew absolutely nothing about.

The way he seemed to look at her, watch her, even move around her... Though she didn't want to admit it, it was frightening and more beastly than anything else.

Her jaw tightened while he held her gaze.

It was malicious, she thought, the way he delighted in the simple act of startling her.

"Careful," he said. His voice was quiet but tense. "If you try to run, I'll have to stop you."

His face moved closer to hers.

"What do you want from me? What does Tamar want from me?" she asked.

"I'm simply following his orders. I don't care why he wants you," he answered.

"So, I'm your prisoner?" said Aleirya.

"A prisoner?" He seemed to halt at her choice of words before he added, "You can call it whatever you'd like. Though I'd prefer to travel as if we were companions, I can certainly accommodate whatever description you favor, if need be."

Something about the slight shift in his tone made her wonder if she had angered him.

The ground shifted beneath them while they stayed in place, and it was only when she felt her back slam into the bark of a tree's trunk that she knew for certain they had moved.

She must have said something wrong.

Aleirya sucked in a breath at the sudden crash and the jolt that shot through her bones upon the impact.

"Apologies," he said with a smirk. "I'll try to be more gentle."

That was a lie.

There was nothing tender or humane about him.

Aleirya hadn't noticed his grip on her collar until he moved his hand to release her.

Goosebumps spread all over her body when she sensed the light touch of his fingers settle beneath her chin; then he raised it, almost as if he meant to be affectionate.

Forcing her to look at him, he spoke in a low but sweet voice. "Don't stray too far from my side, dragon girl."

There... He said it again.

There was no doubt in her mind that he was the one she had encountered inside the cliffs while hunting the draspith.

His fingers slipped from her face just as her gaze dropped and halted on his wrist.

Something dangled from it; paying closer attention to it, she noticed it was a bracelet.

It looked familiar. So much so that she was certain she had seen it before; and then she remembered.

This time, before he could move away from her, she grabbed his arm.

His glare darted from her eyes to her grip and then back up to her face.

A glint flashed across his bright eyes, as if her quick response had somehow excited him.

Her heart beat faster, but she ignored it.

"What is this?" Aleirya asked. Her fingers coiled around his wrist, where several wooden charms hung from his bracelet.

The Metatari said nothing, staring down at his hand and then fixing her with a curious glance.

The spark of light in his eyes dimmed, and his expression hardened before he shook off her hand and stepped away.

"None of your concern," he muttered before turning his back on her.

Aleirya rolled her eyes and followed him.

"I've seen it before... your bracelet," she said.

She stopped and watched him, waiting for him to face her.

It took a moment before he turned around again; when he did, his glare oddly made her shy away from meeting his gaze.

She wasn't one to be timid, and especially not around anyone she knew wouldn't halt from using it against her. But something made her look away, and her gaze dropped to his chest.

It was only then that she noticed the strange clothing he was wearing. In fact, it didn't even look like any sort of cloth at all.

Beneath his black cape, an odd blend of brown and the darkest shade of green leaves, twigs, and blades of grass molded around his body like a leathery armor, covering him all the way down to his booted feet. A belt was strapped around his waist. Fastened to it was a shortsword at his left hip and an array of smaller, strange-looking weapons that were arranged around the front and his right side: Half-moon-shaped blades the size of his fist, a swallow the length of his forearm, each end bearing a small blade shaped like a three-pointed star, and a trio of throwing knives with a decorative design covering the sharp edges.

Curiosity over their make and what he could do with them nagged at her, but she didn't dare ask. She would have to be patient and perhaps slyer if she wanted to learn more about him.

She licked her lips and then slowly dragged her eyes upward to his face.

He was looking back at her when she met his glance, and then she said, "We've met before; several weeks ago… inside the cliffs. You stopped me when I was hunting the draspith. You said I wasn't supposed to be there, and then you disappeared."

Aleirya studied him as she spoke.

Besides the obvious surprise that spread across his face, there was something different about the way he looked at her now, almost as if he had grown sad.

He shook his head but didn't answer her.

It had to be an act, she thought to herself. He was pretending not to remember.

But a part of her began to wonder if he had truly forgotten.

His whole body swayed toward her when he stepped closer.

His expression had changed again to match his usual fierce and ruthless appearance.

"You're mistaken," he replied while looming over her. "Our paths have never crossed before."

Brushing past her, he added, "Now come, we should keep moving. Your dragon will have to track our scent and follow us whenever she deigns to return from her hunt."

Aleirya clenched her fists at the cool and resentful tone of his voice while he spoke of Takhéa.

Whirling after him, she blurted, "I can prove it!"

Again, he moved so fast that she froze. His hand clutched her right shoulder. "Not another word," he growled.

Planting her left palm against his chest, she shoved him backward and scowled.

To her surprise, he let her, but she could tell she had angered him.

Moving as quickly as she could, she tore open her satchel and rummaged inside it until she found what she had been searching for.

Closing her left hand over the object, she exhaled, wondering if this was perhaps a mistake, but then she stretched out her arm toward him and spoke. "I believe this belongs to you."

In her open palm lay the two pieces of the broken wooden charm of the stag she had found at the cliffs and the ruin site of the shelter. She had no doubt it had been crafted from the same wood the rest of his bracelet was made of.

The Metatari's eyes dropped from her face to her hand, and immediately, his features softened. Eyes riveted on the stag charm, he swallowed and then drew closer again.

Carefully, as if her open palm was a trap, he scooped the two pieces up into his own hand.

Gingerly closing his fingers over it, he muttered something inaudible, and when he opened them again, the stag was complete, no longer broken.

He seemed to draw in a sharp breath, and then she watched him reattach it to his bracelet.

Once it hung alongside the rest of the other wooden charms, most of them shaped as something resembling an animal, he took a moment and stared down at it.

Aleirya studied him, realizing that whatever she had found obviously meant a great deal to him. And then another thought struck her, and she suppressed a gasp.

"It was you at the king's banquet before the attack on the dragon shelters? You disguised yourself as a servant. The—the eye patch; the cut across your palm wasn't from the shattered glass; the wound was from our fight in the cliffs. Did you come after me again just to make sure I hadn't told the king? To make sure whatever spell you placed over me to forget had worked?"

Aleirya watched the muscles in his jaw tense before he swallowed and looked at her but said nothing.

Aleirya waited for him to answer, riveting her eyes on him; she felt her fingernails dig into her palms when he continued to hesitate.

"Thank you for returning this to me," he said finally.

For the first time, his tone sounded genuinely kind and soft; there was nothing bitter or harsh hidden in the undertones of his voice.

Aleirya nodded wordlessly in return, taken aback by the gentle answer. She had expected him to deny it or perhaps utter something cruel in return, and yet when he hadn't, she grew angry. Once again, he was pretending not to remember.

The shapeshifter turned to walk away again, tilting his head as his means to urge her to follow.

She did, her arms stiff at her sides, and she scoffed.

Hurrying after him, she shook her head and asked, "What is it with this bracelet of yours?"

Peering past his shoulder, she saw his familiar smirk.

He didn't stop, and he didn't reply.

Clenching her fists, Aleirya stomped after him, picking up her pace to walk beside him.

"You could at least tell me about the piece I returned to you. You know, a favor for a favor? Or does a concept as such not exist amongst your kind?"

Aleirya didn't notice him come to a standstill and stumbled a few steps ahead before she stopped as well and spun toward him.

Eyeing her, he grinned and spoke. "If I answer your question, you must answer one of mine."

Without thinking, Aleirya nodded and replied, "Agreed."

After all, there wasn't anything that interesting or dangerous about her that he could possibly want to know.

Smiling shrewdly, he took a few steps toward her and answered, "I made the charm myself, and the stag reminds me of a friend."

That was disappointing, she thought, irritated at herself. She should have been more precise in the posing of her question.

"Now, my turn," said the shapeshifter. "I'll even be so kind as to use your own words. What does Tamar want from you? The two of you have undoubtedly met before."

Aleirya smirked.

"What a waste of an opportunity," she said. "I couldn't tell you, because I don't know."

Tilting his head back a bit, he replied, "I see. So, truthfulness isn't a concept that exists amongst your people."

Her eyes narrowed, and her jaw tightened at his words.

"I wasn't lying," she answered.

Shrugging his shoulders, he seemed to ignore her and added, "If you won't honor our agreement, I guess I don't have to either. After all, I could just pry the answers from you."

Quicker than she could blink, he stood just inches before her, cupping her face with both his hands while he stared into her eyes.

In any other circumstance, the notion might have been considered romantic, but this wasn't... despite the somewhat tantalizing thrill that jolted through her at his touch.

Aleirya couldn't breathe. Showers of heat and an icy cold ran down her spine.

Thinking fast, she used the moment she thought him to be distracted and whipped a small dagger-like weapon from his belt, raising it immediately to his neck.

The blade nicked the soft and perfectly smooth-looking, alabaster skin and drew her gaze to the fine line of blood that poured down his neck.

A part of her seemed surprised that it looked just like her own, as if she had expected it to appear black or something unheard of.

A chuckle bubbled from his throat, and he spoke. "I like you, dragon girl."

Her whole body seemed to shiver from within when her eyes met his gaze again.

Pressing her lips together, she pushed the weapon harder against his neck.

"I can do far worse to your mind than you to my body with that blade," he went on in that warm and alluring voice of his.

Everything inside her wanted to scream in horror of him. Even if she willed her legs to move and her feet to run from him, she knew she couldn't. Something about his power held her paralyzed in his presence. Like a spider rendered its prey unable to move or escape by its venom, she was helplessly caught in his trap.

Aleirya swallowed, still looking at him.

"No mind tricks," she said, trying to sound firm, but her voice quivered.

She didn't want to beg for mercy. She'd rather he finish her here and now if he really wanted to harm her.

Once again, and only for a moment, the look on his face seemed to oddly soften before his fearsome and unruly countenance returned, and he replied, "Then fight it."

The words came out harsh, indicating that she had angered him.

Her eyes widened at his unexpected answer, and she tried to shake her head. It hardly budged in his grasp when she spoke. "How?"

Aleirya watched the muscles in his jaw contract and relax, and then he lowered his left hand from her face.

The other wandered along the line of her chin. His thumb grazed her cheek and halted at the left corner of her lower lip.

He seemed to study her curiously and then said, "So much power at your fingertips and yet I can overthrow you with the flick of my wrist…"

The corners of his mouth twitched upward to a grin, and he added, "You do not know the gift you possess, dragon girl."

Aleirya felt a pinch as his grip tightened on her face before he let go.

The blood on his neck didn't seem to concern him in the slightest nor that she still held his dagger in her hand.

Her breath quickened while her mind raced, and she tried to make sense of what he had said.

What gift? What in the dragon's name could he possibly mean by that?

When she didn't move, he exhaled, and then gently retrieved his weapon from her.

Aleirya didn't fight him.

She could hear the detritus snap and crumble under the soles of his boots when he moved past her.

"Come now," he said. "That's enough questions for one day."

It had been three full days since Aleirya had last seen Takhéa.

She sat huddled on the cool ground in between the thick twisted roots of the trees surrounding them.

The sun had long set as the night swallowed the endless woods in darkness. Their only light was a fire the Metatari had made to help them keep warm.

They had barely spoken a word to each other ever since she had mentioned the bracelet.

Her stomach grumbled, and she hugged her knees tighter.

The small ration of food he had offered her had hardly been satisfying.

She wanted to hunt. At least that would make for a proper meal, but he wouldn't allow it.

Occasionally, Aleirya let her eyes stray toward the shapeshifter, watching him through the crackling and whipping flames between them.

He wasn't looking back at her, staring blankly at the ground in front of him.

Aleirya thought of their conversation a few days ago and the way he had spoken to her, of her.

Lord Acristus had cursed her for the power she harbored within.

Eskhàra... His choked cry still haunted her memory.

The Metatari, however, had called it a gift.

Had they both spoken of the same thing, she wondered?

Whatever it was, she wanted no part in it.

All she wanted was to return to the life she had lived before, the life in which she knew who she was.

But she didn't, did she? It was all a lie. She had not the faintest idea or shred of the truth to her identity…

Aleirya shivered and rubbed her hands along her arms.

How could she go back to it all, knowing it was just an illusion of what she wanted her life to be?

Wasn't it better to live according to who she truly was than spend a lifetime denying it?

She heard leaves rustle as the shapeshifter rose and moved, but she didn't cast a glance in his direction, fixing her gaze on the fire.

Only when she noticed him standing beside her did she look up.

Watching her wordlessly, she noticed him hold out his cape to her.

The light from the flames flickered across his wide pupils and painted his skin a warm gold that reminded her of the sunset. A sight she had not witnessed ever since they had left Tarragon, having been wandering the depths of the Dhaharran Forest.

Accepting it, she nodded a thank you and saw him imitate the movement before he slowly returned to where he had sat across from her.

"Despite what it may seem, I am no monster," he said.

He wasn't looking at her anymore when he spoke, and Aleirya watched him settle down onto the ground, scooting closer to the fire for warmth, she imagined.

Aleirya sensed something pull at her from within while she cast his cape around her shoulders, her skin tingling comfortably at the warmth it still held from his body.

He must have read her mind the other day… Or was her dislike of his nature perhaps that obvious?

Her stomach twitched when she passed a quick glance in his direction before she stared down at her feet.

"I'm sorry," she said. "I don't think you are… I didn't mean to—"

"It's alright… dragon girl," he interrupted her.

She could see a weak smile spread across his lips before it slowly faded in the quiet that settled between them.

"It's Aleirya," she said after a while.

She caught him shooting her a confused look when she spoke.

Her mouth opened to a smile, and she replied, "My name… It's Aleirya… Not, you know, dragon girl."

She tried to imitate his deep, dark voice when she recited the nickname he had given her, provoking him to laugh.

She joined him until the joyful noise quieted, and the silence embraced them once again.

This time, it dragged on much longer than before.

Her eyes began to grow weary, and she wondered if she might just let herself settle down to sleep when she heard him.

"Hadrian," he said.

The sound of his name made her smile; or perhaps it was rather the fact that she had gotten him to reveal a part of himself to her.

His gaze was still lowered to the ground before him when she looked back at him.

"Hadrian…" she repeated softly. "I've never heard of it…"

Just then, a loud series of cracking noises, like the snapping of bones, broke through the blackness above them, joined by a rustling before something came hurling down toward them.

Aleirya raised her arms above her head in protection and felt another's weight crash against her as, one by one, bits and pieces of the trees' crowns plummeted into the forest ground all around them.

She let out a gasp at the harsh knock that rattled her spine and ribs once she struck the ground while her body was flung backward.

Pinching her eyes shut, she groaned and lifted her head the moment the pounding noises stopped.

It was only then that she noticed the shapeshifter's body bent over hers, and she met him face to face.

He fixed her with a concerned expression for a moment before he pushed himself up onto his feet and helped her up after him.

"Are you alright?" he asked when she stood upright and winced at the throbbing that rose to her head from the nape of her neck.

"Yes," she answered, nodding at him.

He eyed her a bit longer until he dipped his chin at her, seemingly convinced.

"Thanks," she added, and then let him help her climb over the enormous boughs and the remnants of the trees' crowns that had almost crushed them.

Reaching the spot where the forest canopy had been torn open, Aleirya looked up and saw the starlit sky.

She had barely begun to marvel at the brightness of the stars that loomed above them when she heard a deep, familiar growl and whirled toward its source.

Two sparkling eyes found her just as the dragon stepped forth from the shadows.

"Takhéa!" Aleirya cried delightedly and immediately skipped over the piles of branches to get to her dragon.

Reaching her, she hugged her large snout while the dragon hummed and shut her eyes.

"She could have killed us," the Metatari said behind her.

Takhéa growled, baring her teeth just as Aleirya turned around and replied, "She didn't mean to."

The shapeshifter didn't say a word and only eyed them from a distance.

Returning her attention to Takhéa, Aleirya spoke. "I was beginning to worry about you."

She ran her hands over the dragon's smooth scales when Takhéa straightened her neck, withdrawing from her and casting a careful look toward the shapeshifter.

"I'm afraid I have some bad news," said the dragon.

She glanced at Aleirya and then back at the Metatari.

"I would have returned sooner, but I saw a fleet of dragons bearing Tarragon's royal sigil depart from our lands, and I followed them. They are headed toward Erysméa, Aleirya," Takhéa added.

She could sense her dragon's concern, which only multiplied her own.

"I'm afraid the Dragon's Kin and the elves are at war," said Takhéa.

"No," Aleirya caught herself utter breathlessly, and she spun around toward the shapeshifter.

He, too, seemed taken aback by the news.

His features stood out in sharp angles as his whole body appeared to have gone rigid, and his hands were balled into fists at his sides.

"This wasn't supposed to happen," he muttered, as if he hadn't meant for her to hear him.

"What do you mean?" she asked, trudging toward him. She felt her own anger rally within her. Had he known this would happen?

He seemed to drift from them, lost in thought.

Stopping in front of him, she yelled, "Hadrian! What's going on?"

Her gaze bored into him, and she sensed her impatience grow when he hesitated.

She was about to speak again when his head snapped toward her, and he answered fiercely, "I don't know! But Tamar went to speak to the king of the elves to warn him not to strike against your people. We believe someone is turning your kingdoms against each other in a ploy to destroy you both. Tamar took several of us with him. They must still be there."

Aleirya's anger against him abated at the hint of fear in his eyes, and she swallowed.

"Then we must go," she said.

"And do what exactly?" he threw back at her. His fists were still tightly clenched when he went on, "You and I are hardly the sort of force that would break the tie in our favor. Tamar didn't travel with an army of Metatari. Even then, the elves are not a people to be underestimated."

"Well, we can't just sit here and hide!" Aleirya answered.

She could hear his breath come out in harsh bursts.

"If you won't go with me, I'll go alone," she said and then turned away to join Takhéa when he seized her arm.

"Wait," he said.

Aleirya's gaze dropped first to his grip on her and then rose to his eyes.

Exhaling, he stared back at her. He bit his lip and then added, "If we go, then we do this on my terms. Do you understand? I am not about to watch you get yourself killed or let this cost me my life by your reckless nature."

She wanted to smirk at his sudden concern for her but refrained and only nodded in reply.

"Good," he said, observing her response. "We'll travel to Erysméa on dragonback for as long and as far as we can remain undiscovered. Once we're close enough, you and I will portal into the king's city… the city of Mòr Rhíoghain."

Chapter 47

Exhaling, Valeirys tilted his head back against the wall and let his heel drag over the cold ground as he stretched out his leg.

The dangling noise of the chain strapped to his ankle ricocheted softly off the walls of his small cell, and he could hear dripping sounds echoing somewhere in the distance from the moisture that coated the rough stones.

Thin strands of grayish light spilled into the dungeon chamber from a narrow slit, and a chill shook his shoulders.

Valeirys squinted and moaned before lifting a hand to his throbbing forehead.

He could not tell how long he had been here.

Had it been a few hours, a night, a day?

Shutting his eyes, he pinched the bridge of his nose and tried to recall what had happened. His mind was foggy, and a slight hum lingered in his ears as if he had received a good blow to the head.

With a sigh, he then let his arm drop back down to his side, glancing at the bandage wrapped around his hand.

Frowning, he looked away from it and riveted his gaze onto the bland brick wall across from him.

His brow furrowed, his features scrunching together awkwardly, and he winced when a sting chased across the back of his injured hand, and he remembered the pain he had felt when the arrow had struck him.

Piece by piece, the incident with the soldiers at the palace and the fight trickled through the haze of his thoughts.

Valeirys could still see Eyvindr standing upon the palace steps, a bow in hand and another arrow set and ready to fire at him.

He knew his brother had only meant well by what he had done; who was to say what might have happened had he not taken that shot… But the image had permanently etched itself into his mind.

Swallowing, he carefully ran his hand over his side where the guard's blade had gone through him and shut his eyes.

He did not want to think about the fight. After all, there was no way of undoing what had happened.

The sound of a pair of footsteps drew his attention to the dark hall outside his cell, and he turned his head toward the noise.

Peering through the slits of the iron bars, flickers of a torchlight growing brighter swept over his face, and then he saw a figure approach.

Valeirys' mouth ran dry, and his throat tightened before he swallowed and spoke. "What are you doing here?"

Eyvindr placed the torch inside a sconce on the wall across from him and then settled down on the floor by his cell.

Leaning his back against the bars, he lowered his hood with a sigh and spoke. "Well, it isn't every day I get to see you fall from grace."

There was no malice in his voice, and when his brother looked at him, Valeirys felt the entire weight of his concern crash into him.

Eyvindr pursed his lips to speak, but then averted his gaze and let it drop to his hands folded in his lap.

Valeirys stared at him tacitly, allowing the quiet to fill the space between them before he shut his eyes and leaned his head back against the rock.

They sat motionless in the darkness for a while until Eyvindr spoke. "Valeirys?"

Valeirys opened his eyes and caught his brother's gaze just as he went on, "I—I never meant to—"

Valeirys shook his head and interrupted him. "You didn't have a choice."

He caught his brother's features still under his frigid tone and sighed before shaking and dropping his head.

"I don't know what happened, Eyvindr," said Valeirys.

An anguish suddenly coiled his chest and threatened to crush his lungs.

His hands balled into fists that started to tremble so that he pressed them against the ground beneath him to conceal it from his brother. A pressure built in his throat, traveling upward toward his mouth as if he were drowning.

He couldn't bear to deal with whatever had happened; whatever was happening to him.

"What you saw… I can't explain it," he simply said, forcing the words out.

"You were defending someone you loved," his brother answered. "You were defending me."

Valeirys shook his head; guilt, shame, and rage clutching his neck, and he spoke in a choked voice. "No…"

"You're not yourself," Eyvindr interjected. "You haven't been ever since your return from Lyrr…"

He waited until Valeirys met his gaze again, his eyes glowing fiercely against the shadows that enveloped them, and then he went on, "And I believe we are capable of much when we've been broken."

The words stung unexpectedly. Valeirys' lips drew apart to speak when a sudden jumble of noises arose from down the hall again and caused him to fall silent.

His attention darted to his right where he could see two elves coming toward them, one bearing a set of keys that jangled from his belt, the other a sword secured at his side.

Noticing the embossment on the blade's pommel, Valeirys knew its wielder before the lock of his cell clicked, and the pair strode inside.

Valeirys swallowed but did not move when he met Trajan's eyes.

For a moment, they simply stared at each other until Trajan spoke. "Remove his shackle."

The elf obeyed without hesitation, crouching down beside Valeirys' feet and set to undoing the cuff.

Valeirys heard the clatter and clanking while the elf worked to remove his restraint but did not once cast a glance in his direction.

The commander did not avert his gaze from him even as he spoke. "Eyvindr, leave before your father gets word of your presence here."

Eyvindr rose wordlessly to his feet and did as bid, but Valeirys caught the hint of anger laced within the forceful upward tug of his hood and the stiffness in his gait before he disappeared.

Looking up at Trajan, Valeirys could read the commander's frustration off him as easily as he would any written word from a page.

Trajan seemed to bite back a remark, pressing his lips together to a hard line, and once the shackle cracked open, he seized Valeirys rather impatiently by the arm and hauled him to his feet.

Nodding at the elf beside him, the commander turned and then shoved Valeirys forward and out of the cell.

"Move," he said.

Valeirys scoffed but said nothing and followed his order.

They walked in silence out of the dungeon, through the palace's halls and outside its main entrance, only stopping to pause once they stepped out onto the perron. Valeirys saw his horse bridled and saddled at the bottom of the staircase, its reins in the hands of a page.

He was surprised to see his sword fastened to the saddle. He had no doubt it had been the commander's doing that it was returned to him.

Squinting, he glanced up at the heavens as the sun was beginning its descent.

It had been at least a day that he had spent locked up inside that cell.

There was nothing left of the smoldered remains of the scaffold. The barricades had been taken down, even the cobblestones covering the grounds of the King's Square appeared to have been scrubbed clean to remove any trace of the blood spill that had taken place that evening.

Valeirys swallowed, suddenly very much aware of himself.

He could feel Trajan's disappointment weighing on him; nudging him from behind, he heard the commander's voice. "Go on."

Without a word, Valeirys nodded and descended the steps, Trajan following him closely.

Once he had reached the bottom of the staircase, he paused and then turned to face him.

"I need to speak to my father. He's still here, isn't he?"

Trajan nodded and answered, "He has yet to attend a meeting with His Majesty and the royal council. But you are to return home, Valeirys."

"I just need to speak with him. I—"

"You can't be here," Trajan interrupted him.

"But—" said Valeirys.

"No," Trajan cut him off again.

Taking a step toward him, Valeirys spoke. "I only want a moment to speak with my father, only a moment to explain, and then—"

"Valeirys," Trajan said.

His eyes were intently fixed on him, and he remained perfectly still in his stance, as if immovable. His arms hung at his sides, and his feet were planted securely on the ground, a shoulder width apart.

"You can't be here," the commander went on. "It took quite a bit to convince Lord Calaedorn to have you released and sent home until this predicament of yours is settled."

"It certainly took you long enough to get me out of there," Valeirys muttered, interrupting him.

Valeirys saw the muscles in Trajan's jaw twitch before he responded, "Yes. I thought perhaps some time locked up in a cell might do you good, and at the very least, offer you a glimpse of the future that awaits you should you continue down this path."

Something seized Valeirys from within at Trajan's words. Viciously, it began to twist and tear at his gut, making him want to scream.

The pounding from his heart traveled up along his neck, and he gritted his teeth.

"I gave you an order, Valeirys. Now, go home," Trajan warned.

Valeirys snorted and shook his head, briefly thrusting his hands onto his hips and turning away. Approaching his horse, he forcefully removed the scabbard holding his blade from the saddle and attached it to his hip, its familiar weight at his side oddly making him feel whole again.

Aware that Trajan was watching his every move, he paced back and forth before he abruptly stopped and then took an explosive step toward him.

"Don't I have a claim to my future? Is my life not my own? I am prepared to face the consequences of my actions, but I demand the right to speak for myself! Let me speak to Lord Calaedorn, let me speak to my father!" Valeirys uttered fiercely.

There was a scorching heat that built in his limbs, slowly but surely creeping toward the center of his chest.

Lowering his voice, Trajan answered him in an unyielding tone. "No. Return home, Valeirys, or I will have no choice but to arrest you, as are my orders."

His words were enough to raise Valeirys' hackles, and glaring back at Trajan, he spat out angrily, "Your orders—and who gave you those orders? My father? Am I not my father's son, the son of your lord? How dare you threaten me like that!"

At that, Trajan grabbed hold of Valeirys' right arm and pulled him along, stopping beside his horse; with the wave of his other hand, he motioned for the page to leave them.

The boy scurried, and Trajan released Valeirys' arm.

His left hand balled to a fist, and looking at Valeirys, he spoke. "I won't ask you to leave again."

With that, he turned and began to walk away when Valeirys responded bitterly, "I was defending my family's honor. I was fighting for the weak. I was confronting an injustice... I was doing what you taught me to do!"

THE RISE OF ISIGAR

His voice almost cracked at the end, and a dull pain struck his middle as if he had been punched.

He wanted to shake his head at the confusion that tickled his scalp and froze his blood. The truth was, he didn't know why he had done what he had done; how he had been capable of such violence… But he wasn't about to admit that to the commander.

Valeirys noticed Trajan stop and his left hand subtly fold around the hilt of his sword that hung sheathed at his side.

The motion only wounded him more, and he felt as if his body were about to convulse.

When the commander turned to face him again, Valeirys' eyes darted from Trajan's hand to his face just as he answered, "I did not teach you to be merciless. I did not teach you to be violent, Valeirys."

He paused for a moment before adding, "I saw how you fought against those guards that night… You let your anger, you let your emotions control you, and there is nothing honorable about that."

Valeirys bit down on his lip, fuming with anger while he stared daggers at Trajan.

He was about to speak up against him when the commander went on, "You are not the boy I once knew who longed for nothing more than to fight for the good in this world. You are not the soldier I trained. You must stop this, Valeirys."

"Stop what, exactly?" Valeirys blurted. He paused and then nodded. "You're right. I am no longer that boy, and perhaps I'm not a soldier either. Perhaps I was never meant to be one."

Trajan's eyes seem to flicker, and the corners of his mouth pointed downward when he replied, "You are on the precipice of destroying everything you've ever wanted."

"How would you know what I want?" Valeirys yelled.

Something swept across Trajan's face at his words, and for a moment, the commander only stared back at him.

"Do as you wish, Valeirys." Trajan spoke dryly. "Your future should be yours to decide. But alas, be forewarned, only very few of our actions can be undone;

regret haunts us all equally, whether we consider our intentions to have been good or evil."

The slap of a soldier's boots against the stone made Valeirys halt, and he watched the elf rush down the steps and stop at the commander's side.

The soldier whispered something into Trajan's ear, and Valeirys watched the commander's expression harden as he grimaced and clenched his teeth.

Valeirys sensed something was off as his gaze flicked between Trajan and the soldier.

"What's happened?" he asked.

Trajan looked at him, and Valeirys wanted to flinch at his hesitation, the telltale sign that he no longer trusted him.

The commander's hand moved from the hilt of his sword, and he formed a sign in the air, signaling a pair of guards to join him.

"Make sure Lord Altair takes his leave," he said.

Then he returned his attention to the soldier beside him and spoke. "Take with you any soldier who so much as crosses your path and find him! I must inform Lord Altair and the council."

The commander whirled and hurried up the steps when Valeirys called after him, "Trajan!"

The commander stopped and turned to face him again.

He held his gaze for a moment before he finally spoke. "Melquart's gone. He's escaped."

Valeirys froze, a jolt chasing up his spine, and his throat tightened, stalling the breath in his lungs.

Trajan and the soldier had nearly disappeared when he finally made his feet move and turned, realization dawning...

I believe we are capable of much when we've been broken.

A lump formed in his throat, a pit burrowing in his stomach just as a fire stirred within, and his lips moved in a whisper. "Eyvindr."

Chapter 48

Valeirys dug his heels into his stallion's sides, compelling it to move faster as he raced down the cobblestone pathways, ignoring the shouts of the people who leaped aside, frantically trying to get out of his way.

His mind reeled at the well of thoughts that flooded his subconscious. His vision blurred, and his heart throbbed.

Valeirys gritted his teeth and forced a lump down his throat.

It couldn't be, a part of him told himself over and over again in rhythm with the pounding footfalls of his horse.

Eyvindr would never betray him like that. He couldn't have… But the pain that wrenched at his heart told him otherwise.

Valeirys bit down on his lip and yanked at the reins in his hands. His brother couldn't have gotten that far.

The rows of the houses that lined the narrow road ahead melted into one white blur as he sped by them. The wind rushed past the skin of his cheeks, whistling loudly in his ears and tossed his cloak that fluttered at his sides. He could feel the weight of it lift and fall back onto his shoulders in one fluid motion.

There are advantages to being invisible; people tend to underestimate you... Eyvindr's words rang through his thoughts, and he clenched the reins even harder, feeling his fingernails press painfully into his palms.

The skin across his knuckles had turned white, and his hands had gone cold, sending an icy shiver chasing up his arms. But Valeirys didn't care.

He fixed his eyes on the portcullis of Mòr Rhíoghain's gate that finally emerged ahead, and squinting, he spied another rider passing beneath the arch of the barbican.

It had to be him.

A blazing heat consumed his body, and a sharp pain jolted along the bones of his jaw at the ire the sight of his brother roused within him.

Kicking his stallion harder, Valeirys leaned forward and screamed Eyvindr's name.

The rider didn't stop, but Valeirys glimpsed his brother's face when he peered back at him over his shoulder, just as the lattice began to descend toward the ground.

Valeirys could hear the pair of guards who stood watch at the barbican shout, calling out for him to slow down. But he had no intention of stopping.

Frantically, the elves cried out for the portcullis to be raised anew, and Valeirys heard a screech and saw the iron lattice shake before it moved upward.

Bent forward, his feet balanced firmly in his stirrups, he stroked his horse's side and whispered over it a spell of fearlessness and speed.

His mount squealed and then charged.

The gate grew larger and larger as they drew closer, and the guards shouted louder and louder. Their unease was visible as they seemed to scramble back and forth, unsure what to do and how to stop him.

The portcullis dragged upward, emitting an ear-splitting, grinding noise and was not nearly raised high enough for them to pass through it and yet, he did not stop.

Valeirys continued to race toward the gate at a mad pace, and just when it seemed too late, he ducked, burying his face against his stallion's neck.

His heart stammered, and then it felt as if it had slowed its beat to a stop when he heard the lattice creak and squeal above him as they slid beneath it.

The stallion neighed and then leaped once they passed the gate but maintained its stride.

Valeirys drew a breath, and an instant flow of relief flooded his chest with the gulp of air that filled his lungs.

But the alleviating sensation vanished almost immediately when his gaze locked onto the dark shape hunched forward in the saddle of the horse ahead.

His muscles strung taut, and his eyes burning from the whipping wind, Valeirys bounded after Eyvindr.

The sun was setting, lighting the fields in a magnificent golden glow just as they reached the edge of a forest, and he watched Eyvindr disappear into the woodland.

Gritting his teeth, Valeirys followed, ducking under the overhanging branches of a pair of trees as he crossed onto the overgrown trail that led into the forest.

Then, all at once, as if he had meant to lead him into the woods, Eyvindr slowed his pace and turned to face him.

Coming to a stop, Valeirys' chest tightened. They couldn't have been more than a couple paces apart, and yet he felt as if he stared at his brother from the opposite side of a cleft.

For a moment, all he could hear was the rustle of the wind chasing through the endless rows of trees that surrounded them and the sputtering from their horses, their bridles making a clinking noise as they bobbed their heads.

Valeirys forced his hands to relax, unclenching the reins, and squared his shoulders.

"It was you," he said. "All this time, it's been you."

Eyvindr did not shy away, his blue eyes riveted on him, his face solemn as he lifted his chin and answered, "Yes."

"You played me for a fool," Valeirys interrupted him before he could go on. "It must have been quite the spectacle… Tell me, did you enjoy watching me scramble, enjoy watching me, Father, and the entire kingdom struggle to unmask you?"

"It's not what you think," said Eyvindr, his voice steady despite the tension lining his jaw. "I didn't—"

"How could you?" Valeirys yelled.

"You don't understand!" Eyvindr shouted back at him. "And you never will."

Valeirys pressed his lips together and shook his head, his edged gaze relentlessly pinned on his brother.

Eyvindr gave a sigh and dismounted in a practiced swoop, landing carefully so as not to injure his leg.

Standing tall, an unfamiliar confidence in the carriage of his shoulders, Valeirys barely recognized his brother as Eyvindr looked back at him and spoke. "Yes. The rebellion is my responsibility to claim. But however cruel you consider me to be, I never wished any evil against you, Father or the kingdom. I intend to save it."

Valeirys' boots struck the ground as he got off his horse and strode toward Eyvindr, saying, "Save it by assassinating the king? Melquart nearly put an arrow through his head!"

"Did he? Or did the strike not do exactly what it was meant to—miss its apparent target?" said Eyvindr, his eyes narrowing. "You tell me."

Valeirys scoffed, heat rushing to his head, and he clenched his fists.

Memories of the past weeks, even months, sped past his mind's eye, their conversations echoed in his ears. He could not believe this was happening. He could not believe it was Eyvindr all along; and yet, all at once, it made perfect sense. It aligned.

"Melquart was simply a frontman, a face to hide behind, wasn't he? You were feeding the rebellion the information from Father's meetings, our strategies, the plans I shared with you—I trusted you!"

"Valeirys," Eyvindr started.

But Valeirys cut him off again. "That's why the rebellion was always ahead of us. That is why Melquart evaded our detection and escaped time upon time, because he knew everything. You told him everything!"

Valeirys' head spun, anger burning a hole through his gut as he whirled and paced, trying to keep himself from hurling his fists at his brother. "How could you do this? How could you turn against your people? Your family! Me!"

"It had nothing to do with you!" Eyvindr raised his voice.

They stood an arm's reach apart, their breaths audible, chests heaving and gazes wrought sharp as knives.

"King Yevandrielle should not reign," said Eyvindr, breaking the silence. "Despite his good intentions, despite his love for our people, he does not belong on the throne. Erysméa's rulership was to be driven to change—"

"How dare you," said Valeirys. "How dare you stand here and speak in such a way when you know nothing of what it means to rule a kingdom!"

"He did nothing, Valeirys," Eyvindr interjected loudly. "They—the rulership you so adamantly support—they did nothing when our people needed them the most."

Valeirys scoffed and shook his head before he looked up again at his brother.

"Did you know Father turned them away? Fathers and mothers crippled by fear and the loss of their children?" Eyvindr began again, his eyes narrowing. "Melquart spent weeks traveling throughout Erysméa, petitioning before each lord, begging for something to be done when the kidnappings began."

His shoulders lifted as he drew a breath and shook his head, adding, "Our people had to watch their loved ones disappear; for weeks nothing changed, and they were told to be satisfied by the fact that the king and their lords would search for the missing, but nothing truly happened until it was too late.

"And then, when the bodies surfaced… Did you know Father refused to have the victims returned to their families for burial? The people you claim to care about, they were denied the right to grant their dead their final rest."

Valeirys' lips pressed to a line, and he swallowed, hesitating to answer as his brother's words filtered into his mind.

"I found Melquart at our father's doorstep," said Eyvindr. "His son had been taken, and weeks later, after everything he had done to have him returned to him safely, the boy was found dead, his body mutilated, half torched. He was brought to see his son to confirm his identity, and that is it. His name will never be written in the stone of Naitha di Laiona Érjinye, Valeirys. And you know why? Because his death was ruled an obscenity the king and his council, the lords—Father—wanted no one to remember."

His lip curled slightly, and he added, "It was proof of their failing. They were ashamed."

Valeirys studied him quietly for a moment before he said, "So your answer was to turn against your own? To lead hundreds against our king and wreak havoc over those loyal to the throne, ordering your followers to commit one crime after the other? Did you know innocents died during the attack on the banquet? By the blade, I could have died in the battle at Lyrr! Are you so blinded by the cause you've pledged yourself to that you cannot see the evil in your deeds?"

"No one was killed under my command!" Eyvindr shouted. "The night of the banquet did not go as planned, and I will live with the consequences for the rest of my life. And as for the battle in Lyrr... Melquart acted on his own. I never gave the order to attack your unit. Melquart was supposed to surrender."

The space stilled between them, the void Valeirys sensed grew larger and colder as they stared at each other.

"Something had to happen, Valeirys," Eyvindr said, breaking the silence. "If we cannot trust our rulership, how can we hope to survive the evil that has already turned against us? In all earnestness, can you truly stand before me and claim that our king did everything in his power to protect and avenge the people's suffering? Are you truly telling me that there is no fault in the actions of our leaders?"

Valeirys gritted his teeth and bit back a snarl.

"How did Melquart escape that night at the banquet? You helped him. Don't deny it," he said when Eyvindr interrupted, "It wasn't him."

A shudder ran down his shoulders, and Valeirys froze.

"Melquart was never at the banquet," said Eyvindr.

"Then how—I saw him. The gleam in his eyes," Valeirys answered, determined.

THE RISE OF ISIGAR

Eyvindr shook his head and replied, "Khatalaseis chreiana. I put it in my wine. When skillfully used, it changes the color of the eyes to silver. I disguised myself."

"You poisoned yourself," Valeirys said matter-of-factly.

"It's called mithridatism," Eyvindr objected. "I knew you'd recognize me if you saw me. All I had to do was keep out of your sight until the effects wore off."

He paused and then took a step toward him, adding, "As I said before, the arrow fired did exactly what it was supposed to do—it missed. With that kind of shot, I wasn't going to let anyone else do it when I couldn't be certain the king would survive. The king was always supposed to make it out alive, Valeirys. What happened after I disappeared… Trust me, if I could undo it, I would."

Despite himself, Valeirys nodded.

He thought he had noticed a flicker of relief pass over his brother's face but wasn't sure. After all, it seemed he didn't even know the person standing across from him.

His chest ached, and he struggled to decide what he should do. His brother was a traitor. He was to be brought and tried before His Majesty. But how could he drag his own brother to his certain death? The thought made him sick to his stomach.

"So, what now?" Valeirys asked instead. "What's your grand scheme? What did you do to Malik and the kidnapped soldiers? Are they alive?"

Eyvindr's eyes narrowed fiercely, and he interrupted, "Melquart did not take them and neither did I. There's something else at play here, I swear it."

"What if I don't believe you!" Valeirys retorted.

All of a sudden, a crack like the snapping of a branch shot through the darkness.

Valeirys whirled, his whole body gone rigid.

Snap!

Again, the noise rang out. The horses stirred nervously, ears twitching and hooves beating against the detritus that crunched beneath them as they backed up.

Valeirys could hear Eyvindr try to soothe his stallion behind him while his eyes raked through the blackness. But nothing stood out.

A rustle chased through the crowns of the trees ahead, and then again, a crack sounded.

The horses spooked and reared; Valeirys leaped aside just in time before they bolted past him.

Lunging forward, he called after them, but it was too late.

Frustrated, Valeirys tossed his hands up in the air and exhaled heavily.

Eyvindr stood beside him, and they both glanced at each other just as a voice rose from behind them. "Ridiculously skittish beings, if you ask me."

Immediately, Valeirys and Eyvindr drew their weapons and whirled around toward the sound of the voice.

Chapter 49

Valeirys' breath caught the moment he spotted the tall, ominous figure, standing a stone's throw away and enveloped in the darkness of the somber woods.

With features hidden from sight and draped under a black mantle, it did not move, lurking at him from amidst the ranks of the towering trees.

The hairs of his neck stood on end, his muscles stiffened, and a shudder coursed through him once the stranger removed his hood, and Valeirys recognized the Metatari.

"Get behind me," Valeirys growled at Eyvindr.

But his brother only scoffed, and Valeirys heard the high-pitched ring of a pair of throwing knives released from their sheaths just as Eyvindr responded, "After everything, you still think of me as the damsel in need of protection."

Valeirys tilted his head sideways, his jaw set, but he did not look in his brother's direction and risk taking his eyes off the stranger ahead.

"We'll talk about what you are later," he uttered harshly. "For now, I don't want your blood on my hands."

"Well, if it isn't the rebel and the soldier with anger issues," said the shapeshifter, a grin tugging at the corners of his mouth. "There's no need for that," he added and motioned for them to lower their weapons.

Valeirys' mouth went dry, and cold sweat ran down the nape of his neck. How did he know?

Remaining as still as he could, he kept his eyes fixed on the Metatari and replied, "I'll be the judge of that. What are you doing here?"

He had never fought against a shapeshifter before. He did not know what this creature was capable of nor what he would do.

Valeirys' blood ran cold, and his mind scrambled for a plan of how they could get out of the woods.

Looking directly at him, the Metatari cocked his head to the side and answered, "I could ask you the same."

He began to approach when Valeirys lifted his blade higher and shouted, "Not a step closer! I warn you, shapeshifter."

The Metatari's eyes flared bright, though he seemed to remain calm; stopping, he raised his hands before his body and spoke. "If I wanted to harm you, you'd know."

For a moment, he seemed to linger, as if to determine how great a threat Valeirys was.

The hem of his cloak lay spread out over the dark ground and disappeared into the undergrowth like the gnarled roots of the trees surrounding him.

His round pupils were unnaturally dilated as he studied Valeirys, standing motionless across from him as if he were stalking him like prey.

Valeirys did not relent. Beside him, he heard Eyvindr's knives slide back into the sheaths concealed beneath the sleeves of his gambeson, and he noticed his brother's stance shift out of the corner of his eye as Eyvindr straightened beside him.

The shapeshifter's gaze flicked between the two of them and he spoke. "Ah, so you're the sensible one."

Valeirys gritted his teeth and bit back a hiss just when the Metatari gestured toward him and said to Eyvindr, "Is he always like this?"

Eyvindr shrugged his shoulders but said nothing.

"Enough with the games!" Valeirys shouted and raised the tip of his blade higher.

Eyeing Valeirys, the shapeshifter lowered his hands to his sides.

Keeping his distance, he veered left and started to move again.

Valeirys watched him drift in and out of the moon's light, blending seamlessly within the forest's scenery. His stride was soundless and agile while he trod over the uneven ground with ease, as if it were a smooth pathway.

Each step was measured and harbored an elegance that seemed rather incongruent to his sizable form.

Valeirys' skin crawled at the unusual silence that enveloped them while the shapeshifter circled around him like a beast on the prowl.

Gone was the whisper of the wind and the rushing echo of a stream he could have sworn he had heard a minute ago. Instead, a deathly stillness had fallen upon them; although they appeared to be alone, he couldn't shake the feeling that they were being watched, observed by a mysterious audience tucked away in the presence of the night.

The only noises that disrupted the ghostly quiet were the twigs that cracked and the leaves that shifted and rustled beneath his own feet as he continued to turn his body to face the Metatari.

The shapeshifter's feral eyes gleamed against the darkness, and holding Valeirys' gaze he asked, "Why so defensive, Valeirys?"

Flinching at the sound of his name, Valeirys clutched the handle of his weapon and asked in return, "How do you know my name?"

Having come full circle around him, the Metatari replied with a chuckle, "You're quite the interrogator, aren't you?"

Squinting, Valeirys shook his head and spoke. "Just answer the question."

The darker it grew, the more the shapeshifter's form seemed to dissolve within the shadows, making his presence feel even more threatening, and it became increasingly difficult to keep track of his movements.

Suddenly, he stopped, and for a moment, all Valeirys could see was his striking gaze that bored into him.

"You're not helping anyone by poking the beast," Eyvindr hissed quietly under his breath.

But Valeirys ignored him.

"You are bold, young elf, speaking to me in such a tone," said the shapeshifter, his voice sounding like a growl.

Then, all at once, he disappeared from view.

Valeirys felt his gut drop, and a painful throbbing climb to his throat. His heart fluttered out of rhythm while he blinked, and his eyes raked the darkness in front of him in search of the Metatari.

The skin of his neck prickled, and an icy shiver raced down his spine when he heard the shapeshifter's voice rise again from behind him. "Lower your sword. I do not appreciate pointed things being held up to my face while sharing a conversation."

Clutching his weapon even harder, Valeirys whirled around to find the Metatari eyeing him calmly while leaning against a nearby tree.

When he saw Valeirys refused, he added, "Fine; then keep holding that thing up nice and high. I can talk either way."

The Metatari did not seem to bear a shred of concern for Valeirys' raised blade while he strolled across the trail in front of him and approached one of the larger trees that surrounded them.

Carefully, he placed his hand on the wide trunk, almost as if lowering each finger intentionally.

Seconds later, Valeirys and Eyvindr watched as a bright light shimmered beneath the tree's bark at the Metatari's touch.

Valeirys wondered what the shapeshifter had done when the light vanished, and nothing else followed. But then something snapped and rumbled from inside it.

Valeirys and Eyvindr started to back up, and a gasp escaped Valeirys' lips when he watched one of the powerful boughs of the tree that loomed above them crack and then move.

Bending downward, its form was no longer rigid as it drifted toward the Metatari in a serpentine motion. The tips of its branches twisted and turned, slithering through the dark space, before they stretched forth and reached for the shapeshifter's open palm as if coaxed by it.

Seemingly mesmerized by the shapeshifter, the bough yielded to the course of his hand, following its movement like its own shadow.

The sight was enchanting, and Valeirys couldn't help but notice the Metatari smile with delight.

It seemed as if each relished in the other's company, and Valeirys thought he had heard the shapeshifter whispering to it softly as it moved along with him.

At last, the bough dipped toward the ground and then curved upward again, just below the height of the Metatari's hip.

Its end continued to cling to his hand when the shapeshifter turned around to face Valeirys and carefully leaned back, seating himself in the low curve of the branch he had reformed.

Bit by bit, the bark covering the bough darkened just as the fine tips of its branches nestled against the shapeshifter's palm and interlaced with his fingers.

All at once, their movement stopped and the Metatari slowly withdrew his hand.

"Tell me how you know who I am," Valeirys demanded, growing increasingly irritated by the Metatari's evasive behavior.

The Metatari eyed him for a moment, and then folding his arms over his chest, he said, "Is it not the Altair's sigil that you wear?"

He gestured toward the sword-shaped clasp of Valeirys' cloak and then added, "And are you not the son of Lord Uryiel Altair?"

"Yes, but—" Valeirys answered, feeling foolish.

"You do not share a resemblance with your father—or your brother, for that matter," said the shapeshifter, and gestured toward Eyvindr. "Therefore, you must be the orphaned child that was brought to him as a babe and that he took in as his own," the shapeshifter interrupted him.

"How did you know?" Valeirys asked in amazement.

With an amused look on his face, the Metatari replied, "So many speak of the gracefulness of the elves and yet fail to mention their boundless arrogance."

When Valeirys said nothing, he went on, "As leader of my people, it is my duty to know those in power and on whom the rule of His Majesty depends."

He paused, looking back at Valeirys intently before adding, "I have known who you are for a long time."

Once again, it grew very quiet between them when the shapeshifter had finished speaking.

Valeirys continued to study the expression on his face, wondering if he had spoken the truth, until he lowered his sword and sheathed it at his side.

An instant relief flowed through his arm and shoulder after having put his weapon aside, and his body began to relax a bit.

"Forgive me my misjudgment," he said.

The Metatari nodded, and replied with a grin, "It's alright, you wouldn't be the first."

Still curious as to why the shapeshifter had approached them in these woods, Valeirys asked, "What are you doing here? If you truly do not mean to harm us, explain your lurking presence, and apparently, eavesdropping in these woods?"

"I was hunting," the Metatari replied simply. "Despite that King Yevandrielle and I are at peace, I am no honored guest of the king, and the likes of my kind are not welcome in his court. As I am to meet with His Majesty again soon, I chose to lodge here in these woods with my men."

Valeirys' glance immediately leaped from the shapeshifter sitting across from him to the dark depths of the forest beyond him, and his body froze.

As if reading his mind, the Metatari spoke. "You have nothing to fear. We are alone, if that's what you wish to know. And on the matter of eavesdropping; you can hardly call it such, as the argument you two were having was loud enough for any innocent pedestrian in proximity of these woods to hear."

Taking a step back, Valeirys' hand slowly trailed to the hilt of his sword, and with eyes wide, he cast a quick look over his shoulder.

"You should really keep your voice down if you wish not to be heard," the shapeshifter added.

THE RISE OF ISIGAR

Not knowing what to say, and unsure whether he could trust the shapeshifter, Valeirys fell silent and continued to survey the space around him.

Seemingly ignoring his discomfort, the Metatari asked, "Now that I have answered all your questions, would you answer mine?"

Something shook the crowns of the trees above him. At once, Valeirys' head snapped backward, and he searched the black canopy above him.

"What are you running from?" the shapeshifter asked, completely unbothered by the sudden commotion. "Eyvindr's running away makes sense. After all, it was only a matter of time before someone uncovered his secret. But you? Despite the incident with the guards, what's troubling you?"

"Nothing; I'm not running from anything," Valeirys replied.

At his answer, the shapeshifter appeared to examine him for a while before he spoke. "It must be something of great meaning to you, considering that you're lying."

"It's nothing," Valeirys snapped, looking away from him.

He balled his hands into fists and noticed them start to shake.

Taking a deep breath, he tried to conceal the wave of emotions that surged through him upon his frustration. He did not trust the shapeshifter, and something about this place and this moment felt wrong. He knew they shouldn't be here. It wasn't safe.

"Draw your weapon," Valeirys barked at Eyvindr.

"Valeirys," Eyvindr replied, but again, he interrupted him, "Now!"

He fixed his brother with a glare.

"I regret that I have angered you," said the Metatari. "Perhaps I can help?"

Shifting his weight from one foot to the other, Valeirys huffed and answered through gritted teeth, "I do not require any of your assistance."

His eyes darted back toward the shapeshifter, whose expression seemed to have softened as he studied him.

"Valeirys," said the Metatari.

The muscles of his wrists twitched when he yelled back at him, "Stop saying my name as if you know me!"

Valeirys could feel his anger and his fear get the better of him. For all he knew, the odd interest the shapeshifter seemed to take in him was a trick, a hoax to keep him and Eyvindr here alone in the woods, where they were easily overwhelmed and defeated. After all, these grounds were as familiar to the shapeshifter as no other creature.

Valeirys had to get Eyvindr and himself out of the forest.

But how?

If he couldn't escape, would he stand a chance if he stayed and fought?

Valeirys noticed the same power kindle inside him that had driven him throughout the fight at the palace. It tickled the tips of his fingers and nipped at his bones as he buried his heels into the ground, trying to keep the very force of it at bay.

His pulse throbbed painfully at his temples, and his breath quickened while he stared back at the Metatari, contemplating how best to overpower him.

"Valeirys," Eyvindr said, his voice rising slightly at the end as he watched him warily.

But instead of devising a clever plan, his mind grew clouded, and he struggled to focus.

He did not know what would happen next or what he would do once the magic stirring within him took control.

Something built inside him and with it, the urge to unleash the complete extent of his abilities. His limbs tightened, and his whole body seemed to swell.

Valeirys' emotions boiled along with his pride and his desire to best the shapeshifter. Together they outweighed his own sensibility, and he could feel the lust for victory enthrall him as the irresistible power engulfed his heart.

Still riveting his eyes on the shapeshifter who had not moved, Valeirys thought he had noticed the round shape of his pupils change to a vertical slit. His mouth opened slightly, bearing perfect rows of white teeth, and the faintest sound of a low growl rumbled from his throat as if he meant to warn him.

Squinting, Valeirys prepared to snatch the hilt of his sword and run toward the Metatari when, suddenly, an image of the garden of his family's home arose before his mind's eye, diverting his attention from all else.

Confused, Valeirys tried to drive it away, but its appearance stubbornly lingered before him, and it only grew more vivid with every one of his efforts to ignore it.

With a grunt, he shook his head, and fear stifled his breath at the thought of losing his life to the Metatari due to his distraction.

All around him, the forest began to vanish. He could see the garden's neatly cut grass and the beautifully adorned trellises replace the shadowed woods in front of him as an overwhelming plethora of colors crashed into him.

Valeirys wanted to scream and quickly raised his arms before him, as if he could fend off the shapeshifter's attack with his mere hands.

His palms burned, his jaw clenched, and against his own instincts, he shut his eyes.

The whisper of a voice and an unfamiliar string of words sung by it haunted his thoughts and resonated in his ears until they drifted from his lips, and Valeirys felt a dizzying flow of magic leave him.

The ground seemed to soften beneath his feet as if he stood barefoot on the lush grass of the manor's garden. He could feel the dew weigh on his skin, and the distinct scent of lilies filled the air around him. Valeirys wanted to open his eyes, just when a shattering force plowed into him.

He couldn't breathe.

Dark spots shrouded his vision. He lost his footing, and a terrible pain jolted through his arms and legs, tearing through him from the center of his spine.

Unable to see, Valeirys uttered a cry and tried to lift his shoulders from the ground, dragging his body upward.

Hugging his knees, he clutched at his shins, until his agony subsided and his surroundings started to clear again.

Bent forward and panting, Valeirys found himself staring down at the muddied ground covered in leaves and small bits of branches and rocks.

Two figures crouched at his side: Eyvindr at his left, his hand resting on Valeirys' shoulder, and the Metatari at his right.

Pulling away, he quickly dragged himself onto his feet; reaching for his aching head, he asked, "What happened? What did you do?"

He cast an accusatory look at the shapeshifter, just as the Metatari rose and answered, "I did nothing. You, on the other hand, just tried to summon a portal."

He pointed at the scorched ground where Valeirys had previously stood.

Valeirys shook his head unbelievingly and replied breathlessly, "Elves don't summon portals."

"No, not usually," Eyvindr and the shapeshifter spoke simultaneously.

His brother crossed his arms over his chest and raised a brow when Valeirys met his eyes.

"Seems like I'm not the only one keeping secrets," said Eyvindr.

Valeirys shook his head and began to protest when the Metatari chimed in, "Is this perhaps what you're running from?"

"No. No, it can't be," Valeirys said but fell silent, his head still jerking back and forth in denial.

A haziness veiled his thoughts while he continued to stare down at the scorched ground, faint fumes of smoke still rising from the blackened soil.

He did not know what to say, and panic gripped him.

"There are hardly a handful of possibilities to explain what just happened," said Eyvindr, his tone rough. "Now, it finally makes sense. Your transformation. The unbridled violence when you fought those soldiers... Ever since you've returned from Lyrr. It's not just the dreams. Your power—"

"Stop!" Valeirys interrupted.

Their gazes locked, and for a moment, it was as if something shattered between them. Valeirys felt his chest seize in agony. He forgot who he was, and all familiarity vanished from his brother's face as Eyvindr blanched and spoke, "The only elves—" He stopped abruptly before he continued whilst never taking his eyes off Valeirys, "half-elves to wield power strong and versatile enough to summon a portal were—"

"Enough!" Valeirys screamed. His throat tightened, and he swallowed before speaking again. "Eyvindr."

"You could die for this," his brother interrupted him. The look in his eyes had gone so frigid, Valeirys felt his whole body shiver as he held his gaze.

"You lecture me on the decisions I've made, the cause I've pledged myself to, and here you are, harboring a power so evil—"

He paused again and bit down on his lip, averting his gaze, before he scoffed and looked up at Valeirys. "It will destroy you and anyone who gets in your way. You won't be able to control it!"

Valeirys' throat constricted, and his lungs burned as if he were suffocating under the sheer panic that gripped him.

It couldn't be true. It wasn't true.

"I can help you," said the Metatari.

Bewildered, Valeirys turned to look at him, and he caught Eyvindr's shocked expression as well.

At first, he found himself unable to speak once he opened his mouth. But then he answered, "How?"

The shapeshifter drew closer to him and said, "Believe it or not, but I wasn't born with the powers I control today."

Valeirys' interest was piqued by the Metatari's unexpected reply. He continued to look at him, fixing his gaze on the warm shade of his golden iris while the pain in his lungs subsided and the pressure around his neck eased.

"I had to learn to master the power that was irrevocably tethered to my being. I could not escape it. I could not run from it; and so, I learned how to wield it," the shapeshifter added. "Do you think you could trust me?"

Staring back at him, Valeirys hesitated.

Across from him stood a stranger, a creature he knew near to nothing about, and yet he was offering him his help. But why?

It certainly couldn't be out of the goodness of his beastly heart. The Metatari were not known to interfere or mingle with anyone outside their own race. It was why their existence had been shrouded in such mystery and faded into precautionary tales or scary stories children shared amongst each other for the thrill of a little excitement. No, there had to be more to the shapeshifter's odd interest in aiding him. But what was it?

Curiosity tickled his mind, drowning out the voice of reason that this was a dangerous wager. Perhaps he was headed straight into a trap, but...

His thoughts were suddenly interrupted by the loud blare of a horn, and Valeirys' whole body shuddered, goosebumps coating his skin all the way down to his toes.

Instantly, he knew what the noise meant.

It was a warning signal sent out from the palace and strengthened by an incantation that would cause the alarm to echo throughout the entire kingdom.

"We're under attack," said Eyvindr.

His brother had joined his side, and Valeirys looked at him, finding his own horror and confusion mirrored in Eyvindr's earnest expression.

Valeirys gritted his teeth, and his hands clenched into fists as his attention snapped toward the Metatari, and he yelled, "Is this your doing? Why? Why have you turned against us?"

The Metatari's face changed. His features hardened, his eyes glowed, and for a second, his glance appeared empty, as if his mind had drifted elsewhere before the spark in his gaze returned, and he fixed his attention on Valeirys.

But Valeirys didn't give him a chance to speak and stormed off when the shapeshifter stopped him, planting his palm against his chest.

Glaring up at the Metatari, he saw the shapeshifter set his jaw and then heard him answer, "Wait. We'll go together."

Ripples of the Metatari's voice traveled from his arm onto Valeirys' chest, making his bones vibrate, and he shook him off, muttering, "Get your hands off me!"

The shapeshifter let him go but called after him, "The palace is under attack. I have no doubt your king is the intended target."

His words caused Valeirys to stop dead in his tracks, and he spun around toward the Metatari. His gaze darted toward Eyvindr and then back to the shapeshifter when he asked, "How do you know that?"

The Metatari shook his head and walked toward him, replying, "There's no time to explain. We can portal into the city. My men will join us there."

Standing about an arm's reach away from Valeirys, the shapeshifter raised his hands and then a flood of words in a beautifully familiar and yet strange tongue poured from his lips. His pupils narrowed to slits and darted back and forth as if he were drawing a scene with his eyes that flared as bright as a pair of flames; then Valeirys saw the portal take shape.

Nearly invisible, the orb hovered above the ground, tiny veins sparking and then vanishing across its translucent surface. There was no way of telling where it led.

Valeirys' mouth stood agape, and for a moment he forgot what was happening when the Metatari's voice recaptured his attention. "Do you trust me?"

"No!" Valeirys and Eyvindr both blurted.

Valeirys thought he had heard the shapeshifter chuckle under his breath; then, looking at the Metatari, he saw two bright rows of teeth flash from behind his lips as he grinned and spoke. "The both of you have a choice to make. Stay behind or come with me—and just maybe, Valeirys, if we survive, I'll show you how to properly cast a portal."

* * *

The walls of the tower and the floor beneath him shook, knocking Trajan off his feet. Breaking his fall, his forearms smacked against the hard stone when the windows creaked and then exploded.

Glass shards whizzed past his face, cutting his skin as he gasped a breath and then wrapped his hands around his head.

Hot streams of blood trickled down his cheeks from his temples, and he winced, pinching his eyes shut.

A blast of wind howled through the shattered windows of the council chamber, tousling his hair, and making the fresh cuts on his face burn as he staggered to his feet.

A shrill noise pierced his skull, and he blinked, his vision blurred.

But before he could grasp what had happened, another boom struck the tower and the stone tiles of the floor quaked again, making his knees buckle, but he caught himself, eyes darting across the room.

His pulse throbbed against his head, his ears had gone numb, registering only the muffled shouts and disarray of voices as everyone tried to get to their feet.

The king's guard flocked around His Majesty, their shields raised high above the king in a star-shaped formation.

Something clinked just before a crack broke above them, and then the chandelier plummeted into the council table, breaking the wooden surface in two.

A shriek bounced off the walls as everyone ducked and then froze.

For a moment, the quaking ceased, and all grew still.

The skin of Trajan's head began to prickle and crawl as the entire chamber held their breaths; then a noise rose again from the quiet.

Scratching and scuffing sounds swallowed up the space around them before growing louder, and then it thundered and cracked, and all attention rose toward the roof. Dust and bits of rock fell from above as the roof trembled, and then it stopped.

Trajan's glance swept across the ghostly faces of the lords and councilmen spread throughout the chamber, his mind already devising an escape plan as he numbered them. Some clutched at the walls, others clung to the tipped-over chairs or ducked close to the ground, but no one moved.

Then, all at once, a forceful blow struck the tower. Debris scattered, and the structure moaned as an enormous black shape burst through the empty frames of the windows that had once formed the east flank of the council chamber.

Trajan turned at the sounds of the screams that filled the space around him, his eyes locking onto five sharply taloned fingers of a monstrous, onyx-scaled claw that dug into the tower's wall.

His body ached and stung at the jolt that coursed through him at the sight.

Dragon, he thought, just as a deafening roar bellowed above and all around them.

His heart leaped in his chest, and he saw the dragon's fingers start to curl, the stone screeching as the razor-sharp talons burst through the rock. Black lines exploded all over the walls and climbed toward the ceiling as the stone split, and Trajan screamed, "Run!"

CHAPTER 50

The ground beneath Trajan's feet gave way as the tower collapsed behind him.

The battle horns blared in his ears while his feet scuffed and slipped as he ran, struggling under the weight of one of the king's injured councilmen heaved upon his and Uryiel's shoulders.

Ahead, the king's guard had already reached the end of the sky bridge that connected the council chamber to the palace just when the deck beneath him seemed to shift and tilt, bits of rock skidding over the tiles; then the glass casing cracked and blew.

Trajan yelled a curse and tucked his chin into his chest as the tiny sharp fragments sprayed over them like hailstones.

They had seconds left before the bridge collapsed and dragged them to their deaths. Glancing at Uryiel, sweat and blood dripping from his brow, teeth clenched and bared, he nodded and then drove his feet harder against the ground, working against his burning muscles.

He could feel the world around him spin when he heard the soldiers in front of him shout just as the structure creaked, and the abutment behind them failed.

Trajan and Uryiel lunged forward, and he felt several strong arms catch them, hauling them up and dragging them to safety as the sky bridge broke away.

Straightening, Trajan heaved a breath and shook his hands free of the glass shards that clung to his sweaty palms before he turned and stared.

The council chamber was no more. Only a handful of stone pillars remained, poking upward from the depths below like the peak of a mountaintop they had no way of reaching.

For a moment, it seemed as if they had all made it out of the tower and across the bridge in time. But as his glance swept over the group, the sight already betrayed the truth that not all had survived.

He counted six of Erysméa's lords, including Uryiel, three of the king's five councilmen: Lord Calaedorn, Lord Velior, and Lord D'Arthragnan, who bent over the ground on all fours, his cane lost somewhere in the wreckage. How the lord had made it across and into safety with that limp of his astounded Trajan.

King Yevandrielle shouted and tore through the ring of soldiers that surrounded him, capturing everyone's attention.

His hair and clothes were dusted gray from the debris, and his left cheek was smeared with blood from a cut that ran over his left eye.

Staring at each of them, the thin pale lines of his lips contorted into a snarl, and he yelled, "Someone, tell me what just happened!"

Lord Calaedorn coughed. His back was hunched forward awkwardly, and his hands were perched on his thighs while he tried to straighten and look at the king.

Outwardly, he seemed to have made it unscathed, but Trajan could tell by his labored breath and the way one of his hands clutched his chest once he stood and tried to speak that his injuries were perhaps of a much more serious kind.

THE RISE OF ISIGAR

Lord Calaedorn wheezed and spat blood, opening his mouth to answer. "Wretched Metatari." He paused and heaved again. "This—We, we should have never trusted them, Your Majesty."

The remaining members of the council and lords grumbled in unison, but before anyone could add another word, all eyes turned and locked on a group of soldiers hurrying toward them.

The ashen color of their faces and the haunted look in their eyes made Trajan swallow as they stopped, and one of them stepped forward to approach the king.

Their armor clinked as all bowed just before the first soldier spoke. "Your Majesty, lords, royal—"

"Oh, enough with the courtesies!" the king barked, hands balled into fists as he stared at the armed elf. "For the realm's sake, report, soldier! How many of those cursed beasts must we rid of their heads, and how much of the city have they already taken?"

The elf's features twitched, and his lips quivered as he ducked his head and replied, "It's—it's elves, Your Majesty. They—they bear the crest of Izurion."

King Yevandrielle seethed and spat out, "Are you mad, soldier? Look at me and tell me what you saw!"

The elf's head snapped upward, and he met the king's enraged gaze.

The hairs on Trajan's neck stood on end, and goosebumps lined his arms as he noticed the glazed look on the soldier's face.

"It is true, Your Majesty," the elf answered, and drew a nervous breath. "The upturned crown circling the mark of Regulus, it gleams embossed over their shields and plated chests. The banished have returned, my king. What should have been dead is alive and has sought its revenge."

The soldier's lips trembled violently, and Trajan felt his blood run cold as he sensed that there was more the elf had left to say.

With his feet planted firmly on the ground, Trajan braced himself for what was coming just as the soldier stared back into the king's eyes, finally adding, "And there's more… the city burns in dragon's fire."

* * *

The portal opened at the dead end of an alley in the underbelly of Mòr Rhíoghain's city.

Valeirys squinted and inhaled sharply, the pressure receding from his lungs as if he had been held underwater.

At first, he could not tell where they were, having lost all sense of time and feeling.

Gasping, Eyvindr straightened beside him and raised an arm before his mouth, pinching his eyes shut.

The shapeshifter stood across from the two of them, his face turned toward the opposite end of the alley that led onto one of the city's broader streets.

Valeirys could hear people screaming and children crying in the distance, black shapes darting back and forth at the end of the narrow street the portal had brought them to.

The strong smell of sulfur wafted through the air, its sharp biting scent stinging his nose, and he grimaced.

Sweat dripped from his brow, though he had not moved, and it grew awfully warm around him. All at once, he felt the overwhelming urge to draw a breath, but then started coughing instead.

Heaving, he heard the Metatari's voice while he handed Eyvindr and him each a dark piece of cloth. "Take this. The fumes of dragon's fire are lethal to those not born of dragon's blood. They paralyze the body and the lungs if taken in for too long. You'll die before we reach the palace."

Eyvindr grabbed the cloth without hesitation, securing it around his head while Valeirys eyed the shapeshifter a moment before accepting the kerchief. He watched as the Metatari tied his own around his nose and mouth, muttering something that caused the dark fabric to shimmer once before the incantation took effect.

When he glanced at Valeirys again, only his striking pair of eyes were visible, gleaming like two beacons in the night.

"Are you ready?" he asked.

Valeirys nodded.

He could hear rustling coming from the shadows between the closely packed rows of houses that surrounded them; something soared through the sky above him, and he knew they were not alone.

Several others of the Metatari had come to join them and began to step out into the alley. One after the other, dozens of pairs of piercing, heterochromatic eyes found him, but not one of them spoke, awaiting the command of their leader.

The glare of the creatures' bright eyes bounced off the array of the polished edges of their weapons. Javelins, hewing spears, even claw-like gauntlets, and shortswords decorated with symbols joined to a design of concentric geometrical shapes drew his eyes to the beautifully crafted weaponry and distracted him for a moment.

Then Valeirys glanced back at the shapeshifter beside him, who seemed to look over the crowd of men and women who had joined them, studying them wordlessly, until Valeirys realized the Metatari was conveying his plan to them.

One of the shapeshifters across from them came forward, stepping out of the fray and approached.

He handed their leader a long, curved bough like that belonging to a tree. It resembled the shape of a war bow's stave, but there was no string spun between its notches.

The Metatari beside Valeirys accepted the weapon from his soldier and approached Eyvindr.

Another spell left his lips too quickly for Valeirys to comprehend before he fixed Eyvindr with his sharp gaze and spoke. "The arrows will take form under the instruction of your mind. You need only to wish it."

His brother grabbed hold of the weapon, eyes wide, and the moment his fingers fastened around the bow's riser, a silver light sparked and throbbed from out of the bough's grooves before dimming slightly.

"It yields to your command and no one else's," said the shapeshifter, before he nodded and retreated from Eyvindr.

The Metatari cast a glance at the small army before them and dipped his chin before half of the group retreated from their midst, some vanishing as they came between the rows of houses while others leaped into the air, transforming into various creatures of flight. Their calls echoed from afar once they disappeared; then the Metatari turned toward Valeirys and spoke. "Follow me; and keep that sword of yours at the ready. You just might need it."

Nodding, Valeirys drew his blade and caught the hint of a smile in the glint of the shapeshifter's wild eyes just as he began to move and lead the way.

Valeirys' heart sank deeper and deeper with every pounding step as they ran, the shapeshifter navigating through the streets with incredulous ease, as if he had lived in the capital all his life.

The heat felt unbearable, choking the breath from his lungs and dissolving the world around him in flickering white flames fringed in violet and blue.

The screams he had heard before seemed as if all but vanished, swallowed up by the rapacious blaze that transformed a once glorious city into a heap of ash and ruins.

His eyes were drawn to horizontal slits against the blinding light as he went, trying not to notice or trip over the sprawled bodies that covered the public streets.

There was no longer a sky above him, the sight obscured by clouds of black smoke that billowed over them.

Chasing down one narrow street after the other, the Metatari moved soundlessly beside him as they worked their way through the wreckage and cinders.

Shards of glass from broken windows buried beneath thick layers of snowlike ashes crackled and scraped beneath them, their boots stirring clouds of soot and dust up into the air.

Valeirys' eyes watered and stung as he fought the urge to blink, riveting his gaze on the Metatari's bodies ahead, the only moving shapes he could make out in the darkness.

His ears drummed from the shrieks that tore through the fog above them, belonging to the beasts he could not see, and his muscles tensed every time a horrific roar caused the cobblestones beneath his feet to quake.

He could sense them, the dragons, moving through the darkness above them, their terrifying maws torn open wide, the flap of their wings as they drew nearer to the ground and sent wafts of something charred and foul smelling through the air.

THE RISE OF ISIGAR

Every once in a while, a gust of flames burst through the blackness just before someone ahead would shout out a warning, and their group would duck as close to the ground as possible or take shelter behind the crumbled wall of a house.

Remnants of doors, shutters, and scraps from the destruction the fire had wrought and scorched to black gleamed like the embers in a hearth beneath his hands and knees as he pushed himself up onto his feet.

The stench of the burned and death-ridden streets overwhelmed him and roused a sorrow and a boundless anger within him.

Even if they could stop the enemy and put an end to the fire, there would be nothing left to save.

Valeirys' clothes and leather armor stuck uncomfortably to his skin. His throat was parched and itched, and his lips felt charred from the scorching heat while he trudged forward.

He hadn't noticed how strangely still it had gotten until he stumbled and ran right into someone's back.

The space around him was still so heavily clouded in smoke and soot that he couldn't tell what was going on until a shout rang out, and the voice belonging to the person ahead of him cried out for him to strike left.

Without hesitation, Valeirys did as told, an unfamiliar instinct taking control over him while his body moved of its own volition.

Freed from its scabbard, his blade swung in an arc around his body and met its mark.

Valeirys no longer questioned why he had blindly followed the command as a warm, dark trickle of blood ran over his hands and the hilt of his sword, and he sucked in a breath.

There was a gasp, and then he felt the weight of another collapse onto his shoulder. The body plummeted onto the ground just as he moved, twisting to the side.

A bright burst of light exploded from behind him, causing him to squint as the fog around him stirred and broke away, forming a ring around their group Valeirys could now clearly make out.

Eyvindr stood to his right, bow raised, the nearly invisible and yet glittering string of his weapon strung taut, and a translucent arrow notched.

Everyone stood with their backs to each other, aligned in the shape of an oval.

An orb of light hovered and spun in the palm of the Metatari's leader's hand.

Valeirys blinked and then looked down at the slumped corpse at his feet. It was elven, just as the other four dead that lay where several of the shapeshifters had slaughtered them.

Realizing how close he had come to dying, he glared at the Metatari's leader and blurted, "And you couldn't have done that sooner?"

The shapeshifter glanced at him, but didn't speak, the stark lines on his brow indicating that he was concentrating on something greater than Valeirys' words.

In unison, the Metatari moved again, retreating with quiet steps, the oval shape transforming into a tight circle just before their leader screamed a name.

But it was too late.

Valeirys heard a shriek, his head whipping sideways, and he caught a glimpse of a spear shooting forth from the darkness and piercing one of the Metatari through the middle. The woman's orange and silver eyes flared, a soundless whimper leaving her trembling lips before she collapsed into herself, and the shapeshifters howled and screamed.

Arrows whizzed past Valeirys' ears, weapons whirled and flashed like veins of lightning against an overcast sky as the enemy emerged from out of the smoke.

It felt like fighting against a band of ghosts.

Valeirys jabbed and sliced through the dark clouds surrounding him, crimson pools forming at his feet as he fought alongside the shapeshifters, no longer questioning their intentions and moving with them as if they were one.

But their feat seemed lost before it had even begun.

Bit by bit, the smoke and fog cleared, the shapes of the warriors pitted against them sharpening as the darkness receded.

Valeirys' breath caught, and he forced a hard lump down his throat as his eyes froze on the breastplate of the armed elf who started toward him. The upturned twisted crown and the star constellation of the lion dragged his recollections of his people's history, Izurion's tyrannic reign, to the forefront of his mind with a shiver that coursed down his back to the soles of his feet.

Valeirys gritted his teeth and lunged.

THE RISE OF ISIGAR

Tiny black lines sparked from beneath the elf's pale skin, stretching across his brow and cheeks from the corners of his yellowish eyes just before Valeirys severed his head from his body, and the soldier fell.

But instead of leading them one step closer to victory, it seemed as if he had only aided their doom. For the moment he withdrew his blade, Valeirys witnessed a surge of movement from amidst the remaining enemy soldiers.

The line of elves advanced against the ranks of the Metatari, crashing over them like a wave; their strength increased, their maneuvers even swifter than before.

Valeirys cursed as their group was forced to retreat.

Lowering his weapon, he raised his right hand high above his head and uttered a spell.

The shield took form and sent a quake through the ground beneath them, knocking several of the opposing soldiers off their feet and disrupting their progress. But he knew it wouldn't stop them for long.

"What are we to do?" Valeirys yelled, his gaze meeting that of the Metatari's leader.

The shapeshifter shook his head and replied, "You kill the one, it strengthens the other. They are bound; their power is linked. Without knowledge of the source or the spellbinder, there is no end to this fight. Even if we defeat them here, the battle will only grow more difficult elsewhere."

Valeirys' brow furrowed. He shook his head, sweat pouring down the sides of his face, and he spoke. "So, then let's buy time until we find the monster who bound them."

Glancing sideways, he caught a hint of a weary smile in the shapeshifter's eyes before the Metatari answered, "Can you hold the shield?"

Valeirys felt his limbs tremble from the force of his magic that drew on his energy.

But before he could answer, he heard Eyvindr shout from behind him, "Yes, he can!"

His brother fired an arrow that met its mark in between the eyes of an enemy soldier, and lowering his bow, he placed his right hand on Valeirys shoulder and added, "I'll channel my magic to you. Together, we can do it."

Valeirys nodded back at him and redirected his focus onto the shield and the ranks of the Metatari fighting before him. Within seconds, a dizzying surge of power flowed through him, through the link between him and Eyvindr, rushing into his arms held out before his body.

Stepping away from them, the Metatari formed a sign in the air, and within an instant, two others joined his side.

The band of three shapeshifters stood closely together, arms extended, palms facing the ground, the world seemingly forgotten around them.

Valeirys watched, counting the seconds for something to happen while he poured all his and Eyvindr's joint strength into the spell that maintained the shield protecting them.

Then, with a rumble and a crack loud enough to render him deaf, the cobblestones trembled, stone upon stone separating from the others until the ground opened to a ravine and swallowed the enemy whole.

Chapter 51

Aleirya saw the vortex from afar.

What had at first appeared to be a cluster of dark clouds grew to a whirlwind of onyx smoke and ash stirring above the center of Mòr Rhíoghain's city as they drew closer.

Her heartbeat thrummed in her ears beneath the even strokes of her dragon's wings that accelerated as Takhéa struggled against the violent winds of the gale that raged ahead.

The storm howled in her ears, whipping the loose strands of her hair across her face and obscuring the view in front of her.

Aleirya's eyes narrowed while she riveted her focus on the white pointed tips of the buildings and towers peeking through the black clouds of the vortex that had settled over the city. A strange blend of excitement and horror flared in her stomach.

In truth, she had no idea what she was doing, but she couldn't turn back. After everything, she was still a Dragon's Kin, and she refused to abandon her calling as a warrior to serve her king and her people.

Something pressed against her waist, distracting her before she realized it was Hadrian.

She had forgotten the shapeshifter was with her, so lost in thought over what lay ahead that she barely felt the weight of his arms around her waist.

Heat rushed to her cheeks as her mind trailed to the Metatari, and she consciously took in the feel of his hands on her sides.

Aleirya swallowed and buried her concentration on the billowing mass of black that grew more and more threatening by the minute, but she couldn't ignore the shapeshifter's presence for long when he leaned forward, his forehead pressed against the back of her head, and his voice rose. "We need to land now! The city is under attack and burning from dragon's fire. If the elves see Takhéa, they'll strike to kill her while she's still airborne!"

The warmth of his breath tickled her skin and roused the hair on her neck. The sensation wasn't terrible, and Aleirya tensed, her jaw strained as she relayed the message to Takhéa through their bond.

Moments later the dragon growled in response, and Aleirya could hear the rumble of Takhéa's voice and feel its vibrations chase across her scales as she responded angrily, "There's no way I'm leaving you to fight alone."

"Now!" Hadrian shouted from behind Aleirya. "You'll kill us all!"

Aleirya could already see the outer walls of the capital city beneath them, but all concern for their safety seemed swept away when her eyes beheld the blinding streams of light that glowed from below.

Like several rivers intersecting bodies of land, white and gold lines marking the city's streets bled throughout Mòr Rhíoghain in sharp angles and curves.

They were too far up to hear the screams, but Aleirya knew the streets were flooded in blood-curdling cries of those falling victim to the flames.

Shuddering, Aleirya dragged her gaze from the sight below them and stared ahead at the stirring shape of the whirlwind they were steadily approaching.

All at once, she noticed several even darker shapes move from inside the vortex, flashes of green, bronze, and red occasionally breaking through the darkness, and she strained her eyes to identify them.

Her mouth opened to a gasp, and a jolt tore through her chest at the sight of a long black scaled tail that whipped through the clouds just as a roar rattled her frame.

A scream lodged in her throat before she could warn Takhéa, and an enormous shape broke through the vortex, coming toward them, a pair of ferocious eyes locking onto them, the one bright silver, the other a blazing ruby red.

A black dragon spread its wings, its serpentine neck swinging toward them as it tore open its maw, fire glowing in the depths of its throat before it descended onto them. There was no escape.

The beast was double Takhéa's size when it crashed over her, seizing her by the neck and dragging her downward.

Aleirya's scream was stifled, her throat and lungs felt scorched as she tried desperately to breathe while the world spun violently around her.

Blurred streaks of white, gold, black, and red flashed before her, her pupils darting back and forth as she tried to regain a clear sight. Takhéa's roar broke through the deafening cacophony of noise around them. Her cries were a mix of feral anger and pain, and Aleirya felt a crushing weight press against her chest, threatening to collapse her lungs.

Takhéa jerked and twisted beneath her, the hard muscles of her back and neck contracting as she fought, but Aleirya could only catch glimpses of black scaly limbs thrashing about her through her blurred vision.

Her stomach lurched and twisted in agony, bile rising up her throat while a high-pitched screech rang in her ears. Her temples ached as her body was pressed up hard against Takhéa's back. Her eyelids fluttered, and she could feel her consciousness fading when, all of a sudden, her head snapped back, and she screamed as something clawed at her, sharp jabs of pain tearing down the right side of her neck and across her chest as if skin and bone were being ripped apart.

How she managed to cling to her dragon's back, she did not know.

Aleirya felt her head begin to loll to the side as she grew numb from the pain, when she felt the Metatari's body fold over her, and Hadrian's hands clasped hers.

Aleirya. Hadrian's voice rang in her mind. *Aleirya. Hold on to me. Don't let go.*

If she still had control over her body, she would have nodded.

Aleirya gave in to the warmth that ebbed from him onto her, the world around her still twisting and spinning. Her hands clutched, but she was no longer aware of what exactly they clung to. All she could feel was the hard surface of what she assumed was Takhéa's back. All she could hear was Hadrian's voice.

Everything went dark around her, and then Aleirya saw the shapeshifter before her in the woods.

Hadrian's hands cupped her face, forcing her to look into his eyes, and instead of fighting it, Aleirya let go, lowering her defenses.

Her own eyes widened as her mind opened toward him, and she felt an unfamiliar sensation flow through her veins. She could feel Hadrian. She could see him as if they stood directly across from each other.

An invisible bond took shape between them, tendrils forming and stretching from her thoughts to his like fine silver threads; just like the light touch of fingertips before the closing of a pair of hands, their minds connected, and she felt their powers collide, knocking a fresh flow of air into her lungs.

Aleirya heaved and tore her eyes open.

Again, a pair of dragon roars split the air above them, and her eyes locked on the rows of the white houses and cobblestone streets that grew larger at a blinding pace as they neared the ground.

Aleirya clutched Hadrian's hands and pinched her eyes shut, letting the image of a house take form across her closed lids. A strange flow of power rushed through her, and then a flash of bright light enveloped them just before they plummeted into a wall of stone.

With a cough and a gasp, Aleirya awoke. Blinking, her vision veiled in lilac, she sat up and stretched out a hand to touch the membrane of her dragon's wing that shielded her.

Takhéa? she whispered through her thoughts. *Takhéa, are you alright?*

There was no response, and Aleirya's stomach dropped.

Gritting her teeth, she winced and clutched at the heaps of rocks and debris, dragging herself on her belly out from underneath her dragon's wing.

Her whole body felt battered and bruised, and she winced as she climbed to her feet.

A blinding light obscured her vision. Dust and ashes floated in the air; the world shrouded in a sheet of gray.

Aleirya had no idea where she was, standing amidst the crumbled remains of the building they had crashed into through the shapeshifter's portal.

Her pulse throbbed, her breath quickening as she whirled and observed her dragon buried under mounds of stone.

"Takhéa!" Aleirya screamed. Her eyes welled with tears. Her whole body constricted, pain coiling her chest and limbs, squeezing the air from her lungs and threatening to stop her heart from beating.

"Takhéa!" Aleirya screamed again, her vision swimming as she fought her way closer to her dragon, hurling through the rubble and debris.

Aleirya reached her dragon's head, and threw herself against the side of her neck, her hand trembling as it moved carefully toward her dragon's cheek and her closed eye.

A wheezing sound made its way out of her throat in between gulps of air and sobs.

"Takhéa," she breathed. Another sob shook her shoulders, and she sucked in a breath.

"Aleirya?" someone called out from somewhere behind her, and she recognized it as Hadrian's voice. But she didn't turn to look at him.

Her eyes swept over the gashes along her dragon's neck and chest, and she curled in on herself, dropping onto her knees.

A hot stream of tears rolled down her cheeks, her forehead pressing against Takhéa's scales as she wished the world around her to stop turning.

A ravenous ache cut through her torso like a gaping wound, and something between a cry and a scream made its way out of her.

Daring to lift her chin, Aleirya looked up at Takhéa, who continued to lie still. She started to reach out and touch her dragon's wounds, but she stopped herself and simply stared at the jagged, bloodied lines that tore through the black scales.

She had felt it, too…

Her chin quivered, and she bit down on her trembling lip.

A hand came to rest on her shoulder, and she heard Hadrian speak up softly. "Aleirya. She's—"

Aleirya shook her head and interrupted him, "Don't say it; don't—"

But before she could finish speaking, the ground quaked beneath her. The stone and mounds of debris vibrated before they shifted.

Dust and rock crackled and came showering over them, and Aleirya covered her head with her arms.

She tried to get to her feet, but the ground beneath her felt too unsteady, her legs too weak to hold her weight.

Hadrian crouched behind her, and before she could lift her head to see what was happening, she heard the shapeshifter gasp and call out to her, "We need to get out of here!"

Aleirya wanted to protest but failed to get a word out when, all at once, the giant head of the dragon who had attacked them rose from a mass of stone before them.

His huge eyes locked onto them, fury enlivening the deep shade of red and metallic silver that fixated on them. His scales were dusted gray from the debris, the horns and spikes protruding from his head and neck looking as if coated in snow when he stretched to his towering form.

An unearthly rumble reverberated through the ground beneath her, causing her bones to vibrate and her skin to prickle.

Hadrian's hand gripped her arm as he pulled her to her feet and yelled, "Come on, Aleirya!"

The dragon opened his gigantic maw, baring his teeth the length of Aleirya's entire form, and a golden-orange glow flared from his mouth.

Aleirya felt his breath hot against her cheeks, tossing her hair behind her as she stared him dead in the eyes.

Hadrian was right. She knew she should run, even if the chances of escaping were slim to nothing. But she couldn't move.

THE RISE OF ISIGAR

Aleirya knew she should be terrified. But her feet stood planted on the pile of rock beneath her as if she had been carved out of the stone herself.

Aleirya forgot what it meant to feel anything. She no longer cared if she lived or died, and oddly, a strange sense of freedom blossomed from the endless hollowness that ate away at her from her middle.

The world around her broke away. The only thing she saw was the great beast before her and its devilish eyes.

Aleirya felt Hadrian tug at her, trying to pull her away before it was too late.

But it was too late.

A warm pulse sparked and began to throb in rhythm with her heartbeat drumming steadily in her chest.

Aleirya forgot her pain or any sense of weakness that had consumed her body. A rippling force, like energy pent up inside her, flooded every muscle, every cell of her body, racing down her arms and tickling the skin of her fingers. For once, her anger and the part of her that loved the thrill of the fight and the danger had a place. Yanking herself free from Hadrian's grasp, Aleirya drew Valdr from her back and ran.

Her feet seemed to glide over the ground as she charged at the dragon, who watched her with an odd fascination and a deadly gleam in his eyes.

Aleirya's feet found purchase on a collapsed pillar, and she picked up her speed, chasing upward as if running up a ramp.

Her breath came fast and strong, her pulse bounded.

The dragon growled and began to shift, the ground thundering and shaking as he moved, crouched on all fours and facing her.

The dragon tore his maw open wider, and a roar sent a hum through the space.

Aleirya didn't stop, even as the fire built in the dragon's throat, and she felt another blast of his scorching breath crash over her.

The tantalizing thrill of the magic stirring to life inside her drove her onward, a power kindling in her palms, unfamiliar and yet so natural to her, as if she wouldn't know herself without it.

With Valdr raised above her head like a spear, Aleirya gritted her teeth as her eyes sparked blue, and with a scream, she thrust the blade forward. Her left hand shot up before her, her palm raised, and out of it came a blaze of violet-tinted flames that burst forth and engulfed Valdr before the sword buried itself in the dragon's silver eye.

Her feet skidded to a halt just before she reached the end of the pillar.

Aleirya watched as the dragon's slit pupil burst where Valdr's edge cleft its way through it, black twisted lines breaking forth from its center.

The dragon gave a blood-curdling shriek and reared, backing up on his hind legs before he flapped his wings.

Aleirya heard Hadrian shout her name, but it was too late.

One of the dragon's wings struck her as the beast took flight, knocking her from the pillar, and she fell.

Aleirya braced herself for the crash, the numbness consuming her all over again, but before she dared open her eyes to see the ground steadily approaching below, something seized her by the shoulder.

Aleirya gave a scream as a pair of sharp teeth dug into her flesh, and her head snapped upward to see the giant shape of a wolf, its eyes blazing green and silver.

Aleirya felt her body dragged upward and back down the stone pillar as her eyelids fluttered, and she started to drift unconscious.

It wasn't until a cool, soothing sensation flooded her shoulder, vanquishing the agony, that she blinked and caught sight of Hadrian's face bent over her.

Cradled in the crook of his elbow, Aleirya swallowed and held fast to his gaze.

His face was human. Gone was the wolf she had seen; the green and silver of his eyes shining back at her through his long, dark lashes.

Hadrian pursed his lips to speak when Aleirya felt tears stream down her cheeks from out of the corners of her eyes, and she said, "I can't leave her…"

Hadrian was about to answer when something caught his attention, and he looked away from her.

There was a scratching sound followed by the tumbling and cracking noise of rock when Aleirya caught a grin spreading over his lips, and he spoke. "You won't have to."

He helped Aleirya up to her feet, just as her head turned toward the commotion, and she saw Takhéa rise, wagging her head to shake off the grime and rubble from the crash.

Her dragon's eyes found her.

Aleirya sprinted toward Takhéa and threw herself at her, hugging her snout, and broke into sobs anew.

Takhéa hummed softly beneath her and batted her eyes.

"I thought I'd lost you," said Aleirya, stepping back and looking up at her dragon.

Takhéa studied her intently before she released a puff of smoke and answered, "Never."

Aleirya wrapped her arms around her dragon once more, her cheeks cold from the tears that streaked down her face, and she refused to let go while she waited for her heartbeat to steady.

It wasn't until she heard Hadrian speak up behind her that she let go of Takhéa and turned to face him.

"We need to keep moving. Tamar can use all the help he can get—and it looks like we're the only aid that is coming," said the Metatari.

"Alright," Aleirya answered.

Glancing upward at Takhéa and then back at her, the shapeshifter added, "I can place a cloaking spell over your dragon. She's wounded. She will be safe here. That is, as long as she stays put."

A low guttural sound rumbled from the dragon's throat at his suggestion, but Aleirya nodded in agreement and turned around to face Takhéa, placing her hand gently on the dragon's snout. "It'll be alright. And he's right; you can't fight like this."

Takhéa growled again, and Aleirya added, "I will call for you if need be. I promise. I'm not that easy to kill."

She tried to smile convincingly just as the dragon averted her eyes from her and onto the shapeshifter behind her. "I'll find you and roast you alive if she dies."

Hadrian grinned and nodded in reply.

Returning his attention to Aleirya, he asked, "Are you ready?"

Drawing the hood of her cape up over her head, her mind drifting briefly to the sole weight of Ismené strapped to her back, Aleirya dipped her chin once more and answered, "Did you really have to ask?"

His smile was hidden behind the kerchief he had tied around his mouth and nose, but Aleirya could sense his amusement.

Hadrian's fingers then began to stretch and curl as they moved adeptly in an array of lines and circles while he formed the invisible components of a spell. Aleirya watched, mesmerized, as something stirred in the air, and glittering ribbons of light left the skin of his hands, moving toward Takhéa.

The space around the dragon rippled as the rays encircled her, and a dome took shape.

Finally, the light around Takhéa faded. The cloaking spell took effect, and Aleirya's dragon disappeared before her eyes.

Blinking, she suppressed a gasp at the void in front of her where her dragon had crouched before; only slowly did she turn when the shapeshifter started to leave.

Aleirya followed him as he navigated through the heaps of stone from the collapsed house and then climbed the remains of one of its walls.

They had barely made it onto the roof of the neighboring building when the sound of a horn blared above them, and Aleirya saw an organized fleet of dragons approaching the city.

A familiar banner swayed from the long spear of one of the riders. The dragons wore plated armor of gold and sapphire blue, the king's sigil embossed across their powerful chests.

The Dragon's Kin had come. Aleirya only hoped it was to Erysméa's aid and not its demise.

Chapter 52

The walls boomed and quaked as the east wing of the palace continued to collapse.

King Yevandrielle cried out, pain shooting up his right leg, his arms and shoulders aching as he pulled, dragging himself along the floor and away from the mound of stone that had buried the last of his guard.

He did not dare look back, his fingers scratching at the rough tiles covered in dust while he dug them into its grooves.

Another monstrous roar shook the hall, and Yevandrielle could feel the vibrations of its echo reverberate in the core of his bones.

He winced and pinched his eyes shut as a rattle chased across the ceiling above him, shaking small bits of rocks loose that poured over him.

He could hear stone cracking and crumbling not far from him as something struck the palace's façade again.

The dragon had done well, isolating him and his guard, cutting them off from the rest of the lords and his council as they had tried to flee the palace and join the battle outside.

Resting his back against a wall, Yevandrielle told himself he'd only stop for a minute while he tried to catch his breath.

But the air was suffocating and did little to replenish his weary frame. It was hot and dry against his skin, leaving a taste of dust and smoke on his tongue and set fire to his aching lungs.

He did not know how he was to move in his armor that seemed to have tripled its weight since he had had it strapped onto him, the load of his breastplate bearing down onto his chest, ready to crush his ribs any moment now.

With a gasp and a groan, he forced himself onto his feet, staggering while he steadied himself, and his gaze wandered down his bloodied leg.

The sword strung to his hip pressed painfully against his throbbing limb, and he wished he could rid himself of it, but knew all too well that it was his only hope of defending himself should the enemy's soldiers find him.

The sound of his labored breath rose heavy in his ears, and a cold sweat trickled down his back and brow while he surveyed the space around him, his vision obscured and eyes stinging.

These familiar and once homely halls had become a deathtrap.

The dragon had cut off the quickest and most direct path outside the palace. Now, the only way out was through the hidden passage in the garden, raised within an open-roofed courtyard at the center of the royal dwelling. If he could make it there, with a spell, the waters of the fountain at its center would part, revealing a secret entrance that opened into a tunnel that would lead him underground and safely outside the palace.

Yevandrielle pinched his eyes shut, waiting for his heartbeat to slow and willing himself to move despite the fatigue and pain.

His ice-cold hand trailed to the hilt of the sword at his side, his calloused fingers tracing the hilt and pommel while he whispered an incantation. He didn't have the strength to heal his wounds should he be forced to fight, but he could lessen the weight of his weapon and armor, increasing his chances of making it outside the palace without collapsing under exhaustion.

Once the spell took effect, Yevandrielle breathed a sigh and opened his eyes before he took his first step forward.

The dragon had not killed him yet, and he had no intention of dying here buried beneath a heap of stone. If the beast wanted to kill him, it would have to accomplish what it set out to do face to face.

As best as his injuries allowed, Yevandrielle moved through the halls, setting one foot before the other as quickly as he could and maneuvering past the debris toward the palace's central garden.

The shrill clatter and shrieks of grinding metal echoed from distant corners, telling him that the enemy must have breached the palace's gates.

Yevandrielle kept his eyes peeled, scouring through the grayish fog of rock, dust, and smoke from the outside that filled the inner rooms and halls. Never before had he moved through this familiar place so nimbly and alert.

Like the inside of a crypt, death governed the ruins of the palace, bodies of fallen soldiers slumped against the walls or buried beneath the ruins of a collapsed structure.

Despite the heat, his limbs began to grow cold from the loss of blood, but he paid no attention to it; his mind willing him onward at the rush of excitement flowing through him, and the threat of death snatching at his heels.

Having reached the west wing, the staircase leading down into the garden already in sight, Yevandrielle felt the weight on his chest lighten.

But then, all of a sudden, he stopped in his tracks.

His footsteps retreated at the end of the hallway, and adeptly, he slipped behind the stone figure of a statue set within a recess of the wall to his right.

Yevandrielle held his breath and tried to make out the number of the persons he heard approaching. He stood as still as he could, his blade at the ready.

A wave of relief flooded his chest as he glimpsed the shapes of only two shadows before the pair turned the corner.

With a whisper, Yevandrielle's spell took effect, and the marble figure concealing his form trembled and fell.

The statue struck the first of the enemy soldiers just in time, plowing him onto the ground and crushing his skull with a grueling crunch.

Yevandrielle didn't give the other a moment to raise his weapon and lunged, throwing himself onto him. The edge of his sword slashed the elf's throat before he could scream, and Yevandrielle watched him collapse onto the ground, his already lifeless eyes and features turning still.

Eyeing the dead at his feet, he grimaced as his glance swept over the mark of Izurion, glistening beneath the crimson stain that smeared the elf's armor.

These soldiers were ghosts just as much as they looked the part, remnants of a time best erased from his people's history.

With a sneer, Yevandrielle wiped the edge of his blade clean, and then moved on.

He could feel a sudden lapse of strength overcome him when he stopped, halting behind a pillar and daring a glance down the staircase and the space surrounding it.

His senses began to grow hazy as the throbbing in his wounded leg worsened with every footfall.

Breathing hard, he deemed it safe enough to continue onward as nothing emerged from the silence that cloaked him, and he passed down a staircase that bordered into the garden.

Under the dull thud of his boots, he trod over the soft grounds of the garden, almost reaching the pool of the fountain when he veered and ducked behind an overgrown trellis. A chill chased down his spine, and the hairs of his neck stood on end at the sight of a group gathered before the fountain.

Yevandrielle squinted and strained his ears, trying to overhear what they were saying.

"The tides are turning, my lord. We were not aware an alliance was formed with the Metatari; neither were we expecting the Dragon's Kin to come to their aid," one of them spat angrily.

"War always demands a sacrifice. Did your fallen king not teach you that?" said another.

Yevandrielle's back was pressed up against the stone trellis, and holding his breath, he peered over his shoulder to catch a glimpse of the group.

"Gather any who survived and retreat. Leave the rest to me," the same voice rose again. The stranger wore a hooded cloak and stood with his back toward Yevandrielle, facing three others dressed in armor, the crest of Izurion gleaming in black and crimson across their shields and breastplates.

"An alliance with the Dragon's Kin and the Metatari will not save them. It is all still going according to plan," he added.

One of the soldiers then smiled devilishly and said, "So, it is done? The king is dead, slayed by that foul beast of yours?"

"If not by the dragon, then by the point of my blade he will meet his demise. Now, go," the cloaked figure replied.

The soldiers gave a bow and turned away when the first of them spoke up again. "And what about the prince? Should we… dispose of him?"

"No, not yet. Keep him alive for now. Perhaps I will still have use for him before I cut his spoiled throat myself."

A snicker passed through the soldiers' ranks before they turned and left.

Yevandrielle could barely contain himself. His heart ached and burned with rage as he thought of Malik in the grasp of this monster.

His palms twitched, and he clutched his sword before he stepped out of his hiding place without thought or hesitation.

His legs trembled, and he dug his heels firmly into the ground, securing his stance. His strength was failing him, and yet Yevandrielle knew he could not run. He had no choice but to stay and fight; if not for his kingdom, then for Malik.

Malik, his son—Malik, who was still alive.

Yevandrielle's gaze bored into the enemy's back, and he raised his arm, extending the point of his blade toward the stranger who still stood with his back to him.

"Turn around and surrender, and perhaps I shall offer you a merciful death," Yevandrielle said.

The stranger laughed and raised his weaponless hands as if to surrender.

"I was wondering if I'd still get the pleasure," he answered as he began to turn around, and Yevandrielle's whole body shuddered.

All at once, it was as if all confusion of the stranger's identity had broken. He recognized the voice. It sounded much younger than he was used to, and his skin crawled when he finally saw his suspicion confirmed as the elf's face peered out from beneath the shadow of his mantle.

"Go on," he said. "Say my name."

Yevandrielle shook his head, his lips thinning to a line before he bared his teeth and growled, "Gideon."

His jaw clenched while his arm stiffened, and he strengthened his hold on his weapon. "How could you? You monster, you ungrateful—" Yevandrielle began.

But Lord D'Arthragnan lowered his arms and cut him off. "Now, now, enough with the pleasantries. I think we are both past that."

"Kneel, you spineless creature; or if you must, draw your sword so we may finish this," said Yevandrielle.

"So eager to kill me?" Lord D'Arthragnan replied and then chuckled. "You could have done so all these years, but you see, you shall not succeed, and that is because you continue to underestimate me, Yevandrielle."

He began to move, lowering his hands, when he laughed again and added, "A fatal flaw that seems to run within the lines of your family."

Yevandrielle stiffened, eyes narrowing, and he barked, "What did you do to Malik? Why, Gideon? My family—my father gave you everything! How could you do this?"

Immediately, he saw Gideon's smile contort into an ugly frown, and he answered, "Everything?"

He fixed Yevandrielle with a smoldering glare, his anger visibly consuming him whole as his body stiffened, and his hands trembled with rage.

It was then that Yevandrielle noticed his physical form had changed. His face was thinner, sharper angles protruding from his pale complexion. His limp had completely vanished from his gait. His stature was taller and stronger than before, as if he had reversed the effects of time and age. A relentless hatred seeped from him like an aura no one could ignore.

"You did not give me everything. You stole everything from me, Yevandrielle! Or do you not remember?"

"Gideon," Yevandrielle began before he was interrupted.

Sparks crackled and jolted from the center of Lord D'Arthragnan's palms as he seethed, his voice now a thunderous echo in Yevandrielle's ears. "I was the one who dragged your father from the battlefield after the Eskhàra had nearly finished him! I was the one who spared the kingdom from utter ruin, saving the king and salvaging what was left of us. I was the realm's savior, not you; by our laws, the throne should have been mine after your father died!"

His breath hissed as he drew it in through clenched teeth. "But the council—you—you twisted the truth, all to fit your schemes; all to ensure yourself the throne when it was mine by right!"

His right hand slithered to his hip, where it fastened around his blade.

The edge of his sword sung once released from its scabbard, and he spoke. "You are weak, Yevandrielle. You have always been weak. You lack the strength to rule; even before they placed that crown on your head. You let the council pave the way for you by their pretty words, praising you before the people, painting you in a light you could not bear to stand in, while I was scorned. I was cast aside, mistreated as a cripple; my loyal service, my courage, my worthiness and right to the throne ignored, because they wanted a king's son rather than someone who was born to be king."

His weaponless hand glowed, the magical force inside him begging to be released while he went on, "You, my friend, you turned your back on me. After everything… everything you knew I had done and sacrificed throughout my entire life for this kingdom—serving your father as his page, his errand boy; suffering through his tutelage as his squire, and then saving the monster in the end."

He laughed heinously before continuing, "You thought offering me this mockery of a position on your council would rectify all the wrongs you, your father, and this disgrace of a council did to me?"

"Is that what you have told yourself all these years? You were my friend, Gideon," Yevandrielle responded fiercely. "I have always seen, always valued you for who I knew you to be. This is not you."

"You gave me morsels of the respect and recognition I deserved," Lord D'Arthragnan bellowed. "Thinking me so desperate and pitiful, thinking I would be satisfied by simply breathing the same air as you and your councilmen. I was your fool, keeping you company, patting your shoulder, serving as your entertainment whenever it suited you."

Yevandrielle shook his head and answered, "I recognize the cruelty and blind arrogance of our society, Gideon. But after my father passed, I fought for your position at my court, for recognition of your service and talent. This court, this kingdom, was granted to me not by any pretty words, but by my father's sacrifice and example. The people chose me out of their free will just as they could have chosen you. The world is flawed and foolish for overlooking you, yes, but just because something is flawed does not mean it cannot be changed."

Yevandrielle readied himself for their fight, riveting all his focus on his adversary before he spoke at last. "You were never meant to be king, Gideon. But not because the world hated you or because you were overlooked. No, your hatred and the vengeance in your heart made sure of that. It hardened you and distanced you from everyone who loved and saw you; it caused you to bury the goodness, the light you could have shown this world and the greatness you could have offered our people."

Lord D'Arthragnan snarled, but did not give an answer.

Instead, he stared Yevandrielle in the eyes and then lunged.

His movements were agile and much swifter than Yevandrielle could have expected; his thrusts and swings broke against him with an untiring, unimaginable force, driving the air from his lungs and causing him to struggle to maintain his footing.

Yevandrielle shouted, dragging his blade in an arc through the thickening air. Its pointed edge met Lord D'Arthragnan's shoulder, slashing his cloak and sending a screech through the space around them as it slid off the pauldron protecting him.

With a huff and a growl, Lord D'Arthragnan retaliated.

Their blades locked, their gazes frozen on each other, forcing an invisible bond between them that had long been broken.

His head spun just as they drew apart and sweat dripped from his brow, while the metallic taste of his own blood on his lips filled his mouth.

Yevandrielle watched a sneer disfigure Lord D'Arthragnan's face.

"Perhaps it is for the best," he hissed. "After all, if not for yours and the council's schemes to put you on the throne instead of me, I would have never stumbled across the likes of the power that is now mine to beckon. I would have never arisen to fulfill my destiny."

"You mean the alliance between you and that wretched beast of a dragon?" Yevandrielle spat back at him between the gasps of his breath. "You are no Eskhàra. You will never wield power like they did."

A laugh burst from Lord D'Arthragnan's mouth. "You are proof of the sickness that has been festering in the blood of the elves for the past decade. Our blood, our kind, has grown soft and weak, undeserving of the power we were always meant to hold."

His eyes narrowed, and then he lunged for Yevandrielle.

Lord D'Arthragnan's sword almost cut through Yevandrielle's leg just above his knee before he spun out of his reach and went on, "You see, the Eskhàra were the key to our people's great destiny, only lacking a leader, a king, strong enough to rule them. They were a band of lost, volatile if you will, but exemplary souls destined for greatness and power at its truest."

Again, Lord D'Arthragnan advanced onto him, and Yevandrielle gave a scream as his left pauldron was torn from his shoulder and the stinging cut of a steel edge sliced his arm.

Yevandrielle riposted as best he could under the ravenous ache of his wound and retreated.

"You are mad!" Yevandrielle yelled breathlessly. "Even if you triumph over Erysméa, you, your dragon, and Izurion's dead army of traitors will never defeat the Dragon's Kin."

Lord D'Arthragnan snarled, raised his sword anew, and answered, "The Dragon's Kin are a pitiful placeholder, never meant to share in the dragons' power. In time, the dragons will recognize this and abandon them. For they are nothing without them; and I, I will raise a new folk, I will unite the blood of the elves and the dragons. I will reshape the world and rid it of its weakness."

A guttural cry erupted from Lord D'Arthragnan's throat, and then he charged at him.

The subsequent moments transpired within the blink of an eye, and Yevandrielle failed to comprehend or follow their course.

Blow after blow, Yevandrielle clung to the hilt of his weapon, slowly but surely no longer attacking and simply defending, fighting for another minute, another second, trying to delay the inevitable course of his fate.

Lord D'Arthragnan's sword broke over him, and Yevandrielle parried the strike, locking his blade against his adversary; however, not without dropping to his knees.

His gaze tore skyward, past the bind of their weapons and Lord D'Arthragnan's sneer, and stalled on the enormous shadow of a black dragon that swallowed the view of the burning heavens through the open roof of the courtyard.

A roar shook the walls and the ground and numbed his senses just as he glimpsed a sword protruding from the beast's silver eye.

The dragon's cry seemed to distract Lord D'Arthragnan as his expression changed, and he chanced a glance toward the dragon hovering over them.

His hesitation cost him as he moved seconds too slow, and an arrow burrowed its way into his back.

Lord D'Arthragnan gave a shout and whirled, ready to run, but not before he drove his heel against Yevandrielle's chest and released a rippling force through his hand, hurling him backward and into the unknown darkness behind him.

* * *

One horrendous commotion of the high-pitched clatter of steel, shrieks, and roars struck Valeirys like a wave as he stormed into the central courtyard of the palace with Eyvindr and the Metatari at his side.

Cries from His Majesty's soldiers echoed from out of various distant corners of the royal dwelling as the elves chased after the enemy's dwindling forces that fled.

Running, Valeirys' eyes raked through the thick clouds of smoke in search of the king, when, all at once, his feet skidded to a halt, the sheer terror of the sight before him stopping him in his tracks. The sky turned black as pitch, and he saw the giant shape of a dragon hover above them. Its maw tore open to a roar that made his ears ring and sent waves rippling through the air.

Beside him, Eyvindr must have spied the king, for Valeirys heard a shout and then the unmistakable cracking sound of an arrow released from a bow.

THE RISE OF ISIGAR

Valeirys' gaze tore away from the dragon and followed the flight of Eyvindr's shot, catching sight of it as it buried itself into the back of no one other than the Lord Councilor D'Arthragnan.

A bellow rang forth from Lord D'Arthragnan, who stood with his blade raised above His Majesty, and a shudder coursed down Valeirys' spine.

With eyes narrowed on the enemy unmasked, Valeirys let his fury drive him, and he bounded toward the king.

He caught the sneer of Lord D'Arthragnan's face just before the lord stretched out his hand toward King Yevandrielle and propelled him backward.

Valeirys screamed as he watched the king's body disappear, flung into the obsidian walls of smoke that climbed higher, rising toward the open roof of the courtyard.

Valeirys no longer felt the ground beneath him as he charged at Lord D'Arthragnan and then lunged.

His blade barely missed the elf's left hip just as the dragon snatched him away before his eyes.

Valeirys' gaze jerked upward, and squinting, he watched the dragon rise higher into the sky, the wind beating against his face under the strokes of the beast's powerful wings, as if he stood amidst a gale.

The dragon bared its teeth, its terrifying gaze locking onto him and pinning him in place as it halted its ascent.

The glint of a sword's hilt caught Valeirys' attention, the weapon buried deep within the wretched creature's silver eye just as his heart fluttered in his chest, and he saw the dragon's maw glow bright gold.

Valeirys dropped his blade, his whole body stinging from the realization of what was about to happen; then he raised his hands above his head, willing a fire of his own to take shape.

A pillar of amber flames erupted from his hands and rose toward the dragon, meeting the beast's own fiery blaze and forming a sphere that crackled and exploded into shape between them.

Valeirys could hear screams erupting all around him as the sphere widened, and the flames engulfed the grounds of the palace's courtyard, but he didn't dare remove his gaze from the fire that fled his palms.

The heat was excruciating, and the weight of the force pitted against him was crippling, but Valeirys couldn't stop.

A spasm chased along his jaw as he gritted his teeth and shut his eyes, letting the magic that flowed from him consume him until he was simply its vessel.

Valeirys didn't know how much longer he could stand it when, all at once, the fire ceased, and a roar split the air just as he looked up and watched the dragon above him vanish.

Valeirys' body shook, and a violent urge to breathe overcame him just before he heaved a breath and pinched his eyes shut.

His consciousness drifted to the steady, powerful beat of his heart as if to remind him he was still alive, and slowly, he opened his eyes again.

The band of Metatari stood in a half-moon-shaped circle around him, and Valeirys let his gaze pass over their group, resisting the impulse to count their numbers and determine how many had survived.

Beside him, he could hear Eyvindr approach him, just before his brother let the magical shield collapse that had protected him and the shapeshifters from the fire that had razed the courtyard of the palace.

He felt Eyvindr's trembling hand come to rest on his shoulder just before he looked up to meet his brother's gaze. Dark rings gathered beneath Eyvindr's eyes, and his face had gone so pale that his skin almost looked translucent. It was undoubtedly proof of the strain his power had suffered.

Nodding silently at Eyvindr, Valeirys glanced back at the Metatari before him, and relief overcame him at the sight of the king hanging in the arms of two of the shapeshifters. King Yevandrielle's head hung low before his body, but he seemed to be nearly standing on his own.

At last, Valeirys lowered his eyes back onto the ground.

Ruby embers glowed from the scorched remains, and he let his gaze linger on them, the shadow of light stirring something inside him.

His hands curled to fists at his sides. This war was far from over. The enemy would return. But when he did, they'd be ready.

Chapter 53

M òr Rhíoghàin was unrecognizable. The once glowing white streets and houses, the colorful storefronts and sculpted façades were gone; shadows of their memory buried in a desert of ashes.

Sharp pieces of wood stuck out from the ruins like snapped or broken bones, crumbled walls of soot-covered stone lined the indistinguishable streets.

Holding the kerchief over his mouth and nose, Valeirys shielded himself from the powdered black dust that rose to his face as he crossed through the ravaged remains of the city.

The stench of charred wood, sulfur, and smoke still wafted through the air, replacing the familiar memory of enticing smells of fresh wildflowers, sage, lavender, and cinnamon that engulfed his senses whenever he had wandered through these streets.

All throughout the less destroyed parts of Mòr Rhíoghain's city, tents were being drawn up to care for the wounded, soldiers erected pyres to burn the remains of the dead, and dragons soared peacefully through the sky above them; a profoundly unfamiliar sight he still hadn't gotten used to now that the enemy was gone.

Peering through the thin layers of fog that still shrouded the ground, he could already see the outlines of the Great Hall growing sharper as he drew near it.

After everything, it surprised him that its structure had remained mostly intact, only parts of its façade damaged in the fire that had overtaken the city.

With the palace left in ruins, the Great Hall was the only larger and safe structure in proximity. Its inner space now served as a shelter for the survivors, a guesthouse and the king's provisory court.

Reaching the perron that ran along the entire perimeter of the hall, Valeirys climbed the stairs before he paused and halted, sidestepping as a mixed group of elves, Metatari, and Dragon's Kin came down and fanned out in different directions over the staircase before passing him. In their arms, they carried supplies and food to distribute to the scattered groups of people who sat huddled together across the perron.

All around him, the place was a bustle.

People of all races and social classes swarmed the hall and the grounds surrounding it, forced together by their joined misery.

It was quite a scene, and in its own way, it was a reprieve to Valeirys as he watched elves, Dragon's Kin, and Metatari intermingle and aid each other, even if their interactions were quite awkward to observe.

As he gazed over the strange crowds, he couldn't help but smile weakly. It was a welcome change of pace despite its unfamiliarity.

"It seems I'll have to make good on my word," a familiar deep voice rose behind him.

Valeirys turned to find the Metatari standing a few steps above him, a grin lightening his stark features. He drew closer and continued, "You're a good soldier;

if not for your blood, I could have mistaken you for one of my own men. Now you just have to learn how to draw a portal."

Valeirys smirked and replied, "Did you think I was so incapable?"

The Metatari chuckled and answered, "You are far more capable than you know."

It grew quiet between them while both eyed the masses of people crowding the perron of the Great Hall.

The corners of Valeirys' lips quirked up to a smile as he let his gaze wander, unintentionally catching on one Metatari after the other. Their remarkable eyes stood out against the growing shadows as the day neared its end, reminding him of the fireflies he would watch for hours as a child when night had broken over the gardens of his childhood home.

"I've never seen anything like them." The words tumbled from Valeirys' mouth.

Out of the corner of his eye, he glimpsed the Metatari look at him.

The shapeshifter grinned slightly when Valeirys went on to explain, "Never have I seen a group more closely knit; moving, fighting together as if they shared one body and one mind."

Valeirys looked directly into the Metatari's bright eyes and spoke. "They are remarkable."

The Metatari's smile widened, and he nodded wordlessly, conveying his agreement.

Valeirys continued to observe him, another question lingering on his lips when he paused.

He felt something stir in his chest, and a tingle chased down his neck just before he said, "What I did in the woods…"

Valeirys stopped himself. His tongue thickened, and the lump in his throat hurt when he made himself speak. "This power… My magic—"

"I meant it when I told you I can help you," the shapeshifter interrupted him. His blinding gaze of gold and silver pierced through Valeirys while he eyed him with an unsettling intensity. "The source of your power matters less than what you make of it, Valeirys. The force inside you, the magic you sense thriving within the bounds of your being… It's tamable despite how it seems."

A chill rushed over the skin of his limbs. He hesitated, but then nodded.

The shapeshifter studied him thoughtfully for a moment before he spoke. "Come with me. There's someone I want you to meet."

Valeirys frowned, dipping his chin in reply, and followed as the shapeshifter led the way.

A blend of excitement and uneasiness stirred in the pit of his stomach.

Valeirys didn't know if he could trust the shapeshifter with the truth of who he was and his changing powers. Only time would tell.

It was a risk but perhaps also a chance he couldn't afford not to take.

CHAPTER 54

"Where do you think you're going?" Hadrian grumbled, trailing behind her as they forged a path through the ruins of Mòr Rhíoghain's streets.

Aleirya gritted her teeth in annoyance.

They had survived the battle, fought side by side, and yet he still kept her on a tight leash, intent on making sure she didn't escape before he could deliver her to his master.

Aleirya ducked her head as a group of elves and Dragon's Kin passed them by, her gaze dragging along the soot-stained cobblestones.

Uncertain what might happen should any of her people recognize her, Aleirya kept her hood drawn and clung to the shadows.

"Hey!" Hadrian growled and grabbed her arm. "I asked you where you're going?"

Aleirya whirled upon his touch, and with a scowl, she snapped at him, "Sightseeing. Where do you think I'm going? To check on Takhéa, of course."

She moved again when his grip tightened on her, and she felt her back slam against the crumbled wall of a house.

"Your dragon is fine. You can go pet her after you've spoken with Tamar. Until then, you don't stray from my side," he muttered between set teeth.

Heat surged through her body at his firm touch.

Gone was any trace of the tenderness, the understanding, the humanity she had glimpsed in him after the crash; back was the unpredictable, beastly creature he was.

Aleirya's gaze pierced the shapeshifter's glare, and she spoke. "Fine."

The muscles in his jaw strained and bulged, but he said nothing.

With a tug, he dragged her away from the wall and shoved her down the narrow street.

They walked in silence as he led her toward the Great Hall.

The square surrounding it, and the perron that rose before it, was flooded with elves, Dragon's Kin, and Metatari—an awkward and yet not terribly unpleasant sight.

Aleirya could feel the intensity of Hadrian's pointed gaze on her like a dagger pricking the skin of her back as they moved.

She tried to avoid eye contact with anyone as they climbed the steps, headed toward the entrance of the Great Hall, and only jolted to a stop once a familiar face caught her attention.

"So, it seems you have quite the skill to wind up where the trouble is," said Sir Odynn as he came down the steps toward her.

She sensed Hadrian come up behind her just before she heard him speak. "No time for chit-chat."

Aleirya swallowed, ignoring him, and spoke. "Sir Odynn."

He looked very different and somewhat uncomfortable in his armor, and she couldn't help but stare at him.

Sir Odynn came to a stop two steps above her and smiled. "Surprised to see me?"

Still grinning, he added, "You know, just because I have a few more scales on my back doesn't mean my dragon's blood has run slow and cool. I can still swing a sword like the rest of you younglings… maybe even better."

Aleirya couldn't suppress the laugh that rose in her throat.

"Move along, dragon girl," Hadrian grumbled quietly.

Aleirya smiled and took a step toward Sir Odynn instead.

"It is good to see you," she replied.

"I see you've made some new friends," said Sir Odynn, motioning toward Hadrian.

Aleirya turned and shot Hadrian a glance before answering, "Ah, yes. He isn't as beastly as he seems."

At that Hadrian growled, but the sound was so low that she doubted Sir Odynn had heard it. The shapeshifter passed her a sharp look, silently conveying that he would be watching her before he then moved around her and up the stairs, passing Sir Odynn without a word.

"Not much of a talker, I see," Sir Odynn commented, glancing after Hadrian before he turned toward her again.

Aleirya shook her head, unable to keep herself from grinning, and asked, "How did you…"

"How did I end up joining King Ethuriel and his fleet?" Sir Odynn completed the question for her.

Dipping his chin, he went on, "It's a long story, probably best shared another time."

Begrudgingly, Aleirya nodded and smiled.

Joining Sir Odynn, she traveled up the rest of the stairs and crossed onto the colonnade that surrounded the Great Hall, following his lead as they began to circle the building.

Lowering her eyes to her booted feet, she let her thoughts stray in the moment of silence that settled between them.

"I'm going to assume you'd rather not speak of the mess you've gotten yourself into," said Sir Odynn. "Lord Acristus has men searching for you all throughout the kingdom. I dare say you've certainly poked the dragon."

Aleirya's spine tingled, and her heart fluttered in her chest.

Had he heard? Had Lord Acristus shared his suspicions with the king and his council?

She folded her hands behind her back to keep them from trembling.

"However, considering the situation at hand, I doubt you need to worry about King Ethuriel or the council troubling themselves with your case."

Her mind eased almost instantly at his words, and she loosened the tight clasp of her hands, letting her arms relax.

Looking up at him, Aleirya asked, "Do you believe what they have been saying of the enemy?"

She watched Sir Odynn's expression grow solemn before he sighed and answered, "Yes. Our dragons and the young elves were taken for the wretched purpose of the enemy's experiment to recreate an army of Eskhàra, and I believe he's nearly succeeded."

Sir Odynn shook his head.

"The magic binding these soldiers to each other, to the dragons he's enslaved; twisting their wills, forcing them into fealty to himself… He is resurrecting a power of an unfounded darkness, born centuries ago through a group of powerful spellbinders and soldiers of the elven race known as the Ring of Edrador."

Aleirya felt sparks dance across her skin, and her throat suddenly itched, urging her to swallow.

"Though there are severe costs attributed to a use of such magic and despite that the power of those soldiers will never quite match that of those born of true Eskhàra blood—such power—It may destroy us all. There is a reason the Eskhàra were never meant to rise again."

Aleirya felt a shudder pass over her shoulders.

The unwanted memory of Lord Acristus screaming the very name after her as she fled rose before her, but she pushed it aside.

"Is everything alright?" Sir Odynn asked, studying her.

She must have paled or gone awfully still for him to look at her the way he did.

Aleirya nodded and tried to smile convincingly.

She caught his gaze stray from her face just as she heard footsteps approaching from behind her.

"It seems your friend is back," said Sir Odynn. "Or should I say friends?"

Aleirya caught a glimpse of three figures moving toward them, but her thoughts still spun around Sir Odynn's words, and she continued to look at him.

Sir Odynn eyed her once more and then spoke. "Be careful, Aleirya. I do hope we see each other again."

Aleirya blinked, shaking herself out of her reverie, and nodded just before he dipped his chin and patted her shoulder.

She watched him walk away, strolling past the group that was gradually closing in on her.

A chill swept over her shoulders, and her scalp prickled, jerking her senses alert as she recognized one of them as the elf she had fought in the Black Market, the one who had accused her of murdering his kind and then left her for dead.

Balling her hands to fists, she straightened as if to make herself look taller just as the shapeshifters and the elf halted in front of her.

The striking pair of the Metatari's familiar gold and silver eyes rested on her, and a spasm chased along the bones of her jaw as Aleirya fixed him with an equally daring look.

"And so, we meet again," she said first and folded her arms over her chest. "Tamar, is it? If you'd wished to speak with me, you could have simply found me on your own, and not, well, had me arrested."

The Metatari grinned and replied, "It is a pleasure to see you again, too, Aleirya. I trust Hadrian has treated you well?"

Aleirya shrugged her shoulders and answered, "His claws are quite sharp, but otherwise he's been a good boy."

She smirked and glanced at Hadrian just as he clenched his fists and growled. His eyes sparked green and silver, but he stayed put beside Tamar.

"Tell me I am relieved of dragon-sitting this menace?" Hadrian sputtered, his gaze still glued to her.

Tamar chuckled and spoke. "I see the two of you get along well."

He then nodded and added, "You may go, Hadrian."

The shapeshifter huffed and finally tore his lingering stare from her before he walked away. Aleirya's gut twisted awkwardly as she watched him leave as if she were sorry to see him go, wondering if they'd ever see each other again.

Releasing her hands to her sides, she shook off the strange feeling, and her focus snapped back toward Tamar and the elf beside him.

"So, what is this about? What is so important that you had to send your hound after me?" Aleirya probed. "And what is he doing here?"

Aleirya inclined her head toward the elf, shooting him a glare before she added, "So much for leaving me for dead."

The elf did not shy away from her pointed stare and replied, "If I had wanted you dead, I would have killed you."

Aleirya's lips pressed to a hard line, and she took a step toward him. Her eyes searched the elf's face, that odd sensation flaring up inside her that she had met him long before that night in the Black Market.

He looked back at her, seemingly equally fascinated and confused.

Narrowing her eyes, Aleirya crossed her arms over her chest and asked, "Humor me. Why didn't you kill me? Maybe you just didn't have the spine."

In spite of the accusation, she noticed him smirk. Then his features softened, and he answered, "You could have killed my brother right before my eyes. You didn't have reason to spare him, and yet you did."

The genuine sincerity of his tone sent a shiver down her spine, and Aleirya's features relaxed, a faint sense of guilt stirring in her stomach for misjudging him.

Releasing her arms to her sides, she began to step back with a nod.

But before she could withdraw, he extended a hand toward her and said, "I'm Valeirys."

Glancing back at him, she accepted his hand and replied, "Aleirya."

He shook her hand, and upon releasing it, he added, "It's nice to meet you on less hostile terms."

At that, she gave a laugh and caught his wry smile.

"Well, this is going better than I expected," said the shapeshifter, dragging Aleirya's attention back to the tall figure standing beside them.

Eyeing her, the Metatari nodded and then went on, "Come with me. Let's take this somewhere more private."

Aleirya's brow knitted together, and she blurted, "More private? There's no one else here besides us."

But the Metatari had already moved past her and descended the perron when she spun around and followed begrudgingly.

Aleirya trailed after Tamar as they distanced themselves from the Great Hall, occasionally casting a glance at Valeirys who tagged along.

They had wandered inside a grove when her feet slowed as she glanced upward and squinted at the warm rays of ebbing sunlight that trickled through the celadon canopy of the olive trees above her, an earthy and slightly bitter smell engulfing her senses.

Stopping, she watched the Metatari turn around to face her, and she scoffed, "Nervous without your woodsy friends around?"

The shapeshifter said nothing. His hands slipped from his cloak and he snapped his fingers, causing the air to ripple and move until it formed an invisible orb around them.

"Ah, so, I am your prisoner," said Aleirya, and she inspected the magical bubble surrounding them. "A cage with no bars. I like it."

"Consider it more a guard against prying eyes and ears. I won't hold either of you against your will. You may leave whenever you like," the Metatari interjected, passing them each a glance. "Though I would recommend you stay and hear me out."

Narrowing her eyes, Aleirya licked her lips and snapped, "What's wrong with you? And what do you want from me? First, you appear out of nowhere, calling me by name as if you know me. Then you proceed to follow me, pretend to rescue me, and take me off the Black Market, portaling onto the edge of a cliff where you are determined to convince me you are not the enemy. You reveal you knew my true father, only to disappear again before sending your underling after me to kidnap me and drag me right back to you for some cryptic reason."

"That is one way to summarize it," Tamar replied.

Aleirya huffed and shook her head, her arms stretched taut at her sides. "What kind of game is this? Did you really know my father? Is there a real reason behind this scheme of yours?"

"Despite what you may believe, none of this is a game to me, Aleirya," Tamar responded.

Aleirya ran a hand through her hair and sighed.

"I don't have time for this. Whatever you want from me, it's a 'no.' I have bigger things to concern myself with. My people are facing a war, and I won't hide. I must return to Tarragon."

"You can't go home," said Tamar.

Heat rushed down her arms and into her palms, and a spark ignited in her chest as she glared at the Metatari.

Aleirya's eyes darted briefly to the elf who stood silent a stone's throw away to her left. He was staring at the ground, avoiding her gaze as if he already knew the reason for the shapeshifter's strange behavior, the expression on his face a blend of anger and despair.

Aleirya's blood boiled. She wanted no part in this.

Glaring at the Metatari, she snapped at him, "You are not my leader, nor my king. I am not your subject. I do not need to heed your command."

She took another step toward him in defiance and added fiercely, "My people need me. I cannot and I will not abandon them or prove myself cowardly before my king with this enemy on the rise."

She turned and began to walk away when his voice rose behind her. "The Dragon's Kin are not your people, Aleirya. You do not know who you are."

Anger sang in her ears, and she whirled around once more to face him, staring him dead in the eyes.

Tamar's piercing gaze bored into her own before it flicked once more to the elf and then back to her, just as he spoke. "I did know *your* father."

The way he had said it made her stop, paralyzed by the panic that clawed its way up her neck.

"In fact, it was by your mother's dying breath that I vowed to protect you both," the Metatari added.

THE RISE OF ISIGAR

A hum settled in Aleirya's ears, and her limbs seemed to vibrate with tension under the stall of her breath just as the Metatari spoke. "Aleirya and Valeirys... Your people died years ago."

He paused and seemed to draw a deep breath of his own before he said, at last, "You are the last true-born Eskhàra."

AUTHOR'S NOTE

Dear Reader,

I want to thank you from the bottom of my heart for taking a chance on this story. Thank you for trusting and supporting me as a growing and learning indie author!

I hope you enjoyed the world I've created. I hope there were moments you laughed, smiled, and couldn't stop reading. Most of all, I hope this story let you dream a little.

Thank you!

ABOUT THE AUTHOR

J.M.Kidd is a fantasy author from Germany. Though her writing journey began only a few years ago, she has always loved the written world of fantasy and immersing herself in the stories of magical creatures, elves, and especially, dragons.

Coffee dates, a classic cut-throat game of Hearts, and spending time with her friends and family are her favorite past-time activities.

Writing is her favorite escape when life runs fast and busy. It's where she can give the characters and the worlds that inhabit her thoughts and dreams a voice and a place to exist.

If you would like to learn more about the author and upcoming projects, you're invited to check out the author website listed below and connect on social media.

CONNECT WITH J. M. KIDD:

Website: www.authorjmkidd.com
Instagram: www.instagram.com/author.j.m.kidd

SIGN UP FOR MY NEWSLETTER

DRAGONTALES

www.authorjmkidd.com

IF YOU ENJOYED READING THE RISE OF ISIGAR

Please consider leaving a review of my book on your preferred platform.

Thank you so much!

HOW DOES THE STORY CONTINUE?

Preview the first chapter of book two in the Eskhàra Series by clicking the link below!

https://BookHip.com/ZBZXRLL

GLOSSARY

DRAGON'S KIN

Acristus (Uh-chris-Tuss) - Council member of Tarragon's court

Aleirya (Uh-LAIR-ee-uh) - Cadet of the Esdras Academy, Takhéa's rider

Anthea (Anth-EE-Uh) - Warlord of Nihal of Tarragon, Lady Anthea

Bradan (BRAY-dun) - Instructor Sir Bradan, Esdras Academy

Cassian (KASS-ee-AN) - Cadet of the Esdras Academy

Cassiopeia (KASS-ee-OPEYA) - Queen of Tarragon

Damian (DAY-mee-AN) - Cadet of the Esdras Academy

Danae (DUH-nay) - Princess Izidora's cousin

Eldread (Ell-dre-D) - Warlord of Megaera of Tarragon, Lord Eldread

Emmarie (EM-Muh-REE) - First-year cadet of the Esdras Academy

Ethuriel (eth-UR-ee-yell) - King of Tarragon, Leader of Pyrim's army

Hothwin (HAW-th-WIN) - Royal investigator, Sir Hothwin

Izidora (Is-UH-door-UH) - Princess of Tarragon

Kajetan (K-EYE-yuh-TUN) - Cadet of the Esdras Academy

Kalithea (KAL-EE-th-AYE-Uh) - Princess of Tarragon & Royal Dragon Guard

Killian (Kill-EE-An) - Tavern keeper

Luther (LOO-th-UR) - Black Market smuggler, Luther Fynn

Nathanael (NAH-than-EE-Uh-L) - Cadet of the Esdras Academy

Oberon (OH-bur-RUN) - Warlord of Zaurak of Tarragon, Lord Oberon

Odynn (OH-din) - Instructor Sir Odynn, Esdras Academy

Thoran (THOR-Ran) - Aleirya's foster father, Blacksmith, T. Perèdur

Varlam (VAR-Lumm) - Warlord of Gerlach of Tarragon, Lord Varlam

Zadock (ZAH-Dock) - Warlord of Adhara of Tarragon, Lord Zadock

Zannia (ZUH-nee-UH) - Aleirya's foster mother, Blacksmith, Z. Perèdur

DRAGONS

Brandr (BRAN-dur) - Fire dragon, once bonded to Thalos Perèdur, Thoran Perèdur's grandfather.

Galàzios (Ga-LA-ZEE-Us) - Dragon, bonded to King Ethuriel of Tarragon

Takhéa (Tah-KAY-Uh) - Dragon, bonded to Aleirya

ELVES

Alcides (AL-k-EYE-des) - Soldier

Bérètharomyr (BEAR-eth-ARROMERE) - Guardian of the Unforgotten

Calaedorn (Kah-LAY-door-N) - Lord Councilor of the Erysméan court

Cenric (KEN-rick) - Lord of Aram of Erysméa, Lord Cenric

D'Arthragnan (DARTH-rag-NUN) - Lord Councilor of the Erysméan court

Diyara (DEE-yar-Uh) - Princess of Erysméa

Eris (AIR-riss) - Soldier

Eyvindr (EYE-vin-DUR) - Son of Lord & Lady Altair, Valeirys' adoptive brother

Fearghail (FEAR-Guh-L) - Lord of Eihbir of Erysméa, Lord Fearghail

Ganymedes (Gan-EE-mee-DISS) - Tavern keeper

Gwenaël (Gwen-Nah-Ale) – Soldier

Izurion (Is-UR-ree-AN) - Deceased king of Galeya (later: Erysméa)

Malik (Ma-LICK) - Prince of Erysméa

Melquart (Mell-CART) - Alessander Melquart

Rhaegalisron (RAY-Gal-is-RON) - Lord of Alaisdair of Erysméa, Lord Rhaegalisron

Trajan (TRAY-Juh-N) - Commander League of Altair, T. Rheiavirn

Tarquinius (TAR-Quinn-EE-Us) - Lord of Lyrr of Erysméa, Lord Tarquinius

Uryiel (YUR-ee-Yell) - Lord of Inaesa of Erysméa, Lord U. Altair

Valeirys (Vuh-LAIR-riss) - Soldier, adopted son of Lord&Lady Altair

Velior (VEL-ee-OR) - Lord Councilor of the Erysméan Court

Yessenia (YES-enn-ee-AH) - Healer, Lady Altair, Birth mother of Eyvindr, Adoptive Mother of Valeirys

Yeva (YAY-v-Uh) - Lord of Phaedra of Erysméa, Lord Yeva

Zelathiel (Zel-UH-th-EE-L) - Lord of Nyradorn of Erysméa, Lord Amulius Zelathiel

METATARI

Metatari (Meta-TAR-REE) - Shapeshifters

Faelyn (FAY-lynn) - Metatari

Hadrian (HAY-dr-EE-Un) - Metatari

Tamar (TUH-MAR) - Leader of the Metatari

THE KINGDOM OF TARRAGON

Tarragon (T-AIR-Ra-GON) - Kingdom of the dragon's kin

Adhara (UH-dar-Uh) - Region of Tarragon, gov. Lord Zadock

Gerlach (GER-LACK) - Region of Tarragon, gov. Lord Varlam

Megaera (Meg-AIR-Uh) - Region of Tarragon, gov. Lord Eldred

Nihal (NEE-HAL) - Region of Tarragon, gov. Lady Anthea

Pyrim (PEER-RIM) - Region of Tarragon, gov. King Ethuriel

Zaurak (ZAW-RACK) - Region of Tarragon, gov. Lord Oberon

THE KINGDOM OF ERYSMÉA

Erysméa (AIR-riss-MAY-Uh) - Kingdom of the elves/ elven heroine

Alaisdair (AH-lass-DAIR) - Region of Erysméa, gov. Lord Rhaegalisron

Aram (UH-Rum) - Region of Erysméa, gov. Lord Cenric

Eihbir (EYE-Buhr) - Region of Erysméa, gov. Fearghail

Inaesa (In-NAY-ZAH) - Region of Erysméa, gov. Lord Altair

Lyrr (L-UR) - Region of Erysméa, gov. Lord Tarquinius

Lake Diadema (DYE-Ah-DEE-Ma)

Mòr Rhíoghain (MORE -RIO-Gah-N) - Capital of Erysméa

Nyradorn (NEAR-Ruh-Door-N) - Region of Erysméa, gov. Lord Zelathiel

Phaedra (FAY-druh) - Region of Erysméa, gov. Lord Yeva

THE DHAHARRAN FOREST

Dhaharran (DAH-Har-RUN) - Dhaharran Forest, Realm of the Metatari

THE FORSAKEN LANDS OF ISIGAR

Isigar (IS-i-GAR) - Forsaken lands of the eradicated human race

Aidah (AYE-duh) - Region of Isigar

Astellor (AH-stell-OR) - Region of Isigar

Ben Hadoth (BEN- Hah-Duh-th) - Region of Isigar

Ben Terach (BEN -TAIR-ack) - Region of Isigar

Fennick (FEN-Ick) - Region of Isigar

Gothwin (GOTH-Win) - Region of Isigar

Lochlan (LOCK-Lan) - Region of Isigar

Rothvain (ROTH-Vein) - Region of Isigar

Ryṃn (R-IM) - Region of Isigar

Strongard (STRONG-guard) - Region of Isigar

Yurem (YUR-Rem) - Region of Isigar

ESKHÀRA

Eskhàra (es-CAR-Uh) - Hybrid race, half elf, half dragon's kin

ACKNOWLEDGEMENTS

'For I know the plans I have for you, declares the Lord, plans for welfare and not for evil, to give you a future and a hope.'
(Jeremiah 29,11)

To hold this story in my hands in the form of an actual, physical book feels surreal. I cannot begin to describe how grateful I am to everyone who has supported this journey and helped turn this dream into a reality.

First and foremost, my deepest thanks go to my Heavenly Father, who knew this day would come long before I did. He gave me all I needed to write this story, loves me beyond measure, and has blessed me more than I deserve. Thank you, Lord, for knowing my heart inside and out, and for granting me this earthly dream.

I would also like to express a tremendous thank you to my editor, John Matthew Fox, for pulling this story apart and helping me reshape and refine it into the book it's now become. Your insights and advice were invaluable.

Thank you to the team at Fabled Planet and to my copy editor, Cecily Blanch. Your efforts and your keen attention to detail helped me polish this story and made it shine.

Thank you, Krafigs Designs, for bringing my vision for this cover to life with such thoughtful consideration. The result is stunning! I am so excited to share this cover with the world. It is now irrevocably tied to this book, this fantasy realm, and this story! I am so proud to show it off, wrapped inside your breathtaking design.

My heartfelt gratitude goes to my family, my parents, my alpha, beta, and ARC readers, and my resilient and ever-faithful L-Team: Lindy, Laura, Leanna, and Leslie.

Your unwavering support and your faith in me, prayers, and invaluable feedback are treasures I'll forever carry in my heart. I am so blessed to have every one of you in my life and in my corner!

Randy—thank you for being the best possible partner in this daunting and challenging process.

Thank you for being my first audience. Thank you for all the hours of reading out loud so that I could 'hear my story better,' all the little pick-me-ups, every time window you helped carve out of our busy days and lives, and for taking care of our boys so that I could dedicate myself fully to this dream.

Thank you for refusing to let me give up, for loving me well, and most of all, for believing in me when I doubted myself. None of this would be possible without you, my love.

Last but not least, thank you, dear reader. Without you, this story wouldn't have a place to shine. Your trust, your support, and your excitement for this story fill my heart with a joy I cannot possibly put into words.

Sincerely and wholeheartedly, thank you!

Made in the USA
Middletown, DE
14 June 2025

77001269R00316